Between Goodbyes

Also by Anita Bunkley:

Silent Wager

Mirrored Life

Relative Interest

BETWEEN GOODBYES

ANITA BUNKLEY

Dafina Books

KENSINGTON PUBLISHING CORP.

DAFINA BOOKS are published by

Kensington Publishing Corp.
850 Third Avenue
New York, NY 10022

ISBN: 978-0-7394-9092-1

Printed in the United States of America

PART ONE

AMERICA

Prologue

When the doorbell of her Manhattan penthouse chimed, Niya Londres hurriedly clipped on a pair of heavy gold loop earrings, pulled a black cashmere sweater over her head, and stuck her long legs into a pair of white leather pants. With a quick glance into the mirror above her sleek granite vanity, she gave her full red lips a glossing lick, and then turned around to glance over her shoulder to assess her curvaceous backside. An appreciative smile touched her lips.

Not too long ago, Niya would have been irritated that her hips were so prominently rounded below her tiny waist, but not now. The extra pounds she had put on during her month-long stay at a Nevada resort were exactly what she had needed to soften her too-thin figure, and she was perfectly content with her new, curvier image.

At thirty years of age, and pushing thirty-one, Niya was as shapely and hot-looking as any twenty-two-year-old woman and she was proud that her Afro-Cuban heritage was definitely showing out once more. Years of professional dancing had kept her five-foot-eight-inch body lean and toned. Good genes had meant little concern with skincare habits, leaving her with a flawless sepia complexion. Her tousled black hair, shot with golden undertones, now touched the tops of her shoulders, and her dark eyes, which sparkled with spirited energy, created a glow that lit up her heart-shaped face.

Remaining barefoot, Niya hurried from the dressing room off her master bedroom into the short hallway leading to the entry, praying that Ginger Drew had come through for her. Niya hated wasting time with people who were neither organized, committed, nor talented, and she had been informed by four different references that Ginger was the perfect graphic designer to create what Niya wanted, and would happily work double-time in order to meet Niya's deadline.

The doorbell chimed for the second time just as Niya pulled open the teak paneled door.

"Hello!" she welcomed her guest.

"Miss Londres?" the young woman standing at her entrance asked. "I'm Ginger Drew. We had a ten o'clock appointment."

"Yes, yes, Ginger, please come in," Niya replied, assessing the young woman, who had short, blunt-cut dark brown hair, a ruddy complexion, and a small round face which was dwarfed by a pair of large red-framed glasses. "Good to finally meet you, Ginger, and I'm so happy you were able to meet with me here."

"For you, Ms. Londres, no problem. I was happy to come into town. It's only a short train ride into the city from Newark, and I gladly set aside my other projects to do this for you. And what an honor! I loved you in *Morning Stars*. I saw it four times! To be able to say that I designed the wedding invitations for the famous Broadway actress Niya Londres! That's a real coup for any graphic artist."

Smiling, Niya simply nodded, aware that her name was fast becoming as recognizable as that of any movie star, though she paid little attention to the tabloids. Fame. Money. Adulation. They had all fallen her way so quickly and so unexpectedly that she was still adjusting to the notoriety that her critically acclaimed performance on Broadway in the smash hit, *Morning Stars,* had brought. Though pleased to hear that Ginger saw her on stage four times and considered her famous, Niya had no time to chitchat about the theater. She had only one thing on her mind today—focusing on the most personal and important day of her life—her upcoming wedding, and Ginger Drew was going to play a very important role.

"Let's go into the study. I'm anxious to see what you have for me." Niya led the young woman into an oak-paneled room that had two walls lined with books. Silver-framed photographs of Niya with celebrities, friends, and fellow actors in many of her performances had been carefully arranged on tabletops among unusual accessories that gave the room a rich ambiance. Three oil paintings, all of the same island landscape and framed in rustic wood, hung on the wall above a teak writing desk, while a gleaming ebony concert piano occupied a far corner of the room. Open sheet music was scattered across its top.

The room had the quintessential feel and smell of a celebrity's private space, furnished with expensive, tailored leather couches, heavy brass lamps, and intricately designed Oriental rugs. A new flat screen television sat in a corner near the fireplace, where a cozy fire now blazed.

After settling down on the curved black leather sofa, Ginger handed Niya a zippered portfolio, then sat back while Niya eagerly opened the packet. She removed a fragile-looking piece of parchment-like paper edged in gold and held it up to the light.

"Beautiful," Niya murmured, examining the handcrafted piece in the bright November sunlight that was streaming into the room through one of its tall, narrow windows. "Your work is exquisite. This is exactly what I had I mind."

"Thank you. It's real papyrus," Ginger stated with pride. "Two years ago, I took a course in paper making from an Egyptian artist on how to craft authentic papyrus according to the ancient Egyptian methods. One piece at a time. Lovingly. Each sheet is unique. The sample you are holding took me three days to complete and the lettering was done in pure fourteen carat gold. However, if you wish, I could use gold-tone ink and save you quite a bit of money. But I thought you'd probably want the real thing, so I made up this sample for you."

"I'll use the real gold, I assure you," Niya murmured, scrutinizing the paper.

"And my calligraphy is hand executed," Ginger continued with pride. "I don't farm out any of my work."

"Oh, of course," Niya vaguely replied, clearly intrigued by the beautiful sheet of paper. "I love everything about this sample, but could you change the lettering to a less formal script? Perhaps something more whimsical? Maybe with a Caribbean flair?"

"Absolutely," Ginger agreed. "I know exactly what you want."

"And don't worry about the cost. Make them beautiful. These invitations must be breathtaking. And unforgettable."

Ginger reached into her giant-size handbag and pulled out a pad and a pen, ready to write up the order. "How many invitations will you need?" she asked.

After thinking for a moment, Niya decided, "A dozen. Yes, I have exactly twelve guests I plan to invite." She stopped to think, and then added, "No, make that fourteen invitations, one for the groom and one for me. That will be perfect."

"Fine," Ginger stated. "Now, the wording. What would you like on the invitations?"

Settling deeper onto the sofa, Niya thought once more about the words that had tumbled around in her head for the past four days as she'd struggled with what to say, and how to say it. She had paced the floor with a mini tape recorder, stopping to jot down a phrase or two, only to discard them and try again. The final decision about the invitation wording had only just come to her, while dressing this morning, and now she was certain of what she wanted to say.

"My message will be short, uncomplicated, and direct," she began, one finger at her lips. Standing, she walked to a window and faced the city skyline for a few moments, then turned to Ginger, lifted her chin, and began. "This is what I want on the invitations," she started. "Niya Londres invites you to join her in a special day of celebration and to share in her joy at her wedding. Villa Tropical, Acapulco, Mexico, on . . ."

"Uh, Miss Londres," Ginger interrupted. "I think it's customary to include the groom's name in the opening, and then to refer to him in your wording by using the words 'us and we'. I have some samples here, if you'd like to see them." Ginger began rummaging again in her large leather bag and pulled out a bundle of folded papers. "I think, since you are . . . well, mature . . . and your parents aren't giving you away, that a non-traditional type of wording would be appropriate. There are so many ways to . . ."

"I *know* what's traditional and customary," Niya stopped Ginger with a resolute tone. "But my wedding will be neither customary nor ordinary. Trust me, I know what I'm doing."

"Well, fine. It's your wedding, but . . ."

"Right. That it is," Niya confirmed. "So the wording will be as I want it. Now where was I?"

Shrugging, Ginger shook her head. "You were at: Villa Tropical, Acapulco, Mexico," she read from her notes.

"Yes." Niya pursed her lips, and then went on. "On Sunday, December 13, 2006, at five-thirty in the evening. RSVP required. Invited guests only. Reception to follow in the Villa Tropical Ballroom." She held both hands, palms up, at Ginger, signaling that she was finished.

"But, Miss Londres. Really. You don't want to send out a wedding invitation and omit the name of the man you plan to marry."

Niya chuckled aloud, tilting back her head, clearly enjoying the young woman's confusion. "Oh, yes, I do . . . and I plan to."

"But why?" Ginger wanted to know.

"Because I want the invitation to my wedding to be so original, elaborate and intriguingly worded that each person I invite will immediately RSVP, *and* show up."

Ginger made a soft clucking sound with her tongue, but then sighed and scribbled some notes on her pad. "Well, an invitation that looks and reads like yours will certainly guarantee attendance. I'm sure you won't have to worry about no-shows, unless springing for a trip to Mexico is a problem."

"Oh, I'm going to take care of all the travel and lodging expenses," Niya clarified with a wave of her left hand, on which she wore two rings: an emerald-cut yellow diamond surrounded with rubies, and a brilliant round solitaire diamond set in an intricately engraved silver band. "A plane ticket will go out to each person who RSVPs, and I've rented the entire villa for a week. All my guests have to do is show up."

"That's pretty classy." Ginger nodded her approval. "But what about the groom? Won't he be a bit annoyed when he sees that you left his name off the invitation?"

Niya shrugged. "No. The wording on the invitation is of little concern to the man I plan to marry. He's away on business, so he asked me to do whatever I wanted. All he has to do is put on a tuxedo and show up, prepared to walk down the aisle. So you see, I can do exactly as I please."

"Oh, I do see," Ginger agreed, snapping her portfolio shut. "Well, I gotta say . . . this is one of the strangest assignments I've ever worked on, but I have to admit, it's the most intriguing, too. Please, Ms. Londres. Let me know . . . after the wedding, of course, how it all turns out."

"I will," Niya said as she escorted Ginger to the door. Pausing with her hand on the doorknob, she said, "Today's November fifth. Can you get the invitations to me by the fifteenth?"

"Sure," Ginger replied. "I'll get started on them today."

Once Ginger had left, Niya returned to her study and sat down at her dark teak writing table. The red leather address book that contained contact information for Niya's close personal friends and professional acquaintances lay open to the letter *K,* and a cream colored business card with bold black script on it was wedged between two pages. After studying the card for a few seconds, she removed it and rubbed her index finger over the raised lettering.

"Bert Kline," she read from the card. "Private investigator for the discriminating client." Taking a deep breath, she picked up the phone and dialed the number on the card, both nervous and eager to hear what he had to say.

"Do you have the information?" she asked as soon as Kline's secretary put her through to the man she was trusting to determine her future.

"It's on its way to you now," Kline assured her in his familiarly gruff voice.

"Were you successful?" she asked, scooting to the edge of the chair, her head lowered as she focused on the faded blue flowers in the Oriental rug. She had gone to great lengths and paid Bert Kline an exorbitant amount of money to secure his services on short notice. She had been worried that he might refuse her request because he was currently involved in a high profile murder case that required him to testify daily in court. However, because Niya's name carried star-power weight of its own, she had been able to convince him to take her on as a client. Now, Niya expected results. "Tell me what you found."

"I can't do that over the phone," he replied with a professional clip to his words. "I'm sending my report over to you by courier, and it includes everything you asked for. Call me later if you want to discuss anything."

"Will I be pleased?" she prompted.

"It all depends," Kline vaguely replied.

"On what?" Niya pressed, wishing the man would not be quite *so* discriminating.

The sounds of rattling papers came over the line before Kline spoke again. "It all depends on how badly you want to get married. Anything can be worked out, you know?"

Niya tensed her jaw and held her tongue, reflecting on this

non-committal answer. Bert Kline's report was only one piece of a complicated situation, but a piece she needed very much. "Yes, I know," she agreed. "We often have to make trade-offs to get what we want."

"Right. So, call me after you've read my report and we'll go from there."

"I will. And thanks, Bert, for squeezing me in. I know how busy you are."

"My pleasure, Ms. Londres," he tossed back, then clicked off.

Anything can be worked out? Niya thought, the private investigator's comment still hanging in her mind. *What,* she wondered, *did he mean by that?*

Too jittery to concentrate on finalizing the wedding reception menu, she shoved the folder filled with lists of hors d'oeuvres and beverages aside and impulsively opened the side drawer of her desk. She removed a piece of monogrammed stationery and a matching envelope, and began writing a letter to her mother back in Cuba.

After years of silence, they were finally able to communicate, and Niya took pleasure in keeping her mother updated on what was happening in her crazy, fast-paced American life. When Niya left Cuba nearly ten years ago, Olivia's parting words to her daughter had been, "Make a home for yourself in America, but never forget that you are Cuban, first," and Niya had struggled to honor that advice, though it had made her life difficult at times.

Today, Niya's letter to her mother was filled with details about her approaching wedding, and words of sorrow over the fact that her mother would not be there. Even if it had been possible for Olivia Londres to leave Cuba and travel to Mexico, Niya worried that her mother's health might fail if she tried to make the trip.

Finished with the letter, Niya sealed it and set it aside. She pressed her hands together as if making a silent prayer, nodded, and then removed three photographs from beneath the blotter on her desk. Carefully, she lined the pictures up in a row, pausing to study each man's face.

"I love you all," she admitted in a soft, wistful tone. "And I know that you love me, too. Each of you wants to marry me, but which one will hear me say, 'I do'? Which one of you can I trust with my heart?"

She picked up the first photo. A tall man with smooth brown skin, a strong jawline, and keenly carved features, he was standing at a microphone, his head thrown back, his thickly lashed eyes closed, a saxophone at his lips. His white, open-collared shirt was wrinkled and thick drifts of cigarette smoke swirled around his head. Niya could almost feel the pulse of the rhythm he was belting out and hear the music that was coming from the golden horn in his hands.

"Tremont Henderson. My first love," she whispered. "You rescued me from a dreary life without hope and proved to me that I was worthy of being loved. With you, every day was filled with sunshine; our time together was an exciting journey packed with passion, good times, and beautiful music. Life was one big party back then, but it ended very badly, in spite of everything we tried to keep it alive. Is it possible for us to pick up where we left off, or have we lost the spark that fueled our passion?"

After tracing her finger over Tremont's chiseled features, Niya tightened her lips, set the photo aside, and picked up the next one from the desk.

"Granger Cooper," she said with pride, studying the image of a mature white man wearing a black tuxedo who was standing on the sidewalk in front of the famous Metro Theater. The wind had ruffled his longish sandy brown hair and he was smiling as he posed before a giant Playbill poster of his smash hit, *Morning Stars,* which had introduced Niya to Broadway. "My wise manager, my enthusiastic lover, my solid rock who never failed me. When you took me under your wing and into your heart, you turned my life around."

After placing this photo back on the desk, she took up the

third one, a chuckle escaping her lips as she assessed the tanned face and smiling brown eyes of a youthful, well-fit man who was sitting on a beautiful palomino horse, a desert landscape spreading out behind him. "Astin Spence, my rugged Marlboro man," she said, shaking her head with a smile. "So damn full of energy and so damn handsome. You challenged me to take so many risks—emotionally, personally, and even professionally. With you, I was real . . . I was simply me . . . Niya Londres, the little girl from the barrio of Cerro, Cuba, who wanted only to dance. Yet, you made me feel like a star. How could I resist falling in love with you?"

With a sweep of her hand, Niya brushed the three photos back under the desk blotter and then stood. There was nothing to do now but wait for Kline's report and then she would have her answer.

The quietness of the empty apartment suddenly seemed oppressive and she was much too restless to concentrate on anything of importance. Impatiently, she pressed the power button on the television's remote control and flipped to the national news, desperate to occupy her mind as she waited for her door bell to ring.

As the newscaster droned on about the outlandish price of real estate in southern California, Niya let her mind drift back over the years, unable to keep the memories at bay.

Chapter 1

Off the southernmost tip of Florida
Mid-June 1998

Black water lapped at the sides of the dirty gray boat, creating a frightening yet comforting sound as it mixed with rhythmic *swish-swish* of oars being pulled through water. The absence of all other noise meant that, so far, the dark night was protecting them, and that the black stillness surrounding them was as void of life as the inside of a tomb, though the air was strong with anxiety.

The thirty-three refugees who were crowded together on the tiny vessel kept their lips sealed and their ears alert for any signs of danger. No one spoke. No one coughed. No one smacked at the pesky mosquitoes that had suddenly begun attacking them, and no one dared to ease over to the smelly waste buckets shielded from view behind a sheet of dirty canvas that were only used when absolutely necessary.

Though Niya Londres could not see the faces of the dark-skinned people who were huddled together in clumps down in the hull, she knew what they looked like: ragged with exhaustion, nearly broken with terror, yet riveted with an unwavering determination to survive.

A mixture of fear and hope filled Niya, too, and she fought

back the reservoir of unshed tears that had been building inside her for days. She missed her mother, longed for the feel of fresh sheets against her skin, and would kill for a scrap of bread and a sip of water to ease the hunger that gripped her stomach. However, she could not have those things and, no matter what happened, she had to stay strong. She could not break down and lose control and let her brother, Lorenzo, see how frightened she was.

Reaching out in the darkness, Niya groped for Lorenzo's hand, expecting him to pull away; an eighteen-year-old boy might be somewhat reluctant to admit that he needed his big sister's calming touch. However, as soon as Niya's fingers touched Lorenzo's, he grasped her hand tightly and held on without saying a word.

Three years younger than Niya, who would turn twenty-one in just a few days, Lorenzo was a foot taller than his sister, but just as fiercely independent, and much too handsome for his own good. He thought of himself as both a ladies' man and a tough guy . . . a macho male with a devilish smile and little need of comfort from anyone. However, as the inky night wore on, he did not let go of Niya's hand and his faith in her helped Niya remain calm.

Who knew how close the Coast Guard patrol boats might be? she worried. At any moment, a cough, a child's cry, even a muted whisper might bring the authorities bearing down on them with searchlights, orders shouted through loud bullhorns, and gunfire to make them surrender. Back home in Cuba, it had been rumored around the island that not only the United States Coast Guard was out on patrol, but renegade vigilante boats as well, scouting the Florida waters for illegal Haitian immigrants, eager to interrupt their approach. The officials' fast-moving boats were said to be able to glide over the choppy coastal waters as silently as raindrops slipping down a pane of glass. Within seconds, the journey could end in a hail of gunfire, an ordered evacuation that would result in deportation back to the island, detention in a refugee camp, or even death.

For Niya, the only bright spot in the miserable situation was that of the sixty-three passengers aboard the boat, only she and Lorenzo were from Cuba, not Haiti, a fact that she prayed would make it possible for her and her brother to stay in America even if they were caught.

Their journey had started under the cover of darkness at the beach at Caibarien, on the eastern coast of Cuba, when Niya and Lorenzo had hugged their mother goodbye and stepped into the weather-beaten boat that was already jam-packed with Haitians. After slipping out to sea and away from their homeland under the cover of a thunderous, moonless sky, Niya and Lorenzo had managed to commandeer a corner in the stern of the boat where they stowed their plastic bags containing personal items and a change of clothing before hunkering down for the duration of the trip.

Now, as the boat rolled with the waves toward the Florida shoreline, dim lights suddenly appeared on the horizon. Lifting her chin, Niya peeked above the rail and focused on the twinkling lights that illuminated the ragged edges of a far-off shoreline. The lights, like festive Christmas garlands, decorated the land that would soon become her new home. Finally, it lay within reach and, despite her trepidation about what would happen to her once she set foot on shore, Niya swallowed her fear and silently vowed to be courageous, no matter what.

As the eldest, Niya felt responsible for them both, and had promised her mother that she would be brave, careful, and wise, and not let anything happen to Lorenzo. It was a promise Niya meant to keep.

The sighting of coastal lights in the distance caused an unexpected stir among the refugees, and very soon soft whispers of excitement rippled across the deck.

If only we could shout our happiness, Niya thought, near to bursting with joy, herself. Instead, she gave Lorenzo's hand a hard squeeze and allowed the tension in her shoulders to ease a bit, in exhausted, blessed release. *We'll be on land soon,* she thought. *And then everything will be fine. We'll go to New York, find Uncle Eric, and become American citizens like him.*

With a stab of regret, Niya thought of her mother, Olivia Londres, wishing she were with her now. The Haitian boat captain, who had agreed for Niya and Lorenzo to join his group, had made it clear to Niya's mother that he had room for two children only, and had been less than pleased to discover that the "two children" turned out to be a twenty-year-old girl and an eighteen-year-old boy. Reluctantly, the captain had let them aboard.

Now, Niya concentrated on the lights in the distance, eager to shut out the misery of missing her mother. Rising on her knees, she pulled Lorenzo up beside her, and together they strained to make out the dark shapes along the coast as the boat began to pick up speed.

In their eagerness to reach shore, the oarsmen had begun pulling harder, propelling the boat forward at an increased pace. Even the wind picked up and pushed them faster toward America, a good omen, Niya thought.

Unable to resist a view of the approaching shoreline, many of the refugees crowded together at the front of the boat, causing a sudden shift in the distribution of weight, tilting the boat precariously to one side.

"Sit down!" The captain hissed, loud enough to startle everyone. "Sit down or we will flounder."

Suddenly someone screamed; a loud cry of surprise, followed by a splash—as if someone had fallen or jumped overboard. Soon everyone on board, it seemed, was shouting in alarm.

"He fell! Help him. He fell into the water!"

"No, no. I think he jumped!"

"Yes, you see? He's swimming to shore!"

"No! He fell. He did not jump!"

Eyes wide, Niya jerked her head around and followed the voices, but all she could make out in the darkness was a jumble of bodies pressed together at the side of the boat. Soon, some began wailing, others started cursing, and a woman began screaming for someone to save the man who had fallen into the water.

Into this mayhem, a new, loud voice shot out of the darkness and quickly silenced the panicky crowd. "Halt! Halt your vessel or you will be fired upon!" shouted a man, initiating further panic.

The shadowy tangle of people broke apart in an instant, and the splash of more bodies hitting water quickly drowned out the voice on the bullhorn. Niya screamed when groping hands and arms pushed her down onto the deck, but she managed to hold onto Lorenzo and pull him into a safe spot behind a crate where they huddled in fear as the frightened refugees began jumping into the ocean.

Gunfire rang out.

The refugees roared with fright.

The throng trampled forward, and more people flung themselves overboard, pulling loved ones along with them into the freezing water.

Now, pinned against the rail, Niya had no place to go except over the side of the boat, too, and still holding onto Lorenzo's hand she pulled him to his feet.

"Come on, Lorenzo! We've got to jump. Swim for it. If we don't, we're finished."

She stood up, looked down into the black water and took a deep breath, poised to jump. But just as she stepped over the rail, a bullet struck her in the shoulder, forcing her into the icy water headfirst.

"Lorenzo!" she screamed as his hand slipped out of hers. "Lorenzo!" Frantically, she groped for him. But she was alone, and he was gone.

Niya felt herself sinking deep beneath the water and her lungs instinctively tightened with lack of air. For several horrifying seconds she remained in a downward spiral, her head pounding, her limbs useless against the strong undertow. As she continued her descent, she wondered if she would live to see America, her brother, or daylight, again.

When she thought her lungs would certainly burst, she found the strength to fight her way to the surface, and with a push, erupted above the water, only to find that she was totally alone. Not even the boat remained within sight.

Gasping for breath, she dog-paddled to stay afloat, and after forcing herself to calm down, flipped onto her back and floated, letting the waves nudge her body toward shore. Back home in Cuba, she and Lorenzo had often swum as far out as they could, only to float back to shore on the crests of tall, white-capped waves.

Please let Lorenzo be alive. Let him remember how to do this, Niya silently prayed. *Please let him think of the beaches where we played in Cuba. Make him remember not to fight the current but to allow it to carry him safely to shore.* She knew Lorenzo was an excellent swimmer, but would he be able to orient himself well enough to make it to land? Or would he mistakenly swim out to sea until he floundered, drowned, or got eaten by sharks? She could not think of such a horror. She had to concentrate on surviving.

After drifting a while, she calculated that her chances of swimming to land were pretty good, so she flipped over and struck out toward the shoreline, praying that Lorenzo was doing the same thing. With firm strokes, though her shoulder was aflame with pain, Niya continued swimming toward land.

Chapter 2

By the time Olivia Londres arrived back home in Havana, the sun was full up, music was blaring from two amplifiers that a group of teenagers had set up in Cerro Park, and a thick layer of dust had settled on top of the crumpled copies of *El Habanero* that had blown into the entrance of her apartment building.

Everything around Olivia seemed fuzzy and out of focus, as if her trip to Caibarien had occurred during a bad dream. It had been so dark at the clandestine shoreline that she had hardly been able to make out the faces of her children as she had kissed each one goodbye. And after the boat pulled out to sea, she had remained on the beach until the sun had come up, aching for one final glimpse of the vessel that had taken Niya and Lorenzo away. Of course, when the sun rose on the horizon she saw nothing but a sheet of blue water, endless and calm.

Now, Olivia gazed dispiritedly out of the open window of the dirty truck she was riding in, relieved to have safely made it back home, but aching with worry about her children. Where were they now? Had the crowded, less-than-sturdy-looking boat made it safely into the Florida Keys? Were her son and daughter frightened? Hungry? It was difficult to believe that Niya and Lorenzo were actually gone and she would never hear from them again. She had made them promise not to write or call: It would only cause trouble that Olivia did not need. Reluctantly, they had agreed to honor their mother's wishes.

Looking around, Olivia saw that her street, Calzado del Cerro, was bustling with activity as people went about their daily lives, following their normal routines. And that was what she would have to do, too: tend to her chores, go to Mass, and report for work at the Superior Tobacco factory on time every day, as if nothing in her life had changed, preventing anyone from learning the truth about the disappearance of her son and daughter.

The broad street where Olivia lived in a second floor, three-room apartment, was lined with row after row of adjoined one- and two-story buildings with red-tiled roofs and tiny front porches that sagged under crumbling colonial-style columns. She had lived in the Cerro section of Havana all of her adult life but now she suddenly felt like a stranger. With Niya and Lorenzo gone she was not the same; nothing would be the same.

"Thank you for the ride into town, Felix," Olivia told the man at the wheel of the ancient Ford truck, which he was busy maneuvering to the curb. "I don't know what I would have done if you hadn't come along. When the bus broke down outside of Matanzas, all of the passengers were told there was nothing to do but walk back to Havana. And in this heat! I am no longer a young woman, you know."

"It was my pleasure, Olivia," Felix replied, stubbing out his Viceroy cigarette in the truck's already full ashtray. "And you should be glad it was your old friend, Felix Mora, who came along, and not a gang of thugs out to rob an attractive widow woman like you . . . walking all alone on such a dangerous road. You should be more careful. And why would you be going to Matanzas anyway?"

"Niya and Lorenzo wanted to be first in line to apply for jobs at the new shoe factory down there, so I went with them on the bus yesterday morning. The manager used to be my neighbor, you probably know him . . . Senor Ruano, and after I spoke with him, he hired both Lorenzo and Niya on the spot. Such good luck. My children now have good jobs and I'm so relieved, even though my trip back home was such an ordeal. When the bus broke down, I was stuck. There was nothing to do but walk, and *gracias a Dios*, you came along," Olivia finished with her lie, hoping she sounded convincing.

"Where are your son and daughter living?" Felix inquired, squinting against the remnants of smoke that continued to rise from the ashtray.

"At the home of a local cane farmer who has government permission to let out rooms. They'll be very comfortable, and now that they are out of the city and working, it is such a blessing." She glanced at the entryway to her apartment building and frowned. "See what two days away from home brings? If I'm not around, no one sweeps the curb, the trash piles up like a garbage dump, and just look at those rotting melons! What a stench that will make."

Felix leaned forward to peer out the open window of his truck to assess the front of the dirty gray building where Olivia lived. The crumbling apartment had sagging balconies, rotted out window shutters, and cracked ornamental plaster dotting the uneven roofline. Strings of clotheslines holding underwear, diapers and tee shirts connected Olivia's building with a matching structure, where women in housedresses and old men in straw hats were sitting in metal chairs smoking cigarettes, drinking rum and passing the time as they watched the activity in the street below.

Jumping down from the truck, Olivia held open the passenger side door and leaned back in. "Goodbye. And thank you again."

Felix shifted the truck's gears and nodded at Olivia. "You be careful. With your children now living in the country, a widow woman like you must watch out. Call me if you need anything at all." Then he winked boldly, his lips turning up in a knowing grin.

"I can take care of myself, Felix," Olivia quickly tossed back. The last thing she needed was Felix, or any of her deceased husband's friends, getting too close. Things had to settle down. She had to be careful. If the state security agents ever found out that she had smuggled her children out of Cuba she could be fined, jailed, perhaps even executed by a firing squad. It had happened before. "I have managed on my own for five years now, Felix . . . ever since Pedro . . ."

"I know. I know," Felix interrupted. "But please don't say those words, Olivia. Your husband, Pedro, was my best friend, a good man. His death is one that I still cannot accept."

"His *execution*, you mean," Olivia boldly threw back, though she knew she should not say such words. "My husband didn't simply *die*. He was executed by the state for speaking his mind. For telling the truth, when so many were afraid to. He was killed, Felix. So, I *can and must* say those words, my friend, as much as it hurts."

"Just be careful, Olivia. Stay close to home."

"I will. I promise," she shouted. As Felix pulled away from the curb, she wondered if he suspected anything, if he might already know what she had done. *I've tested my story on Felix, and it seemed to go over just fine,* she decided, hoping others would be as easily convinced that Niya and Lorenzo were in the country working.

After the truck disappeared around the corner, Olivia approached her front door, assessing her neighborhood with new eyes. At least her children were finally out of Cerro, the worst, most dilapidated section of Havana, where every structure was an ornate colonial period building that had deteriorated into a ragged shell, creating a type of genteel ghetto that seemed to be valiantly struggling to hold onto its former brilliant glory.

Glancing upward, Olivia focused on the windows of her second-story apartment, which overlooked the busy street. Crisp white curtains hung in her windows, the red geraniums on her balcony were still in bloom, and the thermometer that had been hanging on the wall for years was most likely already registering near triple digit temperatures.

Drawing in a deep breath, Olivia entered the door at street level and began her climb up the cement block stairs leading to the second floor. Poor ventilation made the stairwell nearly unbearable and the buzz of mosquitoes was incessant. Inside her apartment, she found her three rooms musty and too warm after having been shuttered tightly while she had been away. Lorenzo's sneakers were still lying on the floor next to the sofa, where he had kicked them off two days ago. The American movie magazine that Niya had read so many times it was dog-eared and ragged remained on the coffee table, open to a layout on the life of the entertainer, Diana Ross. A lump sprang into Olivia's throat and she swallowed hard, her eyes stinging with unshed tears. Her mind spun. Her hands trembled. And her chest grew tight with alarm. What she hated most was that Niya, her firstborn, would celebrate her twenty-first birthday in two days—and in America, without her. Olivia would never get to know the woman her daughter would become. She was never going to see her beautiful daughter or her handsome son again. Never.

With a thud, Olivia set her heavy straw bag down on the kitchen table, and then went to turn on the tap to let the water run clear before taking a drink. Sediment in the water lines kept the water dark and nearly undrinkable, but in time it usually cleared up.

While standing at her sink, Olivia thought again about Felix, a worry line deepening on her brow. Felix knew exactly what had happened to her husband because he had been at the same protest rally with Pedro on the night of his arrest. However, Felix had run away when the authorities moved in, escaping capture and eventual punishment for participating in the anti-Castro rally to condemn the government for its lack of job opportunities for black Cubans. Her Pedro had not been so lucky. After four months of incarceration in Guantánamo Provincial Prison, Cuba's Council of State (the island's highest ruling body headed by Fidel Castro) refused to grant Pedro clemency. Pedro was tried quickly and executed by a firing squad two days after his trial, leaving Olivia to survive on a meager pension from the state.

Why did the government do this to us? she wondered. Both she and Pedro had been loyal supporters of Fidel Castro at the time that he took office, but soon it became clear that Afro-Cubans like themselves were not destined to benefit from the revolution. Castro's all-white political regime had been awarded top government and tourism jobs, pushing black Cubans into grinding poverty, forcing them to take the dirtiest jobs, or sell bootleg cigars, knock-off imported products stolen from warehouses, or marijuana to survive.

They didn't even let me see my husband or talk to him before they killed him, Olivia recalled with sadness. *I couldn't even tell my dear Pedro goodbye. Well, I've saved my son and daughter from a life of oppression and crushing poverty, and now they will have good lives in America. One day my children will send me Yankee dollars, and then I will have no more worries.*

The prospect lifted Olivia's heartache for a moment: a few American dollars a month would allow her to buy the kind of food she needed to keep her health up and her blood pressure down. She would be able to secure enough kerosene to use her stove more than three times a week. She'd be able to afford a decent dress and a new pair of shoes to wear to Mass, as the soles of her old black pumps were nearly worn through.

Reaching for a water glass from the cabinet above the kerosene stove, Olivia made a silent prayer that all would go well. When people disappeared from Havana, rumors were quick to start, especially when they concerned a family with a reputation for making trouble against the government.

Born and raised in Havana, Olivia had always considered herself to be an intelligent and curious woman. She easily mastered English at a very young age by listening to American radio whenever she had a chance and once dreamed of working as a high-level government translator. However, her racial and social status stood in the way of her making such an economic leap, so she concentrated on making sure her children had a better chance by teaching them to speak American-style English as soon as they could talk.

Now they are in America. Life will be better for them, Olivia thought, going over to the door that led out to her balcony. Opening, it, she was relieved to feel a breeze coming in off the ocean, right up from the Malecon, the spectacular, yet derelict ocean drive. Olivia's gaze went straight to the heart of Havana, beyond the urban landscape that stretched toward the Plaza de la Revolucion. From her balcony she could see the government offices of Fidel Castro and a monument to the poet and national hero, Jose Marti.

Cuba, she mused, facing the ocean where the bright blue sky matched the color of the water. Huge green palms lined the wide boulevard leading to the beach, and the crumbling façades of ornate structures along the way were muted shades of white and gray, blended by the distance. The view from Olivia's balcony did not betray the decay that she knew was eating at the heart of her homeland, but everyone in Cuba knew it was there, and growing fast.

Cuba. So noble, so old and yet still so vibrant, she thought. *You are my life, my soul, and I will surely die here. But my children will not, and that is all that matters.*

Chapter 3

At daybreak, the chatter of a flock of black birds fighting over a rotting swordfish carcass awakened Niya. She jerked upright, but quickly fell back down as a searing pain cut through her upper body. Glancing at her chest, she blinked at the ragged red stain on the front of her shirt, which was fused to her chest by the dried, caked blood that had seeped out during the night. Afraid to touch the wound, she lay back to think, while scratching at her arms which were a blistering mass of red puffy marks, created by the sand flies and mosquitoes that had nibbled on her flesh while she lay unconscious.

Tears sprang into her eyes, but she held them back. What good would it do to start crying now? She had survived the frightening dark waters and she was alive, though her shoulder was throbbing, her arms were still weak from the strain of her long swim to shore, and her mouth was so dry that her tongue felt like a rock in the middle of her mouth.

Forcing herself to remain calm, Niya carefully untangled her long black hair from the thorny underbrush and eased from beneath the bushes. The sunlight that hit her in the face was so strong that she had to shelter her eyes with one hand to look out over the agitated water. White-capped waves crashed onto the shoreline and lapped at the spot where she had washed up during the night. The sheltered area was little more than a swampy inlet about eight feet wide, enclosed in a tangled barrier of green thorny plants.

Weak from loss of blood and exhausted with despair, she squinted out to sea, expecting to see the boat, remnants of the forced evacuation . . . something to connect her to what had happened. But she saw nothing: No traces of life, human life at least, not even a waterlogged sneaker or a sodden plastic bag that had made its way to the beach during the night. For as far as she could see along the narrow strip of land, bleak sand dunes banked up against vicious-looking barriers of spiky jungle-like foliage.

What happened to all those people from the boat? And where was Lorenzo? she worried. Did he drown? Did the Coast Guard get him? If so, would the officials return him to Cuba? But what if it had not been the Coast Guard who fired those shots and ordered the boat to halt? What if it had been one of those vigilante patrols she had heard about, out to intercept illegal aliens who tried to pass through their lines? Could Lorenzo have been murdered, tossed into the sea, never to be heard from again?

As Niya struck out along the narrow beach, she prayed that her brother was alive and had made it safely onto land, because once a Cuban stepped onto American soil, he was safe.

Stumbling along the beach, Niya pulled at her sticky wet blouse, easing it away from her body, alarmed to see that new bloodstains had appeared. Gingerly, she touched the burning spot near her collarbone and winced with pain as the flaming flesh yielded beneath her fingers. Stopping, she quickly removed her sneakers, took off her white cotton socks, squeezed the water from them, and then pressed the damp ball of cloth hard against her wound, trying to stop more blood from seeping out as she continued on.

Lorenzo might have washed up somewhere along this beach, too, she told herself, refusing to believe he was dead. She pushed aside one bristly clump of swamp palms after another and, following the edge of the waterline, she pressed on for nearly a mile. Soon, her narrow path disappeared into the most dense part of the woods, and with no choice but to keep moving forward, she began to tear at the foliage with her bare hands, challenging the dark, damp jungle to let her through.

The thick undergrowth and the needle sharp fronds of the tropical palms made for slow going. The heat and humidity grew more oppressive with each step, and she had to stop every few feet to catch her breath and check her shoulder wound, which ached unmercifully. Very quickly, her hands became a mass of bleeding cuts, her eyes were stinging, and her throat had closed up with thirst. However, Niya persevered, ripping at the foliage that was blocking her path, thinking that she could hear a noise that sounded like cars on a highway.

Frantically, she pressed onward, through a stand of broadleafed trees whose limbs hung low to the ground until she stepped into a patch of sunlight, and nearly shouted her happiness when a dusty red van whizzed past. She stood silent for a moment, her chest heaving with relief as she assessed the situation, and once the dust that the truck had kicked up settled, she saw what looked like a gas station in the distance. Immediately, she started out to find help.

As soon as he stepped onto the boat, Lorenzo knew that the men who had intercepted the Haitians' escape were not officials of the United States Coast Guard, but participants in a vigilante patrol, as he had heard about back home. The six men in charge had plucked all of the refugees that they could catch hold of from the water and had herded them below deck into two rooms the size of closets, separating the men from the women and children. During the sorting, Lorenzo had searched for Niya's face but had not found her, and now he prayed that she had managed to swim to shore and was safe.

With a jerk, he wrapped his scratchy woolen blanket around him and pressed his spine flat against the wall of the cramped, locked cubbyhole, which was packed with half-drowned Haitian men. He was starving, but the smelly waste bucket, near to overflowing in a corner of the room, staunched his appetite and added to the discomfort of the unbearable situation.

What was going to happen to him? Lorenzo worried, his eyes darting from one dazed face to another. The men who shared his cell sat glumly on the floor, tight-lipped and sullen, looking like bundles of dark driftwood plucked from the sea. Each one had belligerently refused to speak or answer any of the questions posed by those in charge—even after being told that they were going to be housed at a detention camp on shore before their return to Haiti. Any man who jumped overboard and tried to swim to shore would be shot.

Upon hearing that, Lorenzo had hurried to explain, in his best American English, that he was not Haitian, but a political refugee from Cuba and he ought to be granted entrance to the United States. However, the impatient man had simply glared at him and shoved Lorenzo into the room with the others, before locking the door and disappearing without comment.

He must have understood me, Lorenzo thought, thankful that his mother had insisted he learn English. *Why won't the bastard talk to me? As a Cuban I have rights.*

Biting back tears, Lorenzo worried about his fate. Though brash and street-smart back home in Cerro, he did not feel very brave now. The intimidating presence of the gun-toting vigilantes, combined with their lack of concern for his circumstances made him feel small and vulnerable, and he knew nothing good was going to come from this situation.

Pulling his blanket tighter around his aching body, Lorenzo squeezed down on the floor between two of the Haitians and tucked his chin to his chest. Feigning sleep, he shut his eyes and began to think about how to get off the boat.

At daybreak, Lorenzo jerked awake when the door to the cramped cell burst open. One of the vigilantes came in with bottles of water, dry rolls, and juice. After placing the rations on the floor, he left without a word.

Hungrily, the men went after the dry bread, greedily devouring the food and drink, and then, much to Lorenzo's surprise, they began clamoring for information about their female companions and what was going to happen to them. It was as if they had all awakened from their trance at the same time.

From outside the locked cell, one of the guards yelled at the captives to shut up and quiet down, but when the Haitians ignored his orders, the guard opened the door and leveled his rifle at the agitated refugees.

"Shut up, you lousy illegal bastards," he ordered, sweeping the long barrel of his gun around the room. The guard was a young blond man with a round face, a short stubby build, and glaringly bright blue eyes. His green-gray Army fatigues swamped his youthful body, and his heavy steel-toed boots seemed to weigh him down.

Lorenzo studied the man carefully, thinking that under different circumstances, the guard might be a student, or a teacher. He certainly didn't look as if he ought to be brandishing anything like an automatic rifle at a bunch of smelly, frightened illegals.

"You will be reunited with your wives and children after we sort this mess out," the young man went on, deliberately pointing his gun at one man, then another. "Depending on each situation, you will either be sent back to Haiti, to an illegal immigration detention camp, or to another country for resettlement. You can forget about ever settling down for good on American soil."

Tensing his jaw, Lorenzo watched the guard carefully, suddenly aware of exactly what he had to do to get off the boat and find Niya.

Chapter 4

"Sandi Lee! Get over here! It's busier 'n hell."

The sound of her father's voice booming out the back door of the truck stop diner did little to motivate Sandi Lee Holt to hurry.

What's to rush for? she thought, not answering her father's demand and not looking forward to another day of frying eggs, pouring coffee, and flipping burgers for a bunch of raunchy truckers. Day after day, she faced the sweaty drivers and the same damn routine, with little to look forward to except aching feet, raw red hands, and the thing she hated most about working in the truck stop diner—hair and clothing that reeked of smoke. The pungent odor permeated everything and lingered long after her work was finished, acting as a constant reminder of how she had spent her day. Once, when her dad, Joe Holt, posted signs requesting that patrons of his diner smoke outside, the truckers had laughed at him and torn down the signs. So who was she to demand that the stupid jerks not smoke around her?

Squinting both eyes nearly shut, Sandi Lee tilted back her head and began to carefully apply a third layer of black mascara around her large jade green eyes. If she had to face the horny lot, at least she was going to look her best. Who knew when a man worth looking good for might actually come into the diner and lure her away?

"Sandi Lee! Get your ass over here!" her father yelled again.

"I'll be over when I'm fuckin' ready, Joe," she shouted back as she carefully drew the gooey black brush over her lashes again. "No way am I steppin' out of this trailer until I feel like it. Those truckers can kiss my ass," she stated with conviction. A giggle suddenly bubbled up and made her grin—a few of the better looking regulars had done just that . . . literally kissed her ass more than once.

With a dispirited sigh, Sandi Lee snapped her tube of mascara shut, applied a generous swipe of pink lipstick to her lips, and then picked up a rat-tail comb. With expert flicks, she began fluffing up the halo of pale blonde hair that erupted from the green satin headband that matched the color of her eyes. Her frizzy hair framed a small oval face with delicate features and a pasty white complexion that was less than perfect. However, Sandi Lee's solution to her not-so-beautiful skin was to obliterate the flaws with tons of makeup.

A small oscillating fan sat on the corner of her cluttered dresser among a jumble of cosmetics, magazines, cheap costume jewelry and tissues. The fan was whirring and struggling to move the stifling hot air around. Though it was not yet eight o'clock in the morning, a thermometer shaped like a Coke bottle, which hung above her bed, registered the temperature inside the trailer at eighty-seven degrees. As the day wore on, Sandi Lee knew it was only going to get hotter. At one time the trailer had been air-conditioned, but when the unit rusted out two months ago, Joe had not bothered to get it fixed.

"There's air conditioning in the truck stop," he had told her. "You can go over there to cool off and save me a lot of money." After hearing that, Sandi Lee had persuaded one of her regulars to buy her the electric fan, and in exchange she had rewarded him with a mind-numbing blow job in a stall in the men's bathroom.

Finished with her hair, Sandi Lee stood, unbuttoned the front clasp of her pink lace bra and leaned over the oscillating fan, allowing the cool air to bathe her more than ample breasts. Sighing in relief, she gave her body a once-over in the dresser mirror as the cool air calmed her nerves.

At nineteen, Sandi Lee Holt had the body of a twenty-five-year-old woman and an attitude to match. Standing five foot five inches tall, she had melon-shaped breasts with pink perky nipples, a tiny waist, and long legs, but absolutely no ass, so she sometimes wore panties with padded inserts on the buttocks, which she ordered from *Body Beautiful* magazine.

Rebellious and tough from having grown up without a mother, she knew how to take care of herself and rarely tolerated bullshit from anyone—not even her father, Joe. Her mother ran off with a truck driver when Sandi Lee was four years old, never to be heard from again, leaving Sandi Lee to be raised by her father. They had always lived in Oyster Cove, no more than a truck stop at the edge of the backwoods swamp off the southern Florida coast. Sandi Lee dropped out of school at the age of fifteen, had never been out of the state, and spent most of her spare time thinking about living any place other than Oyster Cove.

"When the time is right, I'm gonna split," she murmured, re-snapping her bra, then moving to her closet, where she removed a pair of worn jeans and a yellow crop-top blouse. "And when I go, I ain't never coming back."

After squeezing into the outfit, and making sure the top three buttons of her blouse were undone, she snapped off the fan, left the trailer and crossed the eight-foot-long gravel path that led to the truck stop's back door.

As soon as she entered, Joe rushed at her, a dingy dish towel over one shoulder and a black baseball cap on his head. He was a hulk of a man with a huge beer belly and shoulders as wide as the kitchen door. Tufts of gray hair were sticking out from under his cap on either side of his head, and the scowl on his face matched the tone of his voice as he started right in on Sandi Lee.

"What the fuck took you so long? I got six orders of eggs on now and two more waiting. Here," he said, flinging a greasy spatula at Sandi Lee. "Get busy watching that bacon and you better not let it burn, you hear? Bring 'em out when they're ready."

Without a word, Sandi Lee took up the spatula and turned her attention to the sizzling bacon and eggs on the griddle, screwing up her lips to keep from saying something nasty to her father . . . something she might have to pay for later. When Joe got mad at her, he could be a real terror, and she was not in the mood to deal with his shit tonight. No, not tonight.

As soon as the bacon and eggs were ready, Sandi Lee plated the meals with side orders of hash browns, grits and toast, and then pushed through the swinging door that led from the messy kitchen to the eating area where grizzled men in plaid shirts and jeans sat on stools at the counter, hunched over, waiting on her to show up.

With a great deal of attitude, Sandi Lee began plunking down plates in front of one man after another, making sure she made eye contact with each one, enjoying the way they greedily devoured the show of cleavage she provided. It turned her on to see how stupidly they stared at her, and how friggin' much they wanted her. And to know that she was in control made it all the more fun. It was all a game to her, and she *had* to play—who knew when she might discover a diamond in the rough . . . the man who would rescue her from this dreary place and set her free to live the way a girl ought to—in a big city where people wore nice clothes and partied every night?

"I'll be wanting seconds, honey," a middle-aged truck driver with a flat face and a thick neck told Sandi Lee the moment she placed his order on the counter. "Think you can handle that?" he smirked, staring at her breasts.

"I can handle anything you throw at me," Sandi Lee jauntily replied, turning away to clear some dirty dishes. She bent low over the table, giving the man a generous view of her jean-clad butt, secretly smiling to think of how much he must want to reach out and cop a feel. Knowing that his prick was probably growing hard in his pants made her own panties grow wet, and she knew she could get him to do anything she wanted if she had found him worth pursuing.

If only she could find the right guy—one dumb enough to let her use him, yet good-looking enough to tolerate for longer than a few minutes inside the cab of his truck. If she ever came across the perfect target, she'd haul ass to Miami with him tomorrow.

When the bell that was attached to the top of the front door jingled, Sandi Lee looked up, expecting to see a carbon copy of the truckers who were already inside, but instead, the person who entered was a dusky-skinned young woman with tangled black hair and frightened eyes, wearing a blood-soaked shirt and looking as if she'd been scratched up by a pack of wild cats.

"Who are you and what the hell do you want?" Sandi Lee blurted out, straightening up, hands at her hips. She was not about to let this girl, who was obviously in some kind of trouble, sit down.

"My name is Niya. I'm lost. Please help me," the girl implored, in fairly good English. "And I'm hurt, too," she added pointing to her blood-soaked shirt.

"I sure as hell can see that," Sandi Lee snipped, curling her upper lip to one side, assessing the girl, who was a head shorter, but much curvier, than Sandi Lee.

Niya leaned against the edge of the counter, as if to rest.

Sandi Lee looked the girl up and down. "Looks like you're in a damn serious situation. Who beat your ass?"

The girl simply shook her head.

"You been in a car accident?" Sandi Lee pressed.

Before Niya could reply, Joe rushed from behind the counter to see what was going on. All the men in the diner had stopped eating and were staring at the stranger.

"Whatcha want?" Joe snapped striding toward Niya, who stood rigid at the counter, mutely watching him. "What's a matter with you? You high on something'? Your boyfriend beat you up?" he demanded with impatience. Turning to Sandi Lee, he yelled, "What the hell is going on?"

Sandi Lee shrugged her shoulders and rolled her eyes. "I dunno. Says she needs help."

"I can see that, but I ain't no doctor," Joe muttered, frowning. Again, he addressed Niya, in a more brusque tone. "I asked you where you come from and what happened to you? Cops after you? I don't want no trouble in here." Joe stepped forward, as if preparing to physically push the girl out the door.

When Niya shied back and pressed a hand to her lips, Sandi Lee recognized the fright that flashed in her eyes. She knew what it was like to be all alone and desperate for someone to help. How many nights had she lain awake wishing someone would extend a kindness her way, help her out of the mess her life had become? Maybe she ought to do something . . . at least get the poor girl cleaned up. "Maybe I better go get Miss Gladys," Sandi Lee relented. "She's a nurse, I think. She'll know what to do."

"Whatever," Joe muttered. "Anyway, get this gal the hell outta here. This ain't good for business, and you beat it right back, understand? I need you here."

Nodding, Sandi Lee motioned for Niya to follow her, but once they were outside she pulled Niya under a scraggly mango tree and said, "Listen. I'll help you, but I gotta know what's going on. Tell me the truth, you hear? Who are you? What happened? I ain't about to get caught up in your shit and get myself in trouble. The cops looking for you?"

Niya shook her head, no.

"A crazy boyfriend?"

"No," Niya whispered.

"Spill it! Talk to me! You illegal? You might speak English okay, but I can hear that accent. Where're you from?"

"Havana," Niya replied.

"All right. Now I understand, 'cause nobody comes to Oyster Cove on foot. Nobody except boat people. You one of them?"

"Yes," Niya admitted. "I swam ashore last night. Stayed all night on the beach and then I walked through the swamp until I got to the highway. That's the truth. Nobody is after me . . . I'm sure they think I drowned. I lost my brother in the water, too."

"Damn, girl," Sandi Lee muttered, appraising Niya with new appreciation. "If you made it to Oyster Cove on foot through that thick ass swamp, with what looks like a bullet hole in your chest, then you gotta be tough. So, you're sure nobody's gonna come looking for you?"

"I'm sure," Niya assured her.

"Okay. That's my father's trailer over there. We live in the white one with blue stripes. Go on inside and sit down while I get Miss Gladys. She lives next door. She'll know what to do. Okay?"

"Okay," Niya whispered, setting off toward the rickety trailer at the front of the trailer park.

Once inside, Niya stepped directly into the closet-size kitchen, where she turned on the tap water at the sink and held her head under the faucet, drenching her head. Then she put her mouth to the spigot and gulped down large mouthfuls of water, drinking until she thought she would burst. Straightening up, she looked around. The place was a mess but at least there was a table, though littered with bottles of ketchup, mustard and half-empty soda cans, where she could sit down. Flies buzzed an unfinished bowl of cereal that was souring in the heat, which was almost as unbearable as it had been in the swamp.

Wearily, Niya sank into a chair, cleared a spot on the table, closed her eyes and placed her forehead down on the sticky plastic tablecloth, so tired and riddled with pain that she prayed she would pass out.

Since leaving Havana two days ago, she had eaten two apples and a chocolate bar, and had had no fresh water at all.

Her lips were cracked, her eyes were grainy with lack of sleep, and her whole body ached. What in the world was she going to do? And where could Lorenzo be?

"Take a sip, love. Yes, take a big swallow."

Niya stared into the cinnamon-brown face swimming before her eyes, thinking she must be back home in Cuba. The familiar smell of red root tea filled her head, its sweet scent bringing on a rush of homesickness, and the woman holding the cup of brew looked strikingly familiar, too. She had full dark lips, silver hoops hanging from her ears, and a colorful gardenia printed wrap on her head—very similar to one Niya's long deceased grandmother used to wear. The sing-song words the woman was speaking, while urging her concoction on Niya, reinforced her immediate sense of being back in Cuba, where red root tea was commonly given to anyone in need of quick revival.

However, as soon as Niya's focus improved, she quickly saw that the woman was not her grandmother returned from the grave, nor was she back home in Cerro, but still in the trailer, and now lying in a bed.

With a start, she tried to sit up, but the woman placed her palm against Niya's chest and urged her back down.

"At last. We see your eyes," the woman crowed in her island accent. "You are back to us. Very good. Now take a sip, please."

Relenting, Niya opened her lips and accepted the cup, taking a swallow of the tea. Immediately its sweetness spread through her aching body and filled her with a sense of strength. Rising up on one elbow, she strained to look around.

The girl, Sandi Lee, was there, standing to one side and staring at Niya with wide green eyes. A small fan had been moved close to the side of the bed, and it was buzzing and oscillating, providing a bit of relief in the stifling hot room.

"Have I been asleep very long?" Niya asked, struggling to clear her mind.

"Unconscious is more like it," Sandi Lee responded, bending over to give Niya a frank stare. "When I got back to the trailer you were a goner, passed out at the kitchen table. So, Miss Gladys and I had to carry you to bed. You've been out of it for hours. I was hoping you weren't gonna die. A dead body in *my* bed? I don't think so."

Perplexed by the selfish comment, Niya made no reply, but zeroed in on Miss Gladys, who seemed calmly content and eager to heal her patient. "You're a nurse?" Niya asked.

"No, chile, I'm a healer. From Jamaica," Miss Gladys clarified with a pride-filled smile that showed off two big gold teeth. "I tend to the people around here. You see, there's no doctor, no nurse, no clinic for miles. We have to care for ourselves down here."

"Down here?" Niya remarked, anxious for clarification. She had no idea where she was, but she was glad that Sandi Lee and Miss Gladys had come to her aid. "Where am I exactly?"

"I told you, this is Oyster Cove," Sandi Lee replied, moving to sit on the foot of the bed. "As far south as you can go and still be in Florida . . . or the tail end of nowhere as I call it."

"Oh, I thought I might be near Miami," Niya stated, totally confused. She had seen bright city lights along the shoreline before the patrol boat spotted them, but when she awakened, she had seen no signs of civilization at all. During her swim to shore, she must have drifted pretty far down the coast.

"Naw," Sandi Lee said. "This ain't hardly near Miami, honey. That's a long ways away." Sandi Lee tucked her bare feet under her hips, as if settling in for a chat.

Wetting her lips, Miss Gladys studied Niya for a moment, and then asked, "So who shot you, chile? A jealous lover? Or were you robbed on the road and thrown from a car? What happened to you?"

"Who shot me? I . . . I don't know," Niya stammered, glancing over at Sandi Lee, who must not have told Miss Gladys anything about her situation. That was good, she thought, placing one hand over the thick bandage that the healer had applied to her shoulder near her collarbone. The pain was not nearly as severe as it had been earlier, but the wound still pulsed and throbbed like hell. Looking at Miss Gladys, Niya asked, "Did you remove the bullet?"

The Jamaican woman tilted back her head and let out a short laugh, jiggling her full figure as she wagged a long brown finger at Niya. "You, me dear, had no bullet in you. No, love, only a bad flesh wound. Whoever was shooting at you did not have a very good aim!"

Sinking back, Niya murmured, "That's good, I guess," and closed her eyes.

Setting down the cup of red root tea, Miss Gladys stood, preparing to leave. "Well, she'll be sleeping for a while," she told Sandi Lee as she began packing her bandages, scissors, bottles and creams into a gigantic yellow straw bag trimmed with feathers. "The red root will keep her out for a while, and that's what the chile needs more than a lot of talk. She needs rest. Nothing more I can do."

"Rest?" Sandi Lee repeated. "So, how long does this wounded illegal have to stay here in my bed?" she demanded. "No way is Joe gonna let this girl stay, and I am not giving up my bed for very long. When can she leave?"

"Maybe in a week. Ten days. How soon depends on how fast the wound heals and whether or not she gets an infection. It's a bad wound, but not serious. You know? She will recover in time. Come get me if she gets the fever, though. That would not be good." With that, Miss Gladys swept out the trailer door in a flourish of gardenia printed fabric, letting the screen door slam behind her.

"A fuckin' fever?" Sandi Lee grumbled, leaning over to frown at Niya's sleeping form. "You damn well better heal fast and get out faster cause I ain't sleeping on the couch one day longer than I have to."

Chapter 5

The patrol boat lingered off the Florida coast for four nights, until at daybreak on the fifth day, when the vessel moved toward land.

Lorenzo pushed his way through the knot of men, who immediately crowded around the single porthole window in the stifling hot room. After having been locked up for so long, the men were restless, angry, and eager to get off the boat, so the sight of a harbor was both encouraging and frightening. What was going to happen next?

During the time he had been on the boat, Lorenzo had managed to strike up a conversation with a few of the Haitians who spoke limited English and had learned that for many of them, this was the second, third, or even the fourth time that they had been intercepted by a renegade coastal patrol. Each time they had been held on a similar boat for as long as four or five weeks before officials arrived to separate them—some going to detention camps run by the United States government while others had been returned to Haiti.

Moving into the mob, Lorenzo strained to see above the heads of those who were standing at the front, and managed to catch a glimpse of the desolate harbor where a rickety pier jutted out into the water and the shoreline was packed with a dense thicket of tropical foliage. Near the disintegrating wharf, he could make out a small semi-circular clearing, where a lone black car had been parked.

"Florida City. The detention camps are back there . . . in the woods. I know this place," one of the English-speaking Haitians murmured, as if answering Lorenzo's unasked questions. "I been at this place twice before. Both times, they held me for a long time, and then sent me back to Haiti."

Neither Lorenzo nor any of the Haitians had been out of their locked cell since being pulled from the water five days ago, and all were desperate to get out, go up on deck, breathe fresh clean air, and stretch their legs. As they gazed at the approaching shoreline, they held their breath in unison, anticipating whatever was going to happen.

Suddenly, the rattle of keys broke their concentration and the door to the cell swung open. They all turned at once and rushed toward the young blond guard with the startling blue eyes, who forced them back with a sweep of his gun. "Get back. All of you, get back," he ordered, waiting until the Haitians had returned to their spots on the floor before jerking his head toward Lorenzo. "All but you," he said, pointing his gun at Lorenzo's chest. "You. Cubano. Up on deck."

Quickly, Lorenzo followed the guard out of the hold and up the narrow metal stairs onto the deck, were he saw an official looking man in a white shirt and dark trousers standing with the boat's captain. He was holding a folded paper.

An immigration official, Lorenzo surmised, not feeling particularly relieved. Was he finally going to have an opportunity to prove that he ought to be granted amnesty, or would he be held in some detention camp far away from civilization until they decided what to do with him? It could take months, maybe years, for the officials to verify his status as a Cuban political refugee, and he would most likely be detained while the process dragged on. Lorenzo quickly decided that he was not going to wait around and find out exactly what the man had in mind.

With the tip of the guard's rifle pressed into his back,

Lorenzo strode forward, his eyes darting quickly from side to side as he checked out the situation on board the ship, as well as on land. Though he felt like a near-drowned rat in his wrinkled, still-damp clothing and with five days' growth of black stubble covering his chin, he walked with his shoulders back and his head high. At six foot three, with a lean, muscular build and broad shoulders, Lorenzo hoped to give the impression that he was not at all worried about what they planned to do with him, though in reality he was terrified.

As he continued to scope out the scene, Lorenzo saw that the gangplank, lowered for the official's arrival, still connected the boat to the pier, and the black sedan remained in the empty clearing. The Haitian had said that the detention camps were just beyond the woods, so there had to be a highway nearby to transport men, supplies and materials into the camp. If he could find it, he would get away and never get caught. All that lay between himself and a clear shot at freedom was the captain and the man he was talking to.

Increasing his pace, Lorenzo moved quickly across the deck and closed the gap between himself and the two men, but when their eyes met, Lorenzo suddenly spun around, whacked the armed guard with a hard hand-chop to the side of his neck, and sent him and his rifle clattering to the floor. Lorenzo gave the guard a hard kick, slamming the young man's head against a rusted metal container. Blood spilled from his temple and spread like dark wet paint all over the deck.

"What the fuck?" the official yelled, racing forward.

"Help on deck!" the captain shouted, as he raced toward the stairs leading down into the hold. "Get up here! We need help!"

Lorenzo wrestled the official to the ground, quickly put a headlock on the man and gave his neck a fast, hard twist. He could hear the bones crack as they snapped into pieces, and after releasing his choke hold, he dropped the man's body and tore off across the deck. He fled down the gangplank, and onto the pier, praying for a clean escape.

"Stop! You there, stop!" screamed the boat captain, who had hurried to snatch up the young guard's rifle. He lifted the weapon, aimed at Lorenzo and fired.

Ducking the volley of gunfire erupting above his head, Lorenzo yanked off the ropes that held the gangplank to the pier and shoved the flimsy walkway into the water, then jumped from the pier and landed on shore. For a split second he considered taking the black sedan, but decided not to—if the keys were not in the ignition, he would lose precious time.

Calculating that the heavily forested landscape surrounding the isolated wharf was the best route to take, he cut around behind the car just as a bullet clipped his ankle. He stumbled, but recovered and plunged into the jungle-like thicket, unsure of where he was headed.

Above the sound of his pounding heart, Lorenzo could hear the captain cursing, the refugees cheering, and the repeat of gunfire as more shots were fired. His feet slapped the ground and his arms pumped the air as he pushed tangled vines and low branches out of his way. Pain burned into his injured ankle, but he refused to stop. He zigzagged through the thicket, trying to keep the sun to his right side, hoping he was heading north. When he came to a fence made of sharp barbed wire, he easily jumped over it and continued on until the woods began to thin. Seconds later, he emerged into sunlight, and found himself on the shoulder of a two-lane asphalt highway. A fast-moving semi truck whizzed past, nearly knocking him down.

Without pausing to catch his breath, Lorenzo fled across the highway and ran alongside the giant eighteen wheeler until he was at the rear of the truck. He jumped up and grabbed its double door handles. Summoning all his strength, he pulled himself erect and braced his feet against the truck's rear bumper, even though the pain in his ankle was horrific. Holding on for dear life, he prayed that he could stay put until he was far away from Florida City.

Chapter 6

The hot July Miami sun burned into Tremont Henderson's body as he lay stretched out on a chaise lounge by the edge of the pool, his fingers dangling in the sea-green water. He was naked, except for the thick white towel he had draped across his lap and the Gucci sunglasses covering his eyes. Every inch of his well-proportioned, six-foot-two-inch frame glowed with an oily sheen of Sundaze body tanning lotion, which he faithfully used to enhance his naturally cocoa-brown complexion.

A portable CD player on the patio table emitted the edgy riffs of a jazzy saxophone number, sparking the hot, still air with a series of small explosions. Tremont drew in a long breath, filling his lungs with air that was heavily perfumed by the fragrant blossoms of blooming roses that filled the gardens of the gated property, and focused on the gorgeous blue sky overhead. He listened with satisfaction to the rough cut of his latest CD, thinking that he might not have to go back into the studio tomorrow after all. The new drummer he had hired for this recording session had clicked immediately with the other members of his jazz quartet, and every track, so far, sounded perfect. Nodding to the beat, Tremont tapped his fingers on the arm of the chaise and hummed along with the guitar player's solo.

"I like it, too. I think it's your best, ever," a deep voice called out.

With a start, Tremont shifted onto his side and turned his attention to his maternal grandfather, lifting his sunglasses to peer over at G-Daddy Grant, the man who had raised him.

G-Daddy had shocking white hair, deep brown skin, and a set of brilliantly white false teeth. At eighty years of age, his mind was still sharp and his attitude just as feisty as it had been when he was a young, brash man making tons of money in the booming Florida real estate market. And, until a recent fall in which he had chipped a bone in his knee, he had prided himself on power-walking five miles a day without getting winded. A smart, no-nonsense man who pinched pennies and abhorred waste, he lived with his caretaker nurse, Connie, in his shabby, but grand, antebellum house.

"You think it's pretty good, G-Daddy?" Tremont asked, always eager for his grandfather's approval.

"Definitely," the elderly man replied, giving the steering device of his electric wheelchair a quick buzz to maneuver closer to the table, where a spread of fresh fruit and cool drinks had been placed. "You've never played better, Tremont. Whatever you're doing with that horn of yours, keep it up," he remarked, popping a plump red grape into his mouth, and then reaching for a wedge of orange. "Maybe this one will top the charts, finally bring you some decent money. Make you rich and famous."

With a shrug, Tremont lowered his sunshades back over his eyes and lay back to stare at the sky once more. "Rich? Famous?" he muttered, clearly irritated. "You know I don't care about all that crap. I just want to make the kind of music that no one will ever forget."

With a whir, G-Daddy rolled his wheelchair right up beside his grandson and slapped him hard on the thigh.

"Damn, G-Daddy," Tremont hollered, rubbing his leg. "What'd you do that for?"

"Because you *should* be thinking about money and fame. What's wrong with being a rich man, and a famous one at that? You're twenty-nine years old, you live in a high rent apartment without any furniture in it, and drive a car that cost more than what I paid for this property twenty-seven years ago. You play the saxophone better than Kenny G, and I know for a fact that you make very good money, yet you squander every penny you earn on fast women and fast cars—running all over the place like a wild man. You ought to be investing your money . . . or sheltering it from the Internal Revenue Service."

"I'm not worried about money. So, why should you be? And the IRS? Well, it can go to hell," Tremont grumbled.

"Then you've settled that business with the tax man?"

"What business?" Tremont snapped. "I showed him what I wanted him to see and he went away. Anyway, there's no problem. Never was. That's why I always get paid in cash."

G-Daddy arched a brow. "That's a dangerous game, boy. Better watch out."

"I'm gonna enjoy my money and my life," Tremont tossed back, annoyed to have this conversation again. All his grandfather seemed to care about was cold hard cash—and re-telling the story of how he had accumulated his wealth by picking oranges and saving every dime he earned until he bought his first piece of real estate, which he parlayed into a massive estate.

With a snort, G-Daddy expressed his displeasure. "Humph. You need a good woman to settle down with. And not that girl, LaShaun, either. Grant you, she's cute and all that, but she's not wife material. All that child wants to do is shop and eat. Never saw anyone so tiny eat so much. But go ahead, enjoy her now, because you're young and full of energy, but what'll you do when you're too old and tired to race around the country and blow your horn? Huh? Who's gonna be with you then? And what will you have to show for all this beautiful music you're making?"

"I'll manage," Tremont jokingly replied, wishing his grandfather had not interrupted his lazy afternoon by the pool with his usual criticism about the way Tremont lived. As far as he was concerned, the future would take care of itself, and when the right woman came along, he'd know it. Until then he was perfectly content to enjoy his bachelorhood, and that included spending his time and his money any way he wanted.

"Well, if you managed your finances better, you'd be able to afford your own house with a swimming pool, and then you wouldn't have to come over here to lounge around mine every chance you get."

Laughing, Tremont pulled the towel that was covering his private parts tightly around his waist, and then sat up. "You saying you don't want your only grandson coming over to visit anymore?" He made a move as if to stand. "If that's the case, I can leave right now."

G-Daddy gave Tremont another affectionate whack on the leg, forcing his grandson back into his seat, and then shaking his head in irritation, went on. "That's not what I meant at all, Tremont, and you know it. I worked long and hard to get what I have—this property—which I bought it in '52 for a song. Now it's worth millions. You see, I was always thinking ahead, and now I have no financial worries. I wish you'd do more of that."

"But I am thinking ahead . . . thinking about tomorrow, in fact," Tremont replied with a serious tone. "I'm having lunch with Robert York, the owner of Club Cariba, a hot new spot on the beach. He's interested in signing my band to a long-term contract. That would mean I'd have a regular gig in town, cut down on the travel . . . and I'd be able to stick closer to home. You'd like that, wouldn't you?"

"Well," G-Daddy said gruffly as he maneuvered his wheelchair around. "I hope the man pays you a bundle of cash and you'll have enough sense to invest some of it in something other than a good time." With that, he waved both hands at his grandson, and started up the specially designed ramp that led from the pool to the back terrace of his white stucco mini-mansion, where his sharp-eyed, longtime housekeeper, Connie, was waiting to help him with his bath.

As soon as G-Daddy disappeared into the house, Tremont

yanked off his towel and plunged into the pool, embracing the slap of cool water against his hot, oily skin. With ease, he sliced through the water and swam the length of the pool two times before turning onto his back to float, luxuriating in the warmth of the July sun as it bathed his bare skin.

Swimming in the buff was a real treat, and Tremont treasured the privacy of this quiet interlude. He usually brought LaShaun, his current girlfriend, along when he spent a Sunday afternoon at G-Daddy's house, but today he had wanted to come alone. He needed relief from LaShaun, who seemed determined to remain connected to him via his cell phone, which he had deliberately turned off today. He broke off with her two weeks ago, but when she went hysterical on him and threatened suicide, he resumed seeing her, just to keep the peace. However, her impromptu visits to his apartment and incessant phone calls were wearing on his nerves. She needed to get a grip. He didn't belong to her and had no intention of marrying her. Maybe G-Daddy had been right about one thing—it was time to leave LaShaun and move on.

Jumping out of the pool, Tremont strode over to the chaise, picked up his towel, and began to dry off.

I wonder if G-Daddy and Connie ever skinny dip, he mused, glancing up at the windows facing the pool.

Chapter 7

"Take 'em off."

"I told you, no. I'm keeping them on."

"If you don't take off your boots, I'm leaving," Sandi Lee threatened, holding the man's dark eyes with hers in a standoff she knew she would win. It was tight enough in the cramped cab of the man's truck without his huge alligator boots getting in the way. She wasn't a contortionist and he wasn't coming up with enough money for her to get kicked in the legs and bruised by those big boys. If he wanted to have sex with her, he'd comply.

Calmly, Sandi Lee lit a joint, took a long drag, and then blew smoke into the dark interior of the truck, adding to the foggy atmosphere. Though cigarette smoke drove her crazy, a little marijuana now and then suited her just fine, and she never turned it down when it became available. And this guy had a shitload of grass in a plastic bag under the front seat.

Sitting with her bare back against the passenger side window, she looked across the road toward the trailer park, where a lone street lamp illuminated the shadowy cluster of worn out trailers huddled in a semi-circle behind the truck stop diner.

Was Niya asleep? she wondered, surprised that she was even thinking about the girl, who had been in Oyster Cove for two weeks now. Sandi Lee had to admit that Niya wasn't so bad—a bit naive, but at least the girl seemed smart, spoke decent English, and was definitely brave. She had come all the way from Cuba by herself to start a new life in America, even getting shot and losing her brother along the way.

The girl's got guts, Sandi Lee had to admit, wishing she had the nerve to blow this backwater swamp and start over somewhere else. She did run away once, when she was thirteen years old, but her father found her, picked her up, and beat the crap outta her. She never tried leaving again.

But my mother got out of Oyster Cove, she reminded herself, *and no one ever found her or dragged her ass back. Guess I been sticking around, hoping she'd come back for me, but she won't. By now, she's forgotten I exist.*

"All right. All right," the man grumbled, interrupting Sandi Lee's thoughts. "I'll take them off." Obediently, he pried off his boots, tossed them over the seat back and then reached over to tweak Sandi Lee's perky nipples. "Satisfied?" he asked, leaning down to flick his tongue over her firm pale breasts.

"Yes, that's better," Sandi Lee murmured, stubbing out her joint, returning to the moment. Slipping down on the vinyl seat covers, she opened her arms, and immediately, the man was all over her, kissing her neck, stroking her hair, pressing his sweaty hands into her thighs.

Quickly, she released the clasp of his metal belt buckle, slid her hands deep into the front of his pants, and removed his rock-solid hard-on. "Much better," she repeated, spreading her legs to let him in.

Using the thin blue towel that Sandi Lee had given her, Niya cleared a spot in the steamy bathroom mirror above the sink and leaned in to examine the half-dollar size gash at the base of her neck. The wound was definitely healing and, so far, she was no longer in pain, did not have a fever, and had successfully managed to shower for the first time in more than two weeks.

Relieved to be on the mend, Niya reached for the clean bandages that Miss Gladys had left for her, placed a new square of gauze over the wound, and secured it with two long strips of adhesive tape. As she towel-dried her hair she began to hum, slowly moving her hips and murmuring the words to "Para Que Cuba Baile," a song that she had loved to dance to back home in Cerro, while Lorenzo beat out the rhythm on his treasured bata drums.

The drums had belonged to her father, who also had played them for her when she danced. She smiled to think of those carefree days when her father had been alive and her family had been together. They had loved to make music whenever the opportunity arose: in the park, at family gatherings, and even in amateur exhibitions where they often won first place. If she had been in Havana on her twenty-first birthday, what a celebration they would have had. As it was, she had spent the day slipping in and out of a hazy sleep induced by Miss Gladys's red root tea.

In Cuba, everyone enjoyed singing and dancing—the island's music was a national treasure, and the songs and dances of Niya's homeland would always pulse hotly in her blood. She thrived when she was dancing, in the spotlight and accepting the admiring glances of the people who watched her perform. Back home, she had hoped to find work in one of the large hotels as a professional stage performer, but Afro-Cubans with family connections to political dissidents, like hers, were banned from the lucrative jobs in the Cuban hotel entertainment scene.

But here, she had hope: *In America,* she thought, *my dream of becoming a famous dancer could come true.*

Niya was ready and anxious to leave Oyster Cove and head to New York to find her Uncle Eric, and she would have left days ago if it had not been for Miss Gladys's insistence that she wait until her wound had properly healed. Though impatient to move on, Niya had silently agreed with the fussy old woman who hovered over her with unrelenting vigilance. It would be foolish to get out on the road alone, with no money, no transportation, and a bloody gash in her shoulder. Tomorrow, she was going to ask Joe if she could wait tables for tips or do odd jobs around the place for whatever he could pay. All she needed was a little more time to heal and some cash, then she was gone.

Tonight, she was alone, and it was a relief not to have Joe sitting in front of the blaring TV downing one beer after another. He was over at Miss Gladys's trailer playing poker with the Jamaican woman's boyfriend, and who knew where Sandi Lee had gone? All she had said was that she'd be back in a few hours, and then slammed out the door, leaving Joe screaming after her that she had better stop running around and acting like a tramp. Niya wondered what he'd meant by that remark, but wasn't about to ask. Joe and Sandi Lee argued non-stop, and more than once Niya had feared that they might actually come to blows.

However, things could be worse. She had a place to stay, food to eat, and medical care. Even Sandi Lee was no longer upset over having to share her room and her bed. She had told Niya that she could stay as long as she needed to, and had given her some clothes to wear, though Sandi Lee's shorts fit Niya a tad too tightly across the hips and Niya's breasts strained against the front of Sandi Lee's largest T-shirt.

In Sandi Lee, Niya had made her first new friend in America. Joe, however, was an entirely different matter. He complained about everything, never had a kind word for anyone, and was content to wallow in the miserable existence that he created for himself. The man was a mess: He managed to stay sober long enough during the day to operate his truck stop diner, but usually blacked out in front of the television every night, a beer in one hand, a cigarette in the other.

Niya tried hard to stay out of Joe's way, especially after he told her on the first day of her arrival that since she was eating his food, using his electricity, and wasting his water, she ought to be nice to him. Niya had seen the malicious glint in his bleary eyes, and known exactly what he meant.

Now, Niya wrapped the towel around her body and darted

from the tiny shower back into Sandi Lee's bedroom. There, laid out on the bed were new panties and several bras, the price tags still attached, with a note from Miss Gladys hoping she was feeling better.

How nice of Miss Gladys, Niya thought as she dropped her towel and slipped the undergarments on, relieved to finally put on clothing that was actually new, and hers. As soon as she got a hold of some money, she was going to buy her own clothes, makeup, and a stiff hair brush. Sandi Lee did not even own a brush, only a bunch of rat-tail combs that she used to fluff out her baby fine blond hair.

The small oscillating fan was stirring the sultry night air around the bedroom, and Niya went to stand in front of it, welcoming the cool air against her skin. It was never this hot and humid in July in Cuba, where the breezes off the ocean always blew across the island. The stifling humidity in Oyster Cove was not easy to get used to.

Standing in her new panties and bra, she let the cool air bathe her skin, and then went to Sandi Lee's jumbled closet and pulled a black tee-shirt and a pair of white shorts from a tangled pile of clothing. She was about to pull them on when she heard Joe walk into the trailer and open the refrigerator door.

The pop of a beer can.

A loud vulgar belch.

Footsteps heading her way.

Instinctively, Niya went to the bedroom door to lock it, but before she could do so, Joe pushed it open. She stumbled back.

"Whatcha doing in here?" Joe mumbled, glaring at her, blocking the door.

Niya held the tee shirt up to her breasts and stared at Joe, determined not to say anything—it was clear that he was definitely in one of his "moods" as Sandi Lee called the alcoholic binges that made him surly and argumentative.

"I asked you a question, you little wetback. Whatcha doin' in here?"

"Getting dressed," Niya remarked, deliberately tempering the edge in her voice. The last thing she wanted was a confrontation with him. "If you don't mind, I'd like a little privacy."

"Privacy? Shit . . ." Joe grumbled, taking a long swallow of beer. "I do mind," he slurred. "You ain't payin' rent. This is my trailer. You want privacy? All right, I'll shut the door." Joe came into the bedroom and kicked the door shut at his back.

In an effort to appear unruffled, Niya turned her back on him while calculating how serious a threat he might be. He was old, drunk, and already near to passing out. If she pushed him hard enough, he would probably collapse.

"You outta be nicer, Missy. Sandi Lee knows how not to mess with me. Took me a long time to teach her, but she knows how to get along. You outta take some lessons from her."

Before Niya could react, Joe grabbed her by the shoulder and spun her around, forcing her to face him. With a flick of his wrist, he tossed his beer can at Sandi Lee's wastebasket, which was overflowing with used tissues, paper towels, and old magazines. The unfinished beer spilled out onto the floor, releasing an awful stench. Joe yanked Niya up against his chest.

"Get away from me!" she hissed, breaking free and moving to the other side of the bed. Furious, she began to pull on the T-shirt. "If you touch me again, I'll scream."

"Go ahead and scream, nobody's gonna come." Reaching out, he ripped the T-shirt from her hands, threw it on the floor, and then planted himself inches from her face. "We can have a nice time. Me and you, it's okay."

"Okay? You must be crazy!" Niya shouted, pushing hard against Joe's bulky form. When he did not budge, she looked around for something to hit him with, and then snatched the oscillating fan off the dresser and smashed it into the side of his face.

"You bitch!" he growled, stumbling backwards.

Niya jumped onto the unmade bed and scurried across it, desperate to get out of the room, but Joe grabbed her by the ankles, pulled her back, flipped her over and flung himself down on top of her. He pressed his lips on her cheek, slobbering beer-breath saliva on her face. He pressed her deep into the sagging mattress. "Just a little fun," and then he gripped her panties and tried to yank them down.

"Get off of me!" Niya screamed as loudly as she could. Lifting her leg, she tried to knee him in the groin, but he blocked her leg with a heavy hand.

"Oh, no you don't," he ordered, grabbing her by the thigh and pushing her leg to one side. He tried to squeeze his bulk between her legs.

Niya let out a shriek and raked the side of his neck with her fingernails.

His bellow was met with shouts from the other side of the door. "Open up, Joe!" Sandi Lee ordered, banging on the door. "Leave the poor girl alone! You crazy son-of-a-bitch! Leave her alone!"

The sound of splintering wood interrupted Joe's attack as Sandi Lee's hard kick broke the lock on the flimsy door. Once inside, she rushed at Joe, a steak knife in her hand. Standing over him, she yelled once again, "Get up and leave Niya alone!"

Joe did not move.

Sandi Lee brought the knife down in a swift thrust and slashed a long red gash the length of her father's forearm.

"Shit. What'd you do that for?" Joe hollered, now rolling off of Niya, who jumped out of the bed and hurried to pull on the shirt and the shorts.

"Thank God, you got here," Niya told Sandi Lee. "He's drunk. Crazy drunk. He tried to rape me!"

With a sad nod, Sandi Lee looked at Niya, still holding the knife over Joe. "I know. I've been where you are, but nobody ever came to rescue me."

"You mean . . ." Niya started, not wanting to believe what

Sandi Lee had just admitted. Had Joe raped her? Sexually abused his own daughter? More than once? The thought made Niya suddenly sick to her stomach and all she wanted to do was get out of there, fast.

"Yeah," Sandi Lee confirmed through clenched teeth. "That's exactly what I mean. And he's not gonna do it to you."

"Shut up, Sandi Lee," Joe yelled. Reaching up, he tried to snatch the knife out of her hand, but Sandi Lee swung the knife up and out of his reach. "You don't know what you're talking about," Joe shouted. "I never did nothin' to you."

"Liar! You think I've forgotten? I was twelve years old. You sneaked into my bed, put your hand over my mouth, and made me . . ."

"I said shut up!" Joe yelled. "You goddamn tramp. You got me mixed up in your head with all those dirty truckers you carry on with. Think I don't know where you go at night? Think I don't know what you're doing? You ain't no better than your mother!"

Swallowing her fear, Niya began backing up. She eased into the living room, where she paused, her mind spinning. She had to get away, but how? And where could she go at two o'clock in the morning? To Miss Gladys's trailer? Out onto the highway? Oh, God, what kind of people were these?

"I gotta go," Niya decided, speaking to herself while searching for something to put on her feet. After spying a pair of green rubber thong sandals under the kitchen table, she quickly shoved her feet into them and headed to the door.

"Wait!" Sandi Lee called out from the bedroom. "Wait, Niya, please! Don't go!"

The urgency in Sandi Lee's voice made Niya freeze, one hand on the rusty screen door. Her mind whirled—Sandi Lee *had* been good to her. How could she ditch her only friend now? Especially after what she had just learned about Joe?

Cautiously, Niya stepped to the center of the living room and peered down the short dim hallway at Sandi Lee, who was still standing over Joe, now poking at him with the tip of her knife.

"Get your drunk ass up and go get me my money," Sandi Lee demanded.

"Money?" Joe mumbled, slowly sitting up, holding his injured arm while blood dripped all over the bed. "What money you talkin' about?"

"All the money you owe me for sticking around . . . wages, I guess you'd call it. Yeah, wages," Sandi Lee decided, pressing the knife hard against Joe's flushed left cheek. "The safe in the truck stop. Where the money is. You're gonna open it. Now! And don't say another word, you hear? If you say one more thing I'll slit your fuckin' throat."

Terror flashed in Joe's bleary eyes. He stumbled to his feet and lurched out the door, Sandi Lee close behind. Out of curiosity, Niya followed them across the gravel path and into the darkened diner.

Inside, Sandi Lee ordered Joe into the back room and waited while he opened the safe behind the freezer. Without a word, she grabbed handfuls of cash and stuffed the money into the pockets of her jeans.

Turning to Niya, she said, "Come on. We're splitting. For good."

Chapter 8

The Greyhound bus was empty except for a white-haired woman dressed in black who was seated one row behind the bus driver and a young man with headphones over his ears who was slumped down in a seat across the aisle from her. Niya and Sandi Lee had the entire back of the bus to themselves.

"Where are we now?" Niya asked Sandi Lee, peering out the bus window at the foggy coastal landscape as it emerged in the pale morning sunshine.

"Getting close to Florida City, I think," Sandi Lee replied, biting into one of the chocolate doughnuts they had purchased at the bus stop. "But we still got a ways to go."

"You been to Miami before?" Niya asked between quick sips from the paper cup of hot coffee she was holding.

They had been traveling all night. Walking, hitchhiking, and then walking some more until they came to a Greyhound bus stop at a rural country store, where they stocked up on bottled water, chips, candy bars and doughnuts. Now, at last they had food to eat and were on their way to Miami.

"I was there once," Sandi Lee stated. "Five years ago. I was thirteen years old and I'd overheard my father telling a guy in the diner that he thought my mom was living in Miami. So I ran away and went looking for her. I didn't know how I was going to find her, but I just knew I had to go. So I took off with Bobby Ron, one of the regulars who was always chatting me up at the diner. He let me hide in the back of his truck. That was a hell of a trip," she said, shaking her head, a hint of a smile on her lips. "He was real cute, and he was nice to me. He bought me anything I wanted. All he asked me to do was . . ."

"Uh . . . did you find your mom?" Niya interrupted, not interested in the details of Sandi Lee's sexcapades. The girl was always talking about men and sex, and how easy it was for her to get a man to buy her anything she wanted. Niya was no virgin, having had a fairly serious romantic involvement with her neighbor's cousin—a cute student at the university—but she certainly hadn't had the kind of experience that Sandi Lee claimed to have had. It was both sad and shocking to hear her friend brag about her wild encounters.

"Did you find your mom?" Niya repeated.

"Naw," Sandi Lee said. "I wandered around Miami for a few days, bumming food off tourists, sleeping in a park. But then, I stole a pair of shoes from K-Mart and the cops picked me up . . . they called my dad and made him come to get me. He beat the crap outta me when we got home. Told me I better never even think of running away again or he'd kill me."

"Kill you?" Niya repeated, wondering if Sandi Lee was exaggerating, as she had a tendency to do.

"Yep. That's exactly what he said, and I believed him, too. So, ever since then, I been waiting for the chance to split. Last night was it. I've had enough of his shit and it was time to leave."

"Do you still want to find your mom?" Niya prompted, eyeing Sandi Lee with interest, not sure of what to think.

"Nope," Sandi Lee quickly tossed back. "I'm grown now. I don't need her. Miss Gladys gave me all the mothering I needed and I'm not about to waste any more time looking for a woman who don't want to be found."

Niya bit down on her bottom lip and remained quiet. She

definitely felt sorry for her friend, who must have had a difficult time growing up without her mother. And to think that Joe abused her, too! They had grown up in such very different worlds, yet despite their differences, Niya was glad to have Sandi Lee as a friend. She was fun, unpredictable, easy to talk to, and had treated Niya swell, so far.

But can I trust her? Niya wondered, listening as her chatty companion rambled on about how exciting life in Miami was going to be and how they were going to use the three hundred dollars she had taken from Joe to buy clothes and get a cheap motel room where they would live until they got jobs.

"I can't get a job," Niya stated. "I don't have papers. I'm illegal, remember?"

With a gulp, Sandi Lee finished off her doughnut, wiped her mouth with her paper napkin and tossed it to the floor. "No problem. There are places where people like you can go and get help," she said with authority.

"You mean immigration?" Niya asked, thinking that was not an agency she wanted to tangle with. What if they tried to deport her? Detain her? She'd wind up in prison in Cuba, maybe executed—that's what had happened to her father.

"Nope. Not immigration," Sandi Lee replied. "Places that help refugees. I've heard the truckers talking about those agencies all the time 'cause they think there are too many Cubans in south Florida and the government ought to send all of you back home."

Niya flinched, but made no comment, knowing Sandi Lee spoke the truth—as she always did, in her blunt, no-nonsense manner.

Sandi Lee slid down in her seat, stretched out her legs, and put both hands behind her head. "They got all kinds of agencies and organizations in Miami that'll help you get a green card and find . . . what's your brother's name again?"

"Lorenzo," Niya answered.

"Yeah, Lorenzo. So, relax, Niya. You're too damn uptight. I

know you been through hell getting here and all, but stop worrying. You're in America now. Whatever you want . . . you'll get it. Don't worry, I know what I'm talking about."

"I hope so," Niya murmured, turning her attention back to the lush, green landscape that was rapidly slipping past.

Chapter 9

New York City

Rain seeped between the bricks in the wall and puddled at Lorenzo's feet, but he was too despondent to care. His body was stiff from sleeping on a cement floor night after night, his head ached and his stomach cramped with hunger. The swelling in his injured ankle had finally gone down, and the wound seemed to be healing on its own, but it still hurt like hell if he stayed on his feet too long.

With his back braced against the basement wall of the abandoned tenement building, he drew up his knees and stared glumly at the bold gray rat that was gnawing on a piece of rope—the same rat that had been scurrying around the dark, damp cellar for the past five days.

He had never been so miserable in his life. His current situation was even worse than his confinement on the patrol boat. He'd spent a week on the road hitching rides in trucks and in cars with scary-looking strangers until he got to New York, where he had located the address for his uncle that his mother had insisted both he and Niya memorize. However, the building was nothing but a shell; no one lived there anymore and the place had been stripped for demolition.

Now, after two weeks of living in the basement of a nearby

crumbling structure, along with a half-dozen or so other homeless men, he was starving, broke, perpetually damp to the bones, ragged, and afraid.

The neighborhood where he had taken refuge was ruled by dangerous gangs that roamed the area, guns in hand, and engaged in outright warfare at all hours of the day and night. The sound of gunfire was common. Ambulances screamed through the streets nonstop. Vagrants slept in doorways, prostitutes commandeered their corners with the vengeance of cats in heat, and the sporadic presence of police patrol cars did little to control the violence. If only he could get his hands on some money, he would buy food, some decent clothing, and a bus ticket to anywhere other than the hell hole where he was, but for now he had to depend on the garbage cans lining the narrow alleyways if he wanted to survive.

Upon his arrival in the basement shelter, Lorenzo had been welcomed by Pico and Jose, two other Afro-Cuban immigrants like himself who were down on their luck and living on the streets. However, he quickly realized that becoming too friendly with them might bring him more trouble than he needed. Pico, especially, asked too many questions: When and how did you get to America? Where is your family? In Miami or back home, in Cuba? Do you have problems with immigration? Do you want a work permit? A Social Security card? Birth Certificate? For one hundred and fifty dollars he could get Lorenzo any documents he wanted.

Lorenzo had backed off, giving Pico vague replies. After all, immigration spies were everywhere, and who knew when one of them might turn him in for the reward that must be posted by now? What was the punishment for beating, or maybe killing, an immigration official? he wondered, moving to a drier spot in a far corner to let the big gray rat go on its way.

While Lorenzo slept, the rain continued to pound the building and water continued to trickle into the basement. At daybreak, he awakened to find himself soaked through and so stiff that he could hardly stand. With a groan, he pushed himself up off the floor and went to one of the basement windows to look out. The sky was gray and the rain had slowed to a steady drizzle that would most likely last all day.

Lorenzo glanced back at the other ragged mounds of sleeping forms scattered throughout the basement, deciding to get out and see what he could find before the others awakened. Sometimes, just getting to a garbage can first meant the difference between eating or not.

Lorenzo crawled out of the window, pulled up the collar of his already soaked shirt, and lowering his head against the rain, started off down the alley. His first stop was the trash bin behind the Italian deli, where he scored a nearly whole submarine sandwich and a half-full bottle of Dr. Pepper. Feeling better, he continued on his usual route, checking one can after another for anything of value, which he had decided he would take to one of the many pawnshops in the area.

In Cuba, pawnshops were outlawed, though a thriving black market did exist, fueled by goods most often stolen from the state. In Havana, bags of rice, coffee, beans and even cement could conveniently fall off the back of a state-owned truck to wind up for sale on a side street within hours. A taxi driver filling up his car had no problem filling an extra gas can on his employer's bill, and clandestine bars, restaurants, and rooms by the hour for tourists' "entertainment" did a booming business in hard dollars.

Lorenzo had never been inside of a real pawnshop, let alone entered into a transaction with a broker, however, the other men living in the basement had quickly schooled him on the fact that in America the pawnshop was a quick source of cash—if you had something of value to offer.

Hurrying through the rain, Lorenzo cut through a series of connecting alleys until he emerged on a busy main street where the trash cans had been put out for the collectors. The debris was piled high in front of the houses and the stores.

Immediately he began rummaging through one pile after another, praying he might get lucky. If he could find good stuff to pawn, he might be able to get his hands on enough cash to buy those fake identity papers that Pico was always talking about. Why not? Lorenzo, rationalized. He couldn't live like this forever. If he changed his name, perfected his English and lost his Spanish accent, Lorenzo Londres could disappear completely. He'd be free of any connection to Cuba, to immigrations, and he could start life in America without always looking over his shoulder.

Havana

As soon as Olivia answered the door, she knew her luck had run out.

"Señor Crespo," she said in an even tone, greeting the man whom she immediately recognized as the state inspector who had come to her home and arrested her husband five years earlier. Why should she be surprised that the Interior Ministry would send the same man to question her? "What can I do for you?" she asked, as if she did not know what he wanted.

For the past six weeks she had gone about her daily routine with a forced smile on her face, a lie on her lips, and her heart filled with dread. Now the encounter she had known would eventually come was here and she was desperate to maintain a cool facade.

Manuel Crespo smoothed his bushy mustache with two fingers as he rocked back on his heels and studied Olivia with a cagey expression. He was a thick-waisted man with sallow yellow skin and thinning black hair, which he had combed over the top of his head in a wispy veil that did little to hide his baldness. "I need to ask you a few questions, Señora Londres. May I come in?"

Before she could answer, he had pushed the door back and walked into Olivia's tiny living room, where he paused for a moment while looking around. "I have learned that your son and your daughter are no longer living here with you," he started, walking from one room to another as he searched the apartment.

"That's right," Olivia answered, carefully closing the front door at her back. "They both have jobs at the Exito shoe factory in Matanzas and are living in the country." She went to her sofa and placed both hands on its curved back, steadying herself for his next remark.

"And when was the last time you saw them?" Crespo pressed, removing a small spiral-bound notebook from the inside pocket of his rumpled blue suit. He sniffed loudly as he thumbed through the pages until he found a blank one, and then waited for her reply, pen poised.

"Oh, two weeks ago . . . when I visited them in Matanzas," Olivia replied, now moving to sit down. She leaned forward, hands clasped in her lap, obvious concern on her face.

"Matanzas? Have you ever been to Caibarien?"

"Not for a while, why?"

"Because you were seen on the beach at Caibarien on the night of the seventeenth of June. Were you there, perhaps?" Crespo asked.

"Well, yes. I admit, I was there on a short holiday," Olivia confessed, her heart pounding in her chest. "Is there a problem, Señor? Are my children okay?"

"I wouldn't know about that. You see, we've had a report that a Haitian boat was intercepted off the Florida Keys on the night of June seventeenth. The same night that you were seen on the beach. The Haitians were captured and questioned and then returned to their homeland, but several of them said that there were two Cubans aboard the boat, also. A young man and a young woman."

"I have no idea what that could mean," Olivia told the inspector, secretly relieved to hear that Niya and Lorenzo had at least made it to America.

"The girl is missing and the young man escaped from immigration custody. He beat one of the officials very badly, nearly killed him, and no one knows where either one is now."

"And how does this concern me?" Olivia remarked, unable to trust herself to say more. Both of her children were in America and not in immigration custody! That news made up for whatever would happen to her.

"I think that the two young Cubans who escaped from the island were your son and daughter and that you helped them get away."

"Why do you think they are *my* son and daughter? I told you, my children are in Matanzas," Olivia insisted.

"No, I'm afraid they are not," Crespo shot back, a bitter edge now sharpening his tone. "I visited the Exito shoe factory yesterday and interviewed Señor Ruano, the proprietor. He has no records for employees named Lorenzo and Niya Londres."

"Oh," Olivia murmured. "Are you sure? The Exito factory?"

"I am sure," Crespo firmly stated, scribbling a few words on his notepad. He flipped it shut and stared hard at Olivia. "You'll have to come along with me to police headquarters, Señora Londres."

"Why? Am I under arrest?" Olivia boldly asked, now standing to lock eyes with the inspector.

"Yes, you are."

"And the charge?"

"Smuggling your children out of the country."

"That is not true, but even if it were, why not give me a ticket? Isn't a fine the usual punishment doing such a thing?"

"For some people, yes," Crespo agreed.

"And why not for me?"

"Because you are the widow of Pedro Londres."

And I will always pay a high price for that, she thought, silently thanking God that she had had the foresight to get her children out of Cuba before they, too, would be forced to pay for their father's opposition to a government that had never made good on its promises. "Are you going to handcuff me?" Olivia asked, her dark eyes flashing with anger.

"No, Señora. I trust you not to run," Inspector Crespo said as he escorted Olivia out the door.

Chapter 10

Niya tried to concentrate on Deep Diver Sam's rapid-fire instructions, but it was not easy. First of all, he spoke with a thick Southern accent that made his words sound as if they were coated in the Mississippi mud of his hometown and, secondly, he was wearing full scuba gear, mask and all.

"You want me to do what?" Niya asked her co-worker, who was also the son of the owner of Castaway Cove, the busy water park on the outskirts of Miami where she and Sandi Lee had found jobs.

Sam waved a glittery blue-green sequin costume at her while she eyed the man with irritation. He wasn't her boss and he couldn't tell her what to do. He might be the boss's son, but to her he was just an employee at Castaway Cove, like she was. "Sam, I'm supposed to be working the Pirate's Plunge today," she reminded him. "That's what the schedule says."

With an angry jerk, Sam yanked off his scuba mask and glowered at her. "Listen, we got a full park today. Look at the crowd. The Dolphin Dive starts in ten minutes and I need you to help me out, so put the damn costume on and start working the crowd. The kids want to see the dolphins. The women just want to sit down and rest their feet. But the men—and they're the ones coughing up the dough around here—the men come to see the girls. They don't give a rat's ass about watching me dive off a flaming lift and land on a dolphin. They want to see a pretty girl in a skimpy costume prancing around, so get with it. Okay?"

"I don't know if I should," Niya hesitated, scanning the crowded water park. It was a blistering Saturday afternoon, a typical August scorcher, and the line at Pirate's Plunge was three times as long as it had been yesterday, but at least over there she could stand in the shade and take tickets. Why would she want to prance around the edges of the dolphin pool in the sun, wearing a silly mermaid outfit? "Where's Joanne? Isn't that her job?" Niya finally asked.

"She quit."

"Really? When?"

"Yesterday," Sam threw back, frowning.

"Why?"

"None of your business. So, if you want to keep your job, go put that outfit on and cut out all the lip. I gotta go get ready for my show. Okay?"

Knowing she had better not rile Sam, who probably *could* get his father to let her go, she snatched the slinky costume from him and started toward the ladies' restroom.

"And hurry up!" Sam yelled at her back.

"All right, all right," she grumbled under her breath, but she did not increase her pace.

Since coming to work at Castaway Cove, she had worked every area of the popular water park: the fun-brella rental stand, the popcorn machine, the Riptide Raft, and had even sat in for an absent lifeguard at the toddler pool one afternoon. Thank God there had not been any problems, as she was hardly certified to perform CPR.

Sandi Lee was faring very well, after snagging a permanent assignment at the air-conditioned ticket booth where she happily chatted up every good-looking guy who came to the window. She had already had three different boyfriends since arriving in Miami and they had only been in the city for a little over a month. So far, Niya had not been out on a date at all, and that was just fine with her.

But at least they were working, for little more than minimum wage, and were allowed to eat all the hot dogs, popcorn and nachos that they wanted. However, once the water park closed for the season, she did not know what she and Sandi Lee would do.

They were living in a ten-dollar-a-day motel room near the park and were managing to get by. Upon their arrival in Miami, Sandi Lee had taken Niya to the Cuban Immigrant Assistance League (CIAL) so she could tell them her story. There, Niya had met Paige Moore, a buxom woman with platinum hair, dark roots, a ruddy complexion, and a dazzling smile who was a counselor at the agency, and also, as Paige promptly informed Niya, former Miss Miami of 1989. Paige was married to a Cuban, spoke fluent Spanish and was eager to help Niya file the necessary papers for a resident alien card.

"Under the law, you as a new Cuban arrival, are classified as a parolee," Paige had explained. "And that means you will be able to work while waiting for your permanent-residence status card, as long as you stay out of trouble."

With her paperwork in hand, Niya had gotten hired at Castaway Cove, and had begun to feel as if her life was finally settling into some kind of normalcy.

However, after two weeks on the job, Paige Moore called Niya with disturbing news: First, a young man who fit Lorenzo's description had been in immigration custody for a short time, but he beat up an official and escaped. He was shot, but he got away. Also, the address Niya had for her uncle in New York was not a good one: No one lived in that building anymore. And the last piece of news was the most devastating: Niya's mother, arrested for assisting in her children's escape, had been sentenced to twelve years in Manto Negro Prison for Women.

The barrage of bad news had left Niya's heart broken into a million sharp pieces, and she had staggered under the weight of the realization that her brother might be dead, her mother was in prison, and there was no Uncle Eric in New York to whom she could turn for help. However, she was determined not to give up hope. She was healthy, she had her permanent residence papers, and she had a job.

Now, inside the tiny bathroom stall, Niya shed her blue cotton slacks and her red Castaway Cove T-shirt with the name of the water park plastered across the chest, and stepped into the mermaid suit. Immediately she knew she was in trouble: Joanne had been a flat-chested, slim-hipped white girl with long legs and a narrow waist—a walking scarecrow, compared to Niya.

With a great deal of effort, Niya managed to squeeze her voluptuous hips into the skirt of the costume, and then groaned: The skirt had a slit up the front that nearly reached her navel and it flared out around her thighs in two metallic spikes, cheap imitations of fish fins. With a tug, she pulled on the tight-fitting bustier, which pushed her breasts into two mounds of bronze flesh that rose ridiculously high on her chest. At least the glittery seashell crown fit her head and did not look too bad.

Niya jammed her Castaway Cove uniform into her handbag, yanked open the stall door and stomped over to the mirror, anxious to check herself out.

"Damn! You look hot," a plump teenager wearing postage-stamp-size shorts and a tube top exclaimed as she dried her hands under the hot air blower. "You a part of the show?"

"I guess I am now," Niya murmured as she leaned into the mirror and fluffed up her thick black hair.

The people seated in the Dolphin Dive stadium roared with glee when the piped-in music finally came on, blaring Ricky Martin's popular "Macarena." Niya burst from behind a beaded curtain shortly after the music began and flashed the audience a big welcoming smile. Everyone began clapping their hands to the beat of the song and she instinctively began to dance, undulating her hips while making the jerky Macarena moves with her arms.

This isn't so bad, she thought, finding her groove and getting into the music, enjoying the opportunity to dance in front of a crowd. *But I'd feel a lot better if I had on a costume that didn't make me look like the Neptune witch.* Shutting out her worries about her appearance, she concentrated on her dancing.

For weeks, her life had revolved around survival; in Oyster Cove, on the road with Sandi Lee, while searching for a job and a cheap place to live, getting her green card and becoming legal. *Now,* she thought, *it's time to have a little fun.*

She motioned for the audience to join her, and almost immediately everyone jumped up and began to dance along with her, shaking their hips, swinging their arms, generally having a good time. As the music blasted from the loudspeakers, she improvised a jazzy rendition of the Cuban mambo combined with the Macarena and danced her way around the edges of the pool, often bending down to touch an outstretched hand here and there, feeling just like a real stage star.

At one point, her eyes locked with those of a drop-dead gorgeous guy with smooth brown skin and a bright white smile. He was wearing a white straw hat, a white shirt and a thick gold chain around his neck. When he reached out to greet her, she bent down and clasped his fingers, and then laughed when he tightened his grip, nearly pulling her off the stage.

"No, no," she cautioned, throwing back her head and tossing her hair from her face. "No fair pulling."

"What's your name?" the guy called out, still holding onto Niya's fingers, his other hand at the side of his mouth to make sure she could hear him over the music.

Grinning slyly, Niya shook her head, refusing to answer, and pulled her hand from his. Waving at him, she did a quick salsa side-step to the other side of the pool and concentrated on the audience.

The people were enjoying themselves, and that pleased her, though she was not sure if the crowd liked her, the music, or was simply glad that at last the show was about to begin. But either way, she knew that this was the Castaway Cove job she wanted permanently, and was certain that Deep Diver Sam would be more than willing to make sure she got it.

"Why did you do that?"

"What?" Tremont asked, glancing at LaShaun, who had jammed herself so close to his side that her sweet Chloe perfume was making him nauseous.

"Ask for that girl's name," LaShaun said in a huff, narrowing her lips at him. "What'd you want that siesta-sister's name for?"

"Oh, calm down," Tremont threw back, annoyed. "She's a good dancer and York is looking for dancers at the club. I was just thinking . . ."

"Well, you can *stop* thinking about getting *that* hoochie gal's name," LaShaun demanded, jerking her neck back and forth, making her braided extensions flip over her shoulder. "Robert York can do his own recruiting. He's paying you to play your horn, not scout talent for him," LaShaun finished, linking her arm through Tremont's and scooting even closer.

Gritting his teeth, Tremont cut his eyes over at LaShaun, who was wearing oversize dark sunglasses, a low-cut African print sundress, and at least a dozen thin silver bracelets on each arm. He could not read her expression, but knew her ebony eyes were flashing in anger—and for no reason at all. Her insecurities were getting to him, and he had had enough.

"Whatever," he grumbled, unhooking her arm from his, thinking, *She better not make a scene while we're here*.

He had made a big mistake, asking LaShaun out today after swearing he was through with her. Being with her had become more of a habit than a pleasure and he was definitely going to break it off for good. Today.

She ought to be glad I gave up my Saturday afternoon to bring her to this stupid water park when I ought to be rehearsing with my band, anyway, he thought, turning his attention back to the stage.

A loud burst of applause erupted when Deep Diver Sam

leaped from a flaming lift high above the pool and landed onto the back of a dolphin, which quickly swept him under the water.

"Wasn't that fantastic?" LaShaun shouted, rising to her feet, enthusiastically clasping her multi-ringed fingers together. "What a rush! Wouldn't you love to swim with a dolphin?" She looked over her shoulder at Tremont, who had remained seated, not paying much attention. "Well, wouldn't you?" she insisted.

"Not really," he muttered, clearly bored. However, he immediately perked up when he saw the girl in the sequined mermaid costume exit the stadium and start across the grassy esplanade, her head thrown back, her hips swaying, her gorgeous body beckoning to him.

Standing, he told LaShaun, "I'm gonna get a bottle of water. Want something from the concession stand?" He was already moving toward the exit.

"Yeah. A large cotton candy and a Diet Coke," she replied, concentrating on Deep Diver Sam's next trick.

"Be right back," Tremont said, hoping he could catch up with the dancer before she disappeared into the crowd.

It took him a few minutes to find her. She was standing at the ticket booth talking to the blond girl on the other side of the window. He went right over and said, "Hello. Now will you tell me your name?"

Breaking off her conversation with the blond girl inside the booth, she looked over at him and smiled.

That's a good start, Tremont thought as he waited for her to say something. When she didn't, he went on. "I enjoyed your dancing. You certainly livened up the place."

"Thank you," she replied in a rather bemused tone. "I enjoyed it, too."

"My name is Tremont Henderson," he boldly continued, extending his hand, which to his surprise, she accepted.

"I'm Niya," she told him, letting go of his fingers, and then cutting her eyes at the blonde in the booth with a who-in-the hell-is-this-man-and-what-does-he-think-he's-doing kind of look.

Tremont just stared at her, grinning, unable to say anything else. She was the most incredibly beautiful woman he had ever seen. Her skin was flawless, her dark hair was thick and soft and threaded with undertones of gold. Her large dark eyes were heavily fringed with the longest lashes he had ever seen. He had to struggle to keep his eyes from drifting down to the two luscious mounds of tan flesh bulging from the bodice of her mermaid costume. He could tell from her accent that she was not an American, and thought she must be from some island in the Caribbean.

"And you wanted . . . ?" Niya prompted.

With a start, Tremont plunged ahead. "To talk to you."

"About what?" Niya asked, edging away from the ticket booth window to let a woman with three kids step up to purchase tickets.

Tremont stuck close to Niya, hoping she would listen to what he had to say. "I'm a musician. I have my own band and I'm playing at Club Cariba over on the strip. You know it?"

Niya shook her head. "No, sorry. I'm new in town."

"Anyway," Tremont went on. "The owner of the club is looking for dancers, and I thought . . ."

"Dancers?" She shook her head. "I'm not interested. As you can see I *have* a job, and I don't do the club scene. I'm not into taking off my clothes on stage."

"Club Cariba is not that kind of joint. It's a jazz-salsa kind of place. Classy. You'd love it. The owner is looking for dancers to mix with the customers, teach some of the latest dance steps, kind of liven up the place. You know?"

Niya shook her head again and turned, preparing to leave. "Sorry. I'm still not interested. But thanks, anyway."

Tremont quickly removed a business card from his shirt pocket, and held it out to her. "Come by the club tonight and check it out. Ask for me. No cover charge, drinks on me. What do you say?"

Niya took his card, studied it for a moment, and then palmed it. "I can't," she lied with a slight lift of one shoulder. "I've got plans. My friend . . ." she paused and tilted her head toward the ticket booth, "and I are going . . ."

"*Next* Saturday, then," Tremont interrupted. "Please. Bring your friend. Bring two friends. Hell, bring as many friends as you want, but try to drop by, okay?"

"I'll think about it," Niya relented, tossing back her hair. "Right now I gotta get back to work. The next show starts in five minutes." With a quick wave, she hurried away, leaving Tremont staring at the sequin fish fins that swayed with the swish of her hips.

Sandi Lee waited until the lady at the window had pocketed her change and walked away before exiting the ticket booth. "I'll be right back," she told the pimply young man who was her backup.

She hurried through the crush of people, searching for the guy who had been talking to Niya, finally spotting him sitting on a park bench under a tree, sipping a Diet Coke and holding a big puff of cotton candy. She had heard every word of his conversation with Niya and no way was she going to let Niya blow this invitation. Club Cariba was the hippest place on the strip and *the* place to see and be seen.

Plans for tonight? What plans? Sandi Lee fumed. Niya could be so damn naïve sometimes. Didn't she know how difficult it was to gain entrance into a club like the Cariba? No one got in there unless they had a connection, and this was the opportunity of a lifetime. Besides, the guy was definitely worth checking out, too.

"Hey," she called out to Tremont, who looked over at her. Sandi Lee came closer, and then stood, her hands on her hips as she nodded her head. "My friend and I will be there."

"Excuse me?" Tremont blinked up at her.

"Niya and I will be at your club next Saturday night."

"Oh! Yeah. Really?" Tremont beamed and stood up. "You're Niya's friend?"

"Yeah," Sandi Lee replied, checking Tremont out. He was fine! And from the way he talked, she could tell that he was educated, had manners, and was not some creepy jerk out to get over. And his clothes, as well as the sleek watch on his wrist and the heavy gold chain around his neck, screamed cash. Lots of cash. "We'll come on one condition," she added.

"What's that?" Tremont asked.

"Send a car for us. A limo. Okay?"

A quick beat. "No problem," Tremont agreed. "What's your address?"

"Just have the driver pick us up here at the water park. Ten o'clock. At the front gates."

"You got it," Tremont said, a huge grin on his face.

"We'll see you at the club, then," Sandi Lee called out, giving Tremont a double thumbs-up.

Chapter 11

"I thought you said three hundred," Lorenzo protested, frowning hard at Pico, the homeless hustler with whom he shared his damp basement quarters.

"Not for all this, man. I got you a foolproof birth certificate, a Social Security card with a guaranteed untraceable number, a U.S. passport, and a New York driver's license. Five hundred or forget it." With a sneer, Pico shoved the packet of papers back under his ratty bomber jacket and crossed his arms, waiting.

"Four," Lorenzo countered. "That's fair, Pico. Gimme a break." He held his breath, hoping the guy was not going to be a hard-ass about this.

For weeks, Lorenzo had combed every trash pile and dumpster within a ten block radius of the damp basement where he lived in order to scrape together the money for new papers, pawning everything of value that he could find, sometimes taking only a few dollars for an item. His biggest score had been a brown paper bag containing a tangle of gold chains and earrings, many of them set with stones he had assumed were fake. As it turned out, the jewelry was genuine and he had walked out of the pawnshop with a fist full of cash, which he was not about to hand over to Pico. He needed the documents, but he also needed money to live on, didn't he?

"Four-fifty," Pico relented. "And that's a steal. I can move these papers on the street for twice that much. You want 'em or not? That's it, man."

Lorenzo drew in a ragged breath, held it for a long moment, and then let the air out of his lungs in a whoosh. "All right," he finally agreed as he counted out the money. "And these papers better be as good as you say."

Once the transaction was finished, he went directly to Trends, a hip men's clothing store nearby, and purchased new clothes, tossing his old ones into the trash can at the store. Then he headed to the nearest subway station and caught the train to Harlem, anxious to blend into the neighborhood's bustling, anonymous street life.

Lorenzo Londres was gone. In his mind, his sister and his mother might as well be dead, too. He was alone in the world, and he was Larry London, now—just another young black man wearing a throwback jersey, low-slung pants, a baseball cap turned to the side and bright white Air Jordan sneakers.

"Felix, you shouldn't have come here. You will only make trouble for yourself," Olivia hissed, trying to sound angry at her old friend when, in fact, she was overjoyed to see a kind face.

Since her incarceration at Manto Negro Prison for Women six weeks ago, she had been surrounded by angry, frightened, depressed strangers with whom she tried to have as little contact as possible. By staying to herself and not complaining about the filthy water, the lack of light, and the infestation of rats and insects in her cell, she hoped to make her twelve-year sentence easier to bear. Sure, she, too, wished things were different, and silently applauded the women who dared to raise their voices in protest over the conditions in which they had to live. But they were quickly labeled as troublemakers and immediately sent into isolation, which had to be a living hell. At her age, all Olivia wanted to do was survive until her release, but sometimes she doubted that she would live long enough to be free again.

Slowly, Felix Mora shook his head back and forth, dismissing Olivia's protests. "How could I not come to check on you? As soon as I heard you had been arrested, my heart stopped. I was so sick. What have they charged you with, Olivia?"

"Counterrevolutionary activities and contempt of authority."

"Just like they charged Pedro. But is it true that you helped Niya and Lorenzo escape to America?" he wanted to know.

"It is," Olivia admitted. "And I'm not sorry that they are gone. What's here for them, Felix? Nothing. Their father and I must pay the price for their freedom, and gladly."

Felix frowned as he shifted closer to the wire mesh window separating him from Olivia, leaning in as if to shield his words from the stern-faced guard standing watch over them. "How are you treated? What is it like for you?"

"Awful. Just awful. Rats, big ones. Bedbugs, too. They make it impossible to sleep. And it's so dark and crowded. There are eleven women in my cell and only eight beds."

"Are you eating enough? You look thin . . . and tired. Do you need anything?"

Olivia smiled. "You're too kind, Felix. The food is . . . adequate. Enough to keep from starving, but never any fresh fruit. Do I want anything? Yes . . . I'd love a pillow for my bunk. I, at least, have a mattress on my sleeping cot, and a thin blanket. A pillow would be nice."

"I will bring it next week," Felix promised, leaning back when the guard suddenly approached.

"Time is up," the guard announced, remaining close to Felix, who immediately stood, preparing to leave.

"Take care, my friend," he told Olivia. "Take care of yourself and I will see you again, soon."

Nodding, Olivia watched him walk away. Tears filled her eyes to see him go, and her mind flashed back to the one time she had gone to the prison in Cienfuegos to visit her husband shortly after his arrest. Her parting words to him had been,

"Take care. I love you. Take care." She had not been allowed to see him again.

How does a person "take care" in a place like this? she thought, re-entering the dank passageway that led to her cell. She didn't even have a comb to fix her hair, a decent bar of soap with which to wash, or a toothbrush to use with the hard paste that the prisoners were given. *I hope Felix will bring me that pillow*, she thought, glad to have something to look forward to.

Chapter 12

At exactly ten o'clock a white stretch limousine pulled up to the front gates of Castaway Cove. The driver got out and opened the door for the two young ladies who were waiting for him. Niya, wearing a floral handkerchief-hem skirt, five-inch wedge heels, and a clinging silk V-neck blouse, climbed in first. Sandi Lee, dressed in a gauzy black halter top and a tight black skirt, slipped in beside Niya. Both young women smiled sweetly at the chauffeur, who lingered long enough to get a good look at their legs before closing the door.

The drive to the club took less than fifteen minutes, and when they emerged from the limo they were in the heart of Miami Beach's trendy club scene. The gatekeeper at Club Cariba swung open the doors and ushered Niya and Sandi Lee inside, where a tall redhead greeted them and guided them to a table near the dance floor where Tremont's quartet was deep into its music.

The rhythms pulsed. The crowd gyrated. The margaritas, daiquiris, and rum colas flowed. And a steady stream of handsome men quickly descended on both Niya and Sandi Lee, whisking them onto the dance floor where they threw themselves into the party atmosphere, dancing nonstop until Tremont's band finally wrapped up its first set.

Breathless and flushed, Sandi Lee grabbed Niya by the arm. "Look, this is fun, but I'm ducking out for a minute. I met a guy who told me about a party over at the Towers. He wants me to go with him and check it out, okay?"

Niya frowned at her friend, clearly not happy. Sandi Lee, who had set the whole thing up and had been so eager to get there, was splitting? What was going on?

"You're leaving me here alone?" Niya said, furious to be dumped by her friend. She didn't know a soul at the club, but she was having a good time, and after seeing Tremont up there blowing his horn and making beautiful music, she wasn't in a hurry to leave. Besides, she wanted to hear more about this job offer of his. Dancing in a place like Club Cariba would be fabulous! Damn Sandi Lee. The girl was so flighty. So impulsive.

"Don't worry," Sandi Lee said. "It's still early. I'll be back. I promise."

"You'd better," Niya growled, peering at the lanky blond guy in creased jeans, boots and a cowboy hat who was bending down and whispering in Sandi Lee's ear. "You're leaving with him?" Niya asked, pointing at the guy, who grinned and nodded in her direction.

"Yeah. His name is Ace. He's got the invite to the party. A real swank affair. He's cool."

"Whatever." Niya shrugged. "Hey, I'm not your keeper. If you want to leave, go ahead, but I'm staying. And don't you dare take the limo," she warned.

Sandi Lee raised her eyebrows in feigned irritation, and then said in a sarcastic tone, "Don't worry. Ace has a car . . . a Mercedes Benz. So you get the limo all to yourself."

Though Niya was not happy about being ditched she knew there was nothing she could do to prevent Sandi Lee from leaving. Her friend had a rebellious streak that simmered just beneath the surface of her otherwise normal personality, and when it bubbled up, nothing stopped her from going after whatever she wanted. "All right, but be careful, Sandi Lee," Niya warned, giving her a quick hug. "We gotta go to work tomorrow, remember? So don't stay out all night and don't do anything crazy."

"Me? Do something crazy? Never," Sandi Lee laughed as she grabbed Ace's hand and took off.

Recorded music came on, and the dance floor thinned. Tremont left the stage to hurry and greet Niya.

"Hello," Tremont began. "I'm really glad you came, and I see you're having a good time."

"Yeah," Niya said, clearly out of breath, fanning herself with one hand. "This is totally great. A very nice club. I love it. Makes me homesick, though. Reminds me of Havana."

"So, you're Cuban?" Tremont commented.

"Yes, I'm Cuban," Niya replied, watching as Sandi Lee and the guy named Ace exited the front door.

"Come on. I want you to meet the guys in my band," Tremont said, escorting her toward an oversized semi-circular booth at the back where the other musicians had settled down for a break. Pausing, he began the introductions, "Niya, this is Dejen Ray, my guitarist."

Niya nodded at the young man, who was slouched low on his spine, a beer between his hands, which had small tattoos on each finger.

"And this is Jimmy, who plays keyboard, and Kofu, my drummer."

"Hey," both men greeted in unison. "Wanna sit down?"

"Sure," Niya replied, slipping into a seat next to Dejen as the others scooted over to make room. Tremont sat down on the outside, beside her.

The other musicians resumed talking among themselves, leaving Niya and Tremont to their own conversation.

"Been in Miami long?" Tremont asked.

"No, not long. A few months," Niya said.

"You like it?"

"Sure. So far, things have gone great."

"Got any family in the States?"

"Uh, no," she replied, deciding to be careful about how much she revealed. Even though Paige Moore had assured her that she was now a lawful resident and had nothing to worry about, she did not want to tell anybody about Lorenzo.

"So you're finding Miami to be a friendly city?" Tremont was saying.

"Yeah, it is. I don't really feel like a stranger here, with so many people from Cuba around. I can find all of my favorite foods. And the music, too! I'm not as homesick as I thought I'd be."

"Good . . . and thanks for coming tonight," Tremont told her.

"Thanks for inviting me and my friend, and for sending the car. It was very nice of you."

"Didn't I tell you this was a classy joint?"

Niya nodded enthusiastically as she looked around, and then sipped the drink that the waitress set in front of her. "Yeah, you did, and you were telling the truth."

"I always do," he kidded.

"You really can play that horn."

"Thanks." He focused on her, then lowered his eyes. "I played each song especially for you."

"Right," Niya laughed, though pleased by the compliment. He was a charmer, all right, and handsome, too, with a sense of humor and a great smile. His mocha complexion, clear brown eyes, and the hint of a dimple in his chin made him incredibly sexy. How had she gotten so lucky? she thought, now glad that Sandi Lee was gone. Who knew how this evening might turn out?

As her imagination began to kick in, she noticed a man approaching their booth. He stopped and placed one hand on Tremont's shoulder.

"Great set, as usual," the man said.

"Oh, hello Robert," Tremont started, glancing up.

"This the girl you told me about?" Robert asked, now focusing on Niya.

"Right. This is Niya . . . uh, gee," he grimaced and smiled. "You never told me your last name."

Niya smiled and said, "Londres."

"Well, this is Robert York, the owner of the club. I told him how I saw you at the water park and invited you to come by the club," Tremont replied.

Robert leaned over to shake Niya's hand and then took a chair from a nearby table and pulled it up at the front of the booth. "I've been watching you dance. Very impressive. Cuban?"

"Yes, from Havana. I haven't been in the U.S. very long," Niya murmured.

"You're perfect. I can use someone like you here at the club," Robert started right in. "The customers have been bugging me to offer demonstrations of the mambo, the rumba, the merengue . . . you know, salsa dancing is hot. I'd like folks to think of Club Cariba as *the* place to come and learn the latest dance steps."

"And he's thinking of holding dance competitions on Friday and Saturday nights, too" Tremont broke in. "The crowd would love you."

"Are you interested?" Robert asked.

Niya turned to Tremont, who simply winked at her and lifted a shoulder. She scanned the stylish club where trendy, hip people were having so much fun. Working in a place like this would be fantastic. Turning back to Robert, she told him. "You know what? I think I *am* interested. What did you have in mind?"

"You'd have to be here on Friday and Saturday nights. Demonstrate the dances on stage, with Tremont's group backing you up, and then mix with the crowd as they dance. Pump 'em up. Make sure they're having fun. Practice the dances with them. Stuff like that. I'd promote you as an authentic Cuban dance instructor, straight in from Havana."

Niya chuckled and paused, taking in his offer. "Sounds pretty good." She wanted to act cool about this, but she was so pumped up and nervous that her leg began to shake. When she felt Tremont's hand on her thigh, she jumped, but swallowed hard and thought about his move; he wanted her to calm down and successfully negotiate this offer.

"Uh, and the pay?" she ventured. Tremont squeezed her leg in agreement.

"Three hundred a night," Robert said without hesitation.

Tremont coughed.

Unsure of what that signal meant, Niya decided to repeat the offer. "Three hundred?" she said.

Robert York nodded.

"Hey, can't you kick in an extra hundred for costumes, makeup, hair? She's gotta look hot, doesn't she?" Tremont jumped in.

"Okay, okay. Four hundred. Be here at nine next Friday and you stay around till midnight, no later than one," Robert finished.

"You'll pay me four hundred dollars a night to dance for a few hours?" Niya clarified.

"Exactly," Robert assured her. "You in, you out?"

"I accept," Niya told him.

"Fine. Let Tremont know how I can get in touch with you and we'll work out some terms." Robert pushed back his chair and walked away.

"You'll never regret this," Tremont assured Niya, and then he leaned over and whispered in her ear. "You're going to be a hit. A big hit."

"Think so?"

"I know so."

Brightening, Niya began to hum along with the soulful song playing over the sound system: "Always Mine," sung by Juanita Christina, a popular Latina singer.

"Want to dance?" Tremont asked.

"I'd love to," she whispered, taking his hand.

On the dance floor, she let him hold her more tightly than any man she did not know had ever held her before, and she couldn't have been happier. A sense of belonging settled over her, as if she had come back to some kind of safe haven after a long and treacherous journey. She leaned against Tremont, placed her head on his shoulder and closed her eyes, not protesting when he lowered both of his arms around her waist and pulled her even closer. For some reason, she felt completely at ease in this stranger's arms, and knew that he would not be a stranger very long.

When the music stopped, she tilted back her head and studied Tremont's face in the flickering lights that were bouncing off the faceted ball rotating above the dance floor, her body still pressed to his.

"Thank you," she murmured, holding his eyes with a steady gaze, not ready to let him go.

"No, thank you," he replied, his voice hoarse. He touched his index finger to his lips, and then placed it gently to hers, letting it linger there for a few seconds. "I've never had a better time, and I hope we have many more."

"Me too," Niya agreed, aware of the beginnings of Tremont's erection nudge against her thigh.

"But I've got to get back to work," he quickly broke off, as if aware of what was happening. Moving away, he took Niya by the arm and started toward her table.

Suddenly, a woman in long braids, wearing a short African print skirt, a skimpy spaghetti-strap top, and a dozen silver bracelets on each arm planted herself in their path.

"Hello, Tremont," LaShaun said, possessively eyeing Tremont, one hand on her hip.

"LaShaun?" Tremont remarked, clearly surprised. He tightened his grip on Niya's arm. "What are you doing here?"

"Enjoying myself. As I see *you* are," she stated, now leveling a bitchy stare on Niya. "Reggy let me in. Since you took my name *off* the VIP list. Did you really think that would keep me out?"

Tremont rolled his eyes and drew in a deep breath. "Don't start, LaShaun. Not here."

"Don't start what? Telling you about yourself? You need to

be told, you loser. And I see you have a new woman on your arm already," LaShaun went on. "And I'm sure you know her name by now." Without waiting for Tremont to respond, LaShaun turned on Niya. "I've seen you before. You work at the water park, don't you?"

"Why, yes. I do. Why?" Niya answered, stepping back. This girl definitely was out for blood and Niya was not about to get caught up in her drama.

"No reason. Just verifying what I thought was true." Turning to Tremont, both hands now on her hips, she raged on. "You coulda broke off with me in person, Tremont. Walking off on me at the water park! Leavin' me sittin' in the hot-ass sun . . . and then leaving that dumb-ass message on my voice mail. Pleeze! That was some chicken-shit thing to do. But you know what? You can't get me outta your way so easy. I'm gonna be around and"—she paused to focus on Niya—"you, girlfriend, had better watch your back." With a flip of her braids and a scowl at Tremont, LaShaun stalked off and disappeared into the crowd.

Tremont whistled softly through clenched teeth, wiped one hand across his mouth, and then told Niya, "Sorry about that. I had hoped I'd never see her again. La Shaun can be a bit dramatic, but it's all talk. She's not dangerous . . . though I am sure she was the one who let the air out of my tires after the first time I broke off with her. That was months ago. Then we got back together, but we were never serious . . . or exclusive. She knew that."

"She sure sounds dangerous to me," Niya remarked.

"Hmmm. Don't worry. I'll call the police on her ass if she messes with you. Or my Jag again. A few days in jail ought to cure her of this crazy obsession she has about being with me."

"Apparently, she thinks you two are still in a relationship," Niya commented, feeling a bit sorry for Tremont. A jealous ex-girlfriend popping up was not good, but it was not unusual for a guy as handsome and successful as he was. She'd been through similar drama more than once back home in Cuba, where romantic face-offs often deteriorated into physical altercations.

"At least you know who my ex is and that I don't have any unfinished business with her," Tremont candidly confessed, giving a short laugh. "LaShaun is history. I promise."

"That's good to know," Niya agreed, "but you don't have to explain anything to me, Tremont."

"But I want to. LaShaun is in my past and she's gonna stay there. I want to concentrate on the future. Okay?"

"Sure," Niya murmured, moving toward her table, where she sat down and quickly ordered another margarita from a passing waitress.

The recorded music stopped, giving Tremont the signal that he and his band were due back on stage.

"Can you stick around and wait until I'm finished? I'd like to take you home," he said to Niya.

"If you want me to," she replied, in no rush to leave. Why be in a hurry to go back to her empty motel room? Sandi Lee most certainly was not.

"Promise?" he asked, as if afraid that she might escape as soon as he turned his back.

"Sure, I can stick around," she assured him. *Tonight, and for as many nights as you want me to*, she thought, one eye on Tremont as he walked toward the stage, the other on LaShaun, who was now sitting at the bar talking to a masculine-looking woman wearing a dark pinstripe suit.

Outside in the parking lot at the rear of the club, Sandi Lee broke off a long, breath-sucking kiss with Ace and leaned back against the soft leather of the front seat of Ace's Mercedes.

"You move fast, don't you?" she said, trying to catch her breath.

"What's to wait for?" Ace replied, pushing a lock of his limp blond hair out of his face. He sniffed, shrugged, and then slumped low behind the steering wheel. "Wastin' time is not what I like to do."

"Yeah? What do you like to do?" Sandi Lee prompted, really wanting to know, having already made up her mind to get as close to this guy as she could.

"Depends," Ace mumbled.

"On what?"

"On who I'm with and where my head is at the moment," he tossed back, flashing a mischievous, slightly crooked smile.

"Well, you're with me, so where's your head?" she teased.

"Cravin' some blow," he answered after a short pause.

"Oh, no problem there," Sandi Lee glibly answered, reaching for the zipper of his jeans. She yanked it down, reached inside his pants and wrapped her fingers around his already erect penis, eager to ease it out. "If it's a blow . . ."

Immediately, Ace placed his hand on top of hers, stopping her in mid-sentence. "You got it wrong, honey. Not that kind of blow. At least, not right now." Without more comment, he reached over her, popped open the glove compartment in the dashboard, and pulled out a small plastic bag. "This is the kind of blow I'm talking about."

Sandi watched with interest while Ace settled back in his seat and sprinkled a line of white powder onto the back of his hand, which he swiftly snorted up his nose. "Want a line?" he asked, already setting out another.

With narrowed eyes, Sandi Lee studied Ace in the dark interior of his luxury car. Did she really want to do this? With this guy? A blow job and a little grass now and then was nothing to her, but cocaine? This was something entirely different and new. She had heard all kinds of stories about what cocaine was like, but so far, had never had the opportunity nor felt inclined to seek it out to try it.

"If you don't want it, that's fine," Ace calmly informed her as he sniffed the second line of powder off his hand. "I don't want you to do anything you don't *want* to do."

Sandi Lee wet her lips with the tip of her tongue, and thought for a moment. Ace was cute, in a rough-tough, bad-boy kind of way. He obviously had money, or access to it, drove a fine car, and was dressed in designer clothes. She had seen the shirt he was wearing at Tommy Hilfiger and knew it cost one hundred and fifty bucks. With him she could have a damn good time. "Sure," she finally said, trying to sound as if she had done this before. "Why not? Let's keep the party going."

"All right! That's what I like to hear," Ace said, smiling enthusiastically as he laid out a generous line for her.

Lowering her head to the back of Ace's hand, Sandi Lee drew in a quick sharp breath holding one side of her nose, and then the other. Immediately she felt the inside of her head explode in a wonderful whirl of energy and light. A warm wave of pleasure surged through her body. Closing her eyes, she relaxed, allowing herself to enjoy the euphoria, while floating into an incredibly beautiful high. So much better than weed.

"Good, huh?" Ace commented as he placed the plastic bag back into the console and snapped it closed. He licked the back of his hand, zipped up his fly, and then started the engine. "Ready to party?" he asked Sandi Lee, pulling her close to his side.

"For sure," she replied, ready to go anywhere and do anything Ace wanted.

Niya finished off her fourth rum and Coke, checked her watch, and then got up to go to the ladies' room. It was twelve-fifty, and Tremont would be finished at one o'clock. After a full night of dancing and drinking she wanted to freshen up her makeup before they left the club, and hoped he did not plan to take her directly home. She was definitely in the mood to spend some private time with him: Tremont was one man she planned to get to know very well.

Niya pushed through the door to the bathroom, and immediately came face to face with LaShaun, who was on her way out. They exchanged icy stares for a brief moment, then LaShaun crossed her bracelet-covered arms on her chest.

"If you know what's good for you, you'll leave Tremont alone," LaShaun started right in, deliberately blocking Niya's path.

"Get out of my way," Niya ordered, not about to enter into a discussion about Tremont with this crazy woman. She stepped to one side, to go around LaShaun, but LaShaun quickly blocked her path again.

"You better stay away from Tremont," LaShaun repeated. "Don't be messin' in my business. He and I are tight."

"Not from what he told me. If Tremont wanted to be with you instead of me, he wouldn't have sent a limo to pick me up or put *my* name on the VIP list. Get real. He is through with you."

"Oh, no. We're not through. We just had a little disagreement. It's all good with us."

"I doubt that," Niya shot back, trying again to pass. But LaShaun held her ground and refused to budge.

"Please move. What do you want from me, anyway?" Niya demanded, frustration rising in her voice.

"My man," LaShaun spat out.

"From what I understand . . . he's not your man, so get over it, and get out of my way!" Niya moved so close to LaShaun that she could smell her too-sweet perfume, and thought she might be sick.

"Bitch, pleeze. Back up," LaShaun shouted. "Don't start somethin' you can't finish!"

"I think *you* started it, if I remember," Niya replied in a cool tone, now aware that the other women in the restroom had gathered around to see what was going down.

"And I can damn well finish it, then," LaShaun threw back. With a flash, she reached out, as if to grab at Niya.

Niya jerked away, but not fast enough—the many rum colas

she had drunk had affected her reflexes. In a jangle of silver bracelets, LaShaun's hand closed over the sleeve of Niya's blouse and gripped the fabric, tearing it with a hard yank.

"What the hell are you doing?" Niya shouted, shocked at this unexpected assault. She glanced at the torn fabric, took a deep breath, and then hauled off and slapped LaShaun hard across the cheek. "You keep your hands off me!"

"Oh, no. It's on," LaShaun screamed, one hand at her cheek, the other balled into a fist. "You keep your claws off my boyfriend," she growled, swinging wildly at Niya.

This time Niya managed to grab one of LaShaun's long braids, which she yanked as hard as she could.

LaShaun stumbled forward, lost her balance and tripped, landing in a heap of African print fabric on the bathroom floor, leaving Niya holding a handful of fake braided hair.

The women who had been watching the fight broke into screaming laughter and cheered Niya on.

LaShaun simply sat on the floor and glared.

Though her insides were shaking like crazy and she feared she might throw up, Niya forced an outward calm as she went over to LaShaun and tossed the braids into the enraged girl's lap. Then, she went to the sink, washed her hands, and stepped over LaShaun on her way out.

PART TWO

TREMONT

Chapter 13

December 1999

Tremont was in love. It had taken only one date with Niya for him to fall completely, utterly under her spell, and after sixteen months of dating, he was totally infatuated by her—her face, her lips, her hair, her scent, her taste, her voluptuous body, and her seductive smile. She was everything he had ever hoped to find in a woman to love, and he thought about Niya constantly—while driving along a highway, standing in the shower, eating a meal in a lonely hotel room when he was on the road, and especially while he was playing his sax. This obsession with her fueled his music like jet propulsion, pushing him to ever-increasing heights, creating a sense of purpose that often left him marveling at the sounds that came out of his horn.

Not only was Niya gorgeous, sensuous, and exciting to be with, she was smart and very talented. Her dance demonstrations quickly made Club Cariba *the* night spot to visit, and she had developed a wildly supportive fan base of her own. Robert York's business had tripled since he hired Niya Londres.

In addition to dancing at the club, she also gave private lessons to wealthy patrons and often performed at their lavish charity events at their gated estates by the sea, earning thousands of dollars a night. She was an extremely patient teacher and an entertaining performer who made her clients feel intimately connected to her as she taught them the latest dance steps or showed off her intricate routines. Among the jet set, everyone was talking about Niya, who was simply referred to by her first name—the hot, sexy dancer from Havana.

Now, Tremont turned onto his side and focused on Niya, who was fast asleep in bed beside him, her dark hair covering most of her face. She had moved in with him two months after they met and he had never been happier in his life. She was perfect for him. She fit with him. She was levelheaded and practical when she needed to be, yet could party like a wildcat when it was time to have fun. She loved dark rum, but never drank too much, could stay out all night, and still look beautiful the next day, and she was a great cook, but careful not to overindulge—especially on the Cuban empanaditas that she loved to prepare after a long night at the club. They often ate them while sitting on the balcony of his high-rise apartment while sipping rum colas and watching the city lights and talking about the many loves that they had in common: music and dance, Miami, and all things tropical; the sea and the stars; brightly colored clothing, paintings, and anything South American; and food. Oh, how he loved her cooking, and she was always eager to cook for him.

Their relationship had evolved at a breathtaking pace after their first night together at Club Cariba. When he had climbed into the limo with her that night to take her home, she had told him, in a quiet, girlish voice, "You don't have to worry about LaShaun bothering you anymore." And after hearing what had gone down in the restroom, he had laughed out loud at the image of his ex-girlfriend sitting on the floor of the ladies' room, her fake hair in her hand. It pleased him to know that Niya was not the kind of woman who would take crap from a nut case like LaShaun. At that moment, Tremont had been certain that Niya was the woman for him.

She had simply grinned at him and suggested that they go to a quiet place where they could have coffee . . . and talk.

"Sounds perfect," he had agreed, settling her into the crook of his arm, where she remained until the limo stopped in front of a small café on a quiet street a block from the beach.

There, they huddled under a broad blue and white umbrella on the café's breezy patio to drink strong coffee and listen to Brazilian jazz.

During that first night together, Tremont had been eager to talk about himself . . . revealing more than he had expected to, anxious for her to understand that he was not some flighty musician looking to score with a pretty girl, but a man truly interested in getting to know her.

He had told her how his parents had handed him over to his grandfather when he was a child, and then disappeared, leaving G-Daddy to raise their infant son.

"Where did they go?" Niya had asked.

"To Los Angeles. My mother wanted to be an actress, but she and my father wound up living under a freeway overpass and surviving on handouts from strangers." Tremont had been surprised at how easily he had revealed this to Niya. It was a story that still made him ache.

He told her about receiving his first saxophone from his grandfather at the age of ten and how quickly music had become the center of his life. Soon, his world revolved around his horn, his music, and his grandfather, whom he loved very much.

"Nothing else has ever mattered," he'd confessed, and then he had touched Niya's chin, looked directly into her eyes and added, "That is, until I met you."

The next night he took her out to dinner. The following afternoon he took her to lunch at G-Daddy's house and the old man fell in love with her, too. His grandfather pulled Tremont aside and told him sternly, "Now, you're acting like you got some sense. Don't let that girl get away."

On their ninth date, they stayed in, at his apartment, where they ate spaghetti and drank red wine and listened to his new CD, which had just been released that day, and they made love for the first time.

At dawn, Niya had untwined her smooth limbs from his, showered, and quietly left. His entire body ached to see her go.

Later that day, while sipping drinks at a quiet bar, she had finally told him about her life in Cuba, including the arrest and execution of her father, her mother's arrest, her terrifying voyage to America, and how she had lost her brother at sea, including all she knew about his alleged escape from immigration.

"I miss him terribly," she had murmured. "I don't want to believe that Lorenzo was the Cuban boy that immigration says did those things, but in my heart I know he's capable of it. He's strong willed, hot-tempered, and would not easily be detained by any kind of government official. My father's imprisonment and execution nearly destroyed him. I know Lorenzo well. He'd risk his life to get away."

"And your mother?" Tremont had asked, pleased that Niya trusted him enough to share her painful story. "Have you communicated with her? Has she heard anything about your brother?"

Niya had spoken slowly, carefully. "I can't write to her, or try to contact her. It's too dangerous. Cuban authorities monitor the mail, and a phone call is out of the question. Only tourists and government officials have easy access to telephones. A letter from me would only cause trouble. I just hope she's doing okay." After a long pause, she continued. "I've been working with Paige Moore, a counselor at the Cuban Immigrant Assistance League, and she's trying to get information about my mother's situation, but it's difficult to get news about what's really going on."

"I'm sure your mother will be fine," Tremont had offered, trying to comfort her, wishing he could do more.

The telephone rang, interrupting Tremont's reverie and

awakening Niya, who stretched and smiled at him as he rolled to the side of the bed and reached for the phone.

At nine o'clock on a Saturday morning, it was probably Dejen, the only member of his band who might be up at this hour after a long Friday night at the club. Everyone else Tremont knew slept in, almost as late as he did, which was usually until noon.

"Yeah?" he spoke into the phone.

"Tremont. Man, it's Dejen," a deep voice rushed to say.

"Right, I figured it was you. What's up?" Tremont asked, frowning as he sat up and listened to what his guitarist had to say.

"Bad news, man. Skip James is backing out of the live broadcast."

"He can't do that," Tremont shot back, now swinging his feet to the floor. "I've been promoting the hell outta this thing for weeks. The club is gonna be packed. Why's he canceling?"

"Didn't really give me a reason. I ran into him at the Breakfast Kafe this morning. Said to tell you the station can't do it." Dejen paused. "You better get to him. He's at the station now. Better do something fast, Tremont. Without that live broadcast, the CD's gonna die."

"I'll take care of it," Tremont promised, clicking off.

"Anything wrong?" Niya asked.

Tremont looked back at her but did not really see her, his mind was still processing Dejen's upsetting news. "Yeah," he murmured. "KMIA is trying to cancel the live broadcast they promised to do from the club. Dejen said Skip told him the station can't do it. I gotta get over there and talk to him."

Niya placed a hand on Tremont's thigh. "Can't Robert take care of that? It's his club."

"No. I made the commitment and Robert's counting on me to deliver."

When he started to stand, Niya grabbed the elastic waistband of his pajama bottoms and tugged him back.

"Not now," she murmured, yawning.

"But I need to take care of this. Skip promised to do this live broadcast, and it's coming off. And on Saturday, too!"

"Can't you go a little later?" she cooed, now reaching into his pajama bottoms to massage his buttocks.

"Naw. This needs to be handled right away."

"So, he'll be there for a while. You don't have to go just yet." She snuggled closer, eased her body on top of Tremont's and wrapped her sleep-warm arms around his bare chest.

Tremont felt his himself grow instantly hard at her touch and knew he was in deep trouble. "Niya," he weakly protested as she began slipping his pj's over his hips and down his legs. "I have business to take care of," he said, his voice hoarse, his desire for her so hot he was already perspiring.

She sat back and pulled her nightgown over her head and tossed it aside, and then slid her naked body over his.

Fully aroused, Tremont knew it was no use protesting further. Skip James would just have to wait.

Flipping her onto her back, he covered her lips with his, then he eased down to suckle each perfectly erect nipple, his tongue tracing soft circles around the dusky flesh. Her moans urged him lower, down to her navel and into the soft brush of hair between her thighs, where he settled in to pleasure her exactly the way he knew she liked him to.

As he kissed and stroked and touched her, she grew wild with excitement, and didn't hesitate to give him full access to the most intimate parts of her body. Making love to Niya was a pleasure-journey filled with delightful twists and turns that drove him to heights he had never known before, and a journey he hoped would last forever.

After making love, Niya went to take a shower.

"Are we still going shopping this afternoon?" Niya asked, drying off. With only two weeks until Christmas, they still needed to find the perfect gift for G-Daddy and the members of his band, whom he treated more like brothers than fellow musicians and friends.

"Sure. When I get back," Tremont said, stepping into a pair of tan Cavali slacks while grabbing a pair of socks out of a drawer. "Did I really say I was going to ruin a perfectly good Saturday afternoon by traipsing through the mall with you?" he replied, tucking in his navy polo shirt.

Niya took a sip from the cup of coffee sitting on her dresser and mocked a frown. "Yes, you did. So hurry back. We'll have a late lunch, and then off we'll go."

"Steak sandwiches?" Tremont prompted as he fastened the leather band of his Cyma watch.

Niya thought for a moment. He loved her *pan con bistec*, and she loved preparing it for him, but she'd have to make a quick run to the Cuban market for the bread while he was gone. "If that's what you want, sure. And after we finish at the mall, we've *got* to go talk to the caterer at Pierre's."

"Pierre's?" Tremont repeated.

"The caterer that your grandfather wants to use for his New Year's Eve party. I was there when you promised G-Daddy that you would take care of everything. Did you forget already?"

"Yeah, I guess so," Tremont mumbled.

"What would you do without me to keep you organized?" she teased.

He strode over to her and bent down and kissed her. "I never want to find out. You've become totally indispensable."

"That's good to know," she tossed back, running her tongue over her lips. "Hurry back, okay?"

"I'll try, but Skip is not one to hurry with negotiations. I can't rush him, but I'll be back as soon as I can . . . promise," he replied, kissing her again before taking off.

After she finished dressing, Niya went out onto the private wraparound balcony of the spacious six-room condo in the heart of Miami that she shared with Tremont. From the twenty-sixth floor of Turquoise Towers, a luxury high-rise on

Ocean View Drive, she had spectacular views of Lake Catalina and nearby downtown Miami. She never tired of standing on the balcony enjoying the luscious scene spread out before her: the modern tall buildings, lush green landscapes, shiny expensive cars on the streets, and beautiful people everywhere.

During the months they had been together, Tremont had taken her on the road with him a few times—to Tampa, Atlanta, and New Orleans—fascinating cities that looked exactly like the photographs she had seen in magazines back home. However, none of them made her feel quite so comfortable and secure as Miami, where all she had to do was walk a few blocks from their apartment to find the foods and smells and music of her homeland, as well as people in the streets who spoke the same language. Walking through Little Havana was like a visit to home.

"But I've come a far, far way from Cerro," she murmured, still surprised by all that had happened to her in such a short time. Her life in Havana and the hopelessness she had felt while living there were fast becoming distant memories. The present was beautiful. Tremont was captivating, and so easy to love. He made Niya happy, and she knew she was a lucky girl.

She now earned more than enough money at the club and from her private dance lessons to support herself in style, but living with Tremont was what he had wanted, and she had not been able to resist his invitation. She had fallen in love with him that first night on the dance floor, and had rarely been separated from him since. He was thoughtful, loving, talented, and generous—at times, too generous, for her taste.

He loved buying gifts for her: jewelry, flowers, perfume, and even clothes. He had excellent taste and always bought the best. When she protested about the amount of money he spent on a Louis Vuitton bag for her twenty-second birthday, he'd turned angry, and nearly snarled when he said, "Never do that again. It's my money to spend. Let me be happy, making you happy. Please?" Realizing that she had touched a raw spot, she had backed off and never said anything again about how he spent his money.

With Tremont she felt whole and safe, and was careful never to crowd him. Images of LaShaun sitting on the floor of the ladies' room was enough to keep her from ever taking her man for granted. So far, her life was perfect. Almost. She only wished things were turning out as well for Sandi Lee.

Chapter 14

Sandi Lee ducked her head and remained behind the wheel of Ace's black Mercedes until Tremont passed by, but as soon as his Jag disappeared down the exit ramp of the parking garage, she felt safe enough to get out. She slammed the heavy car door shut and hurried toward the elevator, praying she would not run into Niya. That was the last thing she needed to happen. She had not wanted to come to Turquoise Towers for just that reason, but Ace had insisted.

"What are the chances of you running into Niya or her musician boyfriend?" Ace had snapped when she told him why she did not want to go there "Zilch! Nada. I promise you. Hundreds of people live in Turquoise Towers. You're not gonna see a soul who knows you, and this connection is too good to mess up. You gotta go."

He better be right, and this better be worth it, Sandi Lee mentally grumbled while waiting for the elevator to arrive.

It had been almost a year since she had seen Niya, though they had spoken on the phone a few times. After that first visit to Club Cariba everything had changed for both of them, though at times Sandi Lee wished that she and Niya were still crowded into that cramped motel room, working at Castaway Cove, and living off nachos, popcorn and hot dogs. Life had been fun and simple then. All she'd had to do was show up at the water park and sit in a ticket booth all day, and then get dressed up and party all night. Though she was crazy about Ace, life with him was not always as easy or fun as it had been when they first met.

Sandi Lee was glad that Niya had fallen hard for Tremont and had moved in with him, and while she had fallen hard for Ace, she had also developed a love affair with the pretty white powder that he made sure she never was without. The stuff made her crazy, made her float, made her happy, made her sad, and made her do things she sometimes wished she didn't have to do. But she couldn't give it up. Getting high was all she cared about, and when she was floating along with Ace, the ugly parts of her life with him and before him disappeared, leaving her suspended in the euphoria of the moment.

Inside the elevator, Sandi Lee opened her purse and removed the small pink notebook which she carried everywhere, and after checking an entry, pressed twenty-two. She leaned against the wall as the elevator zoomed upward, glad to be alone. As many times as she had done this, she still got nervous, but there was no way she could back out now.

At the twenty-second floor she got out. The corridor was empty, quiet, and decorated with expensive looking lamps, vases, and paintings. She paused in front of a spectacular gilt-framed mirror to check her hair, which she decided was looking a bit limp, so she bent over and gave her head a hard shake, then straightened up and went to the last door at the end of the hallway.

Sandi Lee drew in a deep breath, pressed the buzzer, and began counting to herself. If no one answered by the time she got to ten, she'd leave. That was the way it worked.

The door swung open right away. "Well, hello! Sandi Lee?" a middle-aged man in a navy velour jogging suit asked.

"Yeah, that's me," Sandi Lee coolly replied, thinking that at least he looked like a nice man. Sometimes they looked mean and angry, or depressed, which always spelled trouble.

"Come in. Come in," he told her, his huge grin exposing nearly all of his big white teeth.

Sandi Lee entered the spacious living room, which was surprisingly modern—furnished with sleek light wood and glass furniture that looked European—Swedish, perhaps, she thought.

The man offered her a drink, which she refused, deciding to get right to the point.

"Uh, if we can take care of the business . . ." she began, hoping to nudge the man to get on with it. Ace had told her she had twenty-five minutes to get this done and get back home, and if she was late returning, she'd be sorry.

"Oh, sure," he said. The man went over to a chrome and glass desk, opened a bottom drawer and took out a yellow paper bag, which he immediately handed to her.

Sandi Lee sat down on the low tan leather sofa and crossed her legs as she opened her purse and counted out her money, making sure the man saw that it was correct. Then she examined the contents of the package while the man, who was hovering over her, watched. She stuck in a finger and tasted the white powder to be sure it was the real thing.

"Okay?" he asked.

"Okay," she replied.

"Want a hit? To be sure?" the man prompted, pocketing the cash, and then moving to sit down beside her.

"Can't. Not outta this," Sandi Lee tossed back. Ace would know right away if any of his buy had been tampered with. She had done that once before and never would again. She had been black and blue for weeks and still had a scar on her upper arm where he'd dug his fingernails into her flesh.

"Oh, no. Not your stuff. I got my own stash," the man offered. He reached under the sofa and pulled out a metal tray containing a glass pipe and several large white rocks.

"Well, shit, yeah," Sandi Lee exclaimed, perking up. As long as it was his, why not? Just a quick hit and then she'd be gone.

"Can you . . . uh . . . get comfortable?" the man prompted, one bushy eyebrow arched as he dropped one of the white rocks into the glass pipe. He flicked his Bic lighter and waited.

Without a word, Sandi Lee stood up, stripped off her skirt and top, and then sat back down beside him in her panties and bra. "In here? The bedroom? Where do you want to take this party?" she asked, reaching for the pipe.

Tremont swiveled back and forth in the blue club chair in front of Skip James's desk, determined to remain calm. After thirty minutes of small talk about his latest release, the new club scene, and the music industry in general, Skip still had not gotten to the problem at hand, and Tremont was getting anxious. He should have known it would play out like this. Tremont was used to his colleague's rambling, long-winded discourses and thought Skip acted that way in order to maintain control over the person he was talking with—some kind of a radio talk-show host throwback that Skip could not let go, even though he was now part-owner and general manager of the station.

Tremont had known Skip for fifteen years and was silently fuming mad over what Dejen had told him. There had to be a way out of this mess and he was not leaving until he found it.

"Okay. The problem," Skip stated, finally getting around to the reason Tremont was there. "I know the station agreed to launch your CD during a live broadcast from Club Cariba, Tremont, but it's not going to play out that way after all." He fiddled with the gold nugget cuff links in his pristine French cuffed shirt and then leaned away from his desk and lifted his chin, peering at Tremont through eyes that had turned into dark challenging slits while waiting for a reaction.

Tremont knew the game that Skip was playing, and it hurt him to realize that his old friend was putting him to the test. The music business was like any other; there was always a way to get what you wanted if you were willing to play the right game. "Let's get right to it, Skip. How much? How much for a live broadcast?"

Quickly, Skip leaned forward again, his ebony eyes now fully open and lit with interest. "Here's the deal . . . KMIA is owned by Clear Wave Radio, who owns twenty-seven stations across the country in major markets. Why should management throw cash at one market here in Florida when your CD could be playing nonstop, simultaneously all over the country?"

"And you can make that happen?" Tremont clarified.

"Shit, yeah. Man, I got all the DJs in my pocket. By this time tomorrow, every Clear Wave station disk jockey in America could be making sure your music becomes so well known, you'll get sick of hearing it on the air."

"How much you need to make this happen?" Tremont ventured, holding his breath.

Skip scribbled a figure on a piece of paper and shoved it across the desk at Tremont, who looked at it, grimaced, and then thought about his grandfather's constant criticism over how he spent, or wasted, his money. He could afford to pay what Skip asked, but was this what he wanted to do? Paying off DJs across the country would strip him of a chunk of cash, but maybe for once he'd be putting his money to good use. And there was another matter that he had to address: He had told his grandfather that he was straight with the IRS, but they were still nosing around, asking questions about his income. He had to be cautious about where he tossed his cash, but what choice did he have? He had to make the CD fly. "If that's what it takes, I'm in," he decided.

"You sure?"

"I'm sure. As long as I'm free to book other venues in each city and get a take of the door."

"Sure. I got no problem with you making extra money on the side. Glad you see things my way. You gotta realize, Tremont . . . Afro-Latin Jazz is hot in Miami, but it'll take some serious air play to move you out there in other markets. There could be more expenses ahead. Understand?"

Tremont nodded. *Like all the venue owners and local promoters who'll be eager to hype my appearance, as long as I grease their palms,* Tremont thought, fully aware of what it was going to take to get where he wanted to be in the business.

"Can you go on the road after the holidays?" Skip broke in.

"Sure, my contract with York is fluid enough. He'll let me off to make appearances in other markets. I just gotta give him a few weeks' notice."

"Okay. I'm thinking of a two-month tour starting early January. East coast and midwest, first . . . then California and Texas later. This album is your best, man. It could earn you a Grammy nomination, but you got competition. Constant air play is key, and you got hip-hop, rap, R&B, and country taking up the airwaves. And don't forget gospel . . . gospel's the fastest growing segment of the market right now. Can you believe it?"

"Yeah, I can."

"So, you do what you have to, to get some serious air time, right?"

"Right . . . uh. You want cash, I suppose?" Tremont prompted, knowing Skip spoke the truth. This CD represented everything he had ever wanted in a recording and it had received excellent local reviews. However, it would be up to him to push it deeper into the marketplace if he wanted to make some real money and get national recognition. If Skip James could help him do that, Tremont was willing to give the guy whatever he wanted.

"Cash? Hell yes," Skip shot back, pulling a serious expression. "I don't want no paper trail, or any trouble, and neither do you, I'm sure."

"I'll bring the money by tomorrow," Tremont told Skip, hoping he was doing the right thing.

"Not here," Skip decided. "Call me. I'll come pick it up."

"Fine."

"All right," Skip said, grabbing his pen, scribbling as he continued speaking. "Now, let's outline exactly how the tour is gonna go. I think Philly should be the first stop, then D.C., okay?" Pausing, Skip glanced up in question at Tremont.

"Sure, sure," Tremont vaguely replied, realizing there was no way he was going to get home for lunch with Niya today.

* * *

Niya balanced her paper bag of groceries in one hand and dug into her purse for her door keys with the other as she crossed the Turquoise Towers' spacious lobby and headed to the elevators. In addition to the Cuban bread, she had bought bananas, apples, pears, and a huge bouquet of fresh *plumeria* for her kitchen table. In Miami, just as in Cuba, fresh flowers were a necessary part of everyday life.

The elevator filled quickly, but Niya managed to squeeze inside, with her nose nearly pressed against the door. At each floor, the crowd thinned out until only she and a woman holding a toddler were left. At the twenty-second floor the woman got off and the doors began to close, but then a voice called out, "Hold it, please!"

Instinctively, Niya put out her hand to block the doors for the passenger, and was shocked when Sandi Lee stepped in.

"Well, Sandi Lee. You finally came to see me!" Niya remarked, wondering why her friend would be roaming around on twenty-two when she knew she lived on twenty-nine. "Did you get lost? Tremont and I live on twenty-nine. Good thing I ran into you."

The elevator doors closed.

"What?" Sandi Lee remarked, staring blankly at Niya. "What the hell are you talking about, Niya? I been visiting . . . a friend . . . a different friend."

Niya stepped closer and looked into her old friend's face, which was flushed pink and covered with blotchy marks. Her pale blond hair was damp and her mascara was smudged. She looked as if she'd been in a fight.

"You're stoned," Niya said matter-of-factly.

"Yes, I am," Sandi Lee giggled, putting one hand over her mouth. "And it was the bomb. Really the bomb, Niya. You shoulda been there." Then she closed her eyes, leaned against the back wall of the elevator, and slowly slid to the floor.

Chapter 15

"Hey, Larry, go over to Crizie's and get me a double pepperoni with extra sauce!"

Lorenzo's head snapped up, as he automatically responded to his new name, though it had taken several weeks to get used to hearing himself called Larry. He was Larry London from Philadelphia now, and he loved to hear those words. They made him feel proud, in control of his life, and free of Lorenzo Londres, the scared kid from the slums of Havana who was an illegal alien and a fugitive from the law.

It was a relief to be an unknown—an anonymous black man in a huge country like America. Such a thing could never have happened in Cuba, where everyone was trapped on a piece of land the size of California, and too many people were related by blood, marriage, or simply proximity. However, he missed his mother and his sister terribly, though he tried not to think about them. Especially Niya.

Where was she? he wondered. Did she drown? Or was she alive and well and getting on with her life? Perhaps, in Miami? She had not come to Brooklyn looking for their uncle, he was certain. He would have heard about it if she had been in the area, asking questions. Did she think of him as often as he tried not to think of her?

Their abrupt separation was still far too painful to dwell on, so he always pushed the experience out of his mind as soon as thoughts about it surfaced.

His sister and his mother *had* to stay in his past: They were the only connections to the identity and the life he had been forced to abandon. According to his fake birth certificate and passport he was Larry London, American citizen, and as such, could never return to Cuba. He was on his own.

When Larry first arrived in Harlem, he had mistakenly befriended some street people whom he later found out sold drugs on the corners and took bets on drag races in back alleys. He had stupidly committed a few petty crimes with them in order to get his hands on some quick cash, but quickly realized that living so close to the edge was very dangerous. After he dumped the neo-gangland lifestyle, he took a series of odd jobs that paid honest money, found a clean, but small room in which to live in an area where he felt relatively safe, and bought a color TV.

There was nothing Larry loved more than American television and American music, especially the new hip-hop rappers who were edgy, raw, and mesmerizing. He was enthralled by their jerky, rhyming lyrics, impressed by the huge numbers of sexy girls who turned out for their concerts showing off so much skin, and loved the rhythms that pulsed in his blood long after he'd seen a performance.

Larry had begun composing songs, which he scribbled on small pieces of paper scattered all over his apartment, and when he felt like it, he would grab a flashlight—pretending that it was a microphone—stand in front of his bathroom mirror, and sing to his reflection. He knew he was good looking, had the kind of face and physique that drove the ladies wild, and was just as good a singer as Marley Marl or Mr. Magic. One day he would be a star, too.

Back home in Havana, after his dad was arrested and executed, Larry had put minimal effort into school, and had eventually dropped out to take leather tanning classes at a trade school. It had been okay, but he had preferred to hang out in the streets with his friends, listen to the radio and watch the girls pass by while smoking strong Viceroy cigarettes.

He had paid no attention to his mother's or his sister's words of caution and had simply done as he pleased, with little regard for anyone other than himself. He walked with a swagger that bordered on rebellion, and was quick to tell everyone that he could take care of himself.

The only thing Larry had ever really cared about was music, and he had been one of the best singers and bata drum players in his neighborhood, and his sister, Niya, one of the best dancers. Their father had been a bata player, too, so it came as no surprise that the syncopated, stylistic lyrics and verses of American hip-hop music would be so attractive to him. With MTV or VH1 blaring on his tiny television, he loved to sing along with the musicians, shouting out to his invisible audience as he boasted and dissed and criticized and praised, imitating the styles of Natural Flow, NK-4, Motha Big, and Ice Blu, his favorite.

Now, Larry set aside the electric broom he had been using to vacuum up the peanut shells that constantly littered the floor at the Spectrum Game Room, grabbed his jacket, and started toward the guy who had called out to him.

"Sure, Ice," Larry said to the young man who was lounging on an orange plush sofa, engrossed in playing an ear-splitting video soccer match on the big-screen TV. "Anything else you want?"

"Yeah. Camels. No filters. Got that?" Ice Blu tersely added as he dug into the pocket of his fashionably faded jeans and pulled out a crumpled one hundred dollar bill, which he held out to Larry without ever taking his eyes off the television screen. "And tell King to start stocking Camels in the machine. Okay? I been complaining about this for months."

"Yeah, yeah, you got it," Larry hurried to reply, shrugging on his black leather jacket as he walked to the exit, secretly pleased that the flashy singer had remembered his name and had asked *him* to run this errand.

Ice Blu, who always wore five carat diamond earrings in both ears, a tangle of gold chains, dog tags, and spinners around his neck, and a three thousand dollar Chronoswiss watch on his wrist, was a regular at the Spectrum Game Room, where Larry worked as an assistant to the manager.

Larry's duties at the high-tech game room where the hip-hop crowd, sports figures, and regular guys with money to throw around came to pass the time, included anything that his boss, King Jones, or the flashy customers wanted him to do.

Larry was in heaven. So what if he had to vacuum the floors, clean the toilets, and wash glasses when the bartender ran out? Where else could a guy get paid to spend time in a place where he had access to famous people, as well as the latest video, digital, and sports-related satellite entertainment devices in the world?

Out on the street, Larry plunged into the foggy December drizzle shrouding 8th Avenue, hunched his shoulders up to his ears and folded Ice Blu's Benjamin into a small square. He jammed the bill into his pants pocket—Ice never asked for change and Larry had more than enough cash in his wallet to cover the cost of the pizza and cigarettes.

Why bother breakin' a one hundred dollar bill? he thought, pleased with his latest score.

At the Spectrum Game Room, huge tips were definitely the biggest perk of all, and Larry was fast accumulating quite a bit of folding money by running errands for the flamboyant customers who came to drink, play games, and shoot the breeze.

Catching Ice Blu's attention had been a real coup. When the up-and-coming African-American hip-hop rapper had first come in, Larry had boldly struck up a conversation, letting him know how much he enjoyed watching his music videos on TV, and that he, too, was a musician of sorts. He had spontaneously rapped a few lines, making Ice Blu chuckle, and from that day on, Ice never let anyone but Larry run his errands.

Ice Blu, whose real name was Harold Harris, was fast becoming a true celebrity. He walked around with an entourage of twelve or more hangers-on, wore top label clothing, tons of real bling, and walked with an expression that screamed don't-talk-to-me-because-I-am-somebody. Stories about him in the trades reported that he had plenty of cash from the blow-up success of his latest recording—"Natural Matter," which he produced on his own private label. Local DJs and those who monitored the hip-hop music scene predicted that Ice Blu, a native of Queensbridge, would soon replace Marley Marl's Juice Crew as the king of hip-hop music. Larry envied the hell out of him.

Ice Blu had risen from the ghetto to make a lot of noise, earn big money and gain instant fame. He was bulldozing his way through life, doing his thing and taking crap from no one. Larry wanted the same for himself and really *did* think it was possible, especially after Ice tossed out a nonchalant promise to let Larry sit in on one of his sessions at a local radio station one day. Larry was not about to let the rapper forget what he had said. Oh yes, he was going to hold Ice to *that* promise.

At 145th Street Larry cut through the intersection and walked half a block to Crizie's Pizza, only to find it was closed! He yanked hard on the door several times, and then checked his watch. It was only twelve-twenty in the afternoon, but a handwritten sign on the door said the place was temporarily closed. In his hurry to accommodate Ice Blu's request, he had failed to think about calling ahead. This was not good at all.

Larry thought for a moment. He could go over to Carlo's Deli and get a pizza—but that was six blocks away and Ice had specifically requested Crizie's. Larry had to do something, fast.

"This is fucked," he cursed, leaning close to the glass door. He put his hands up to the sides of his face and peered inside. The lights were on. "Somebody's gotta be in there," he muttered, now banging on the door.

Instantly, a girl wearing a red-and-white striped apron

emerged from the back of the store and looked out the glass door. Frowning, she made a signal with her hands for him to go away.

"I can't," Larry called through the door, knowing she could hear him. He had seen her in the pizza parlor before when he'd come by to pick up an order and had always thought she was pretty, in an earthy, robust kind of way. She was an attractive Italian-looking girl with olive skin, long black hair, rosy cheeks, and a healthy bosom that strained against the top of her red and white apron. Somehow, he had to convince her to open up the kitchen and throw a pizza together that he could take back to the game room. "Please, let me in," he begged. "Please."

"Sorry. We're closed," the girl called back. "Come back tomorrow."

"You gotta open the door," Larry pleaded, dropping to his knees on the damp cement. He put his hands together as if he were praying, and mocked a desperate expression. "I gotta have a double pepperoni with extra sauce. It's a life or death situation! I'm gonna be jacked if I don't get one."

Laughing, the girl unlocked the door and stuck out her head. "The ovens are off. Just got them repaired. I'm here by myself, and I don't plan to stick around. Sorry. Come back tomorrow and I'll give you a special deal."

Hearing this, Lorenzo realized that this was a girl he could bargain with and grabbed the opening, knowing he could convince her to let him in. "How about I pay you extra for your trouble," he offered, fishing two twenty dollar bills out of his wallet. After smoothing them out, he held them up and flashed his most seductive smile.

"No way," she told him, trying to close the door. "I just came over to let the repairmen in. They finished. They're gone. I'm going home."

Quickly, Larry shoved the two twenties back in his pocket and took out the one hundred dollar bill Ice Blu had given him. He winked and flashed the Benjamin at her. "How's this? The change is your tip . . . if you let me in." He knew girls always weakened when he winked at them and he had no doubt that the cash would give him the leverage he needed with this one.

Without a word, the girl stepped back and let Larry enter.

"It'll take me fifteen minutes to get your order ready," she told him, snatching the money from his hand. She stuffed the bill into the pocket of her striped apron, and then turned away.

Relieved, and impressed with his fast thinking, Larry watched the girl's hips swish back and forth as she headed toward the kitchen, and on a whim, decided to follow her.

"What are you doing?" she asked, suddenly whirling around, squinting angry eyes at him. "You wait out front."

"Just thought I'd keep you company," he stated nonchalantly.

"Why would I need any company?" she tossed back, proceeding into the kitchen, where she pulled a large metal pan off a shelf.

"I dunno. You just look like the kind of girl who doesn't like to be alone."

"You're whacked," she told him, opening the refrigerator to take out a ball of dough, which she tossed on the metal pan, one eyebrow raised at Larry. "That's crazy! Why'd you think I'd need *your* company? You don't know a thing about me." With a whack, she punched the pizza dough and then began to push it around.

"Maybe you bring me up to speed while you're making my pizza," he softly teased. "How about starting with your name."

After giving the dough a final stretch to pull it to the sides of the pan, she began slathering tomato sauce onto it, and then finally answered. "Gina. Gina Crizie. My father owns this place."

Lorenzo nodded and smiled. He knew he had seen her before, but from a distance, and he remembered thinking that she was cute, but now that he was so close to her, he realized that she was really very pretty. She had beautiful white teeth and the kind of thick black hair that he would love to run his hands through. And now that she had told him her name, he knew he'd made it to first base. Going the rest of the way would be easy.

"I'm Larry London," he told her, circling the table to come up behind her. "I've seen you in here before, Gina."

"Really?" she replied, not impressed. "I don't remember ever seeing you."

"Too bad," he murmured, standing very close, watching her hands while she finished putting the pizza together.

When Gina turned around, preparing to take her creation to the oven on the other side of the kitchen, Larry blocked her path. When he did not move, she scowled at him. "You gonna just stand there?" she demanded, holding the pizza pan between them. "You want me to cook this thing, or not?"

With a shrug, Larry stepped out of her way.

Gina crossed the kitchen, placed the pizza on a long wooden paddle and slipped the pan into the brick oven. Then she slammed the heavy black iron door shut.

That was when Larry made his move. He eased up behind her before she could turn and put his arms around her waist, praying she would not whirl around and slap him with the wooden spatula that she was still holding.

She didn't.

Cautiously, he inched his hands up to her breasts and gently fondled her nipples, which immediately jumped hard and prominent against the apron's bib.

To his relief, Gina didn't pull away. In fact, she dropped the wooden paddle to the floor and began pressing her buttocks hard against his groin, with an urgency that nearly knocked him off balance. However, he held on tightly and within seconds, he was hard and they were on the floor.

He ripped off her apron, yanked up her skirt, and grinned

when she started tugging on his black leather jacket until she had pulled it off his shoulders.

Just think of the women I'm gonna have screamin' and creamin' for me when I'm a famous singer! Larry thought as he eased Gina's panties down.

Chapter 16

"A job? What would I want with a stupid job? Ace doesn't want me to work, anyway," Sandi Lee told Niya while shoving her makeup back into her purse.

Niya arched a brow but did not comment. At least Sandi Lee was talking coherently. It had been a struggle but Niya had managed to get her friend into the apartment, into the shower, and sobered up with cup after cup of strong coffee and the hearty steak sandwich she had prepared for Tremont's lunch.

Niya was still irritated at Tremont for blowing off their lunch and shopping trip so he could work through the afternoon with Skip James. However, the good thing was he had not been around to witness Sandi Lee's drug-induced meltdown.

"What does Ace actually do for a living?" Niya asked Sandi Lee, coming back to the moment, relieved that her friend seemed to be in much better shape, though she was still jittery and looked kind of spaced out.

"He travels a lot and he wants me to be free to go with him," Sandi Lee rambled on. "We're going to Orlando tomorrow and to Tampa next weekend. And he promised to take me to Las Vegas for New Year's. That's going to be wild."

"So he has his own business?" Niya pressed, her eyes on Sandi Lee, who was fidgeting with her still-damp hair, visibly agitated, confirming Niya's suspicion that Ace was not doing much of anything, and certainly nothing good for Sandi Lee.

"Yes, he's self-employed," Sandi Lee snapped, flicking her wrist in a dismissive gesture. "He manages a lot of different businesses for clients who live out of town. Something about insurance, I think."

Niya let it drop, but not before commenting on how worried she was about her friend. "You were in bad shape in the elevator," Niya blurted out. "You could have died."

"Don't be so damn dramatic. It was nothing."

"You need to leave the drugs alone."

"I'm just having a little fun."

"Fun? You may think you're just having fun, but it can get out of hand, Sandi Lee. I work in the clubs. I see what can happen. Before you know it, you're hooked."

"I'm fine. I fainted because I've been dieting, but I sure blew it with that steak sandwich. It was the bomb. I never knew you could cook."

"We never had a stove in our motel room, remember?"

Sandi Lee laughed and shook her head.

"You need to eat more! Promise me. You're too thin." Niya admonished.

"A girl can't be too thin," Sandi Lee glibly tossed back while zipping her purse closed, but then added, while eyeing Niya's voluptuous figure. "However, curves . . . in the right places, of course, are great, too."

And Tremont seems to think so, Niya thought, wondering if Sandi Lee had any idea of what she had gotten herself into by moving in with Ace.

A wave of emptiness surged through Niya as she watched Sandi Lee get ready to leave. What would have happened if a stranger had been in the elevator, and not a friend who had been willing to take her in, feed her, and sober her up? Sandi Lee was clearly in trouble. The bruises on her fair skin showed right through her makeup, and though Niya had no proof, she suspected that Ace was responsible for the ugly purple welts, as well as this dangerous involvement with drugs.

"I wish you didn't have to rush off," Niya said.

"Rush off? I've been here for hours. Ace is going to be furious. I've got to get going, but it's been great chatting, Niya. Thanks for helping me pull my act together. I mean . . . I guess . . . Well, I've missed you, girl."

"I've missed you, too." Niya put her arms around Sandi Lee and held on for a long moment, remembering how much fun they had had when they first arrived in Miami. How carefree and optimistic they had been! A shiver of fear cut through Niya to realize that their friendship would never be the same. They were both making choices while stepping out into the world, and taking two very different paths, it seemed.

"Maybe we can get together over the holidays," Niya offered, more out of something to say to break the tension than anything else. She stepped back and let go of her friend. "I'm going Christmas shopping today for the first time in my life," Niya added, trying to brighten the mood. "Wish you could come with me. It would be a lot of fun."

"Some other time. I've got your number. I'll call next week," Sandi Lee replied already moving toward the door.

Niya gave Sandi Lee another quick hug, opened the door and then watched until her best and only girlfriend disappeared into the elevator.

Sighing, Niya returned to the kitchen and poured a second glass of lemonade for herself, suddenly looking forward to the holiday festivities. *Christmas. Gifts. Laughter. Dinner with Tremont and G-Daddy. A New Year's Eve party.* How her life had changed.

In Cuba, no one celebrated Christmas, except tourists in the luxury hotels. It had been a holiday until 1969 when Fidel Castro decided it was interfering with the sugar harvest. So, authorities banned the public display of Christmas trees and nativity scenes, and ordered the holiday dropped from the Cuban calendar.

With a mental shake, she cleared her mind, determined not to dwell on life in Cuba. She was in America now and she was going to buy Christmas presents for Tremont, his friends, his grandfather, and Sandi Lee, too, though she did not know when or if she'd ever see her again.

Chapter 17

When the guard called her name, Olivia's head jerked up in surprise. A visitor? So late in the day? She swung her feet off her cot and stood, taking a moment to catch her breath and smooth back her hair.

"Come along," the guard hurried her. "Move along."

Olivia struggled to focus. Why did she feel so light-headed? So tired? She had not done anything but lie in her bunk all day, as she had every day for months.

It couldn't be Felix, she thought. He never visited twice in one month. He had come to see her last week, and had finally brought her a new pillow. The first one he brought her over a year ago had been stolen by one of the inmates.

Maybe it was that lawyer he had told her about, the one who Felix thought might be able to get her sentence reduced. Or perhaps it was a doctor? She had been begging the guards to allow a doctor to come and to listen to her heart. Something was wrong. She was so tired all the time—she had even stopped going outside during the brief exercise periods that she used to look forward to.

The man who was waiting for Olivia at the visitor's table was a stranger. Slim and dignified, in a dark, though outdated, business suit, he stood when she approached. He bowed slightly at the waist, and then sat back down on the iron stool in front of the grated window.

"Hello, Mrs. Londres. I am Eduardo Robles, and I have a message for you."

Olivia sat down and stared wearily at the man. "A message from who?"

"The Cuban Immigrant Assistance League in Miami."

"Miami? Really?"

"Yes. Your daughter, Niya, has been working with one of their counselors who sent me a message to give to you."

Tears immediately sprang into Olivia's eyes and glazed her vision. "Niya? So, my daughter *is* alive?"

"Yes, and doing well. She is working as a professional dancer and has settled into her life in America with no problems. She wanted me to tell you that she loves you and misses you and for you not to worry about her. She is fine."

"*Gracias a Dios*," Olivia murmured, lowering her head, shaking it back and forth as she made the sign of the cross on her chest. "My Niya is well . . . and happy." After a moment, she looked up at the man and asked, "And Lorenzo?"

Mr. Robles shook his head. "Nothing. No one knows where he is."

In a hushed tone, Olivia told him, "I see. But if you hear anything about him you will come and let me know?"

"Ah, of course. Immediately," Robles assured her, then he stood and made another short bow. "I hope the news about your daughter is helpful."

Olivia smiled. "Yes. Yes. Thank you so much. I will sleep much better now."

"Good. I hope to come back again soon with more news." He paused, and then added, "Happy New Year, Mrs. Londres."

Olivia blinked, then smiled. "Yes . . . yes . . . it's New Year's Eve, isn't it?" she whispered, as if to herself. "I never know what day it is in here . . . but I will surely remember this one."

On her way back to her cell, she realized that Christmas had come and gone without her even noticing, and that Niya . . . and Lorenzo—wherever he might be—were celebrating the holiday for the first time.

* * *

All fifteen rooms in Ice Blu's luxurious New Jersey home were vibrating with hip-hop rhymes, shrieks of laughter, energetic dancing, and the loud voices of the partiers that filled his house. Their shout-outs bounced off the walls and ramped up the fun as the rapper's New Year's Eve party rocked on toward midnight.

Larry, who was still in shock over having been invited to the awesome celebration, locked the door to the bedroom that Ice had offered him and popped the cork on two bottles of champagne. Grinning, he ran to the bed and leaned over the doe-eyed honey-blonde who was sitting naked in the middle of the bed and poured the golden liquid over her bare breasts. Jumping on top of her, he began licking the bubbly off her huge pink nipples with quick flicks of his tongue, making her giggle and squirm with delight. When she pushed him back and squealed with laughter, he shifted his attention to the plump olive breasts of the dark-haired beauty on the other side of his bed. Gina Crizie shrieked her pleasure, grabbed Larry by the neck and pulled his mouth down on hers.

After untangling himself from Gina's choke hold, Larry lifted both bottles of champagne high into the air and yelled, "Happy New Year, y'all! Now let's get this party going!"

Niya took a flute of champagne from the silver tray that Connie was passing around, and then went to stand beside G-Daddy in the doorway of his kitchen. "This is one great party," she told him, leaning close to his ear.

With a grin, G-Daddy nodded and then linked his arm through hers. "I'm glad I'm finally free of that damn walking cane and I'm glad you're here to enjoy my party." He walked her to a corner of the festively decorated dining room, where his many friends and neighbors, of all ages and walks of life, were happily devouring his lavish New Year's spread. Tremont, Dejen, Kofu, and Jimmy had gathered around the grand piano in the living room, and were creating beautiful music for his guests.

"You're making Tremont very happy . . . and me, too," G-Daddy told Niya. "Since he got a hold of you, he's finally acting like he's got some sense."

Niya laughed.

G-Daddy wagged a long finger at her. "Don't laugh. It's the truth. After you two get back from that tour of his, I want you to make him buy you a house. A big house with a pool, so he can stay at home and skinny dip with you."

Niya chuckled under her breath and slapped playfully at Tremont's devilish grandfather. "Skinny dip? You're terrible."

"That's what he does when he comes over here, so why should he do it alone, when he has a pretty girl like you around? He's a lucky guy. You'll be a good influence on him, especially while he's on tour."

"Tremont is so hyped about this tour," Niya went on. "I can't believe how many cities we're visiting in just two months. His CD is going to do very well."

"Yes, it will," G-Daddy stated with assurance. "It's his best. Ought to make him rich . . . and for God's sake, while you're on the road, make him give you his paycheck . . . he can't manage two nickels . . . never could. You've got to watch out for him, young lady."

"If he'll let me," Niya replied, doubting that Tremont would ever hand over his paycheck to her. If there was one subject he never discussed with her, it was money. And besides, what paycheck? He always insisted that he get paid in cash, whether it was at Club Cariba or any venue where he and his group performed. And what he did with his money after it was put into his hands, she had no idea.

"Well, I tried to raise him right, you know? All I want is for him to have a fine life, and with you I think he will. Stick by him. He can be stubborn, but he's a generous softie, too." He sighed, and then he kissed Niya on the cheek. "What a great way to start the new year." Studying her, he went on. "Keep him happy. You promise?"

"Yes, I promise," Niya vowed, glancing down at the brilliant round solitaire diamond set in an intricately carved silver band that glittered on the third finger of her left hand.

The croupier called out, "Seventeen!"

"Yes!" an elderly Japanese man shouted as he gleefully raked in his winnings.

"Shit," Ace cursed, shoving back from the table, and then stomping off in a huff, both hands in his pockets.

"Rotten luck," Sandi Lee said to no one in particular as she hurried to catch up with Ace, who was already halfway across the noisy casino. She caught up with him at the cashier's station.

"We're down to our last hundred," Ace announced while handing a one-hundred dollar bill to the cashier for change.

Sandi Lee leaned against the glass window, clearly puzzled. "What about the money I gave you to hold for me? The five hundred in twenties?"

"Shit, we blew that yesterday."

"We?"

"Yeah, you were too messed up to remember. Over at Bally's . . . playing blackjack."

"No, I don't remember, and I was not *that* messed up. *I* didn't even go to Bally's with you. You bastard! That was *my* money you were playing with." She yanked hard on his shirt-sleeve, her green eyes hard and as cold as flinty emeralds.

In an instant, Ace whirled around and slapped Sandi Lee hard across the cheek, sending her stumbling backwards. He took a long step toward her, but then backed off, calmly stuffing his change into the pocket of his tight jeans. He anchored both fists at his waist, his thumbs hooked into his belt loops, as he glowered at Sandi Lee. "Don't start that shit with me," he growled. "You're stoned. Go up to the room and lay down.

And stop your goddamn bitching. We're together. What's yours is mine, so don't go actin' crazy on me."

Rubbing her face, Sandi Lee tucked in her lips and bit down hard to stop herself from screaming. Some New Year's Eve! They had been arguing, getting high, and then arguing some more ever since they got off the plane two days ago, and now he'd run through *her* money? And slapped her in public?

It was bad enough when he pushed her around behind closed doors—no way was he going to humiliate her in the middle of the Aladdin Hotel casino and expect her to just take it. She had earned that money the hard way—all the hands, lips, tongues and dicks she'd had to suffer through made it hers. Ace had a lot of nerve calling it *his*.

"Give me my plane ticket," she boldly decided, ready to roll. "I'm going back to Miami."

With a curt laugh, Ace started walking away. "Fine. Go on. But I ain't givin' you shit. Not when I can cash your ticket in and get me some good blow, you know? Go on, if you want to. Get home the best way you can."

"I will!" Sandi Lee shouted back.

People at the nearby slot machines stopped punching their betting buttons to turn and stare. Furious, Sandi Lee ran into the nearest ladies' room and grabbed a handful of paper towels, which she soaked in cold water and held to her cheek until the imprint of Ace's hand disappeared.

She could hardly look at herself in the mirror. Her whole body was shaking, her mouth was so dry she could not swallow, her eyes were glazed and swollen, her face was flushed, and her cheeks had become two gaunt, sunken hollows. What the hell was she doing? Killing herself? She had not slept in more than thirty-six hours and her nerves were shot to hell.

You're totally fucked up, she silently admonished the stranger in the mirror. *You've got to get a grip or you're gonna die right here in* Vegas.

With shaking hands, she repaired her makeup, fluffed out

her hair and straightened out her clothes. *You know what you gotta do*, she said to her reflection, praying she could really pull it off.

Emerging from the restroom, she went into the casino's Horseshoe Bar and scanned the place for any man who was sitting alone. A once-handsome, once-young man with salt and pepper hair, nursing a beer at the bar, caught her eye. She walked right up to him, placed both hands on his shoulders, and leaned close. "Want some company?" she asked in her sexiest voice.

Chapter 18

January 2, 2000

Dear Mama,

I hope my letter gets to you and that you are well . . . as well as any poor soul could be in your situation. My heart is breaking for you. I have heard that Mr. Robles saw you and gave you my message—the news that you are well keeps me going. I promise to do everything I can to get you out of that place. One day soon you will be free, I promise.

On a happy note—I am settled in Miami and am engaged to a wonderful, handsome, talented man who is a musician at the club where I dance. His name is Tremont Henderson and tomorrow, I leave Miami to go on tour with him—all across the country, Mama. I am so excited and happy, but I feel bad that you have had to suffer so that I can enjoy my life here in America. I wish you were here and I wish I knew where Lorenzo was. The Cuban Immigrant Assistance League has tried to find him, but no luck. I don't think he drowned. I think he's alive and all three of us will be reunited again one day.

I will write again soon, and pray that my letters reach you. Keep strong and don't despair.

Your loving daughter, Niya

Chapter 19

After seven weeks on the road, Niya was not surprised that the chaos of rushing through airports, late night rehearsals, high-energy performances—sometimes twice a night—and the stress of dealing with the never-ending hassles that came with an extensive tour were all taking their toll on Tremont.

From the moment they left Atlanta's Sunset Arena and got into the car, Niya noticed that Tremont was somber-faced and quiet. He and his quartet had just finished a particularly exhausting concert in one of Atlanta's most popular venues, and Niya thought he would have been bubbling with enthusiasm over the huge turn-out, the crowd's wild reception, and how well he and his musicians had played. However, he was quiet, almost sullen, and Niya was worried that this foul mood had something to do with the conversation she had overheard earlier that evening.

Fifteen minutes before Tremont had been due to go on stage, he had had an unusually heated argument with Ronnie White, the local radio station manager who had promoted Tremont's Atlanta appearance. Niya had been standing in the corridor outside of Tremont's dressing room and had been shaken by the words she had overheard.

"Take it up with Skip," Ronnie had yelled at Tremont. "All

I know is somebody's got to come up with the fifty-five hundred right now or I can make sure the curtain stays down."

"Fuck you and fuck Skip," Tremont had hurled back at Ronnie. "I paid him enough to cover your expenses. He said you guys were straight."

"I guess he lied," Ronnie had replied in a nasty tone. "I been pumping your CD on air for two weeks. I got the crowd out . . . now you've got to come through. You can't leave me hanging like this."

"No one promised you anything more than what Skip guaranteed!"

"Hey, that's the way it works, man. You want air time? You gotta pay."

"Right. Like I been doing in every city on this goddamn tour . . . sixty-five hundred in New Orleans, fifty-two in Columbus, the same in San Francisco, and L.A.? My God, Jelly Jam Green had the nerve to try and stick me for more than what I paid for my car. This fucking tour is costing me a fucking fortune, and I'm gonna break Skip's neck when I get home."

"That's not my problem. Take it up with Skip. For now, whatta you gonna do? You want me to go out there and tell a packed house that you're too sick to play? That the concert is cancelled? Or what?"

"Hell no. I'm not cancelling!" Tremont had shouted back. A pause. "Here's your goddamned money," he had growled. "And you can be sure I'll never work with you again."

Niya had fled down the hallway just as the door to Tremont's dressing room had opened and Ronnie White stomped out, counting the money that Tremont had given him.

Now, in an effort to lift Tremont's mood, she began chatting excitedly about how much she was looking forward to Memphis, the next stop on the tour, and how she had always fanaticized about visiting Graceland one day.

"You'll be disappointed," Tremont murmured, continuing to stare out the window at the dark city streets.

"Why?" Niya asked.

"It's a lot smaller than people expect."

"I don't care. I'm sure it's beautiful."

"Kind of ordinary, if you ask me."

"I still plan to see it."

"Go ahead. Do whatever you want. I'll be in rehearsals all day, anyway."

Niya did not reply, in fact, she did not speak to Tremont again until they had entered their hotel suite and were getting ready for bed.

"I know what's bothering you," she started right in as soon as Tremont came out of the shower.

He didn't even look at her.

"I heard you and Ronnie White arguing," she ventured.

Now Tremont turned to her and squinted in question while he continued to towel-dry his hair. "You were listening to my conversation with Ronnie?"

"It's not like you two were whispering. Anybody in the hall outside your door could have heard every word you said."

A beat. "Well, forget whatever you *think* you heard. It's not your business."

"It is when it gets you down like this. We're engaged, Tremont. I'm going to be your wife. Why are you keeping all of this from me? And . . . why should you have to pay so much money to those greedy station managers and disc jockeys to get them to play your music on the radio?"

Tremont threw his towel to the floor and stepped closer to Niya, clearly angry. "Don't ever say that! You hear? You could cause a lot of trouble for me . . . for everyone."

Though unsure of what that meant, Niya nodded, eyes wide.

"You don't know what you're talking about, Niya, and I never want to hear you say anything about what you overheard tonight." He yanked off his white terry robe, and grabbed his pajamas. He sat down on the side of the bed as he dressed.

"But you're spending so much money," she said, unable to

let the subject drop. In fact, she was beginning to feel guilty for allowing Tremont to spend so lavishly on her. In every city they had visited so far, he had taken her shopping, filling her suitcases to bursting with everything that caught her eye. And he always paid in cash. In fact, he had a small black snakeskin bag that was filled with cash and he never let it out of his sight. Clearly, he loved the rush of doling out bills to buy expensive gifts for her, and she loved him for doing it, but she also knew that he ought to be more careful about the way he spent his money.

G-Daddy's words of caution, along with her promise to him that she would monitor Tremont's spending, came to mind, and she hated to think that she was letting the old man down.

"Don't start meddling, Niya," Tremont advised in a voice she had never heard before. Finished dressing, he turned to face her.

"I'm not meddling," she boldly answered. "I'm concerned."

"Don't be. It's *my* money. So, stay out of it. Don't I buy you everything you want? You've got designer dresses, shoes, purses, jewels, furs . . . a driver and a car in every city. We're staying in the best hotels . . ."

"I never asked for any of this, Tremont."

"Well, I like things nice—top of the line. And I will spend whatever I have to, to have it that way."

"Well, G-Daddy said . . ." Niya started.

"G-Daddy?" Tremont interrupted, spitting out the word as he stood. "You better *not* start quoting him to me!" He paced over to the window, where he crossed his arms on his chest and faced the city's lights, his rigid back to Niya. "Don't get me wrong . . . I love my grandfather." He turned. "Besides you, he's the only person who ever really loved me. I owe him everything, but I won't live my life by his rules. Growing up, he never spent a dime more than he *had* to on anything—food, clothing, cars. Everything he ever bought was secondhand or at rock-bottom prices from some cheesy discount store. And all the while his money was piling up in his many bank accounts. He's a multi-millionaire, you know. Yet he still cuts coupons and gives them to Connie when she goes shopping. His favorite meal is hot dogs and beans. He wears clothes he has had for twenty years. He refuses to allow himself to enjoy his money, and he has convinced himself that his way of doing things is the only way to live."

Niya went over to Tremont and put her arms around him and was shocked to see the tears in his eyes. She held him close and let him hold onto her, aware that his turmoil was deep-seated and hard. All she could do was love him. Be there for him and let him love her. Changing him was not an option.

"When I was a boy," he went on, "I never knew what it was like to have anything new, and now that I have my own money, I'll damn well spend it as I please. Niya, if you mess with me on this, you'll ruin everything."

Niya's heart sank as she stepped back and let go of Tremont. "I love you, Tremont. And I don't want to mess things up."

"Then promise me that you'll never again tell me how to manage my money, and I'll do the same for you."

"I promise," she whispered.

"Thank you," Tremont replied, then he walked out of the bedroom and into the kitchenette of their suite.

She could hear him slamming cabinet doors and the clatter of ice cubes hitting glass, and knew that she had touched a place inside of Tremont that was too raw and painful for her to try to heal.

With a sigh, she climbed into bed and switched off the light.

Chapter 20

"Lights out" always scared the hell out of Sandi Lee, and tonight was no exception even though she had been at the Penway Charity Recovery Center for Women for two months and the evening drill was permanently imprinted on her brain. Two short blinks of the hallway lights, and then the night attendant's stern announcement over the PA system. A cursory bed check, followed by total darkness.

Sandi Lee's self-imposed exile to the recovery center had begun on the third day of the New Year, after she returned from Las Vegas broke, bruised, depressed, and facing the fact that she had to straighten out her act, or die. Acknowledging the downward spiral that her life had become had been a painful, humiliating, and depressing awakening, but one she had had to face. If she had not returned to Miami and begged for a bed at Penway, she would most likely have wound up dead in the Nevada desert, and no one would ever have known what happened to her.

In Vegas, she had smoked her last crack pipe and turned her last trick with the man she picked up in the bar, who had been happy to have some company. He had been pleasant enough on the eyes and flush with cash, so Sandi Lee had immediately hooked up with him, and together they had had a wild good time that lasted for two days. Little did she know that the stranger she was partying with would turn out to be her savior.

During their two-day binge of drinking, drugging, dancing and sex, she had managed to tell him her life story and for some odd reason, he had seemed particularly interested in what she had had to say. When she informed him that she was never going back to Miami, and that she had decided to stay in Vegas and work the bars, he had gripped her hard by the shoulders and leveled a stern, rather fatherly stare at her.

"Listen. I'm a fifty-two year-old insurance underwriter from Illinois who leads a boring life," he had begun. "I have an overbearing boss, no wife, no kids, and once a year I come to Las Vegas for two weeks and do anything I want to do. This is not who I am. This is my fantasy, kid. When I'm at home, I don't do drugs, sleep with strange girls or drink anything stronger than beer. I follow my routine and work my job for eleven months a year with no regrets about whatever I do while I am here. But you, Sandi Lee, are much too young and too pretty to continue down this path. Honey, don't waste your life. Go home. Get clean. Don't stay here in Vegas."

The next morning, he gave her his business card and three hundred dollars in cash. He drove her to the airport and made her promise to go directly into rehab. If she could not find a free clinic, he had said to call him, he would foot the bill.

Upon her arrival back in Miami, Sandi Lee had done as promised and, after pocketing the three hundred dollars, had talked her way into a bed at Penway, remaining clean and sober ever since.

"Lights out," came over the loudspeaker once more, making Sandi Lee shudder. She stayed busy during the daytime and had little time to dwell on the mental and physical cravings that still plagued her, so when the attendants called "lights out" again, a familiar surge of panic shot through her.

When the entire floor went black and the nighttime noises began, the women at Penway—the only free recovery center in Dade County and the most dangerous, too—didn't fall asleep immediately. The nine p.m. curfew was simply a signal for the beginning of a night filled with a variety of illicit activities:

theft of personal belongings, forbidden couplings, growling arguments, and the ranting voices of desperate, strung-out recovering addicts crying for a fix.

In survival mode, Sandi Lee feigned sleep, kept her mouth shut, and held her small manicure scissors, blades open, clutched in her right hand.

However, the days weren't so bad—she stayed busy doing her mandated chores: kitchen duty, mopping floors, and emptying trash barrels throughout the one-story building, and after her chores she went to group therapy, in which she had reluctantly participated at first.

Now she found it rather amusing. She enjoyed shocking the other participants in her group, so she made up horror stories about her days of booze and drugs, not only to get a reaction out of the women, but also to impress them. With a reputation as a bad-ass girl, no one messed with her. She was given respect, not thought of as weak, and never walked around like a sad, frightened shadow, talking to herself and whimpering all day.

The favorite part of Sandi Lee's day was her computer class, which she took three times a week—and she'd been seriously thinking about getting a real job, in an office or a bank, when she left Penway. Waiting tables and selling tickets at a water park did not seem that attractive, and she wanted to do more with her life now that she was sober.

The second favorite time of her day was outdoor recreation, when she could sit in the sun and soak up the rays, letting her mind float free, eyes closed as she imagined herself to be any place other than Penway.

"Lights out, Miss Holt!" A stocky black woman in matronly slacks and a white shirt stuck her head into Sandi Lee's closet-size room, and then stepped right in. She remained by the door and scanned the space, while waiting for Sandi Lee to turn out her light. "Just cause you're leaving tomorrow doesn't mean you get privileges," she stated haughtily.

Sandi Lee set aside the magazine she had been leafing through and focused on Milly, the night attendant assigned to her wing. "All right, all right, Milly," she grumbled, throwing the magazine onto the bedside table, when in fact, she was pleased that Milly had come in.

When Sandi Lee first arrived at Penway, Milly had been assigned as her watch-counselor during those terrible first hours of withdrawal. Milly had doggedly remained at Sandi Lee's bedside, suffering the verbal abuse, threats, and wild thrashings that came with withdrawal. Milly had been patient, kind, and had taught Sandi Lee how to meditate in order to control her mood swings and cravings.

During those first few days, when Sandi Lee couldn't sleep, Milly had broken the lights out rule more than once to come in and play cards with her, remaining until Sandi Lee got drowsy. Sandi Lee was going to miss Milly's tough, yet motherly presence, and was not looking forward to going back out into the world alone.

"Well, after tonight, you won't have me to boss around anymore," Sandi Lee tried to joke.

"There'll be a new girl in your bed before we can change the sheets," Milly threw back with a laugh.

Sandi Lee rolled her eyes. "Good luck to her."

"She'll need it, just like you did . . . and you've done pretty well," Milly replied, moving deeper into the room. "You kept your nose clean, stayed out of other folks' mess, and took this sobering up business seriously. I wasn't so sure you'd stick around for the full sixty days, but I'm sure glad you did."

"Whew. Me, too," Sandi Lee mumbled, feeling proud of herself, yet fearful that she might begin to cry. Getting free of the hold that the drugs had had on her had been hell, but having a caring soul like Milly around had helped ease her through the journey.

"Still going to Orlando to look for an office job?" Milly asked.

"Yep. I got my level one computer training certificate and I don't want to stay in Miami. Too many temptations," she admitted, doubting she'd ever get caught up in Ace's crazy world again.

He had walked out on her, left her broke and hurting in the middle of the casino. She didn't care if she ever saw his ass again. "I don't have any family here in Miami," she told Milly. "No friends, either. So, I can go wherever I want. I was thinking it ought to be easy to get a job in Orlando, with Disney World there and all."

"Probably. You just stay out of trouble and pick your friends carefully. I don't want to see you back here again."

"You won't," Sandi Lee quickly promised. "When I get to Orlando things are gonna change. My life is gonna be a whole lot different."

The manager of the Denny's restaurant off Interstate 4—the heavily traveled frontage road leading to Disney World—read over Sandi Lee's application for employment and then set it aside. "I need another reference. Where have you worked besides Castaway Cove?" she finally said.

Slipping down on her spine, Sandi Lee blinked her green eyes at the heavily made-up woman who was sitting behind a messy desk. After a week of rejections for every clerical position she'd applied for, she sure as hell thought she could get hired as a waitress at Denny's with only one reference. With forty-two dollars left out of the three hundred she had been holding onto, she needed this job—today.

After thinking for a moment, her lips puckered as she searched for the right way to answer, she said, "Yeah, I've worked other jobs, but no place you'd know."

"Try me," the woman remarked, removing a pencil from a bright red plastic cup that was crammed with an assortment of pens, scissors, rulers and drinking straws.

With a shrug, Sandi Lee said, "Joe's Diner in Oyster Cove."

The woman scribbled the words at the bottom of Sandi Lee's application and then looked up. "How long did you work there?"

"Too long."

"Why did you leave?"

"You might say the owner and I didn't exactly get along."

"Did you quit or get fired?"

"I quit."

"Would the owner give you a reference if I called him?"

"I doubt it."

"Why?"

"Because I slashed his arm pretty bad before I left."

The woman shoved the pencil back into the red plastic cup and crossed her arms on the edge of the desk. "Did you have a good reason to do that?"

"Yeah, a damn good one. Trust me. He was a dog, if you get my drift."

A faint smile touched the woman's lips. She nodded in a knowing way, and then murmured, "I do." A beat. "Can you start work today? I'm really shorthanded in the kitchen."

"Sure can. Do I need a uniform?"

"There's one in the women's dressing room that ought to fit you. Put it on and report to Linda in the kitchen."

"You got it! And thanks," Sandi Lee said in a breathless rush as she stood up and prepared to leave.

The phone on the manager's desk rang, and the woman reached for it while nodding at Sandi Lee. With one hand over the mouthpiece, she whispered, "And put on a hairnet, you hear? That blond frizz of yours could get me in trouble."

"No problem," Sandi Lee glibly tossed back as she headed out the door.

Chapter 21

"Let's see what you can do with this," Ice Blu challenged in his deep, melodious voice as he tossed out a string of rhyming words about a shootout in the Village and a dead teenage boy.

"You mean right now?" Larry asked, hitching up his baggy jeans while he glanced from Ice Blu to Spinner T, the DJ who was sitting behind the microphone in the control room at the WDSE-FM radio station. Larry paused and rubbed his chin, wondering at his luck. Had he just been given permission to create a song on the radio, and with lyrics by Ice Blu?

"Yeah, man. I'll let you close out my show," Spinner T agreed, and then he hunched over his microphone, one hand at his ear and shouted out to his invisible audience, "Listen up out there. And if you like what you hear, drop a dime on me and let me know. Closin' out my hour . . . here's . . . Larry Lo . . . the hot new voice . . . discovered by Ice Blu."

Larry grinned at Spinner T while shaking his head up and down. *Yes!* he thought. *Larry Lo! That's fly! That's me from now on.* He grabbed the headphones that Spinner T offered, moved in close to the microphone and began to spew out lyrics that had been locked in his head for months. The words tumbled from his mouth in precise, rhythmic order, flowing like small round gems that burst into vivid colors in front of his eyes. He felt light-headed, energized, and free. Nothing had ever felt like this before and he owed it to his new, famous friend.

Larry had been hanging out with Ice Blu and his posse ever since the New Year's Eve party—which had been jam-packed with luscious babes rounded up for the rapper and his friends. What a wild, crazy time they had had. Beautiful girls everywhere, champagne by the case, and Gina! She had turned out to be a real freak! How lucky could a guy get?

Over the past two months, Larry had gotten very close to Ice, and jumped on every opportunity to express his aspirations in the hip-hop world, even trying out a few of his lyrics on him now and then. Coming to the radio station appearance had been exactly what he had been waiting for.

Now, Larry began weaving the words that Ice had tossed his way into an original composition, creating a new song on the spot.

Reasonable doubt
That's his plea,
Cause it coulda set him free
From a lifetime of makin' noise
'Bout all he used to be.
Whatever throne he think he got
Might just turned out to be
Nothin' but a . . .

"Go ahead, man," Spinner T prompted, nodding his head, a lazy smile on his lips as he got into the music. "Come on now, bring it home, show my fans out there what you can do."

Without missing a beat, Larry continued to improvise his message about the young dead man, his confidence soaring with each word that came out of his mouth. He swung his arms, raised his shoulders, cut his hands in sideways gestures, and twisted his neck from side to side as he put the song together, determined to show Ice that he could pull off a real live on-the-spot performance.

He worked the beat for a full five minutes, so engrossed in his own magic that Spinner T had to wave his hands in front of Larry's face to get him to stop.

"Hey! Time's up, ya'll," Spinner T shouted out to his listeners. "But I know you wanna hear more from Larry Lo 'cause the switchboard is blinkin' like a Christmas tree on crack!" He laughed at his own joke and then added, "Catch Ice Blu onstage next Friday at the Hip-Hop Face Off. Remember, you heard Larry Lo here first . . . Fresh with Spinner T on WDSE-FM." And then he began his sign-off spiel.

Ice Blu zeroed in on Larry. "That was hot, man. Really fly."

Larry licked his lips, wiped perspiration from his forehead, and watched Ice Blu, who had a serious expression on his face, as if pondering a dilemma.

"Yeah," Ice finally said again. "Fly."

Spinner T, who had begun taking one call after another, gave Larry a thumbs-up after each one. "Damn, man, these ladies are asking where to get your album."

"I wish," Larry tossed back, trying to suppress his joy.

"Where you been hidin' all that energy, man?" Ice asked Larry. "I thought you were joking with me when you started yapping about getting into the hip-hop scene. You really got rhythm, Dude, and attitude, too. The words were all good, too. There's hope, man. There's hope."

Larry stepped closer to Ice Blu and flashed him a bright, too-eager smile. "Think so?" he asked.

"Yeah, I do," Ice replied. "But you still got a lot to learn about presentation, man. On stage you gotta get your flaunt on . . . you know, your stuff has gotta be sharp."

"You could help me?" Larry ventured, tilting his head to one side as he peeped up at Ice Blu from beneath the brim of his baseball cap.

"Maybe," Ice hedged. "But it ain't gonna be easy. And you know it'll cost you, too."

"How much?" Larry tossed back, holding his breath. He had no money, and knew that whatever figure Ice threw out would be way too much for him.

"Thirty percent."

"Of what?" Larry wanted to know.

"Of whatever I help you make," Ice answered, studying the flashy rings on his right hand. "Teaching you is gonna take up my time, but you might be worth the investment." He moved to the far side of the control room and rested one hip against a leather-topped stool. He sniffed loudly and jerked back a shoulder. "I'm gearing up for the Hip-Hop Face Off at the Coliseum next Friday. Get your act together and I'll give you two minutes of my time on stage."

"You'd do that?"

"Sure. If you think you can handle it."

"Just watch me," Larry replied cockily, though his heart was pounding and his mouth felt as dry as dirt.

This was the break he had known would come one day. He'd prayed for it, planned for it, and now he sure as hell was not going to pass it up.

"I've got tons of material, Ice. I been writing forever, just waiting for a chance to show everybody what I can do. I'm gonna blow the audience away."

"Yeah, I'll bet you will," Ice replied, holding his chin between two fingers as he studied Larry through half-closed eyes.

Chapter 22

As soon as the seat belt light went out, Niya stood and grabbed her carry-on bag from the overhead compartment, anxious to deplane. She didn't like flying very much, and especially not alone. She had been a nervous wreck during the long flight from San Jose to Orlando, and was still upset that Tremont had remained in California to work out some money issues with a concert promoter before joining her in Florida for the final appearance of his tour.

He had not told her what was going on in San Jose, and she had not asked. After their argument in Atlanta she no longer initiated any discussions about finances. Though the tour had been a huge success and Tremont was earning quite a lot of money, she was worried. While in Los Angeles, she had overheard him talking to someone on the phone about back taxes and money that needed to be paid right away. Though she knew little about tax laws in the United States, she knew no one wanted trouble with the IRS.

Since Orlando had been on her and Tremont's itinerary, Niya had agreed to perform at a charity event at a private estate on the coast, and was relieved that this was the last stop of the tour. Her trip across the United States had been a wonderful adventure, a real eye-opener about what her new adopted country was all about. Niya's only complaint was the weather: The East Coast had been rainy and cold; the Midwest, still nearly frozen; and even San Francisco's foggy damp days had left her longing for Florida sunshine.

Niya made her way toward Baggage Claim, moving quickly, anxious to settle into the hotel, relax, and call Tremont, whom she missed already. This was the first time they had been separated since their engagement and she realized that it was not going to be easy waiting until next week to see him.

The sunlight streaming through the large airport windows warmed her skin and made her realize how glad she was to be back in Florida after so many weeks on the road.

At the Wyndam Orlando Hotel, she was quickly ushered into a three-room suite on the thirty-fifth floor. A gorgeous bouquet of pink and white roses had been placed on the polished dining table. After tipping the bellman she opened the card and smiled:

> *I hope you are missing me as much as I am missing you. Look in the top drawer of the dresser for a surprise.*
>
> *All my love, Tremont*

Holding the card, she moved to the dresser and opened the drawer to find a pink Victoria's Secret bag. Opening it, she pulled out a silky gown of sheer lace and satin in a delicate shade of coral. The note pinned to it read: *I'll be there soon, Love, T.*

As she gazed at the beautiful creation her eyes teared up. He was always surprising her. The expensive gift was so like Tremont, as was the five-star hotel, the three-room suite, and the driver who had met her at the airport and who would remain on call during her stay. How could she complain about his lavish spending? She loved him, and knew he'd never change.

Feeling hungry, but not in the mood for hotel room service—which seemed the same no matter where she stayed—Niya picked up the phone, called her driver, and asked him to bring the car around. She had seen a Denny's restaurant on the drive into town from the airport, and was suddenly in the mood for an old-fashioned breakfast.

"Blueberry pancakes, here I come," she murmured with satisfaction as she pulled on her sunglasses and grabbed her purse.

Sandi Lee recognized Niya as soon as her friend emerged from the sleek gray town car that pulled up outside the restaurant. Watching through the front window, her mouth dropped open, her eyes widened, and she temporarily forgot about the woman who was rattling off her order.

It was Niya, all right. And she looked like a movie star. A chauffeured car! At Denny's. Things had really jumped off for her girlfriend.

Sandi Lee watched Niya come into the restaurant, impressed with what she saw. Niya was wearing a short leopard print jacket, a black silk shirt, black leather pants, strappy five-inch heels, gold jewelry and sunglasses that screamed CHA-CHING!!!

"Uh, excuse me," Sandi Lee interrupted. "Let me see if the cook has fresh pineapple, okay?" Before the woman could respond, Sandi Lee was at the booth where the hostess had seated Niya, her order pad in hand.

"Can I take your order?" she asked in her most proper manner.

Niya looked up, and then screamed. "Sandi Lee!" She jumped out of her seat and embraced her friend. "My God. It's really you! In Orlando?"

"Yep. It's me, all right."

"Girl, you look great."

"I ought to. I'm not the same person you dragged out of that elevator in Miami. I've been clean for nearly three months and I plan to stay that way."

"That's good news. Wow, this is such a surprise," Niya gushed.

"What are you doing in Orlando?" Sandi Lee asked.

"I'm dancing at a private party of conventioneers—some kind of organization of spa and resort owners."

"Where?"

"At Brentwood Estate. Some rich guy's palace by the sea, I understand. Ever heard of it?"

Sandi Lee shook her head. "Sorry, I don't run in those circles. And where's Tremont?"

"He's flying in next week. He has a three week engagement at Level Four—starting next Saturday night. So, we'll be around for a while. You've gotta come and hear him play. We've been on tour for weeks. His new CD is flying out of stores!"

"I know. I've heard it on the radio. It's really hot, and getting tons of play around here. He must be thrilled."

"He is," Niya confirmed with pride. Lowering her voice she mocked a mischievous whisper behind her hand. "And he's making tons of money."

"And I can see that you're helping him spend it, girl, " Sandi Lee added, giving Niya a calculated once-over. "Looking mighty prosperous, girlfriend."

Without hesitating, Niya responded, "Things are *too* good." Then she extended her left hand, wiggling her fingers, drawing attention to her engagement ring.

Sandi Lee leaned in to get a better look. "That's huge, girl."

"I know. Isn't it fabulous? Can you sit down? Can we talk?" Niya hurriedly asked.

Sandi Lee glanced back at the woman she had been waiting on, who was now glaring at her in confusion. "For sure. But later. I get a fifteen-minute break after I finish this lady's order. I'll be right back." Then she rushed back to the woman and told her, "Sorry, no fresh pineapple today, ma'am. Will canned do?"

Brentwood Estate sat on one hundred and twelve magical acres by the sea, and included six separate guest cottages, an office complex, horse stables, a championship tennis court, and a mosaic tiled swimming pool—the centerpiece for waterfront entertaining in unforgettable splendor with boundless views of the ocean. The grand outdoor entertainment area was where Niya and two other acts were scheduled to perform that night.

Upon her arrival at the estate, she was greeted by a tall man with ginger-brown skin, a pleasingly crooked smile, and the swagger of someone who was completely comfortable with himself. She was surprised to see that he was wearing heavily tooled black leather cowboy boots with his immaculate tuxedo. When Niya's eyes met his, she immediately glanced away, unable to match the intensity of his gaze.

"I'm Astin Spence," he told her clasping both of her hands in his. "Welcome to Brentwood. I'm the national president of SARO, International—Spa and Resort Owners, International, that is, for those not in the business." He chuckled and paused. "The members of our organization are looking forward to your appearance tonight, Ms. Londres."

"I'm happy to be a part of your entertainment," Niya murmured, easing her hands from his, fully aware of how tightly Astin Spence had been holding onto them.

"I flew in from Nevada only an hour ago," he went on, "and I am thrilled to have been asked to serve as your escort for the evening." He lifted both hands in an expansive gesture. "Isn't this a fabulous estate? Bob Brentwood is our national treasurer and it was so good of him to open up his home for our party."

"It's beautiful," Niya agreed, looking around, feeling as if she had just stepped into an unreal Hollywood set. Everything about the place—the tropical plants, the vivid blooming flowers, the exotic Spanish architecture, and the spectacular views—were picture-postcard perfect, too gorgeous to believe.

"You will perform midway through the evening," Astin told her, as he launched into an overview of the evening's festivities while walking her through the wide double doors of the main house, into the grand salon, past a richly paneled English pub room, and up the floating staircase that dominated the lower floor. "We will hold the live auction first, followed by a few songs by Sammy Jarvis, and then your performance, and finally, our main act, Bill Cosby."

"The comedian? The guy from TV?" Niya asked, impressed.

"The same," Astin replied, taking Niya's elbow as they mounted the steps together. "He's a longtime friend of Bob's. I think they golf together whenever Mr. Cosby is in Florida."

Niya suddenly felt slightly nervous to hear that such a high-powered celebrity would be in attendance tonight, and knew that she had to give the best performance of her life.

"I must say, you are lovelier than your photos," Astin gushed as he reached the top of the stairs. "I'm so happy that you could fit this performance into your schedule."

Niya smiled and nodded. "It has been a hectic time . . . on the road. Waking up in a different city every few days. It's good to be back in Florida."

"Yes, I know, I understand that you've been touring with your fiancé, Tremont Henderson, the musician, right?"

"Yes," Niya replied, realizing that this man had done his homework. What else did he know about her? she wondered.

"Where to next?" Astin asked.

"After this stop in Orlando we'll be going back home to Miami. I'm looking forward to a few days of doing absolutely nothing."

Astin grinned, nodded, and then reached into the breast pocket of his tux. He produced a white business card, which he handed to her. "I understand completely. And if you ever need a private place to rejuvenate, restore, or simply relax, come out to Nevada. I own Diamond Marsh Resort, just east of Carson City . . . a three hundred acre spa resort with every luxury you could ask for. If you think Brentwood Estate is beautiful, you need to see my spread. Gorgeous country, Nevada. The opposite of Florida, of course. Dry. Rugged.

Mountains all around. But even more exciting, in my opinion. I'd love to have you come out as my guest."

Niya took the card, studied it, and then studied her host a bit closer. He looked to be in his mid-thirties, and was exceptionally handsome, with lively brown eyes, a thin mustache, a chiseled jaw, and the kind of rugged features that reminded her of a black Clint Eastwood. His double-breasted tuxedo jacket, which accented his broad shoulders, had discretely placed rows of silver studs along the edges of the lapels in a unique Southwestern pattern. He had the appearance of a charmingly suave yet flamboyant man who knew exactly who he was.

"Well, here you are," Astin told her, opening the door to a suite with an ocean view overlooking the estate. "Make yourself comfortable, and if there is anything you need, just pick up the phone and press one. We want you to be happy."

"I'm sure everything is fine," Niya told him, giving him a quick lift of her hand as she bid him goodbye and eased the door shut.

She stood for a moment looking around. The house was one that truly provided a grand lifestyle for someone who wanted only the finest. The sumptuous suite was an opulent mix of traditional furnishings accented with the bright punch of trendy, contemporary pieces.

What a place, she thought, wandering around the luxurious room. She picked up a bottle of Fathom perfume and held it to her nose, aware that the scent cost five hundred dollars an ounce. "If Diamond Marsh Resort is more beautiful than this, I can't imagine what it's like," she murmured, fingering the raised letters on Astin Spence's business card.

The crowd of seven hundred conventioneers rose to their feet when Niya finished her act, and they did not sit down until she returned to the stage for an encore. Panting with excitement, as well as the exertion of her forty-minute routine, she smiled and waved at her audience.

Looking out, she caught Astin's eye and he gave her a big

thumbs-up, and then whistled through his teeth before he resumed clapping. When she realized that her audience was not going to let her leave the spotlight without a final number, she motioned for a microphone from an assistant at the side of the outdoor stage.

"I'd like a volunteer from the audience to help me close out my performance for you tonight," she requested in a breathy voice. "And I need someone who can rumba!" she shouted.

Before she even had time to scan the packed seating area under the stars to settle on one of the many raised hands, Astin had bolted onto the stage and wrapped a possessive arm around her waist.

"Look no further," he shouted at his colleagues, waving at them. "I'm your man!"

The audience roared its approval.

Niya turned toward Astin and propped her hands at her hips, which were snugly encased in a yellow beaded skirt that rested low on her hips, showing off her firm, bare midriff. "You sure you can rumba?" she teased, smiling. "I'm talking real Cuban rumba. Think you can keep up with me?"

"Just watch me," he tossed back, accepting the challenge.

"Okay, let's see what you can do!" With a flick of her wrist, she cued the band to begin, and the bata drums quickly started pounding out the familiar Afro-Cuban beat that was always accompanied by the click-click of hardwood sticks that set the pace for the staccato rhythm. The audience cheered and began clapping along, shouting taunts at Astin.

Moving an arm's length from Astin, Niya lifted her chest and extended her right hand, which Astin quickly enclosed with his left. With an easy motion he sent her into a spot turn to the right, after which Niya whipped her head around and grinned. Moving gracefully, she eyed her partner with new appreciation, seeing that he was completely at ease with this spontaneous rhythmic encounter. Hand to hand, quarter turn after quarter turn, they twisted their hips, fanned out and merged, flirted and chased, and rocked in a seductive curving of their bodies, as if they had danced together many times before. His timing matched hers, as did his understanding of the importance of posture, gesture, and facial expression and, as the audience continued to cheer with enthusiasm, the exciting exhibition unfolded.

By the end of the evening, Niya knew that Astin Spence was indeed, no ordinary man.

Chapter 23

It did not take long for Niya and Sandi Lee to rekindle their friendship, and when Tremont arrived in Orlando, he was glad to find Niya happily reunited with her best friend. Niya had told him about Sandi Lee's problems with Ace and how he had gotten her hooked on drugs, but that now she was clean and sober.

Tremont insisted that Niya spend as much time with Sandi Lee as she wanted. When Niya and Sandi Lee went shopping, he generously handed them hundred dollar bills, impressing Sandi Lee and letting her see that Niya wanted for nothing. All Tremont wanted was for Niya to be happy, and when Sandi Lee was around she seemed to be.

Tremont was well aware that Niya thought he should not spend so lavishly on them, but she was wrong. He worked hard and he was going to make sure his woman, and her friend, enjoyed themselves. Niya ought to be grateful, he thought.

He invited Sandi Lee to attend his opening night performance at Level Four, where she sat with Niya at their table near the stage.

On his rare evenings off, the three of them went out together, and he spent lavishly on meals at pricey restaurants, exotic drinks, and front row tickets to concerts. He insisted that Sandi Lee allow him to pay for the fancy dresses she needed for their outings, and loved the look on her face as she modeled her purchases for him.

He was happy that Niya had some female company, keenly aware of the toll that being on the road with four guys was taking. Living in hotels in strange cities, with no friends or family around had been stressful on her, and he knew that, at times, he had not been the most pleasant companion. He was grateful that Niya had been willing to put her own professional commitments on hold to travel with him, and having her along had made the grind of the tour much easier to bear.

However, they were in Orlando, the last stop on the tour, and it was a great relief for Tremont, who was still livid about the amount of money he had had to shell out to Skip James's boys. When he got back to Miami, he was going to have it out with Skip and make sure that none of his musician friends did any business with him.

In three weeks, he and Niya would be home, and back to as normal a life as they could lead.

Niya sipped her iced tea and then stirred it with the straw, wishing this was not her last day in Orlando. Though ready to go home and back to her job at Club Cariba, she was going to miss Sandi Lee and, surprisingly, the hectic, gypsy lifestyle of being on the road as well. She had visited so many places, seen so much of America, enjoyed so many new experiences, and made quite a few short-lived friendships that she had known at the time would not last.

Being in Orlando with Sandi Lee had been the best part of the tour. They had reconnected right away, as if they had never drifted apart. Going shopping, out to dinner and to movies with her friend had initiated memories of their early days together in Miami, though things were very different now. Niya was engaged to a wonderful man, had no financial worries, and was not the lonely frightened girl she had been when she and Sandi Lee first met. Sandi Lee, however, was still all alone, still struggling to make a life for herself, and Niya wanted to help.

"Come back to Miami with me and Tremont," Niya impulsively offered, watching Sandi Lee through dark sunglasses. "I'll pay your airfare, you can stay with us until you find another job. Please come. I can't leave you here like this."

Sandi Lee shook her head. "Too many temptations in Miami."

"Ace?" Niya commented.

"Yes, and others," Sandi Lee added.

"Oh, Ace has probably moved on to another city, or gotten hooked up with some other girl that he can push around. You're past all of that. Besides, Miami is a big city. You'd probably never run into him, or anyone else from those days."

"I don't know . . . I've got a good thing here, Niya. Maybe being a waitress at Denny's doesn't sound like much to you, but it pays my bills and lets me take care of myself."

"There are Denny's in Miami, if waiting tables is what you really want to do."

"I know that, but here, I've got control of things—a nice, cheap apartment, an '81 Honda. And a job that is legitimate, even if it doesn't pay much. The tips are good. I stay busy, and that's important. Too much time on my hands can be deadly. And I don't want to go back to . . . that, you know?"

Niya nodded. "I know. But I had to try, didn't I?"

"Sure. Now, you go on back to Miami and get married. You're a lucky girl, Niya. You've got a terrific guy who loves the hell outta you, no financial worries, and you got talent. I'll bet you'll become a famous dancer one day."

Grinning, Niya swept her index finger along the frosty side of her glass as she glanced around the crowded restaurant. "Who knows? And if you're right, I'd want to share my success with you."

"You already have. It's been great getting together again, but it's time for both of us to move on. We'll stay in touch. I'm not that far away."

* * *

One month after Niya left Orlando, Sandi Lee met Brian Simms, a steadily employed, twenty-five-year-old certified public accountant who worked for a large accounting firm, drove a brand new BMW, and lived in a studio apartment in a trendy part of town. She met him at Denny's, where he ate lunch every day, sitting alone at the same booth in her section, often waiting thirty minutes for the seat. He was clean cut and nice-looking in a preppy sort of way, and when he finally asked her out on a date, she immediately agreed.

Brian took her to play miniature golf, and afterwards, to eat pizza and drink beer at a California Pizza house in his neighborhood. Two weeks after their first date, he asked Sandi Lee to move in with him and, ready for a steady boyfriend who treated her nice, kept her away from her old lifestyle and made her feel as if she were important, she took him up on his offer.

Once she had settled in, they went to the movies or stayed home and played Scrabble, or went out for burgers or attended barbeques at his friends' suburban homes. Brian loved to party, but he couldn't hold his liquor worth a damn, and he was not a very good dancer. However, Sandi Lee found him attractive. She also found the low stress lifestyle that came along with being Brian's girlfriend was exactly what she needed—and she convinced herself that she was happy.

Four months into their relationship, Brian got a promotion at his firm and became the supervisor of his unit. To celebrate, he treated Sandi Lee to a rare dinner at a fancy restaurant, and over their meal of lobster tails, steak, and garlic mashed potatoes—washed down with a respectable bottle of red wine—Brian told Sandi Lee that he predicted he would become the senior manager of his department within six months.

"That would be great," she acknowledged, digging into her potatoes. "Be a whole lot more money."

"Yeah, I could triple my savings bonds."

"You really sock away the cash in bonds, don't you?" Sandi Lee remarked, having noticed how many of the little green checks arrived regularly in the mail.

"The safest investment there is."

"Do you ever wish you were rich? Really filthy rich?" Sandi Lee suddenly prompted, sipping her champagne.

"Why would you ask that?"

"I dunno. Just asking. Do you?"

"Nope. Can't say I ever thought about being filthy rich. I just want to be secure," Brian mumbled, chewing on a piece of steak. "Being financially secure is better than being rich."

"Oh, well. I was thinking about a friend of mine . . . her fiancé is rich."

"Yeah? Who's that?" Brian asked.

"Niya. Remember? My girlfriend from Cuba that I told you about?"

"Yeah, and who's the guy again? Her fiancé?"

"Tremont Henderson."

"Right. The jazz musician."

"Yeah. I'm sure he's rich," Sandi Lee glibly decided.

"Maybe he is. Maybe not. Some successful people just act the part but they don't have the cash to back it up."

"I guess he could be acting, but he sure throws the cash around. I was talking to Niya on the phone a few days ago, and you know what?"

"What?"

"Tremont bought a yacht. They sail all the time now. I wonder how much a yacht costs. I wonder how rich Tremont really is," Sandi Lee casually commented.

"I could find out what he makes," Brian boasted.

"Really?"

"Sure."

"How?"

"By checking his tax returns, of course."

"You could do that?" Sandi Lee wanted to know.

"If I wanted to. I have access to all kinds of information on my computer at work."

Sandi Lee poured Brian another glass of wine, filling his glass to the rim. "Would you do that? I'm just curious."

"Sure. As long as you keep it to yourself."

"Oh, yeah. Who would I tell, anyway?"

The next day, Sandi Lee answered the phone in the break room at Denny's and was surprised by the information that Brian had for her.

"You know that musician guy, Tremont Henderson?" he started. "The one we were talking about last night?"

"Yeah. What'd you find out?" Sandi Lee asked.

"He's never filed an income tax return."

"Never? That's impossible. The guy makes tons of money."

"Maybe so," Brian agreed, "but he's never declared any of it, as far as I can tell."

"Well," Sandi Lee replied. "That's really strange, isn't it?"

Chapter 24

For Niya and Tremont, the remainder of the year flew by in a blur of pulsing music, long nights in smoky clubs, and carefree off days spent in bed catching up on their sleep or at sea aboard *The Pearl*, the yacht that Tremont had leased for the summer. They hung out with a group of close musician-artist friends, whose upside-down lifestyle was similar to theirs.

Niya, who resumed dancing at Club Cariba as soon as she got back to Miami, was getting more private engagement offers than she could possibly accept, while Tremont, whose CD had won a Grammy for the Best New Afro-Jazz Album for 1999, packed the house wherever he played.

When Niya couldn't accompany Tremont on the road, she enjoyed spending time with G-Daddy, who pressed her relentlessly about when she and his grandson were going to get married. The one-year anniversary of their engagement was two weeks away, and Niya, who never tired of being with Tremont, loved the crazy life they lived, and was deeply in love with her fiancé, was in no hurry to walk down the aisle.

Luckily, Tremont was leaving it up to her to set the date. He was a patient man who knew that she loved him and who also knew that she wanted to have her mother with her for the most important day of her life. Though *he* knew it would be impossible, he also knew that Niya needed time to come to terms with the realization that her mother would not witness her only daughter's marriage.

Niya wrote letters to her mother once a month, which she delivered to Paige Moore, who somehow got them into the hands of a man who supposedly could get them into Manto Negro Prison. Niya never received a reply from her mother, but trusted Paige's assurances that her contact in Havana was doing his best to deliver the correspondence. Niya would wait it out. It didn't matter how long she would have to wait. One day her mother would be freed, and when that happened Niya was going to find a way to get Olivia Londres to America for her wedding.

"And by the way," Brian went on, tilting back a glass of eggnog at his CPA firm's holiday party while grinning at Sandi Lee. "In January, my unit is being transferred to our Omaha office."

"Omaha?" Sandi Lee responded, trying to keep the edge of disappointment out of her voice. "Like in Nebraska?"

"Yep," Brian replied. "Big salary increase and this puts me on a fast track for regional manager. Isn't that great?"

"Omaha?" Sandi Lee repeated, gulping down the last of her Diet Coke. She had not had a drink of alcohol or an illegal drug in her system since arriving in Orlando and Brian's presence had had everything to do with her sobriety. Her life with him was a predictable routine, and as stable as that of an old married couple. But now, it sounded as if this cocoon of security was about to crack wide open. "Uh, when are you . . . we . . . moving?"

"I have to be there by the fifteenth of January. But you've got to stay here, at least for a few months . . . until I get settled."

"Oh," Sandi Lee murmured. "A few months? Can I stay at the apartment?"

"Nope, sorry," Brian replied. "I've already given the manager notice and it'll be rented out by the time I leave."

"So I've got to find a place to live?"

"I'll help you," Brian stated, placing his empty eggnog cup on a nearby tray, and then accepting congratulations about his upcoming transfer from one of his co-workers. Turning back to Sandi Lee, he went on. "I've been to Omaha many times. It's really a very nice city. You'll love it."

"Right," Sandi Lee murmured, fearful about starting a search for a new place to live.

As his news settled in, she stared glumly at the gaily decorated Christmas tree in the corner of the room, realizing that she was tired of Brian and bored with their relationship. Why the hell would she want to leave sunny Florida to live in a cold-ass place like Nebraska? With him? He wasn't worth that much of a sacrifice. Ever since renewing her friendship with Niya, she'd been thinking seriously about returning to Miami. Now she had the perfect excuse.

The bright stage lights blinded Larry Lo and blacked out the audience, and for that he was grateful. He could hear the shouting, clapping, stomping noises of his fans' wild appreciation, and was relieved that he did not have to make eye contact with any of them. He knew what they looked like—frenzied, energized, blown away, and totally caught up in his music—as they had been in every jam-packed auditorium, club, concert hall and stage he had performed on for the past year. He was live tonight and he wanted this holiday concert to be the one his fans would remember and talk about for years.

After his first radio performance with Ice Blu, Larry had moved swiftly into the spotlight, rapidly building a fan base that was shockingly loyal, very young, rowdy, and demanding. The raw emotion on their faces often overwhelmed him, leaving him frightened—not of them, but of what might happen if he disappointed the crowd.

Becoming a hip-hop star overnight was a scary reality that Larry still did not fully comprehend, and he knew he had to be careful. Anything could blow up at any moment and he was still learning how to handle this kind of fame. He tried to focus on his music, his stage presence, and writing new lyrics, though he had to admit that the gorgeous girls who were always hanging around were a distracting weakness he could not ignore. The honeys were ever-present, aggressive, and hungry—moving from one hip-hop star to another as they chalked up notches on their sequin-covered, low-slung belts. Larry sampled them all, though he knew all hell would break out if he accidentally tasted a rival rapper's treat.

It was easy to initiate a beef over some half-naked girl or a misspoken word or a gesture casually made. It did not take much for a rival rapper to feel as if he had been dissed, and this generally led to a fistfight or a shooting—both of which Larry had narrowly escaped more than once.

His new song tonight was "Let's Break Through," a direct message of thanks and goodbye to Ice Blu for bringing Larry into the spotlight, and Larry hoped his mentor would receive the message in the spirit that he intended. Ice Blu had been a generous mentor and had given him a start, but it was time for Larry to break out of the senior rapper's shadow and go it alone.

Larry had paid Ice Blu thirty percent of everything he'd made from live performances all year, but now that he was being courted by noted record producer, Timmy Kym, it was time to roll, and to get a real agent.

Bending low, his gold spinners swinging from his neck, he launched into his fast-rhyming, sizzling hot, loud-spoken composition, "Let's Break Through," his public thank-you to Ice Blu.

The crowd whooped and whistled and shouted its approval. Larry Lo beamed into the darkness, raised a clenched fist at his fans and then tapped it twice against his chest as he nodded his head up and down. From the side of the stage, he heard Ice Blu shout out some words that were quickly lost to the noise, making Larry glance over at his friend, and then raise both his hands in question.

In a blur, Ice bolted from where he had been standing in the wings, grabbed Larry in a bear hug, and buried his face against his protégé's neck.

"Hey man," Larry started, "glad you liked the track. Just for you, man. I really do thank you for everything you did. It's been . . ."

Ice Blu, keeping his back to the crowd, tightened his grip. "You piss-ass leachin' motherfucker," he hissed. "Think you can blow me off in public and walk outta here alive? Don't even think about it."

"Hey, dude, you got it wrong," Larry started, but stopped talking when he felt the hard nose of a gun poking into his stomach. "This ain't no kiss-off song. Naw, man, you took it all wrong."

Ice Blu pressed the gun deeper into Larry's side.

With a jerk, Larry stepped back and managed to break free.

The gun went off, its loud bang resonating above the cheering crowd as the bullet tore a big hole in the stage floor.

The audience erupted into a screaming, crying mass of people scrambling in confusion for a safe place to hide.

Four security guards rushed forward just as Larry jumped off the edge of the stage and landed on his feet. He fought his way through the terrified crowd to the double doors at the back of the club where arms and hands and clothing created a tangled block at the door.

"Move it!" he shouted, thrashing at the frantic fans. "Let me outta here!" With a hard jab of his elbow, he sent an hysterical woman off to one side and slammed her into a wall. Head down, he pushed his way through the door.

Outside, the cold December air hit him in the face and the sprinkling of snow flurries swirling in the air touched his cheeks and momentarily calmed his nerves. After hesitating for a second, he flagged down the first taxi that came along, jumped into the backseat, and ducked down onto the floor.

PART THREE

G-DADDY

Chapter 25

The emergency room of Miami Community Hospital was so crowded that Niya had to sit on the steps of a narrow steel staircase just inside the main door while doctors, nurses, patients and frightened family members came and went.

As the people rushed past, she tried to imagine what was going through their minds and what illness or injury had brought them to the hospital. Playing this guessing game kept her thoughts off of G-Daddy, who was lying in one of the sterile cubicles beyond her view, unconscious and alone.

I've got to call Tremont and tell him what's happened, she kept thinking, but could not bring herself to get up and go find a pay phone, having forgotten her cell phone in her rush to get to the hospital. *I'll call him after I've spoken to the doctor*, she decided, determined to stay put until someone came to tell her how badly G-Daddy had been injured.

Connie's shrill, disjointed words still filled Niya's mind: there had been a horrible accident and G-Daddy was bleeding and unconscious. An ambulance was on the way. Hurry and meet them at the hospital.

A tangle of questions had tumbled around in Niya's head during her frantic drive to Miami Community. *Why did G-Daddy dare to climb up on a ladder, knowing he had a very weak knee? Where was Connie, who was paid to watch the elderly man and prevent such things from happening, while he was busy hanging silver streamers from the dining room chandelier? And why wouldn't the emergency room attendants at least let me or Connie be with G-Daddy?* Niya fretted.

She had arrived just as the ambulance was pulling up to the hospital entrance and had only been able to touch G-Daddy on the arm before the attendants wheeled him into the hospital and down a long corridor. He had looked so small and fragile with his eyes closed and his body as still as death.

Niya checked her watch for the hundredth time, looked down the bright white corridor where Connie had gone to confer with the admitting clerk and sighed. It seemed as if she had been there forever, but in fact it had only been two hours. Exhausted and numb with worry, she slumped against the wall and closed her eyes.

"Niya. Wake up."

Jolting alert, Niya looked up to see Connie standing over her, a young Asian man in a white coat at her side. With a start, she stood up, fingertips at her lips as she waited to hear what the doctor had to say.

"I'm Doctor Yin," he said, extending his hand.

"Niya Londres," she replied, shaking it.

"I understand that you are engaged to Mr. Grant's grandson?"

"That's right," Niya said. "Tremont Henderson. He's out of town on business."

"I see. Have you spoken to him?"

"No. I wanted to wait until I knew what was going on. How is G-Daddy . . . I mean Mr. Grant?"

"Still unconscious. He suffered a concussion, fractured his collarbone, and has a very serious gash on the right side of his head, which required quite a few stitches."

"But he will come around, won't he?" Niya asked.

"I can't say right now," Dr. Yin truthfully replied. "To be honest, at his age, it could be very serious. Even if he regains consciousness, he may have some brain damage. It's too early to tell. Right now, we're doing more tests to determine how extensive his injuries are, and then we'll see where to go from there. However, I suggest you get in touch with Mr. Grant's grandson. Is he the closest living relative?"

Connie nodded.

"Well, Mr. Henderson should get here as quickly as possible. There are papers that only he can sign, as next of kin, and it's best to be prepared for whatever happens."

"Of course," Niya replied, locking eyes with Connie, whose face was lined with sadness and regret.

Tremont arrived at the hospital seven hours later, after canceling his performance and flying in from Detroit. Niya was sitting in the near-empty waiting room, while Connie went back to the house to get some papers that the admitting clerk needed.

When Tremont saw Niya, he rushed over and took her by the arm, holding onto her, as if to steady himself, while she told him all that she knew.

"He's a tough old bird," Tremont finally replied, easing down into a chair beside Niya. "He's going to come through this just fine. He has to."

"Yes, he has to," Niya agreed, gripping Tremont's hand, prepared to keep vigil with him for as long as he needed her there.

Over the next four weeks, Niya, Tremont, and Connie took turns sitting in the chair beside G-Daddy's hospital bed, talking to him, singing to him, reading to him—anything that might make the coma-stricken patient open his eyes. They ate their meals at his bedside, left the television running when they were not there, and Miami Community Hospital soon became a second home.

When G-Daddy finally regained consciousness five weeks

after the accident, both Niya and Tremont were there. They leaned close to G-Daddy to hear what the elderly man immediately began to mumble.

"Did you take the turkey out of the oven?" G-Daddy asked, looking straight at Niya.

"What turkey?" she asked.

"The one I'm cooking for my New Year's Eve party," he told her, rising up, steadying himself with both of his elbows.

"New Year's is long past," Tremont told his grandfather. "You had a bad fall. You've been unconscious for over a month."

"Unconscious? You mean I missed my party?" G-Daddy snapped, bewildered.

"You didn't miss it . . . we cancelled the party," Tremont told him. "But don't worry, there's always next year." He placed a hand on G-Daddy's frail chest. "Now, lean back and rest."

G-Daddy shook his head slowly, sank down, closed his eyes and promptly went to sleep.

Two days later, after a final battery of tests, Doctor Yin told Tremont that his grandfather was fine, physically, but would never be as mentally sound as he had been before the accident. The blow to the elderly man's head had been serious and he might not be capable of making important decisions. Dr. Yin urged Tremont to take the appropriate legal steps to become G-Daddy's guardian.

Back home in his aging mansion, G-Daddy was lost. It hurt Niya to realize how much his mental faculties had dimmed. He became easily confused and often wandered through the big old house while searching for the kitchen or the bathroom. He was forbidden to go anywhere alone, not even as far as the mailbox at the end of the driveway, and became hostile because she or Connie or Tremont followed his every move. When he got upset, he vented his anger by throwing whatever was at hand or cursing like a hellion, shouting obscenities at old friends who came to visit, swearing he had never seen them before. He wanted all the doors and windows to the house locked at all times and would not let anyone but Connie, Niya or Tremont get near him.

Two weeks after G-Daddy returned home, Connie had to leave for San Diego to be with her daughter, who had endured a difficult labor while delivering Connie's first grandchild.

The following week, Tremont had to leave for Paris to begin a six-week European tour that could not be rescheduled, leaving Niya to move in with G-Daddy and watch over him until Connie's return.

Before Tremont left the country, he arranged for Niya to become G-Daddy's legal guardian, including full access to his many bank accounts.

Chapter 26

Sandi Lee slipped behind the wheel of Ace Leland's two-week-old silver Mercedes Benz and started the engine. The soft purr of the luxury car brought a smile to her lips as the part of her brain that craved pleasure kicked in. She was back in Miami, back in her element, and happy about reuniting with the only guy she had ever truly cared about.

Looking back, she viewed her time with Brian Simms as little more than a transitional relationship that she had needed to pull herself together. He had provided her a safe haven in which to get her head straight, refocus and stay sober. She didn't really miss him . . . after all, he had been such a boring, predictable person, but she hoped he was happy living in Omaha because she was thrilled to be back in the city she loved, where life was fast, dangerous, and full of good times.

On the second of January, Sandi Lee kissed Brian goodbye, packed her '81 Honda with all of her belongings and headed straight to Miami, where she immediately telephoned Niya to tell her she was back in town. Niya had been so stressed out dealing with Tremont's grandfather's accident that Sandi Lee had been reluctant to impose.

"But I want you to come and stay with me," Niya had told her, after expressing her joy that her old friend was back in town. "This house is huge and I really get kinda creepy-feeling at night when it starts cracking and making all kinds of sounds. Come on. You can have your pick of six bedrooms."

"Nope," Sandi Lee had insisted. "Sounds like you got enough on your hands. I've got some cash. I can get a place, and I've already got a job lined up at the Denny's over on Seaton Avenue. We'll get together soon," Sandi Lee had promised.

That had been four months ago and she and Niya had not hooked up yet. However, later that same day, she had stumbled into Ace Leland.

She had truly run into Ace by accident in the parking lot of a convenience store near the restaurant where she had gone to meet her new manager and arrange her work schedule. He had hugged her right away, kissed her hard on the lips, and promptly apologized for the shabby way he had treated her in Las Vegas.

When she told him about her stint in rehab and her move to Orlando, he had shrugged, as if cleaning up her act meant little to him, and then he had rattled on about how swell he was doing before inviting her to lunch.

They went to a cozy Mexican restaurant, where they ate enchiladas, joked around and laughed, just like old times, and finished off two pitchers of margaritas. By the time Sandi Lee followed Ace home to his condo on Oceanside Drive, she was totally smashed, revved up about seeing him, and as horny as hell.

Their first night together, they made love for three hours in every room of his condo and did so many lines of coke that the evening swirled into a blur of white powder, white wine and tangled sheets.

"You're the only girl I ever really trusted," Ace had confessed between snorts.

"That so?" Sandi Lee replied, accepting the straw that Ace handed to her. She pressed it into the mound of white powder and drew in a sharp breath. Her head immediately exploded in that sweet foggy high that swept through her like silver lightning. She had missed this wondrous, fleeting magic so damn much, and knew immediately that she was back in heaven.

"Yeah," she murmured, leaning back to savor the rising crescendo inside her. "Yeah. This is the best."

"I'm not gonna let you get away again," Ace had vowed. "We belong together, babe."

He's right, Sandi Lee now thought as she pulled away from the curb. *We belong together. I need him . . . I crave the excitement, action, and thrill that only Ace can bring. Ace understands me, and as long as he treats me right, I'll stick around.*

As far as she could tell, Ace *was* a changed man: more easygoing, less impatient, and a bit more romantic. Now, he brought her presents when he came home; no longer yelled at her or pushed her around; and he let her do whatever she wanted, as long as she gave him what he wanted in bed, and that was certainly no chore because sex with Ace had always been the best part of their relationship—well, second best, she decided, her body tingling with that edgy search that only a bit of blow could control.

She did start working the morning shift at the Denny's on Seaton Avenue, but quit two days later, when Ace insisted that she'd do a lot better working for him. Now, she spent her days running errands for Ace, never asking questions about the contents of the packages that she was instructed to drop off and pick up all over the city.

Sandi Lee turned into a narrow alley, drove up to the graffiti-covered back door of a Chinese restaurant and stopped the car. Leaving the motor running, she waited. Soon, a short, caramel-colored youth dressed in dirty white pants and a baggy green sweatshirt came out the back door and approached the car. She pressed the button to let the window down.

"On time, as usual," the guy said, grinning at Sandi Lee.

"That's right, DuPree. You can count on me being on time," Sandi Lee casually replied, watching as he pulled two paper-wrapped packets from beneath his sweatshirt.

"One for Ace . . . the other's for you," DuPree told her, winking, while running his tongue over his lips.

She checked him for a quick second, aware of what was going down. DuPree Jones had been hitting on her for weeks—asking her out and making lewd come-on remarks, which she steadfastly ignored. *Does this short, bald-ass teenager think that an extra ounce on the side will make me give up some pussy?* she thought. *Not hardly. He ought to be glad I haven't told Ace about him, cause Ace would have no problem shoving his foot up this punk's ass.*

"For me? Why?" she asked innocently.

"Because I like you, baby," DuPree replied, leaning into the open window, his lips parted. "You're hot. And I want you to have a little sumthin'-sumthin' for yourself. Somethin' wrong with that?"

"Nope. Not at all, since you're offering," Sandi Lee replied, accepting both parcels. "But don't expect me to *pay* you later. Got it? Don't be throwing this shit up in my face later on, DuPree. I ain't gonna go there."

"Why you think I'd do that?" he replied, extending his tongue and then flicking it at her.

"Cause I know just what kinda punk-ass guy you are," she sweetly tossed back.

DuPree frowned.

Sandi Lee smiled, and with a quick nod, she slipped her gift into her purse and then took out a sealed packet which she handed to DuPree. "See you next time," she said in a cool tone as she rolled up the window and took off, grinning into the rearview mirror as she watched DuPree Jones watching her.

At the end of the alley, she pulled into the vacant parking lot behind the Laundromat, put the car into park, and opened the parcel that Dupree had given her. With a flick of her fingernail she dug down, scooped up a hit and drew it into her nose.

"Good shit," she murmured, grinning as she tucked a strand of hair behind her ear, glad that she would not have to answer to Ace for this indulgence. Maybe DuPree wasn't so bad after all.

After two more generous snorts, Sandi Lee wiped her nose, turned up the music—filling the car with Natalie Cole's voice—put the car into drive, and made a left turn onto North Shore Way Boulevard.

The music and the coke were creating a delicious buzz inside her head, and she was proud of the way she had handled DuPree. Maybe she could string the stupid punk along a few more weeks . . . score a decent stash for herself before things got ugly.

Musing the idea, she entered the busy thoroughfare. However, as soon as she looked up, she knew she was in trouble. North Shore Way Boulevard was a one-way street and she was definitely going against traffic. Totally disoriented, dizzy and confused, she blinked at the cars that were dodging around her, missing her by inches, while oncoming traffic became a blur of vivid colors.

"Shit!" Sandi Lee screamed. With a jolt, she slammed her right foot hard on the brake pedal and held it there, certain she was about to be killed. The sound of screeching tires drowned out Natalie's highest notes and immediately sobered Sandi Lee up. Horns honked, rubber burned the pavement, and drivers shouted curses at her, demanding that she get out of their way.

Somehow, Sandi Lee managed to keep control of the car, and with a hard jerk to the right, she spun it around and entered the flow of traffic, but in the process, she sideswiped the rear end of a blue Pepsi Cola truck. The front end of Ace's silver Mercedes crumpled before her eyes, and the sound of shattering glass and twisting metal made her heart begin to race. Confused, she slowed down and pulled alongside the Pepsi truck to see what had happened, but when the driver jumped out of his cab and began shouting at her to stop, Sandi Lee slammed down on the accelerator and sped up.

No way . . . not with the shit that I've got in this car, she decided, speeding away from the scene of the accident.

The hood of the car was bent so badly that she could hardly

see the road, and she knew the grill, the front bumper and the headlights must have been shattered, but as long as the motor still purred, she was not about to stop.

Once she got off the main highway and was a safe distance from the accident, she turned into a weed-filled lot and tossed both of the packages that DuPree had given her into a pile of trash in the field. After glancing around to make sure no one had seen her, she took off down a trail, into a wooded area and emerged into one of the crowded neighborhoods with narrow side streets that would take her back to Ace's condo, dreading the confrontation she knew was inevitable.

"What the fuck were you thinking?" Ace screamed, coming around the kitchen table to grab Sandi Lee by the shoulders. He slapped her with an open palm for the second time. "You stupid bitch." He grabbed her purse and emptied it onto the table. "Nothing! No money, No dope. *Nada*. This is gonna cause a lot of problems. You got a lot of nerve fucking around out there when you were supposed to be working. The cops coulda caught you . . . and you were driving *my* new Benz, too. They coulda taken my car, you know . . . and then both of us would be in jail."

"But I got away," Sandi Lee meekly offered.

"For now! And without the shit!"

Sandi Lee gritted her teeth, afraid to say anything.

"There are other people involved, you know? And they don't wanna hear nothing about why you tossed their goods." He drummed his fingers on the counter, then made a fist. "And there were probably a thousand witnesses on Shore Way who can ID my car now." He punched her in the side and glared hard at her, as if daring her to make a sound.

Sandi Lee doubled over and stumbled back, one hand outstretched as if to dodge another blow. "I'm sorry. I was just . . ."

"Just playing the fool," Ace finished. "Think I don't know DuPree Jones is hot to fuck you? Givin' you a "gift". Shit. He just wants to get in your panties, and for all I know he's already been there."

Holding onto her side, Sandi Lee frowned. "That's not true. I don't care nothin' about DuPree. I was just playing him. Look, Ace, I'm sorry about the car and the stash. Somehow, I'll make it right."

"Damn straight you will," Ace shouted, towering over Sandi Lee. "I oughta kill you. I could snap your skinny neck with one hand if I wanted to and be done with you for good. But I won't. Oh, no. You're gonna get your ass out there and bring back enough money to fix my car and pay for everything you tossed in that field. I can't believe you did that!" He pushed her hard toward the door, opened it and shoved her onto the sidewalk in front of the condo. "Out! Get the hell outta here."

He threw her purse at her, and the keys to her '81 Honda flew out when her bag landed on the lawn.

"Where am I gonna get that kind of cash?" Sandi Lee whimpered, stunned that Ace was doing this to her, though she knew the car repairs were the least of his worries. The missing cocaine was going to cause real trouble.

"I don't care how you get the dough. Sell some pussy. Tap your rich Cuban girlfriend. Didn't you say her fiancé is rolling in cash? Do anything you want, bitch, but don't show your face around here again until you've got the cash to clean up this mess. You wanted to play, baby? Okay, then, let's play."

Chapter 27

Niya was not surprised to see Sandi Lee when she opened the front door of G-Daddy's house, but she was surprised to see the ugly bruises and the swollen jaw on her friend's face.

"Are you back with Ace?" Niya asked before Sandi Lee even came inside.

Sandi Lee lifted a shoulder in response, and then lowered her eyes.

"Damn, girl, when are you gonna learn?" Niya tossed out, stepping aside to allow Sandi Lee to pass. "Come on in. Now I see why you insisted on coming all the way out here to see me today."

An uncomfortable silence hung between the two women as Niya prepared coffee and made small talk about G-Daddy's condition, which was steadily deteriorating.

"All he likes to do is sit outside by the pool all day, like he's doing right now, or tend to his roses. Doesn't even talk to me anymore," Niya said, going over to the window to look out. "I'd introduce you, but he doesn't like strangers coming around. Might get him upset."

"I understand," Sandi Lee replied, coming up behind Niya to study the lone figure sitting in a chaise lounge by the sea green water. "Beautiful place," she commented, glancing around. "Musta cost a bundle."

"He's been living in this house forever. Refuses to leave.

Tremont had thought about putting him in a private nursing home, or something like that, but we know he'd never stay. He'd just walk away. He likes to wander, so I have to watch him like a hawk."

It wasn't until they had settled down across from each other at the small round table in the sunroom that Niya zeroed in on Sandi Lee, questioning the reason for her frantic phone call and impromptu visit.

"What happened and what can I do to help?" she said, watching Sandi Lee closely. "Obviously you and Ace are back at it. Not doing drugs again, I hope," she ventured.

"No," Sandi Lee snapped. "Nothing like that. We had an argument, that's all."

"About what?" Niya asked.

"Well, I wrecked his car this morning and he wants me to pay for the damage. I know I was at fault, and I will pay him, but . . ."

"But you don't have the money. Right?" Niya finished.

"Right," Sandi Lee admitted.

Niya shifted her weight to one side and thought about how to respond. Sandi Lee looked a mess: her left cheek had a deep gash beneath her eye, which was red and swollen. Her blond hair was a tangled nest of wiry strands and she was clearly high on something. Drugs had to be at the root of her problem, and Niya wanted no part of it. "Ace is no good," Niya gently started in. "Leave him alone, Sandi Lee. You'll ruin your life if you stick with him."

"I know, and I *am* gonna leave him . . . I promise, I am. But I can't do that until I settle this business about the car. If I don't, he'll hunt me down." She paused. "He even threatened to kill me if I didn't get the money."

"He doesn't have car insurance?"

"I dunno. Probably not."

"Are you sure there's not something else going on?" Niya pressed, wondering why Ace would threaten to kill Sandi Lee over a banged-up car, even if it was a Mercedes Benz.

"You know how he is . . . just crazy. He's mad at me and said he'd kill me if I didn't make things right."

"Girl, you need to go to the police."

"I can't do that. All I want to do is pay him off and get out of town. And believe me, this time I won't come back." Sandi Lee sipped her coffee, bit down on her bottom lip, and leveled worried eyes on Niya. "Can you help me out, Niya? Please?"

Niya paused, remembering the time when she had taken refuge in Sandi Lee's trailer, and how relieved she had been to find a friend to help her when she needed it. Sandi Lee was not a bad person, she just made bad choices and was easily misguided as she struggled to survive. "As much as I hate to say this, maybe you *should* leave Miami. If I give you some money to clear this up, will you promise to leave Ace for good?"

"I will, I promise," Sandi Lee nodded eagerly. "If you can help me outta this jam, I'm gone."

"All right, how much do you need?" Niya asked.

"Twenty thousand."

"Twenty thousand dollars?" Niya gasped, almost laughing. She had been prepared to give her friend five or six thousand dollars—max. "I don't believe you just asked me for that much money. Sandi Lee, isn't that a lot to pay for repairs to a car?"

"Not for a brand new Mercedes," Sandi Lee offered.

"Well, I won't give you that kind of cash," Niya replied. "That's asking a lot."

"What about the old man?" Sandi Lee asked, getting up to look out the window at Tremont's grandfather. "You said he's loaded. Couldn't you pull some money from one of his accounts? He'd never know it was gone and I'll pay you back, Niya. No matter how long it takes, I will pay you back every cent. If you want me to sign a paper . . . anything . . ."

"No way," Niya stated firmly. "I can't do that. Tremont trusted me to oversee his grandfather's affairs while he's in Europe, and I don't want to mess things up."

"But I have to have that money tonight, and you *know* you

could get your hands on it if you wanted to," Sandi Lee snarled, clearly agitated.

Slowly, Niya nodded, turning Sandi Lee's words over in her mind, realizing how desperate she was. There must be a drug deal involved somehow, Niya thought, thinking she should have known better than to believe Sandi Lee's version of what was going on. "Yes, I probably could get my hands on any amount of money I wanted to, but I'm not going to do it. Not for you to give to Ace, who is probably going to use it to buy drugs. I think you'd better leave, Sandi Lee, and come back when you're free of Ace, and whatever else that has a hold on you."

With a huff, Sandi Lee walked to Niya and stood over her, breathing fast, her body trembling in anger. "So, you're putting me out?"

"Yes. Please, go."

"After all I did for you when you needed help? This is what I get in return? Tossed out? That's a real bitchy thing to do, Niya." Sandi Lee grabbed her purse, pulled out her car keys and jangled them nervously as she glared back at Niya. "Fine. I'm gone. And thanks for nothing, girlfriend. See you around." Sandi Lee was out of the sunroom and out the front door before Niya could respond.

With concern, Niya rushed to the open doorway and watched her friend drive away, suddenly feeling very alone, sad, and somewhat regretful.

Sandi Lee had been the best friend that she could, in her own crazy way. She had stopped her father, a degenerate sexaholic, from raping Niya, and she had kept her company when Tremont was on the road. Niya had thought that they would always be close, never stray too far apart, but now they were more like enemies than friends. As she slowly closed the door she realized that the stranger who had just left was not the Sandi Lee that Niya wanted to remember.

* * *

Sandi Lee blinked back tears as she drove down the curved driveway that led from G-Daddy's house to the main highway. How could Niya treat her like this? Niya ought to have been happy to do everything in her power to help her best friend out of a jam.

She's got access to money, Sandi Lee fumed. While in Orlando, Sandi Lee had been standing in Tremont's dressing room when the manager of the club had given Tremont ten thousand dollars in cash. She had seen how Tremont threw money around, paying his way through life with wads of cash. He had once openly bragged to her that he never took a check from anyone and always got paid in cash. And she had also overheard more than one of Niya and Tremont's arguments about money, and about his free-spending lifestyle. *Tremont has plenty of dough*, she thought, *but Brian says he's never paid taxes. The crooked bastard and his snooty fiancée are living the good life while I gotta go sell my body to get a few bucks together to calm Ace down tonight.*

The longer Sandi Lee drove around town in her aging Honda, the angrier she became. Why did everything turn ugly for her, while Niya had such a beautiful life? Niya . . . the illegal immigrant who had washed ashore with nothing, now had a handsome, successful boyfriend, a beautiful apartment, a career as a dancer, a soon-to-be-grandfather-in-law who was filthy rich—but somewhat demented, according to Niya. When the old man died, everything would go to Tremont and Niya, and they needed absolutely nothing.

Resentment flooded through Sandi Lee, and the sobs that she could no longer hold back spilled out, forcing her to turn into a Burger King parking lot to pull herself together. She wiped her eyes and sat staring out the windshield, thinking back over the past three years. "Niya may think she's so smart and so secure, but I've got news for her." With a yank on the door handle Sandi Lee got out of the car, went to the pay phone on the corner, and dialed O.

"Give me the number for the Internal Revenue Service," she told the operator in a determined, don't-mess-with-me voice.

The woman who came on the line was very polite, efficient, and interested in what Sandi Lee had to say about the large cash payment she had witnessed Tremont Henderson accepting from a club owner in Orlando. And she listened patiently while Sandi Lee described how Tremont Henderson regularly threw money at DJs and radio station managers to make sure his music got played on the air.

"We already have an open file on Mr. Henderson," the woman told Sandi Lee.

"You do?" Sandi Lee replied, somewhat surprised.

"Yes. But thank you for calling. We'll follow up on this additional information."

Feeling smug and self-satisfied, Sandi Lee dropped another quarter into the pay phone and called Ace, who had finally calmed down.

"Did you get the money from your friend?" he asked right away.

"No, Niya refused to come through. The selfish bitch," Sandi Lee told him. "She's living up there in a big mansion, taking care of Tremont's demented grandfather while he's over in Paris, making more money. She could get it, but do you think she'd give up a few dollars for me? No way."

"Yeah? She's alone in the house . . . taking care of the rich guy, huh?"

"Yeah. And he's loaded."

"Then I know what I gotta do. Where are you?" Ace asked.

"I'm at the Burger King on Central."

"Okay. I want you to go over to a garage at Smith and Naranja. Ask for Scotty. He'll give you a van. Something plain and dark. Leave your car there and come pick me up, okay?"

"Why should I?"

"Because you got me into this mess, you dumb-shit, and you gotta get me out," Ace snarled, then he hung up.

Sandi Lee remained where she was, still holding onto the

phone as she considered Ace's request. She *had* wrecked his car and dumped his coke, so she ought to do as he asked, but she sure as hell wasn't going to leave her car at some funky garage over on Naranja Street. Who was this guy, Scotty, and why should she trust him not to strip her car for parts as soon as she drove off in his van? Her '81 Honda might be dented and dusty but it was hers. She slammed the receiver back into its cradle, stepped out of the phone booth, and flagged down a passing taxi.

Ace watched G-Daddy walk from the chaise lounge by the pool to the blooming rose bushes four times before he got out of the car. He jumped the low white slat fence that separated the grounds from the rarely used access road behind the house and hurried across the newly cut lawn, walking right up to the elderly man.

"Beautiful rose garden," Ace told G-Daddy, who simply stared in confusion at the stranger. "I'm from West Side Landscaping. I've got those miniature rose bushes you ordered."

G-Daddy's face brightened.

"Why don't you check them out before I bring them in?" Ace prompted, already guiding G-Daddy toward the back gate. "My delivery van is right over here."

G-Daddy eagerly followed Ace across the lawn, through the fence gate, and over to a black van that was parked on the shoulder of the access road.

As soon as G-Daddy was standing near the passenger door, it suddenly slid open. With a hard shove, Ace pushed the elderly man inside, locked the door, and then hurried around to get behind the wheel.

"You didn't have to shove him so hard!" Sandi Lee shouted from the back of the van.

"Shut up!" Ace shouted, tossing a roll of gray duct tape over his shoulder. "Tie him up good. I don't want any trouble."

* * *

They drove around the city for hours, while Ace snorted cocaine from a straw that he had poked into a plastic bag, and rattled on nervously about all the cash he was going to get from Tremont for the old man's return. When they were forced to stop and get gas, Ace locked her and G-Daddy inside the sweltering van, filled up the tank, and then went inside to use the restroom.

Waiting inside the vehicle, Sandi Lee began to panic as she watched G-Daddy sweat profusely. His eyes were half closed, his brown face was dark red, and his clothing was soaked through. She wiped his brow with her bare hand and patted him on the shoulder, fearing that he might actually pass out.

Glaring at the entrance to the gas station, she prayed that Ace would show up with a bottle of water, a cold Coke. Anything to drink. There was no reason to be so damn hard on the old guy. He was harmless, totally lost, and no threat.

Ace's erratic behavior was getting to her, and she feared he might blow everything sky high and get them caught. How could she have been so stupid? Why had she even gotten involved? Why couldn't she do what Niya had urged her to do—dump the loser and clean up her act?

The sense of failure that swept through Sandi Lee was so overwhelming it made her feel dizzy. After all she had gone through to get away from Oyster Cove, to get sober, to clean up her act, and now she was involved in a major criminal act! The flashy, exciting lifestyle that she had had with Ace suddenly didn't seem so pretty anymore, and she wished like hell that she was living in the suburbs of Omaha, Nebraska, with Brian, bored out of her skull.

When Ace retuned to the van, swigging a beer that he had bought inside, she began screaming at him, fed up. "Why didn't you bring us some water?"

He slid behind the wheel and held up his beer can without turning around. "Want a sip?" he asked.

"Hell no!" Sandi Lee shouted. "What the fuck are you doing? Trying to kill the old man, and me? We been driving around for four hours with a kidnapped old coot who is about to die on us. What's your plan, Ace? Huh? Do you even have one?"

He reached around and tried to smack her, but she ducked out of his way. "Shut the fuck up, and watch Gramps, or get the fuck out."

Well, maybe I'll do just that, Sandi Lee silently grumbled, now realizing that Ace had never had a plan, didn't know what to do, and was so high that he didn't even realize the danger he was putting them in.

As soon as Ace had pushed G-Daddy inside the van and slammed the door shut, Sandi Lee had known they were in trouble. She wanted out. G-Daddy was such a gentle, trusting soul that she doubted he understood the trouble he was in. He simply sat quietly and stared out the window as if he were going on a trip to the beach. She wanted to get out, run away, but doing that would not be easy, and persuading Ace to set G-Daddy free was out of the question. Ace was in too deep, too paranoid, and too confident that he could make things up as he went along to listen to her. In his deep drug-fog, he really believed that everything was going to work out just fine.

"Ace! If we dump the old man in front of a hospital or something, he probably won't be able to tell anybody anything."

"That's the stupidest thing I ever heard," Ace shot back, racing the engine before pulling away from the gas station. "He's a smart old codger. He's just playin' dumb to get you to feel sorry for him."

"You're fucked! I shoulda known you'd mess this up, Ace. Keep the old man if you want to, but I want out."

"You ain't goin' nowhere, so shut up," he growled, braking hard to stop at a red light.

Sandi Lee scanned the intersection and saw that the Miami bus station was on the opposite corner. Seeing the only opportunity to save herself, she jerked on the door handle, slid back the van's heavy door, and jumped out, landing on her stomach in front of a car that screeched to a halt. She jumped up and cut around the back of the van, and tore off, leaving horns blaring after her as cars reentered traffic.

Frantically, Sandi Lee fled across the street like a woman pursued by a pack of pit bulls and raced into the bus station. At the first window she came to, she stopped, bent over double and tried to catch her breath, before yelling breathlessly at the attendant, "I want a ticket!"

"To?" an obese woman with a teased beehive of dyed black hair asked in bored response.

"I don't care where to. Put me on the next bus out."

"That would be the three-fifty-six to New Orleans," the attendant replied. "It's about to leave. You'd have to hurry."

"Okay. Okay. I don't care."

"Round trip or one way?"

"One way, bitch! Can't you see I'm in a hurry?" Sandi Lee screamed at the woman, thrusting a handful of crumpled bills at her.

"You don't have to be nasty," the shocked clerk replied. "That'll be $72.50." She picked up the bills and counted them, and then pushed the ticket under the glass window, along with some change.

Leaving her change, Sandi Lee snatched the ticket and ran to the appropriate gate. After boarding the bus to New Orleans, which was already running and set to pull out, she flopped into a seat, inched down and peeked out the window. She saw that Ace had pulled into the Greyhound Bus terminal parking lot, but had not gotten out of the van. Her eyes nervously swept the parking lot, the busy highway, the nearby side streets, paranoid that police were lurking everywhere. Zeroing in on the black van, she kept her eye on it until the bus entered traffic and she was far enough away to realize that Ace had no intention of following her.

A muffled cry of relief slipped from Sandi Lee's throat and tears sprang into her eyes as she silently bid Miami goodbye.

Chapter 28

G-Daddy's sudden disappearance shook Niya to the core, and after searching the neighborhood, she realized that his disappearance was not accidental. Something was going on and it was connected to Sandi Lee's strange visit earlier in the day. If only she had not gone upstairs to put the laundry away. If only she had kept her eye on G-Daddy, as she had promised Tremont she would do.

Niya immediately called the police and told them about Sandi Lee's visit, her request for money, and all about Ace Leland, whom she suspected might have masterminded this awful tragedy. Once the police heard her story, a search for G-Daddy began immediately, as well as a search for Sandi Lee Holt and her boyfriend, Ace Leland.

Niya called Tremont in Paris and told him what had happened, assuring him that the police were doing all that they could to locate G-Daddy. Tremont instructed Niya to get funds from his grandfather's bank account if she had to, to pay any ransom demand that might come in. He was flying home on the next flight he could get.

At two o'clock in the morning Niya finally got a call from the kidnapper, who demanded, in a muffled voice, two hundred thousand dollars in cash. He instructed her to take the money to Polo Tio, a Cuban restaurant on Santa Clara Avenue the next day at noon and to leave it in a booth—to come alone and not to involve the police. There, she would find instructions on where to find G-Daddy.

The next morning, without telling anyone, Niya went to the bank, withdrew the money from G-Daddy's bank account and headed to the restaurant. Once inside, she found the appropriate booth where directions to a warehouse on Gilbert Road had been taped under the tabletop. As instructed, she left the money in the booth, drove to the warehouse and found G-Daddy. His hands and feet had been bound with duct tape, a red mechanic's rag was stuck in his mouth, and a piece of rope was knotted around his neck.

Niya hurried to check his pulse, and then froze. She was too late. He was dead.

Tremont arrived back in Miami to find his grandfather's house overrun with police, invaded by concerned neighbors, and crammed with shocked friends, while Niya, exhausted from dealing with the authorities as well as her sharp grief, tried to manage the chaos. She was moving like a zombie, suffering from a serious lack of sleep, and was so high-strung and edgy she burst into tears every fifteen minutes. Tremont took over right away and sent her to bed. Then he cleared the house and promised the police that he would be available to answer any questions.

With the house quiet, he roamed the rooms, memories of his grandfather so fresh and sharp that he began to speak to him. "You're gonna be fine wherever you are, G-Daddy," he whispered as he stood at a window and admired the blooming roses. "I lost you when you went into the hospital, but now I feel as if I have you back. As long as I live, I will never be able to thank you for taking me in when my mother tossed me away, for raising me, for loving me when no one else wanted to. I'll never stop until I find who did this. Never. It wouldn't be right for anyone to get away with what they did to you. Rest easy, G-Daddy. In my heart you're still alive."

* * *

Two days later, the police investigating the kidnapping and murder came to see Tremont. They had found Ace Leland—dead of a drug overdose in a motel room in Hialeah. A good portion of the ransom money, scattered about the room, had been recovered.

The following day they reported that Sandi Lee Holt's car had been located on the parking lot of a Burger King on Central Avenue. The car was clean, and so far, they had no leads on her whereabouts.

Chapter 29

Tremont buried his grandfather in a private cemetery near G-Daddy's property—in a sunny spot beneath a pink rose bush. Tremont was devastated at losing his beloved grandfather and was inconsolable for days. However, his misery soon increased threefold.

At the reading of G-Daddy's will Tremont was shocked to learn that his grandfather had left all of his money to the Dade County Horticultural Society to establish a rose garden in his name, but had left his shabby grand mansion to his only grandson with a stipulation that the property was not to be sold out of the family. With no money to restore or maintain the house, Tremont covered the furnishings with sheets, shuttered the place and padlocked the huge front gate.

The next blow came when, soon after he'd settled G-Daddy's affairs, an IRS agent in a dark blue suit personally served Tremont with papers charging him with income tax evasion.

And finally, a month later, the Department of Justice leveled a charge of racketeering against Tremont, two radio station managers, and four disc jockeys, all of whom admitted to taking cash from Tremont to promote his recordings on the air.

When Tremont's case finally went to court six months later, he received a two hundred thousand dollar fine and fifteen years in prison, five of which he had to serve before he would be eligible for parole.

Niya was devastated. She fell into a deep depression that kept her at home, sitting mutely in front of the television for hours, unable to accept the stunning circumstances that had shaken her life. Tremont, who nervously fussed over her and urged her to have faith, kept telling her that everything would be fine. She did not believe him and wanted no part of his cheerful encouragement—she wanted her life to return to what it had been before G-Daddy's accident, before Sandi Lee came back to Miami with all of her drama, before the authorities walked into Tremont's life and ruined everything for them.

The lengthy court case drained both her and Tremont's bank accounts, leaving them broke, anxious, and adrift. Neither knew what the future would hold. When Niya brought up the subject of getting married before Tremont went to prison, he adamantly refused to tie her to an absentee husband, condemning her to a bleak future of prison visits and lonely nights.

When the time came for Tremont to say goodbye to Niya, he held onto her tightly and told her, "I love you too much to ask you to wait for me. It wouldn't be fair."

"Let me decide that," Niya answered between sobs. It seemed as if she had been crying forever and now Tremont wanted to break their engagement? How unfair was that?

"Fifteen years is a long time, Niya."

"You might get out earlier."

"Maybe so, maybe not."

"I don't care. I'll wait for you. I'll visit you every . . ."

"No," Tremont snapped, cutting her off. "I told you before . . . I can't go away thinking that all you are going to do is wait for me. Don't visit me. Don't call me. Don't write me any letters. I let you down. I let G-Daddy down. This is the punishment I deserve and I gotta serve it. Forget about me and go on with your life. You're too young and talented to waste time waiting for me. Get out there and live, Niya. Really live." Then he picked up his bag and left.

Niya was too numb to cry. Tremont was going to prison,

her mother remained in Cuba in jail. G-Daddy was dead. Her brother was missing. Even Sandi Lee had disappeared.

I've got to leave Miami, Niya decided, having made up her mind to go to New York on the chance that she might track down a lead on her brother. *Lorenzo,* she thought, grasping at hope. *I've got to know what happened to you. You're all the family I have now.*

PART FOUR

GRANGER

Chapter 30

New York City, 2002

Opening nights on Broadway always terrified Granger Cooper, and tonight was no exception, even though *Union of Sorts* was his seventh production to make it to the Great White Way in his twenty years as a producer.

Tonight's play had received mildly positive reviews during its lengthy East Coast tour and from the audience's applause tonight, after six curtain calls and a lot of whooping and whistling, he felt certain that the changes he had made in casting, along with major tweaks to the script, had paid off.

Now, he sprang from his front row seat, anxious to go backstage to congratulate the cast, and began shaking hands with important financial backers, longtime theater devotees, and friends who wished him well as he made his way through the animated throng.

He stepped into the corridor leading into the bowels of the theater and immediately ran into Ricky Monroe, a freelance artistic director and creative type who was devoted to the theater. Granger was not surprised to see that Ricky, a lanky guy of thirty-nine with fading, swarthy Italian good looks, had a new young girl on his arm—a slim one with cropped blond hair, a tattoo of a teardrop on her cheek, a jangle of glass beads around her neck and a red boa feather purse swinging from the crook of her elbow. Both Ricky and the girl were smoking slim black cigarettes.

Granger greeted Ricky with a firm handshake and then gave him a one-armed hug around the neck.

"Looks like you've got another hit on your hands," Ricky said, his blue eyes crinkling with approval while he rubbed the neck of the nubile girl, who ground out her cigarette in a dusty potted palm and then linked her arm possessively through Ricky's.

"Sure does," Granger replied. He glanced down at the girl.

"Oh, this is Meg," Ricky hurried to introduce. "Meg, this is Granger Cooper, my best friend and the producer of the show."

"Hello," Granger offered, running his gaze over the girl, who was so incredibly tiny that he imagined a strong westerly wind could pick her up and blow her all the way to Los Angeles. Her nose turned up in a pixie kind of tilt and her eyes seemed much too large for her face, which was completely devoid of makeup. She reminded him of a diminutive Mia Farrow. "Hope you enjoyed the show," he added.

"Yeah, I did," Meg gushed in a high-pitched voice. "It was awesome. I never saw a show on Broadway before."

"Well, you'll have to come again," Granger offered. "I'm sure Ricky can see to that. I think it's going to have a decent run."

"Decent? It's gonna be huge! Maybe I shoulda invested, after all," Ricky joked, now lounging against the wall.

"Don't worry; there'll be others you can put your money in. I can always use another backer," Granger assured him, laughingly rubbing his thumb and forefinger together.

Ricky, the son of a well-known New York real estate businessman with rumored connections to the mob, was also a budding playwright who had worked as the artistic director on three of Granger's plays. He often bragged to Granger that he had access to investment money from his mob-connected father, and would love to form a partnership with Granger to produce one of his plays. So far, they had never been able to settle on a project.

"Gonna join me later?" Ricky asked Granger. "I'm going back to my place. Having a few folks over . . . to wait for the reviews." He slipped his hand up to Meg's shoulder and gave it a squeeze, pulling her along as he began to walk away.

Granger shrugged and lifted a brow, but made no comment.

Ricky turned around and started walking backwards, still talking to Granger. "Ah, come on. Relax. Okay? I'll have Cristal on ice . . . and anything else you might want." A pause while Ricky stared frankly at Granger. "After an opening night like this you deserve to unwind and have some fun."

"I . . . I don't know how long I'll be," Granger hesitated, watching Ricky and Meg make their way down the hall. "The after-party with the cast is at Driscoll's, then interviews with the press . . . the obligatory appearances. You know the drill, Ricky."

"Well, come late. It won't matter how late," Ricky offered, and then he raised one hand in a casual wave and slipped through a side door.

"Maybe," Granger said to himself as the door slammed shut.

A chill of emptiness cut through him, deflating his earlier euphoria. What was wrong with him? Why did he suddenly feel as if he wanted to cry? *Union of Sorts* was going to be huge. He was a wealthy, successful producer who moved in the right social circles and lived at the right address. Within his world, at forty-four years of age, he possessed the kind of influential maturity and financial power to get whatever he wanted. So, why was he feeling so hollow—and so angry at himself for not wanting to spend time tonight with those who had worked so hard to make *Union of Sorts* a success?

He had chosen to attend the opening alone, even though he could have brought along Alexis DeMulle as his date. She was nice enough, though she could be tiring at times—with her nonstop chitchat about her cheating ex-husband and her snobby friends' petty problems. But at least he would not have been solo.

What was it going to take to pull out of this fractured state of uncertainty? Granger wondered. *Find the right woman and marry her.*

The parade of attractive, mature, intelligent women who passed briefly through his life never seemed to be able to ease the restless hunger that constantly plagued him, and tonight it seemed particularly acute.

"Maybe I will drop by Ricky's place," he said to no one in particular. "But only for one glass of champagne. Just one glass. That's all."

It was two-fifteen in the morning when Granger finally broke free of his many well-wishers and rang the doorbell to Ricky Monroe's Greenwich Village apartment. The moment he heard the chime ring out, he tensed, tempted to leave. But Ricky immediately swung open the door and pulled Granger inside before he had time to change his mind, and within a matter of seconds, it seemed, Granger had removed his tuxedo jacket, torn off his black bow tie and was lounging on Ricky's exotic overstuffed tiger skin sofa, sipping a glass of Cristal.

By now, the crowd had thinned to five people: Ricky and Meg; Jon Ricard, a well-known watercolor artist from whom Granger had bought many paintings; Davita Dunham, Jon's super-tall, super-model fiancée; and Bud Glass, a local black comedian who was entertaining Ricky's guests with a blow-by-blow account of his recent trip to Los Angeles to appear on West Coast Comedy Central.

When Bud finished his outrageous tale, everyone burst into laughter and assured him that he had been terribly funny during his five-minute spot on national television and was definitely on his way to superstardom.

"I don't know about that," Bud commented, "but congratulations to you, Granger," he said, lifting his glass of Scotch. "I didn't catch your opening tonight, but I've got tickets for tomorrow."

"Good. I think you'll enjoy it," Granger nonchalantly replied, accepting the toast and sipping his champagne.

"But for now . . . I gotta go," Bud added, draining the last of his drink. "It's a long drive back to White Plains."

Soon after Bud left, Jon and Davita took off, too, and without having to ask Granger if he wanted to stay over, Ricky went to the hall closet, removed a pillow and a blanket, and tossed them at his friend.

"You read my mind," Granger replied, as he kicked off his shoes.

"No reason to leave," Ricky replied, groping for a cigarette, which he lit, and then blew smoke toward the ceiling. "You know you're always welcome." After another long drag, he and Meg disappeared into the bedroom.

Granger turned down the lights and stretched out on Ricky's sofa, thinking about the evening, still high from the excitement of the opening and the frenetic pace he had kept up for the past month as rehearsals pressed on. The aftermath of opening nights always left him feeling adrift, a bit sad that the anticipation was over and his baby had been born. Unable to sleep, he shifted and tossed and sighed and squeezed his eyes shut, determined not to let his mind turn to what he knew he wanted to do.

The sounds of Ricky and Meg moving around in the bedroom only added to his restlessness. Their proximity sent his heart racing. Their muted voices seeped into his brain. The rustle of sheets and the soft creak of the bedsprings as they swung into a steady rhythm made Granger nearly gasp with alarm.

Granger had stood by Ricky during both of his divorces, and put him up in his Central Park apartment during the aftermath of the last one. Having learned his lesson, Ricky's chaotic love life now consisted of an endless stream of girls who had little to offer except their bodies, which Granger suspected Ricky secretly videotaped for his personal erotica library.

Granger drew in a ragged breath, balled his fingers into fists and willed himself to ignore the noise coming from the bedroom. It was impossible.

He eased back the blanket and stood. A beat—while he gathered his courage. Walking softly in sock-clad feet, he ventured down the hallway toward Ricky's room. The door was open. Light was spilling out, and as if in a state of sleepwalking, Granger continued on until he could see into the room. He remained in the shadows, his body rigid and drenched with sweat, his gaze unwavering as he took in the familiar scene in Ricky's bedroom. He glanced at the red blinking light coming from Ricky's video camera, which was always sitting on top of his dresser, always aimed toward the bed to catch any action that might occur. He watched the two naked bodies shift and fuse into one explicitly erotic position after another, and he didn't even move when Meg peeked over Ricky's naked shoulder and caught him watching her.

Chapter 31

April 2002

Dear Mama:

Even though I've been in New York a while, I still am not used to the cold weather, the traffic, the crowds, the expense of living here, and so many people always rushing around. But I don't regret leaving Miami. I had to start over someplace and put my disappointment with Tremont behind me. I write to him, but my letters come back unopened. I guess I didn't know him as well as I thought I did.

I have a small apartment, clean and safe, and I just started work—dancing in the chorus line of a show at a club called Miracle Mile. Dancing is hard work, but I love it, and it seems to be the only good thing left in my life right now.

I have no news about Lorenzo. I located Uncle Eric's address as soon I got to New York. Paige Moore was right. It's a vacant lot now. I asked some homeless men who were living in the rubble if they had heard of a man named Eric Como or Lorenzo Londres. They said they didn't, so I contacted an organization in New York that helps refugees reunite with family members and talked with them. They

promised to do what they could to help, but were not very encouraging. Still, I am hopeful that Lorenzo is alive. Thank God for Paige Moore—my lifeline to you. She told me that her contact in Havana has visited you several times and that you are holding up as well as possible. Stay strong, Mama. Your time in Manto Negro is counting down and I believe we will see each other again somehow.
Your loving daughter,
Niya—Oh, here is my phone number in New York—212-001-0001. I want you to have it just in case there is ever a chance you can call.

Olivia folded the letter into a small square and shoved it inside her threadbare pillowcase, placing it on top of the other letters that Mr. Robles had managed to smuggle into the prison for her. This letter, the last one she had received from Niya, was creased and worn from the many times Olivia had read and reread it.

She cherished her only contact with her daughter, and still cried over that fact that, six years after entering Manto Negro, she still she had no word from her son.

A mist of tears came to her eyes, though she was grateful that poor Mr. Robles had been able to get these precious letters to her. He was gone now, dropped dead of a heart attack at the Miami airport during his last visit to the States, she had heard. With him gone, her only contact with Niya had vanished, too, and Olivia doubted she would ever hear from her daughter again.

The single lightbulb hanging in the center of her cell went out, plunging the place into inky darkness. Olivia relaxed, still thinking about her daughter. It was good to know that Niya was dancing again. That had always made her happy. And how could that crooked musician break her daughter's heart like that? Olivia tightened her lips, relieved that Niya had had the gumption to leave Miami. Good thing she did not marry that flashy, unpredictable man, who was not the kind of man she wanted for her daughter. No, Niya should marry a doctor or a lawyer, or a wealthy businessman, Olivia mused—a stable man who would take care of her

Olivia stretched out on her bunk bed and closed her eyes. At least the electricity had stayed on long enough for her to reread Niya's letters. They were such a comfort. Sometimes there was no light in the prison for weeks at a time, but lately things had been better. The drinking water was not quite so cloudy and the women had been served chicken for dinner three times this month, but six years of incarceration was taking a terrible toll on her health.

The prison doctor who had examined her months ago told her that a weak heart was the source of her chronic fatigue, and had recommended a lighter workload for her at the prison laundry. That had never happened. In fact, she was working longer hours and doing more chores than when she first arrived.

A creeping sense of panic began to arise inside of Olivia. Would she live long enough to walk through that thick steel door to freedom, or would she die behind bars and be buried in the field behind the prison where paupers and criminals with no family to claim their bodies were dumped into the ground without even a prayer?

With a grunt, Olivia shifted around on her hard cot as she tried to find a comfortable spot on her lumpy mattress. Her life had been full of so many unexpected twists and turns. She had no one now. No husband, no children, no friendly neighbors with which to pass the time. Who would have thought that she, Olivia Londres, would be sleeping on a filthy cot in a prison cell, surrounded by strangers? Or that both of her children would be living so far away from her in a place she would most likely never see? But that's the way it was, and so far, Olivia was managing to make the best of it.

"Niya," Olivia whispered, trying to bring her daughter's face into focus against the pitch black solitude that enveloped her. "Lorenzo. My beautiful children. I miss you so." A tear slipped from the corner of Olivia's right eye. *Niya is a survivor, like me*, Olivia thought, sinking towards sleep. *She'll be fine, no matter what happens. But what about Lorenzo? Sometimes I think it would be better if I knew for certain that he was dead. At least he'd be in heaven with his father and have someone to watch over him.*

Los Angeles

"Larry Lo. Larry Lo. Welcome to the show," Sam Clark told his guest as he stood, leaned over his desk and shook Larry's hand. "What's going on, man?"

Before taking a seat in the red plush chair next to the TV talk show host's desk, Larry shook the flamboyant man's hand. Then, with a wave to the live audience, he slipped down into the chair, settled his hips under him, turned his black cap with the letters "LL" emblazoned in sequins on the front to one side, and grinned directly into the television camera. "Too much, Sam. Too much. What can I say?"

"You've got it all goin' on, Larry. I understand your new CD, *Don't Be Crazy*, is blowing up all over the place."

"Yeah," Larry breathed, still looking into the camera. "Took me by surprise. All I can say is thanks to all my fans out there who are dropping the cash at the record stores. It's all good, you know?"

"Larry," Sam started, adjusting the microphone to move it closer to his guest. "You blew up overnight. One day no one had ever heard of you, the next, you're everywhere. Got yourself a huge contract with XXO Records, I understand. Tell me, how did all of this happen?"

"Hey, I'm still in shock myself, man," Larry replied, now focusing on Sam. "I came out here from New York a few years back, and I . . ."

"So, were you born in New York?" Sam interrupted.

"Right. Born in Harlem," Larry lied. "You know, Ice Blu gave me a break back in the city, but I wanted to get out here and hustle my songs in L.A. Next thing I know I'm hangin' out and singing with some of the best musicians around. Then I got a break last year when I signed with Timmy Kym and before I knew it I had this record deal with XXO. It's all good, Sam. All good."

Sam hunched his shoulders and edged closer to his guest. "Now is it true that one of the tracks on *Don't Be Crazy*—the one called 'Gotta Go' is fueling an east coast/west coast beef with Ice Blu?"

"Hey, I don't know nothin' about no beef."

"But I've heard rumors . . . some upset rappers are predicting trouble at the Hip-Hop Awards show next month. They say you are really dissing Ice Blu on that track. Any truth to that?"

"Naw, man. Ice Blu's boys are taking it all wrong. We been friends from way back. I got nothin' but respect for the dude. He gave me my first break. Yo, all I can say to him . . ." a beat while Larry looked directly into the camera, ". . . is I'm sorry if you think I'm dissin' you, Ice. It ain't that way at all."

Sam nodded vigorously, a toothy grin that showed off a lot of gum. "*Word Review* calls you the hottest new talent on the music scene." Sam paused. "At twenty-four, I gotta say, you're drop-dead handsome, built like an athlete, brash, and about to become filthy rich. And I see you do love your bling."

Larry laughed and glanced down at the shiny watch on his wrist, and then fingered the round diamonds in both ears. "Yeah, I gotta have my bling," he jokingly replied.

"So, what's next?" Sam asked. "When will you perform live again?"

"Big concert comin' up at Dirty Shame on Thanksgiving night. Come on out, Sam. There'll be great music, an endless stream of gorgeous babes, and I understand Tupac is supposed to drop by. It'll be wild, man, wild."

"I'll be there, I promise," Sam told Larry, holding up one hand as he looked out at his live audience. "And I want all of you out there in KBU-TV land to drop by, too. Now," he focused again on Larry. "You gonna give us a taste of what we can expect at your concert?"

"Absolutely," Larry replied as he stood and accepted a cordless microphone from a stagehand. "Thought I'd drop a few lines from a track on my new CD . . . 'You're All That.' Okay?"

"Sure. Sure. Sounds great," Sam agreed as Larry sauntered off toward the center of the stage. "Ladies and gentlemen . . . Larry Lo!"

Larry was disappointed that the rain had not slacked off while he'd been inside the KBU-TV studio. He had wanted to go jogging in the park later that day and get in a few rounds of golf—his newest passions to stay in great shape. But all that exercise business would have to wait.

He snapped his fingers at the chauffeur who was waiting for him, and the man instantly produced a huge black umbrella that he used to shelter Larry as they hurried toward the limo, which was only a few steps away from the station's front door.

Inside the limo, Larry flopped down on the black leather upholstery while the driver started the engine.

"Pour me a Chivas on the rocks," he told the buxom, coffee-cream brunette with legs that went on forever who was sitting in the limo across from him.

Without comment, the girl did as he asked, and then handed the heavy crystal glass to Larry, who took it, sipped from it, and then set it aside.

"How about some sugar?" he asked the girl, who immediately moved over and slipped down beside him. She kissed him greedily on the lips, her tongue moving deep inside his mouth before darting across his cheeks. While she kissed him, she began unbuttoning his shirt.

Larry remained completely still while she opened his shirt and trailed her tongue across his chest. Then he took her right hand and eased it down into his pants. "Lower, baby. We can go much lower, okay?" he murmured, stretching out, realizing that he did not know the girl's name. But that was not unusual for Larry. The sexy groupies came and went so fast that he no longer bothered trying to remember all their names. As long as the girls made him happy, didn't talk too much, and were easy to drop when he got tired of them, who cared about names?

For Larry Lo, wild sex, wild parties, lots of booze, beautiful women, chauffeured limos, and top-drawer everything were now his way of life. The only thing Larry did not do was drugs, and if any man or woman within his inner circle put shit up their noses or into their veins, they were immediately booted out of his world and never allowed near him again. Those who were privileged to be a part of Larry's entourage were vigilant about keeping the druggies and the crazies away, though now and then a disgruntled fan or overly infatuated sister-girl did manage to get too close.

As the limo sped through the slick streets of Los Angeles, Larry allowed himself to be pleasured by the expert touch of the buxom brunette while thinking about his upcoming appearance at Dirty Shame, a hot club in the heart of Los Angeles. Would P. Diddy really show up? If he did, Larry was going to invite the popular rapper to come out on stage to perform with him. That would be fresh! The next day, all the trades would have photos of Larry Lo and P. Diddy together on stage. Ice Blu could never top that.

Ice Blu. An east coast/west coast beef, Sam had said. Yeah, Larry knew all about that crazy shit, but he wasn't worried. Threats about violence at a concert or some other hip-hop happening were common. While performing at Club Xenon last week, a fight did break out in the audience, but it had been a minor fracas. Larry did not even stop singing as the fans began to shove and hit each other, and no one really got hurt. However, he would not be surprised if a bunch of legal problems followed: lawsuits were just a normal part of being in show business, and for that reason, Larry kept two high-priced lawyers on retainer to handle that kind of stuff.

Larry's heart began to race as the brunette worked her magic on him with her warm slick tongue. He groaned and tensed his jaw, determined to hold back as long as he could. He forced his mind away from the gentle teasing that was driving him wild and thought back again to Sam Clark's reference to an east coast/west coast beef.

It was true. He *was* dissing Ice Blu on his track, "Gotta Go," and Larry was not sorry for telling the world that Ice had used him to shore up his own sagging career. Larry knew that his "answer records" to Ice Blu's accusations that he had sold out to Hollywood were only adding to the tension between himself and his one-time mentor.

So what if I'm west coast now? he mused. *I've got a contract with XXO Records for three million dollars to do three albums and I bumped Ice Blu off the cover of* Word Review Magazine.

For Larry, living in la la land was the best—great weather, creative types all over the place, gorgeous girls—and being there improved his odds of making it into the movies one day. Definitely his next step.

The brunette moaned, buried her head deeper between Larry's thighs, and dug her fingernails into the calves of his legs. He gasped and placed his hands on top of her head, holding onto her spring dark curls. While the heat in his groin exploded in spasms of mind-numbing light, he realized that his song, "Gotta Go," was playing on the limo radio.

Chapter 32

New York

When Candace Stevens twisted her ankle during rehearsal, Niya was promoted to lead dancer at Miracle Mile, a club in East Village that had gone through so many personalities over the years that patrons no longer knew or cared about what it had originally been long ago. For years, musicians, artists, and a variety of theatrical types had worshipped at the shabbily chic club, which moonlighted regularly as an off-off-Broadway venue for dated burlesque-type shows.

The shadowy downstairs lounge was a gathering spot for unshaven men in black leather jackets and overweight cigar smokers wearing pinstriped suits who hurried down the stairs and often did not emerge for days. Niya had no idea what went on down there and during her two and a half years at the club had never ventured below the stage.

Her move to lead dancer meant an increase in pay, as well as better tips, a dressing room of her own, and much more visibility than she had had in the chorus line of the cabaret-style show.

Tonight, Niya stepped off the stage after her final performance and hurried toward her dressing room. She was flushed, excited, and pleased with the audience's reception of her as replacement for Candace, who had been the lead dancer in the floor show at Miracle Mile for eight months. However, before Niya could enter her dressing room, Contessa, the Puerto Rican sister-girl who took care of her costumes, stopped her. She was holding an exotic floral arrangement of red roses, white lilies, and orange bird of paradise.

"Wow," Niya remarked eyeing the bouquet. "Who are those from?"

"I don't know his name, but he's fine as hell, and he said to tell you that he'll be waiting for you out front."

"Really?" Niya remarked, searching the bouquet for a card.

"There's no card, girl. I already checked," Contessa admitted, smirking, and flashing a dimple.

"Flowers from a stranger, huh?" Niya commented as she continued toward her dressing room, anxious to get changed and find out who her mystery admirer was.

"I'll bet he won't be a stranger long," Contessa murmured, following Niya inside. She put the flowers on the far end of Niya's makeup station and then began collecting discarded costumes from around the room, hanging them on a rolling garment rack in the corner.

"Why do you say that?" Niya commented as she removed her sequin-covered bustier.

"Uh . . . as I said, the guy is hella-fine. Movie star kind of looks."

"Oh? In a Denzel kind of way?" Niya prompted.

Contessa propped both hands at her hips and tilted her head to one side. "No, honey. More in a Richard Gere kind of way."

"He's white?"

"Um-hum. A bit mature, a touch of gray here and there, but he's definitely got it goin' on."

"Interesting," was all Niya said as Contessa picked up the costume that Niya had just shed and handed her a simple black sheath.

"Well, he's waiting out front," Contessa went on as Niya slipped into the dress. "Better go thank him in person and see what's on his mind," she added, pushing the garment rack filled with costumes out the door.

After a quick repair to her makeup, Niya went into the semi-dark club and sat down in a booth near the stage, where she often sat between sets. The ceiling fans were whirring full blast, helping the aging air-conditioning unit to stir the late August heat from the room.

She patted her forehead with a tissue and glanced around, hoping to spot a man who fit Contessa's description, but it was so dark in the club that it was hard to make out the faces of the men who were standing toward the front.

A waitress approached, leaned down and handed Niya a small white card. "He wants to talk to you," she said.

"Granger Cooper," Niya read aloud as she examined the card. "Skylight Productions. Where is he?" she asked, still scanning the room.

"Coming this way right now," the waitress said as she turned to leave, and then murmured under her breath, "I wish he was coming to see me."

Niya grinned and nodded as she watched a tall, slim man in a dark suit make his way toward her booth. "I see why," Niya responded, checking the stranger out.

The man walking toward her was as gorgeous as Contessa had described, in an elegant, sophisticated way. His brown hair, slightly wavy and streaked with gray, nearly touched his shoulders and it swayed slightly with each step he took. His aristocratic features were delicate, but sharp, holding her attention and making it impossible for her to look away. Even from a distance, Niya could feel the power he radiated. He exuded class, confidence, and—from the cut of his suit—a great deal of wealth.

"I'm Granger Cooper. May I join you?" he asked, pausing slightly before slipping into the booth across from Niya, who simply nodded and stared. "Did the young lady give you my flowers?" he asked in the most melodious, perfectly upper-crust voice Niya had ever heard.

"Yes," she managed, finding her own voice. "And they're lovely. Thank you, but I'm not quite sure why . . ."

"Why I sent them?" he finished, a glint in his slate gray eyes as he tilted his head to one side.

"Yes," Niya said, giving him a half smile while inspecting him more closely under the soft lights above the booth. She decided that he might be about forty years old, maybe a bit older. He had a pale, but healthy complexion, a bit of stubble on his chin, which relaxed his otherwise proper appearance, and his high planed cheekbones gave way to a softly pointed chin. His watch, cuff links and tie clasp were all studded with shiny stones, which Niya felt sure must be real diamonds.

"So, why *did* you send me flowers, Mr. Cooper?" she finally asked.

"I see management has moved you from the chorus line to lead dancer," he casually remarked, ignoring her question.

"Right. So, that means you've been watching me?" Niya tossed back, now wondering if she should be worried about a stranger who had been observing her so closely.

"Yes, I have. Ever since you first started working here."

Niya tensed. "Why?"

He picked up the card that the waitress had given Niya and held it up between them. "I own Skylight Productions, an entertainment production company, and I'm always scouting new talent."

"For what kind of work?" Niya warily asked, thinking if this man was looking for a hoochie-mama stripper, he was definitely talking to the wrong woman.

"To act on the stage. In off-Broadway productions that have a future."

"What does that mean?"

"I scout talent and dabble in producing, too. It's not uncommon for many of my clients to work in shows that stage successfully off-Broadway, but that later go on to have a run at a major Broadway theater. Are you familiar with any of the current plays on Broadway?"

"No, can't say that I am."

"*Union of Sorts* . . . it's been running for over two years now, is one of my plays." When she didn't respond, he went on. "So, I'm ready to launch a new project and want to talk to you."

"Oh, well, you're wasting your time. I'm a dancer, not an actress, Mr. Cooper, and I don't know anything about stage work."

"All performers are actors," he quickly countered. "You could easily transition to the stage. I've been watching you. You have a kind of presence that is magnetic, you handle yourself with a sassy confidence, but you're graceful, too. I can see you as an actress in a play that I am casting right now to be staged at the Feldon Street Theater, a small house that I've supported and worked with for many years."

Niya paused. "In a way, I guess you're right . . . about dancers being actors. It's all about performing, but I'm not into learning lines and speaking parts. Besides, I'm happy where I am."

"Really?" Granger replied. "Are you really happy?"

"As much as I can be, I guess."

"That can't be nearly enough," Granger stated, going on to tell Niya about his new play.

For the next ten minutes, Niya listened to Granger Cooper as he described the upcoming production, which would feature unknown actors, most of whom he had personally discovered in New York. It was to be a dramatic show called *Rise,* and it was set to open in January 2005, introducing five talented unknown performers to the theater. Rehearsals had already begun and he had two roles left that needed to be filled, and thought Niya would be perfect for the role of a young woman who had once been a promising dancer who is recovering from an automobile accident. She falls tragically in love with the married surgeon who eventually makes it possible for her to dance again.

"Sounds like a difficult part, one for an experienced actress," she told him when he finished. "That's not me. I'm an exotic dancer."

"Don't worry. You will get the necessary training, if you are selected to be in the cast. But first you have to audition."

"You haven't said anything about money," Niya interjected, growing a tad more interested in Granger Cooper's proposal. "What's the pay?"

"The pay?" He laughed aloud, and then took Niya's hand. "I'm sure that whatever I offer will be much, much more than you are earning here. All of that will be settled if you get the part."

"And who decides if I get the role or not?" Niya asked.

"Mostly, I do . . . though my artistic director on this project, a man named Ricky Monroe, gets a say, too. Please come to the address on the card and audition. Tomorrow at noon. You won't be sorry." Standing, he studied Niya for a moment, and then told her, "I hope to see you again, even if you decide to pass on the audition tomorrow." Then he left.

The next day, Niya got up early and began telephoning theatrical booking agencies to find out what she could about Granger Cooper. She discovered that he was indeed a legitimate, successful talent agent and respected producer and that snagging a role in one of his plays launched at Feldon Street was almost impossible: The auditions were by personal invitation only. The critics were predicting that his upcoming production, *Rise*, was going to make stars of whomever he cast and it would become an instant success.

Niya paced her third-floor, walk-up apartment all morning, mulling her options. An actress? Maybe on Broadway one day? Was it really possible, and most of all was it what she wanted to do?

Since arriving in New York, she had struggled so hard to

make it on her own, and her gig at Miracle Mile was key to her survival. The management treated her fine, the hours were long, but the salary allowed her to live in a neat, safe apartment on the edge of East Village, close enough to the club so that she could walk to work. She was independent, doing what she loved most to do—dance—and was certainly more secure than many other dancers who were still waiting for a break. Did she dare give that up to take a chance on the stage, where she would be a complete novice?

The idea of starting over in a strange new venue was frightening, yet tempting all the same. What if things worked out as Granger predicted? What if she did discover that she had what it took to transition to the stage? And how would she know if she didn't try? There was only one way to find out—go to the audition and see what happened.

At noon, Niya was standing on the stage at the Feldon Street Theater holding a script and reading lines to a young man from South Carolina who had already been cast in the role of her physical therapist. The chemistry was great. The reading was a breeze, over within a matter of minutes. When Granger came onto the stage afterward, he told her how well she had done, that he loved her, and that she was perfect for the role. All he had to do now was get her to agree to come onboard. Of course, Niya immediately agreed.

Afterward while Granger was explaining what the next step would be, he told her, "We'll send over your contract in a day or two." He put an arm around Niya's shoulder and walked her to the side of the stage. "I am going to personally manage you, Niya. And if you do as I say, I have a hunch that you will become very, very famous. Very fast. Trust me."

She did.

As the weeks passed and rehearsals continued for *Rise*, Granger kept his promise, arranging for acting lessons, voice lessons, and anything else that Niya needed to make a professional debut on the stage. He also began to take much more than a professional interest in his discovery and, on a cold November morning, after the first heavy snow, he made his first real move.

"I'd like you to come with me tomorrow to my house in Connecticut for the weekend," he told her. "You've been working so hard. You need to get out of the city, take a break."

"Who else will be there?" Niya immediately asked, thinking he was planning a break for all of the cast members.

"No one else. Only you and me," he casually replied.

"Oh," Niya murmured, realizing that he was moving forward pretty fast. His romantic interest in her had been evident from the first moment they met, and she had known for some time that he wanted to get closer to her, more intimate with her than she had wanted to admit. The prospect of going away with him for a secluded weekend made her nervous, yet she knew she wanted to go, if only to find out how she would handle him.

Since starting rehearsals months ago, she had been thrown into Granger's life and presence every day, making escape nearly impossible. Over the hectic weeks of preparing for the play's opening, they spent long hours together in the theater, in the voice coach's studio, during working lunches and dinners, and at late night run-throughs that often lasted past midnight.

Now, his intentions were right up front, and how she handled this invitation would set the course for whatever was to come.

"Maybe I shouldn't do that," she resisted, her mind going back to the disastrous way her relationship with Tremont had ended. She had trusted Tremont to protect their love, to do everything in his power to ensure their future together, but he had been careless with her heart. His selfishness had dealt her a terrible blow, and a romantic entanglement with her agent-producer could not be a good thing to start.

"Why not?" Granger persisted. "You must know how I feel about you."

"And how *is* that?" she wanted to know.

"I care deeply for you, Niya," Granger started. "I watched you dancing at Miracle Mile for months before I approached you about joining the cast of *Rise*. I think I fell in love with you then. You're stunning to look at, talented, and when we're apart, I feel lost. I hate being separated from you. Come with me to the country. You're always complaining about the nasty weather in the city. Spend the weekend in Connecticut with me, Niya. Let me show you what being a part of my world is like."

Surprisingly, his plea struck a chord with Niya, who was grateful for all that Granger was doing for her, and so in need of the kind of attention that only a man could deliver that it did not take long for her to make up her mind. "I'll go to the country with you," she said, watching him closely as her heart pounded furiously. "But I can't promise anything . . . if you know what I mean."

"I do," he murmured. "And I promise not to do anything that will make you uncomfortable."

They left before daybreak on a blustery Saturday morning and arrived at his cottage on the lake in Connecticut at sunrise. A gentle snow was falling, adding another layer of fluffy white to the limbs of the stately pines that forested the countryside.

The country house sat on twenty lushly landscaped acres of prime real estate. The "cottage" turned out to be a four bedroom, pine-paneled house with a loft, a huge fireplace, and warm wooden floors covered with bright tatted rugs. The kitchen was surprisingly modern with stainless steel appliances and granite counters throughout, and expansive windows that looked out over the lake.

After showing her around the house, they took a long walk to circle the lake before cooking breakfast together in his spacious country kitchen. They meshed immediately, laughing, joking, and even singing along with golden oldies on the radio as they prepared Belgian waffles with blueberries and cream.

After eating, they snuggled down on his bear skin rug in

front of the stone fireplace, coffee mugs in hand. Granger casually picked up a small sketch pad and a piece of charcoal and began to sketch Niya in profile.

"You're an artist, too?" she commented taking a sip of Granger's strong coffee.

"A hobby I rarely have time for," he replied as he made several quick strokes on the page.

"Are you good?" Niya teased, scooting over to try to see what he was doing.

"No peeking . . . and sit back . . . hold still," he admonished, moving the sketch pad away as Niya leaned back against a brown leather ottoman and curled her feet beneath her hips. "Am I any good?" Granger repeated. "I don't know . . . I've never shown my work to anyone who could give me an opinion. I just do it to relax."

"What kinds of things do you sketch?"

"Landscapes, buildings, trees, flowers. Things like that. Yours is the first portrait I've tackled," he said as he continued to trace the charcoal over the paper in a leisurely yet confident manner.

"I'm honored," Niya replied, holding very still.

While Granger sketched, they talked, filling the next hour with stories about their childhoods, their families, their successes, aspirations, and disappointments in life.

Niya told Granger everything about her life in Cuba, her escape from the island, and her mother's incarceration, but few details about her romantic entanglement with a now-convicted felon who was serving time in a Florida prison. When she told Granger about her brother's disappearance, he listened closely, and then frowned.

"I doubt you'll ever find him, Niya," he solemnly offered.

"Why do you say that?"

"The authorities don't have him. If he had remained in the Miami area, he would have found *you* by now. You were visible, and you said you even registered with a refugee service . . . if he had wanted to find you he could have. On the other hand, if he survived the swim to shore, he must have left the area and decided to stay away for a reason. Clearly, he's not looking for you. I think you ought to face the fact that he's probably dead. If I were you, I'd forget about him."

Lowering her chin, Niya tried to hide the fact that his blunt reply had hurt her. He might be speaking the truth, but no one had ever said the words aloud, to her face. A slow burn of uneasiness began to rise inside her. It was easy for Granger, whose life was full of friends, gaiety, and excitement to casually dismiss her need to hold onto a shred of hope that her brother might be alive. Granger was happily living among everything familiar while she was still trying to find her way in a strange country full of surprises.

However, instead of saying something to make him feel bad, she swallowed back her disappointment and said, "You may be right, but I won't give up hope. I loved my brother. We were very close . . . and I miss him. And I promised my mother that I would watch out for him. I feel like such a failure." Her voice cracked and her tears sheened her eyes.

Granger took her hand. "Trust me. The best thing you can do is forget about your brother."

"That's impossible."

"Maybe not," Granger replied, drawing out his response. "Not if you let me help you."

"How?"

"I have big plans for you, Niya. You're going to be so busy with your new career that you'll have little time to dwell on painful matters like the loss of your brother. You're too young and beautiful to carry such a heavy burden, anyway, so let it go. You had no control over what happened out there in the ocean, so you can't feel guilty about the fact that your brother, most likely, grabbed his chance at freedom and either lost, or ran away with it. I plan to make your life one that will more than obliterate all the painful things that are worrying you now."

"You can do that for me?" Niya pressed, beginning to realize how powerful and generous Granger was, and how lucky she was to have him in her life.

"Of course," Granger told her, stroking the back of her hand. "Anything to make you happy."

He opened his arms to her and Niya snuggled against his chest, reveling in the wave of contentment that washed over her. Granger was giving her the first real sense of peace that she had known in a long time. Even while she had been with Tremont, she had never felt so optimistic about moving into the future. With Tremont, it had been a day-by-day kind of existence, with no real plan. Now she had something to look forward to.

"Now, tell me about *your* family," she urged, suddenly ready to learn all she could about Granger Cooper.

As he talked, Niya learned that he was the only child of very wealthy parents, both deceased. Both his father and mother died when he was a teenager. When they passed away, Granger inherited the country house, the apartment overlooking Central Park, and a substantial trust fund that gave him the freedom to take risks with his theatrical productions.

His social status and financial independence placed him firmly among the ranks of the wealthiest, and most firmly established of New York society. He had never been married, had traveled the world, and was at a place in his life where he admitted that he was thinking of settling down, if he could find the right woman. He felt Niya might be the one.

"Why would you say something like that?" Niya asked, slightly perturbed that he was confessing his feelings for her so openly, so soon. "You hardly know me."

"I know that you are totally alive," he countered. "Everything about you radiates youthful energy and passion, something that has often been lacking in other women I've known. You are uniquely beautiful, and courageous, too. The fact that you came to America, jumped right in and created a life for yourself, and then took on the hard work to become an actress with little complaint, is enormous. You're fearless, Niya. And I love that in you. I would never tire of talking to you, traveling with you, looking at you, loving you . . . and I need that in a partner. I really do." Setting his charcoal aside, he ripped off the sketch and assessed it. "For you." He paused. "And not so bad, if I do say so myself, for my first try at a portrait." He handed it to Niya.

"You are very good!" she exclaimed, smiling. "I can have it?"

"Of course. It's for you." He placed his sketch pad to one side and leaned to kiss her. Niya did not protest, but sank into the soft cocoon of his embrace and melted against his chest.

That evening, they drove into town and had dinner at a quirky French restaurant, where the waiters wore floppy red berets and sported thick black mustaches. They drank less-than-fine wine and laughed about all of the craziness surrounding the upcoming opening of *Rise*, which was already being touted in the press as the hottest ticket off-Broadway.

They returned to the country house very late that night, and without hesitation, Niya slipped into bed with Granger and fell completely under his spell.

The next day, they did not leave the bedroom, except to pull fresh bottles of champagne or another box of chocolate covered strawberries from the refrigerator in the kitchen.

Back in New York, with Granger as her manager, as well as her lover, Niya was happy. *Rise* opened to rave reviews in January and she became a celebrity overnight, as well as a part of Granger's ultra-sophisticated world, and as the months slipped by, she allowed him to take full control of her life.

He persuaded her to cut her long wavy hair into a chic boyish style, to use less makeup when not on stage, and to adopt a modest mode of dress, discarding the bold, colorful outfits she loved so much. No more flighty ruffled clothing or five-inch heels, or dangling earrings, or pulsing Cuban music playing in her car. Granger said that he wanted her to be stunningly conservative, creating an image that better suited Niya now that she was a celebrity and part of his social circle. He discouraged her from eating her favorite Cuban dishes: beans and rice and her beloved *media noches*—sandwiches filled with pork, ham, and soft Swiss cheese—so it did not take long for her curvaceous Latina figure to become a svelte shadow of its former self. And with each change, Niya began to feel more elegant and more worldly, even though she was rapidly distancing herself from her Afro-Cuban roots.

If this is what makes Granger happy, so what? she often thought, eager to do whatever he asked of her, very content to be his lover. This new outlook on life made it easy for Niya to focus on her future as an actress, as well as her blossoming romance with Granger. For the first time since the disastrous end of her relationship with Tremont, Niya felt secure, loved, and safe once more. With Granger the future looked bright.

Their lovemaking was passionately fulfilling, and she had never felt so completely free of worry in her life. Granger was mature, wise, stable, and caring—exactly what she needed, she kept telling herself.

Chapter 33

The ten mile drive from Venice Beach to the Crown Plaza Beverly Hills Hotel should have taken less than half an hour, but tonight, due to an overturned Greyhound bus on I-10, traffic was backed up for miles.

Sandi Lee gripped the steering wheel of her green Chevy Blazer and inched along the freeway, one eye on the clock on her dashboard. No way could she be late. Not after the stern directive she had issued her staff about arriving two hours before the event, which was scheduled to begin at ten o'clock sharp. Everything had to be perfect. This was the most important party that her upstart bartending company, Divine, had ever served, and all four bars at Larry Lo's Valentine's Day party had to be fully stocked and fully staffed by eight o'clock.

The SUV in front of her suddenly changed lanes, veering off toward the exit lane, providing Sandi Lee a clear view of the traffic-clogging accident. As she pulled alongside the overturned bus, she could not help but slow down and stare at the twisted, smoking pile of metal and the ugly bloodstains on the cement. The sight jolted her back to the last time she had been on a Greyhound bus; more than two years ago, the day she fled Miami after failing to convince Ace to let Tremont's grandfather go free.

What a fuckin' mess that was, she thought, recalling how confused and frightened both she and the old man had been.

After making it to New Orleans, she had gotten off the bus only long enough to buy a ticket to Houston, and from there she made her way west to Los Angeles. *The bus ride from hell,* she now thought with a shudder, wondering again, how she had managed to survive holed up on one cramped, smelly bus after another for seven days and nights, eating junk food out of vending machines, first freezing her ass off, then sweating like a pig as she struggled to kick her drug habit cold turkey. It had been a nightmare, but worth it, and she had been drug-free ever since.

After arriving in L.A. she had gone straight to the public library, logged onto the Internet, and searched the Miami papers for any information about G-Daddy's fate. It had taken only a few seconds for her to learn that Ace had actually strangled the old man, and then killed himself by shooting too much shit into his veins. *The dumb jerk*, she had thought, not surprised that he had not had enough sense to take the money and run.

As the months slipped past Sandi Lee kept checking the Miami papers to see if her photograph might appear with a "Wanted" notice beneath it. It never turned up, but she did learn that Tremont Henderson had been convicted of income tax evasion and racketeering, and was serving fifteen years in a minimum security facility outside of Miami. After much thought, she had written him a letter, explaining what had happened, and apologizing for all the hurt she had caused, including her calling the IRS on him. She had not put a return address on it.

Now, as she moved past the accident, Sandi Lee sped up, anxious to get to the hotel. Larry Lo was a huge celebrity and she was looking forward to providing him with the best bartending services he had ever had. She had researched the singer thoroughly, knew that he drank Chivas on the rocks, but only from Waterford crystal, and preferred an old-fashioned glass. She knew what each member of his entourage preferred to eat and drink, and had had flashy commemorative cocktail napkins printed with the initials LL in gold letters on each one.

The event was serious business for Sandi Lee, who felt lucky that 2006 was starting off on such a good note and that the Crown Plaza had decided to contract with her company for tonight. Pulling off this event without a hitch could put Divine on the lips of other celebrities, ensuring the success of her venture.

Shortly after her arrival in California, she had taken a job tending bar in a weather-beaten tavern on Venice Beach, where she now lived in two sunny rooms above the bar. When the owner of the establishment died suddenly of a heart attack, his widow begged Sandi Lee to stay on as the manager and encouraged her to take private bartending jobs on the side. That was how Divine, Sandi Lee's private party bartending service, began.

Tonight, Sandi Lee was feeling confident. She knew she looked professional in her black and white tuxedo-style pants suit and her jaunty black velvet cap, which she always wore while serving bar. Each member of her staff also wore the stylish black caps to prevent their hair from ever accidentally falling into a customer's drink. She knew what was expected. After all, whether slinging platters of bacon and eggs or pouring expensive champagne, it was all about pleasing the customer—and she had had plenty of practice doing that at Denny's, and back home in Oyster Cove.

Larry Lo's latest release, "Slide My Way," blared from huge speakers in each corner of the room, where tall champagne fountains, dressed with twining red roses and bold silver hearts bubbled continuously. The dance floor was packed with gyrating, trendy partiers dressed in every shade of red imaginable—in suede, leather, silk and fur—and so much glittery bling that Sandi Lee felt as if she had stepped into a jewel box.

With a great deal of interest, she watched the guest of honor wrap his hands around the waist of a waif-thin girl in tight blue spandex pants and pull her round buttocks up against his crotch in a bumping, grinding dance move that left little to the imagination. A wave of heat flashed into Sandi Lee's chest as she watched Larry Lo swivel his hips and grin while the girl pressed her body into his. When the girl giggled, turned around, and rubbed her breasts against his chest, Sandi Lee felt her heart begin to pound. When the girl kissed him on the lips, Sandi Lee's stomach did a flip. Larry Lo was a raw, strikingly handsome figure whose magnetism was contagious.

When the music stopped, Larry shoved his dance partner aside, grabbed a glass of Chivas on ice from one of Sandi Lee's roving waiters, who had been instructed to always keep the star's drink nearby, and rejoined his entourage at his table near the dance floor.

With a pop, Sandi Lee uncorked another bottle of Dom Perigon and poured it into one of the fountains, her eyes still glued on Larry. He was such a charismatic, dynamic guy—no wonder every woman in the room had fallen under his spell and had the hots for him. He flirted shamefully with all of them—black, white, Asian, Latina, hoochie-girl, sophisticate, gorgeous, or plain. It was clear to Sandi Lee that he was definitely approachable, and different from the stuck-up celebrity types she had been around before.

After emptying the champagne bottle, she headed back toward the main bar, deliberately cutting across the dance floor to pass in front of Larry's table. She managed to catch him between dances and between women. He looked up at her and smiled.

"Mr. Lo?" Sandi Lee started, pausing at his table.

"Hey, call me Larry, sugar." He sipped his Chivas and squinted at her. "You know you got some damn pretty eyes," he said. "I never seen eyes that color of green."

Though his remark caught Sandi Lee by surprise, she managed to maintain her composure. "Thanks. They're often called jade."

"Jade. I like that. Hey, is that your name? Jade?"

"No, I'm Sandi Lee . . . and I'm the owner of Divine."

"Divine?" he repeated, looking puzzled.

"The company servicing your bar tonight."

"Oh! Yeah. Well." He glanced around. "Top drawer, babe. Good job. You got my drink right, and that means a lot."

"Good. I just wanted to say hello and leave my card. Perhaps in the future . . ."

"For sure . . . yeah." He turned and pointed to a young man who was seated next to him, dressed in red and white with a fist-sized, stone-studded heart swinging from a chain around his neck. "Give it to my man, Stevie. We'll use you again. It's all good."

"Thanks," Sandi Lee replied, handing her card over to Stevie. "Is there anything else I can do for you?" she finished, pleased to have made such a personal connection. An endorsement from Larry Lo would be huge for future business!

Larry looked her up and down, paused, and then stood. He dug into the pocket of his stylish, baggy pants and took out a hotel room key. "I'm sure there is. I gotta go up to my room for a minute. Drop by."

"Now?"

"Yeah, now. Why not? I'm sure my mini-bar needs restocking, and while we're there I'm sure I can find something else that you can do for me."

"I'd love to," Sandi Lee replied, inclining her head slightly as she touched the brim of her cap and accepted his hotel room key. "I'll be up as soon as I get rid of this empty champagne bottle."

Larry leaned against the headboard of his king size bed and shot an impatient glance at the door leading to the massive bathroom in his luxury suite, wishing like hell that Sandi Lee would hurry up with whatever she was doing in there. She was a nice enough looking chic with great breasts and eyes that mesmerized him, but he didn't have time to wait around while she prettied herself up. This sure as hell was not going to be some kind of romantic Valentine's Day liaison and he had a swinging party to get back to.

He flipped open the drawer on the bedside table and sifted through the wide assortment of condoms he always kept nearby, finally settling on a Honey Heaven, a ribbed style in bright red. He loved Honey Heavens. They were almost like wearing nothing at all! Very light, very thin, very strong, and very sensitive. He took a sip from the drink that Sandi Lee had fixed for him, and just as he was tearing open the condom packet, the bathroom door opened and Sandi Lee emerged.

She had wrapped a tiny white towel around her torso, but it barely covered her pale pubic hair and only the nipples of her heavy white breasts. Her blonde hair, now released from her signature cap, touched her shoulders and framed her face in an angelic explosion of soft curls. Her skin, as pale as the towel that she was holding onto, shimmered from a dusting of fine silver powder. She was holding her drink, a vodka martini, as she walked slowly toward him, allowing Larry plenty of time to savor her approach. Her green eyes were half closed, her bright red lips parted, and she kept her chin down as she glanced up at him.

Larry lay back against the headboard and let every muscle in his body go limp while his erection grew so fast and hard it even surprised him. He had planned on getting this little bar-girl tryst over and done with in a matter of minutes, but now he re-thought his plan. This chick was no novice, and he sensed that this was not going to be an ordinary lay. She was probably as kinky as he was.

Sandi Lee placed her martini on the bedside table, sat down on the side of the bed and reached over to caress Larry's stiff erection. "Nice," she murmured, locking eyes with him. "Real nice."

He could not trust himself to speak.

"But I can make it even nicer," she murmured.

Larry simply nodded.

Sandi Lee reached into the front of the white towel draped over her body and pulled out a small vial of oil, which she uncapped with her teeth. "Peppermint," she told him as she drizzled the pink liquid over his private parts, his chest, his arms and legs.

The sweet scent that exploded under his nose made Larry go tense, and for a split second he feared he might let go before he even had time to enjoy this luscious playmate.

Sandi Lee lowered her head and began to lick him all over, her tongue keeping time with her fingers, which were probing, pressing and massaging parts of his body that he knew no woman had ever touched before.

Larry groaned, grit his teeth, and then sent up a little prayer of thanks to whoever had sent him Sandi Lee.

"Whew! Where'd you learn all those luscious tricks?" Larry asked Sandi Lee after nearly an hour of the greatest sex he had ever had. He grabbed a corner of a tangled sheet and wiped perspiration from his face.

"Around," she murmured, stretching, and then reaching for her martini glass on his bedside table.

"Around where?" Larry pressed, looking over at her. "Where you from, girl? I gotta say, you sure can deliver." He swung his legs over the side of the bed and then stood, keeping his naked back to Sandi Lee.

"A small town in south Florida," she replied, sipping from her glass. "Ever been to Florida?"

"Nope," Larry tossed back. "Never been there."

"You oughta go down there sometimes. Blue water. Beautiful beaches. You like to swim?"

Larry spun around and stared hard at Sandi Lee, memories of the short, ugly time he had spent off the coast of Florida confined to a renegade vigilante ship with a bunch of ragged Haitians flooding back. Why'd she have to go and bring that subject up? Spoil the mood and everything.

"No. I don't swim," he snapped. "I don't like water and I hate the beach. And I sure as hell never plan to go to Florida. They treat black folks like shit down there. I like it fine right here where I am."

"Whoa. Excuse me," Sandi Lee brashly replied. "You got friends in Florida?"

"Naw," Larry hedged, "but I've heard about the way immigration treats those boat people . . . the black ones from Haiti, especially. Like they don't deserve a chance."

"I knew a black girl from Cuba once. She was a boat girl. Used to be my best friend. Real pretty. Her name was . . ."

"Listen!" Larry interrupted. "I don't wanna hear nothin' about your Cuban girlfriend. Okay?"

"Okay!" Sandi Lee shouted back. "I was just making conversation, that's all."

"Well, don't," he ordered as he strode toward the shower. "I got no use for a lot of silly chitchat." Before entering the bathroom, he turned around and told Sandi Lee, "You can go now. Ah-right? I'll give you a call sometime."

"Promise?" she asked, finishing off her martini.

"Yeah, yeah. I promise," he replied before disappearing behind the bathroom door.

Sandi Lee fell hard for Larry Lo. After their first night together, she began spending less and less time in her two sunny rooms above the tavern on Venice Beach and more time in his bed at his sprawling mini-mansion in the Hollywood hills, which was a nonstop party palace with booze, babes and hip-hop music blasting day and night.

She knew he saw other women, because he told her so, but whenever Larry called and invited Sandi Lee over, she dropped whatever she was doing and went—and stayed as long as he wanted her there. Unable to stay away from him, he became her new drug of choice, and addicted to him, she resigned herself to accepting whatever attention he threw her way, proud to be at his side as he rose higher in the frantic, pulsing, often dangerous world of hip-hop music.

Her work at the tavern suffered. Her company, Divine, suffered, too, but she didn't care. She did anything he asked of her, whenever he asked, and became totally obsessed with loving Larry Lo.

Chapter 34

New York, 1999

"Happy?" Granger asked, gazing down at Niya, who was fused to his outstretched arm. He began to lazily trace his index finger along the curve of her neck.

"Totally," Niya murmured, adjusting the red satin sheet that was covering her nakedness.

"You remind me of liquid gold, Niya," Granger said, leaning closer to brush his lips over her cheek. "All silky and smooth and glowing. You make an old man like me very happy."

"Forty-six isn't old," she playfully replied, tapping him on the arm. "You've still got it going on, Granger. In every way that counts."

"Are you sure?" he pressed.

"I'm sure," she whispered, tilting her face up to his.

"I really give you what you want?"

"Always."

"Good. Because you're all I need, and I never want to lose you. Promise me, Niya. You'll never leave me."

"Never," she promised, sucking in a gasp of longing when Granger suddenly slanted his lips over hers.

He kissed her with renewed energy and urgency and then

eased his naked body over hers once more and, as his weight pushed her deeper into the soft folds of the red satin sheets, she could feel the heat from his body seeping into hers, the slick perspiration from their earlier lovemaking mingling once again. She closed her eyes tightly and ran her hands along the length of his back, over his rock-hard buttocks and back up to his shoulders. Granger might be seventeen years her senior, but he had the body of a much younger man. A body that totally captivated her.

Her fingers inched into his silky hair, which was long enough to graze the sides of her face as he kissed her. She loved his hair. She loved the way it rested against the collars of his custom made shirts, tempering his edge of sophistication, providing a glimpse of the youthful guy that still lived inside.

Ever so slowly, she removed one of her hands from his hair and touched his neck. His flesh was warm, inviting. Breaking off their kiss, she buried her face against his cheek and breathed in the peppery-sweet scent of his expensive cologne, the slight bristle on his chin exciting her, bringing on a heavy dampness that gathered between her legs.

"I love you, Granger," she heard herself say.

"I love you, too, Niya," he responded, his voice strong, gentle and sure. "I don't know how I could ever live without you. I need you in my life. I . . ."

But she did not let him finish what he was about to say. With a gentle shove she urged him beneath her, changing positions so that she was settled on top of him. Within seconds he was inside her, filling her up with his love and, as she arched her back and closed her eyes, a moan escaped her lips, an unconscious response to the insistent desire that swept through her and sent her heart racing.

Granger tightened his grip on her waist, his slim hands nearly encircling her tiny body. His touch shocked her with its heat, its light, and its agonizing need to be as close to her as possible.

She leaned down and traced her tongue across his chest,

into the hollow of his neck, and along the curve of his ear, teasing him softly, gently, and then withdrawing to savor the taste of him on her tongue. Their strident breathing soon filled the room, adding to the heavy, pulsing sensation that fused them together. A flash of heat ran through Niya's veins, and in an instant she realized that she had never enjoyed making love to Granger quite so much before.

When he suddenly loosened his grip, she relaxed and let him ease her to one side and then pull her quickly down beneath him, exchanging positions without missing a stroke. Niya's eyes flew open, and she giggled at his deft maneuver before settling into a new and faster rhythm, her legs now wrapped around his waist, her hands fastened around his neck.

The sight of her own coppery brown arms against his pale smooth shoulders gave her pause for a split second, but she closed her eyes once again and concentrated on making love to Granger.

She hadn't expected to fall so completely in love with him, so quickly . . . and a romantic involvement with a white man had never entered her mind. But it had happened. Very naturally and easily. And why not? How could she not love him? He was handsome, tender, kind, and he understood her drive to be a success. He made her feel completely whole, loved, and alive.

Granger had kept his word: he had turned her into an actress—a good actress who received accolades from reviewers in all the trades that mattered. Her belief in him had never wavered. The acting lessons, voice coaching, and the total makeover he had urged her to undergo had been exactly what she had needed in order to perfect her dream. Granger had been right about everything . . . and she owed all of her happiness to him. He was her manager, her agent, her friend and her lover. How could she ever repay him for all that he had done for her? By loving him, of course.

Granger groaned, cried out, and then shuddered to a climax.

My future belongs to Granger, and no man will ever take his place, Niya told herself as a glorious spasm of completion rippled throughout her body.

After an invigorating shower, Niya sat at the breakfast table in Granger's designer kitchen and read, with a good deal of satisfaction, the review of the closing performance of *Morning Stars*, the production that had catapulted her to fame after her stage debut in *Rise*. Now, after only two years on the stage, she was a certified actress, whose talent and beauty captivated her audiences—as well as members of the press, who were relentless in their search for new tidbits of information that they could print about her.

Fame, money, and adulation had come to Niya so quickly that she could hardly believe it was happening to her. Even Granger's love seemed ethereal and magical, as if it could vanish as easily as it had appeared.

Included in the current newspaper article was a mention of Niya's next project, a play entitled *Perfectly* written by Ricky Monroe and produced by the new partnership of Cooper and Monroe. It would be Granger's first musical production and it was set to debut in London in the fall for a limited two-week run at the Royal Tower Theatre before coming to Broadway.

After eighteen months on stage with *Morning Stars*, Niya was saddened to see the play end, but still excited about moving to Europe to do *Perfectly*, an original musical written especially for her by Granger's best friend and now, partner. However, before departing for Europe, she planned to take a much needed, month-long break at Diamond Marsh Resort, the desert getaway near Carson City, Nevada, owned by Astin Spence.

Niya had never forgotten her magical evening under the stars with Astin, who had been the consummate gentleman and escort the night of her performance at Brentwood Estates in Orlando. How they had danced! How they had laughed and enjoyed the festive affair! And when the time came for her to leave, he had insisted that she promise to come to Nevada one day and let him pamper her at his spa. Now she planned to take him up on his offer.

When she telephoned him last month to arrange her upcoming visit, he had instantly remembered her and expressed his delight that she was coming for a long stay.

Now, she closed the paper, took her coffee cup to the sink, and then leaned over Granger's shoulder and kissed him on the neck. "Gotta run," she told him, ruffling his hair. "I have a million things to do before I leave for Nevada. I have to let the cleaning lady in to blitz my apartment, and then I'm meeting Contessa at the theater to clear out my dressing room. I need to stop my mail, contact the answering service . . ."

"I wish you'd give up that apartment of yours and move in with me," Granger cut in, setting his newspaper aside. "You don't need to spend your time worrying about such mundane things. If you lived here with me, I could have all of that taken care of."

"Granger, we've talked about this too many times. I lived in six different cubbyhole-sized apartments until I could afford my Manhattan penthouse. I love it, and I'll never sell it. It took me a long time to get it, and for now, I'm going to keep it. Don't press me, okay?"

"All right," he mumbled. "But it's a terrible waste of money."

She kissed him on the cheek and playfully tugged his ear. "Thanks to your wise guidance of my career, I can afford it."

Laughing, he reached around and grabbed her, pulling her onto his lap. He rested his head against her shoulder. "God, I love you. And I wish like hell that you were flying to London with me. I'm not looking forward to that long flight alone."

"I'll be there soon enough. While I'm resting in Nevada, you and Ricky will be busy with all of that pre-production business . . . you won't even have time to miss me," she lazily replied. "Besides, I can rehearse my lines, as well as the dance routines for *Perfectly* while I'm in Nevada. I understand they have a studio that I can use, and I couldn't face a long overseas flight right now, anyway. I'm totally exhausted, Granger. I need time to regroup."

"I know, I know," Granger reluctantly agreed. "It's just that I hate the thought of being separated from you for nearly a month. You know that's the longest we'll have ever been apart."

Niya looked down at Granger, taken aback by the concern in his voice. He seemed truly anxious about going ahead without her. "Time will fly," she assured him. "I'll be in London before you know it."

"You'd better. I'm going to be very unhappy without you," Granger mumbled.

"Well, don't let some pretty young stranger swoop in and gobble you up while I'm not there. Okay?" she teased.

With a squint, Granger jerked erect and studied Niya for a long moment. "Why would you say something like that?" he asked, taking care to stress each word.

Carelessly, Niya put her arms around his neck. "I don't know. It just popped out. Calm down, honey. Just joking." She nuzzled his cheek. "You know I love you . . . and a few weeks apart is not going to hurt us. Might even do us some good. Absence only makes love stronger, isn't that the way it goes?"

"Not for me," he tossed back. "I never want to be away from you . . . I wish you'd marry me. We could do it tomorrow . . . at City Hall, before I leave. That would make me very happy."

Niya bit down on her bottom lip, thinking about how to respond. He had proposed marriage to her twice before, but she always put off giving him an answer. Why? she now wondered, her thoughts straying from the moment. Why couldn't she take the plunge and become Mrs. Granger Cooper? She needed him . . . and loved him . . . but she had loved Tremont Henderson, too, and look how that had turned out. He had turned cold and hard toward her as soon as his world spun out of control, and their time together now seemed like a dream. However, she had no right to let that disappointing relationship shape her future with Granger. If she ever wanted happiness, she'd have to clear away the pain of the past and take a chance on tomorrow.

Removing her hands from Granger's neck, she turned serious. "Maybe . . . maybe we could get married after we return from London," she ventured.

"You mean it?"

"Yes, we'll have a fabulous winter wedding during the holiday season, right here in the city. Then, we can fly to sunny Acapulco for our honeymoon. You know I've always wanted to go to Mexico. What do you think?"

"Perfect," he told her, giving her a quick kiss.

"Well," she murmured, a hint of a frown on Niya's brow. "It would be *perfect* if my mother could be here with me. I can't imagine getting married without her."

"Niya, I wish I could make that happen, but getting her out of Cuba . . . well, that's not possible. I've written some letters and made some contacts to initiate an investigation of her prison sentence, but that's about all I can do."

"I know . . . I know. And I appreciate it. You've done so much for me already. You're too sweet," Niya cooed, dismissing the subject as she planted kisses all over Granger's face. Leaning back, she blew him a final kiss, untangled herself from his embrace and stood. "Now, I've got to go. Contessa is going to meet me at the theater in less than an hour. When we finish, I think I'll go over to Stephanos and look at wedding dresses."

After Niya left, Granger paced his elegantly appointed Central Park apartment, frustrated that Niya was refusing to fly to London with him. There were plenty of spas in London that she could go to to unwind. Why did she insist on traipsing out into the Nevada desert, forcing him to make the trip overseas alone? He didn't ask much of her, and he gave her everything she asked for. Why couldn't she make this one concession and be with him when he needed her so much?

When he had taken her under his wing, he vowed to do all

that he could to ensure her success and he had not let her down. She was a nobody when he found her, and he sank a lot of money, time, and attention into her, successfully turning her into a legitimate money-making star. She belonged to him. She owed him. He couldn't afford to let her slip away.

The London production was going to be an experimental play featuring new London actors and financed completely by himself and Ricky Monroe, who had managed to pull together his quarter-million dollar share of the investment money by selling a chunk of his AT&T stock.

It was a risky proposition, *Perfectly,* with only a short, two-week run, and its success depended on a sold out house every night and no glitches in their budget.

Ricky was a nervous wreck, but there was no doubt in Granger's mind that the play would be a hit in London, creating opportunities for other theaters to book his production. A major European tour of *Perfectly* was in the future, Granger felt certain of that.

Now, Granger went to the wall safe in the dining room, which was hidden behind an original self-portrait of the artist Frida Kahlo, opened it, and removed a square silver box. Inside was a spectacular yellow diamond ring with a double row of glistening rubies surrounding the stone. He solemnly studied the ring that had been in his family for three generations.

"I know you would have hated Niya, Mother," he whispered into the empty space. "Just as you hated every girl I ever brought home to meet you. And I am sure that you are spinning in your grave right now. Your son, marrying a woman of color? A dancer? A nobody without social status and breeding?" He let out a sarcastic chuckle and clenched his jaw. "But one day she *will* wear this ring, and she *will* be Mrs. Granger Cooper. My wife. And there is nothing you can do about it."

Granger placed the ring back into its box and put it in the safe. While doing so, his fingers brushed a stack of sketch papers bound with a rubber band. He pulled his hand back, as if he had been shocked, and shuddered as he stared at the bundle. Gingerly, he touched one piece of paper, and then another, and then he clenched his fingers into a fist as a flash of heat enveloped his body, nearly cutting off his breath.

After a long moment, he removed the stack of sketches and slowly looked at each one. "Betty Andrews . . . too pale, too thin, and probably unable to give me a son. That's what you said about her, Mother. Remember?" He took up another, shook his head and murmured, "Sophia Charles . . . beautiful, but too ethnic, too poor, and definitely not in our class, you had said." Looking at the next, he whispered, "Terri Morgan . . . you liked her a lot, Mother, and you even agreed to let me give her this yellow diamond ring, that was until you found out she was the *illegitimate* daughter of Senator Morgan."

Unable to look at the remaining sketches that he had made of the women whom his mother had run out of his life, he tossed them back into the safe. None of them had met her exacting standards or been able to stand up against her withering verbal attacks, and he had not been strong enough to go against his mother's wishes to find happiness with a woman. "Not Niya. Not now," he told himself, flinging the safe door shut.

His mother, who had died only two months before he met Niya, and not when he was a teenager—as he had told Niya—had been an interfering, demanding, and possessive creature. His mother had ruined his life.

Mothers did things like that to their children, all in the name of protecting them. He knew how it worked, and he definitely was not going to help Niya's mother come to New York to mess things up for them. He had done all he planned to do for Olivia Londres, whom he doubted would be happy that her daughter was planning to marry a white man. Granger knew what would happen if he managed to get Olivia to America. If she showed up, his life would once again spiral into that scary place from which Niya had managed to rescue him. He wasn't going back there.

* * *

The dressing room was so cold that Niya did not remove her camel-colored cashmere coat as she went about collecting the last of her personal items. She picked up the simply framed charcoal sketch of her that Granger had made, recalling how easily she had fallen for him, and how naturally making love to him had come to her. Their time at his house in the country had been one of the most memorable times of her life and she was glad she had the drawing to remember it by.

Giving herself a mental shake, she put the sketch into her handbag and began dumping makeup, hairbrushes, curling irons, and an assortment of jewelry into the large baskets that Contessa, who had become Niya's unofficial personal assistant, had brought in, taking little time to clear the top of her vanity. At least fifteen pairs of shoes had been piled in the center of the room, with no less than six umbrellas stacked on top. Just as Niya was about to start emptying the closet, Contessa returned with two cups of herbal tea.

"Thanks," Niya said, accepting a cup. "I can really use this."

Contessa, perched on the arm of a chair beside Niya, eyed the overflowing baskets and piles of items with interest. "Niya, I hope you're not planning on taking all of this stuff to London. I've been told that your dressing room over there is really tiny. A cramped little cubbyhole, sorry."

Niya laughed as she opened the bottom drawer of her makeup station and stared at the jumble of papers and photographs inside. "Don't worry, Contessa. Only the photos are coming. And since Granger will be going on ahead of me, I'm going to send some things with him. Are you absolutely sure you don't want to come with us?"

Contessa moved to the narrow dressing room closet and began sorting through items still hanging inside. "No, my cousin from D.C. and I are going to take that cross-country road trip to the Grand Canyon that we've been wanting to do for ages, and when I get back to the city, I'm going to take that temporary receptionist position at Miracle Mile that Mike called me about last week."

"Just can't leave that place, can you?"

"It's not so bad. But when you return from London, look me up, girl. I'd love to work for you again."

"You know I will," Niya replied. "And with a wedding to plan . . ."

"A wedding? Really? So you and Granger are finally going to get married?" Contessa remarked excitedly.

"Yep. And it's going to be a real big affair. I'm going to stop by Stephanos when I leave here and start looking for my dress. I'll be so busy . . . and exhausted when I get back from London, it would be a relief not to have to go hunting for my dress right away. It's going to be a hectic time, Contessa, and I'll need your help for sure."

"No problem. I'll be happy to help. Good for you. Granger's a great catch, girl. I knew he was special the minute I saw him standing out there in the hall holding those flowers," Contessa replied. "I know your wedding will really be over the top!" She chuckled, and then asked, holding up a makeup-stained dressing gown, which was one of Niya's favorites. "And what about this? It's a bit worn out, if you ask me."

"Right," Niya replied. "That, you can toss."

"Good," Contessa sighed, rolling the gown into a ball. "So, let's get this done." She pulled an empty wastebasket from behind the chair, knelt down and grabbed a handful of papers from the bottom drawer. Concentrating, she began to sort through the clutter. When she tossed a packet of letters bound with a thick rubber band into the trash, Niya gasped and immediately retrieved them.

"Looks like you've found something you want to keep," Contessa mused, eyes lowered as she continued sorting.

Niya did not reply. She and Contessa had been together for a long time and over the years had grown very close. Contessa's Puerto Rican heritage had made for a common bond between the two women and she had quickly become the friend Niya turned to when things got rocky and unsettled, or celebrated with when all was going well. Contessa had heard the sad tale of the love story between Niya and Tremont: how he had swept Niya off her feet and then broken her heart by shutting her out. Contessa knew all about Sandi Lee and her betrayal of both Niya and Tremont. And she never failed to remind Niya that she had been there when Granger first arrived on the scene, bouquet in hand to turn Niya's life upside down.

Now, Niya lingered with the letters in her hand, knowing she should throw them in the trash, but couldn't.

"They're your letters to Tremont, aren't they?" Contessa quietly ventured.

Niya nodded as she slipped off the rubber band. They were addressed to Tremont Henderson, Moore Haven Correctional Facility, and each one had the words REFUSED BY INMATE stamped in red on the front. The latest refusal was dated over four years ago. "I don't know why I've kept them," she muttered, gripping the letters, a sick feeling coming over her.

"Because you loved him . . . once upon a time," Contessa commented.

"Yeah, once upon a time, I loved that man so much. I thought he was everything I'd ever dreamed of. I thought I'd be his wife and have his kids, but it didn't turn out that way, did it?" Niya said, bitterness creeping into her voice. "Yeah. That about sums it up. Just like some stupid fairy tale."

"We all make mistakes, honey. Just be glad that chapter is closed. It's been five years since he went to prison, and if he truly loved you, Niya, he would have been talking to you on the phone, writing you letters, looking forward to your visits, and making plans for a life together after his release."

"I know," Niya whispered. "I can't believe he never really loved me."

"Who knows how he felt? At this point in your life, who cares? Let it go," Contessa urged. "Maybe if you toss the letters, you can toss the memories. Besides, by now he's probably out on parole and got himself a new girlfriend, or he's so messed up from being in that place that you wouldn't want him anyway."

Niya gave Contessa a puzzled glance, thinking her friend was probably right. Tremont had served enough of his sentence to have been paroled. She could easily check it out, see what was going on. But did she really want to know?

No, Niya decided, tossing the letters, one by one, into the waste basket. *Between goodbyes, we both have changed too much to ever recapture what we once had.*

The windy beach was dark and deserted, and the salty night air was much cooler than Tremont had anticipated, but he quickly shed his shoes and socks anyway, rolled up his pants legs and walked barefoot into the surf. The feel of sand between his toes, the smell of the sea in his nostrils, and the jolt of cool water lapping around his ankles felt heavenly to him. After living in a seven-by-ten-foot concrete wall cell, he was free, though his early release had come with the stipulation that he remain in Florida, get a job, and report to a parole officer twice a month.

Finally able to indulge in the fantasy that had kept him awake so many nights, he hunched his shoulders up around his ears, stuck his hands into his pants pockets, and drew in a long, deep breath, filling his lungs with the wet, humid air of his beloved Florida coast. He glanced up at the moon and studied it for a long moment, as if seeing it for the first time, and wondered if, someplace far away, Niya might be looking at it, too.

A stab of loneliness contracted in his stomach, but he quickly swallowed it back, pushing thoughts of her aside as he continued on his walk along the shore, with no destination in mind.

It was dark when Niya let herself into Granger's apartment with the key he had given her. She had stopped by her place first to deposit the heavy shopping bags filled with items from her dressing room, as well as from Stephanos, where she had found the perfect wedding dress: a tea-length white silk creation with a bodice encrusted with seed pearls and tiny satin bows. It had a medium size lace-edged train and a full bridal veil that was trimmed in matching pearls. The dress was a bit fussier than she knew Granger would have preferred, but what the hell? She was the one who was going to wear it, not him, and when it came to her wedding dress, he didn't have a say.

The dress had fit her perfectly, and since Stephanos' designs were one of a kind, she had bought it on the spot, as well as her shoes, her veil and all the necessary undergarments. With her attire for the big day securely tucked away in her closet, she was excited about planning the upcoming wedding, and eager to become Granger's wife.

As soon as she entered Granger's foyer, she sensed that something was different. Soft music was coming from somewhere in the house and she definitely smelled lemon chicken, one of her favorite dishes.

Niya removed her coat and tossed it over the sofa in the living room. The drapes were open, providing a spectacular view of Central Park, and she took a moment to enjoy it. Looking out over the city, she felt a spasm of longing pass through her, and realized that she had finally grown to love the huge bustling city and would miss the gridlock traffic, the dazzling lights of Broadway, and the energy of it all when she left for Europe.

Coming here had allowed her to dance, act, fall in love again, and fulfill so many of her dreams. However, she also knew that she could never love New York in the same way that she loved Havana, with its shabby old-world charm and slow, tropical pace. Even Miami had felt more like Havana than this strange, cold place. But this was her home now, and she would never see Havana again, so it felt right that she had finally come to terms with the place she hoped to call home forever.

"Did you get everything taken care of?"

Niya whirled around to see Granger emerge from the dining room, a glass of white wine in each hand.

"Yes." Niya replied, accepting the drink that he handed to her. "Contessa was a big help, but it still took longer than I thought it would."

"Well, it's done, at least," he commented, and then asked, "Hungry?"

"Starved," she told him, sniffing the air. "Is that lemon chicken I smell?"

"It is," Granger told her, smiling. "I had it delivered from Shrazz while you were out. Chocolate mousse, too." He sipped his wine and studied her for a moment before going on. "I thought it would be nice to stay in tonight."

"Fine. All of my favorites," she said, twirling her glass between two fingers, thinking that Granger looked rather smug, as if he had something more than dinner on his mind. "It'll be good to simply kick back and relax. Seems like we're always on the run." She looked down at her blue jeans and baggy sweatshirt, glad that she kept several casual outfits in Granger's spare bedroom closet. "I should change before we eat," she decided, starting toward the bedroom, but Granger placed a hand on her arm and stopped her.

"Come and sit down. Before we eat, I want to talk."

"Uh-oh," she murmured, giving him a puzzled glance, but she went to sit down on the gray suede sofa facing the view of Central Park, hoping he was not going to start up again about her not leaving for London with him. The matter was settled as far as she was concerned: She was going to Nevada and would join him later.

He sat beside her, closer to her than usual, took her hand in his, and then got down on one knee. As he reached into his shirt pocket, Niya held her breath. The large yellow diamond surrounded by rubies that he produced made her gasp.

"This morning you said that we would get married after we returned from Europe, but I don't want to leave for London without making it official." He slipped the ring on her finger before she could reply.

"Granger. It's beautiful."

"Not nearly as beautiful as you are," he said.

When he pulled her to her feet and kissed her, she knew that this was the man she would love forever, the man with whom she wanted to spend the rest of her life.

Chapter 35

Larry Lo paced the length of his master bedroom, his cordless phone pressed to his ear while Sandi Lee snuggled up to a king-size pillow in the middle of his bed and watched him stride from one side of the room to the other. She was not really interested in Larry's conversation with Tiny Fizz, the overzealous bodyguard who watched Larry's back and had just interrupted their hot and heavy lovemaking. She was interested in getting Larry back into bed before his interest cooled.

They had been together steadily now for six months straight, and Sandi Lee was feeling very happy, very secure. But she had begun to realize that his attention span was shorter than before, and any interruption to whatever he was doing at the time threw him quickly off course. People were always after him to go someplace, do some TV or radio show, to make a personal appearance, return a call, and though he had people to handle most of his appointments, he could not escape the pressure that came with being a recording star.

"Listen, Fizz," Larry said in a stern tone, "I don't care how it happened. I'm not the one at fault. Take care of it. Make sure I know what's going on." He stopped pacing long enough to rub one hand across his lower jaw and take in a deep breath as he listened to what his bodyguard was saying. "That's Ice

Blu's kind of talk," he went on. "Nothin' will come of it. Nothin'." He moved to the side of the bed and sank down. "All right, man. All right. Keep me posted." He pressed the OFF button, terminated the conversation, and tossed the phone into a chair across the room.

With a moan, he flopped down on his back. Sandi Lee immediately scooted close, leaned over him, and began massaging his shoulders. "Something wrong?" she ventured as she pressed her thumbs into the hollows beneath his shoulder blades.

"That was Fizz."

"I guessed that."

"He said a girl got hurt . . . hurt pretty bad when that fight broke out last night."

"What's it to you?" Sandi Lee casually replied. "You were on stage singing. If the people in the audience want to fight, what can you do about it?"

Larry suddenly sat up and pushed Sandi Lee aside. "She's in a coma."

"Oh. Too bad," Sandi Lee replied, pulling her satin camisole over her bare breasts. It was clear that they were not going to resume what they had been doing before Tiny Fizz called. At least not right away.

"Yeah, and the girl is Cat Jack Morris's daughter," Larry groaned.

"Cat Jack? The singer?"

"Yeah, and he's Ice Blu's cousin. He's making a lot of noise about takin' me to court, suing me for millions, getting even and all that kind of crazy shit. Hey, I got nothing to do with the girl getting hurt. I had security on site. Every ticket to my concert has a statement on the front telling folks that they comin' in at their own risk. I can't be policin' folks, you know? If Cat Jack wants to start up with me, let him."

"Probably all talk," Sandi Lee murmured, sidling closer to Larry. "Forget about it, baby. Nothin' you can do about it tonight." She got up, went to the mini-bar in the corner, and poured Larry a Chivas on the rocks. "Here, have a drink. Relax. Put that craziness out of your mind."

She crossed the room, handed the drink to Larry, and then sat down on his lap, straddling his body. She jerked off her camisole and rubbed her breasts against his bare chest. "Come on, Larry. Forget about the girl. You got lawyers to handle that stuff. Don't let it spoil our fun."

Larry took a big gulp of Scotch from his glass and nodded. "Right." He set the glass on the floor. "You're right. Ain't nothing I can do about it now." He leaned down and captured a pink nipple between his teeth, while Sandi Lee giggled in delight.

She tightened her thighs around his waist and together they fell back into bed and back to what they had been doing before the telephone rang.

Two weeks later, Larry received a summons to appear in court to tell his version of what had happened at the concert. Flanked by two lawyers, his agent, and his bodyguard, he entered the courtroom and faced the judge.

Once Cat Jack's case had been heard, the judge ruled that Larry Lo was not responsible for the injuries that the girl suffered, praised him for having had private security guards at the concert that night, asked for his autograph, and then dismissed the case.

Incensed at the ruling, Cat jumped up, crossed the courtroom in three steps and tried to punch Larry in the face, but Tiny Fizz blocked his swing. Furious, Cat fled from the building, but once outside, Cat reappeared, screaming and vowing to make Larry pay for what he'd done. He raced along the sidewalk, taunting the star until Tiny Fizz, a bulky bear of a man with a bushy beard and a head the size of a watermelon, suddenly turned around and snatched Cat by the back of his leather jacket, lifted him off his feet, and gave him a violent shake.

"Let him go!" Larry shouted, wedging himself between the two men. "This ain't worth getting arrested for."

Tiny Fizz did as Larry ordered and quickly dropped Cat to the sidewalk, letting the man bang his head on the hard cement. Blood spurted out of his nose and sprayed the toes of Larry's six-hundred-dollar shoes.

"Get up and get outta here," Tiny Fizz spat out, kicking Cat in the side.

"If you think this is over, you're wrong!" Cat yelled at Larry as he struggled to get up, one hand to his bloody nose. He dusted off his pants and pressed his hand harder to the bloody mess. "My baby girl is brain dead, and you're running around grinnin' and singin' and actin' like you didn't have nothin' to do with that fight! You love it when your fans act out, and you push 'em till they go crazy. You're gonna be sorry, man. Really sorry. Blu's gonna make sure you fall hard and I'm gonna be there to see it."

Larry reached over and pulled Cat right up to his face, so close that Larry could smell the blood all over the angry man's face. "Be glad I told Tiny to drop you, man," Larry growled, "and that all you got is a damn bloody nose. This kinda shit don't play around here. Go on back to New York and tell Blu I ain't worried. Bring it on, man, bring it on."

Chapter 36

Olivia was pulled from her dream by the sound of her own name. Someone was calling to her, again and again, in a voice so loud that it hurt her ears and made her squeeze her eyes tightly shut. As the yelling continued, she finally opened her eyes and was greeted by a bright light coming from outside her dark cell.

"Olivia Londres!" the harsh voice called again. The bright light moved in an arc, sweeping every corner of the dark space until it came to rest on Olivia's face.

"Over here," Olivia managed, easing to a sitting position. She blinked several times and then pushed herself upright, moving cautiously and slowly, careful not to trip and fall in the pre-morning darkness. Lately, every step she took required a measure of care and energy that she was no longer certain she had to give.

"Come with me," the voice ordered.

Olivia stared at the spot where the voice was coming from and now saw a female guard holding a flashlight in one hand while unlocking the cell door with the other. Olivia stuck her bare feet into a pair of straw sandals, gave her thin cotton shift a tug to straighten it out, and ran shaky fingers through her matted hair in an attempt to untangle the mess.

Once outside her cell, the guard walked quickly, forcing Olivia to struggle to keep up. When they passed the dark, empty visitors' room, Olivia raised a brow, realizing she was not being taken to meet someone, and wondered if she might be going to the medical wing to be checked by a doctor. However, the guard proceeded past the clinic with an increased pace and did not stop until they arrived at a section of the vast prison that Olivia had never seen before. The walls were newly painted and free of the awful mold and graffiti that covered most of the areas accessible to inmates. The floors here were covered in shiny red tile, and not the flimsy straw scattered over hard cold cement that was standard in all of the cells. Electric lights blazed from large panels in the ceiling. Male guards in freshly pressed uniforms were standing around holding their rifles loosely at their sides as they chatted to one another and smoked cigarettes. None of them paid any attention to Olivia as she and the guard swept past.

"In here," the guard told Olivia, opening a green door at the end of a hallway.

Olivia entered the room, which was stuffy, square, and furnished with a gray metal table and two metal chairs.

"Sit down," the guard ordered.

Olivia sat down in the chair with its back to the window, but not before taking notice that the faintest streaks of daylight had begun to creep into the sky.

The guard left, locking the door behind her.

Olivia fisted her hands, terrified. What was going to happen to her? A transfer to another prison? A beating? A grueling interrogation that might last for days? She had suffered all of that, and more, upon her arrival at Manto Negro and had been left alone for so long. What could the authorities possibly want her to tell them now?

When she heard the rattle of keys in the lock, she stiffened, eyes wide, her poor heart pumping much too fast for its weakened condition.

A stout bearded man dressed entirely in green khaki with numerous fancy badges pinned to his chest came in, sat down across from Olivia, took a pair of glasses from his shirt pocket, and opened a thick brown folder. "Are you Olivia Londres?" He peered at her over the tops of his glasses, and then checked the plastic armband that she was required to wear.

"Yes," Olivia whispered.

"I see." He shoved two papers across the table at her, and then said, "Sign these, please."

Olivia stared at the papers, wishing she had her glasses, which had broken long ago and never been replaced. She was an intelligent woman, and smart enough to know better than to sign any document before reading it.

"What is this?" she asked, squinting at the blur of black lines on the white papers, very suspicious of this pre-dawn meeting. If she was about to be whisked away to the far side of the island, to disappear forever, she wanted to read the order for herself and understand what was about to happen to her.

"These are your documents of release," the official answered.

"Release? I don't believe you," Olivia dared to challenge the man, fully aware that all political prisoners were required to serve their full sentences. In Cuba there was no such thing as parole or early release for good behavior for someone like her. A sentence was served until the end or until the prisoner died. "I know it has not been twelve years yet. What is the date?"

"Today is June 20, 2006."

"You see? I arrived here in September 1998. I know it has not been twelve years. How can you say I am to be released?"

"It seems you have friends who are very influential," he sneered.

"You mean the man Mr. Robles?" Olivia queried warily. "You can't mean him. Mr. Robles died."

"I know nothing about that." The official heaved his shoulders in impatience and lifted his bearded chin. "Do you want to leave Manto Negro or not?" he snapped.

"Of course, I do," Olivia stated, drawing herself up to sit more erect.

"Then sign."

"But I can't sign a paper that I can't read. Can you read it to me, please?"

"Here is a bus token," the official replied, ignoring her request. He shoved a round dark coin across the table. "The bus going to Havana arrives in half an hour. If you sign these papers, you can be on it. If not you will go back to your cell."

Olivia turned around in her chair and looked out the window and saw the sun rising beyond the palm trees in the distance. Free? Could it be possible? She saw the shapes of people walking along the dusty road on their way to work the cane fields. An ancient open-back truck lumbered along, cut around the pedestrians and then swung back onto the road. Olivia knew that beyond the barbed wire fencing that surrounded Manto Negro people were going to work, to school, to the dance halls, to the restaurants to eat meals with their families, and going on with their lives while she was wasting away in a dark, dank cell. What did it matter if she signed some document that might come back to haunt her? Hadn't she already suffered the worst fate that could come to someone like her?

"I will sign your papers. Hand me the pen," she told the official. With great care she wrote her name at the bottom of each page and then picked up the smooth round coin, ready to go home.

The bus ride to Havana took twice as long as it should have, but instead of becoming irritated and impatient when the driver pulled over to pick up or discharge more passengers or to wait for the grandmother of a rider to show up—as she would have been in the past—she simply smiled and resettled herself into her seat by the window, not even bothered by the thick coating of dust that inhibited her view.

Nothing was going to dampen her happiness at finally being out of prison and on her way back to the safety of her beloved home, where memories of her life with her children and husband awaited.

Back in Cerro, Olivia hurried down the middle of Calzada

del Cerro, the broad street that was flanked by one-story homes with red-tiled roofs with front porches that looked as faded and rotted as old bones that had lain outside in the sun too long. In Cerro, everyone walked in the street, dodging cars that accommodated the people who competed for the road.

She turned into a side street and anxiously approached her apartment building, noticing from a block away that not much had changed while she had been in prison. The crumbling façade had lost a bit more of its ornate plasterwork and trash still littered the entry. The faces of the children and the colors of the dogs and cats that meandered through the street looked about the same. She climbed the steps to her apartment slowly, taking her time, and then pulled her key out of the paper bag of personal items that the attendant at the prison had handed to her. She grinned as the key clicked and turned in the lock. However, once the door opened, her smile disappeared and she was horrified to find a roomful of strangers staring back at her. Some of them were sitting at her kitchen table, others were lounging on her sofa, and children of all ages were running everywhere.

"Who are you?" Olivia asked a fat man in an undershirt who ventured over to the door, a glass of beer in his hand. "What are you doing in my apartment?"

"Your apartment?" the man replied. He took a leisurely sip from his glass. "I am Salvador Chavez, and this is *my* home. For the past eight years, it has been mine. You must be mistaken, lady. I think you are in the wrong building."

"No, I'm not. I used to live here," Olivia persisted. "You see, I have a key." She lifted the key to show the man. "And those are my dishes, my paintings on the walls, my rugs."

"Not anymore," Salvador told her, turning up one side of his mouth. "The Ministry of Housing assured me that everything inside came with the apartment. I'm sorry. You don't live here now."

Stunned, Olivia tottered back, clearly jolted by the news.

Her heart raced, her stomach heaved, and she felt as if she would faint. Grabbing onto the rusted iron stair railing near the door, she tried to steady herself. All of her possessions now belonged to these strangers and she no longer had a home? Impossible. What was she going to do?

With a quick nod of understanding that there was nothing more to say, she turned and left, eager to get over to the Ministry of Housing and protest this action against her. The officials were required to notify her, she knew that much. Even in prison, the government had to let her know what they planned to do with her personal effects. Her friend Felix Mora, who lived only blocks away, could have come to salvage some of her things and hold them for her until she was home again.

Olivia walked as fast as she could down the tree lined boulevard toward the Plaza de la Revolucion, where all of the government offices of *El Commandante,* Fidel Castro, were located. She did not look up, as she usually did, when she passed the towering statue of national hero, Jose Marti, or into the faces of the people she passed because no one would recognize her, anyway. She was a bone-thin, scraggly ex-convict who was homeless and afraid.

Arriving in the center of the city, she stopped in front of the heart of Cuba, where ornate government buildings were clustered together in a kind of aging fortress. She scanned the facades of the age-stained structures, trying to recall which one housed the Ministry of Housing. Raising her eyes to the tiny windows in the huge old buildings, Olivia swallowed back her fear, considering the consequences of making an appearance before the officials who had stripped her of her home and her possessions.

There were several possibilities for people like her: The officials could assign her to living quarters in the city with another family; she could be transferred to a rural area far from Havana; they could send her to a work camp for women, which would not be much better than Manto Negro had been; or they could put her name on a waiting list for an apartment in Cerro and simply send her on her way to fend for herself in the streets. None of these options seemed acceptable.

A man hurrying up the steps bumped into Olivia and jostled her from her thoughts.

"Oh, pardon, señora," he apologized, tipping his head in her direction without stopping to look at her face before continuing up the steps at a brisk pace.

"No problema," she responded, watching him go on his way. Suddenly, a surge of relief swept over her as she instantly recognized the man, and for a moment she was speechless. "Felix! Felix Mora. Is it really you?" she managed to call out.

The man stopped in mid-step and looked back at her. "Olivia," he stated in calm acknowledgement. "Olivia. You are free?"

"Yes, yes," she rushed to tell him.

He hurried down the steep steps and stared at her. "How can it be?"

Olivia quickly described the circumstances of her early release. "I'm sure that Niya or one of her powerful friends in America had a hand in it and I want so much to contact her, to let her know I am free."

Felix hugged his friend warmly, and then stepped back, looking her up and down. "I know a man who has a telephone that you can use, and he'll help you place the call. Do you have Niya's phone number in America?"

Patting the paper bag filled with the few personal items she had brought from Manto Negro, Olivia told Felix, "Yes, Niya wrote it in the last letter I got from her . . . but it was some years ago."

"Good, good," Felix said. "We can try. Will Niya send you dollars?"

"I'm sure she will."

"Excellent. The only way to get anything of value in Cuba nowadays is if you have American dollars. My friend will let you use the phone for free, this time. But once you get in touch with Niya, get her to send you some money right away. In 1993, the government broke down and made it legal for us ordinary Cubans to hold U.S. dollars, and the black market is flourishing like weeds in a vacant lot. Cubans like you, with relatives in America, can live decently now, and everything can be had *por la izquierda*. Through the left hand, Olivia, you can have *anything* you want if you have *yanqui dolares*."

"I see," Olivia murmured, praying that she would be able to get through to her daughter.

"So, what are you doing standing out here?" Felix asked.

"I have no place to live, Felix. The government confiscated my apartment and everything in it while I was in prison."

"I'm not surprised," he admitted, in a voice that cracked with regret. "I've seen strange people coming and going from your building. Real pigs!" He spat into the grassy patch near the street. "Thieving pigs!" Linking one arm through hers, he guided her into the shade of a grand old palm tree at the edge of the boulevard. "You must not go in there." He pointed toward the Ministry of Housing building. "They will not do anything for you but bring you more grief. My wife and I don't have much, but whatever we have we will gladly share with you. You're coming home with me, Olivia, but first, I will take you to my friend's place of business where you can place your call to America."

Olivia blinked back tears of relief and did not protest when Felix took her by the hand and led her to his battered Ford truck, which looked exactly as she remembered.

After a short drive across the city, Felix pulled up in front of a graffiti-covered, dirty-gray, one-story building with a sign over the door that read, *Relojs, Cameras, y Radios*.

Olivia got out of the truck and followed Felix inside, where the owner, a lanky dark-skinned man with a pointed goatee, who had been busy repairing a round pocket watch, looked up, greeted Felix with a smile, and immediately agreed that Olivia could use his telephone in the back of his establishment.

Nervously, Olivia placed the call. She could count on one

hand the number of times she had used a telephone, and had certainly never placed a call off of the island. After giving the operator Niya's number in New York, the pleasant sounding woman put Olivia's call through. The phone at the other end of the line rang six times, and then Olivia heard three sharp, short beeps that interrupted the call.

"The number you are calling is no longer in service," a voice from far away informed Olivia. She frowned and pressed the handset of the phone closer to her ear, and kept it there long enough to listen to the message four more times before she relented and finally hung up.

Chapter 37

Nevada, July 2006

Thirty-six year-old Astin Spence, developer, landowner and entrepreneur, concluded his early morning meeting with key members of his staff at Diamond Marsh Resort with a stern but friendly warning.

"I want no glitches," he informed them, sounding quite serious. "I expect Ms. Londres' stay to be flawless. All amenities of the spa are to be available to her twenty-four hours a day. I've researched her preferences related to food, drink, and recreational activities and have prepared a list for each of you. Please review this with your staff. I want you to be vigilant, attentive, but not overly solicitous. Niya Londres is coming here for a rest, and I want her to experience the magic of Diamond Marsh at her own pace. She's an old friend of mine, as well as a very famous dancer and actress, so after she arrives today and is settled in her suite, I want each of you to meet with her individually and assure her that you are available at all times. I personally plan to oversee every aspect of her stay, but don't hesitate to call me if you are not sure about what she wants or needs."

"How long will Ms. Londres be with us?" asked Don Farling, the gourmet chef who had overseen the food preparation at Diamond Marsh Resort since the day Astin opened it twelve years ago.

"Until August 25th," Astin replied.

"Almost a month, huh?" Don remarked. "I'll make up sample menus featuring some of our signature dishes so she can help me plan her meals."

"Good idea. Make sure she has a wide selection of foods to choose from," Astin said, as he began handing sheets of paper to the people seated at the conference table.

They were gathered in the meeting room adjoining his office on the top floor of the twenty-seven-story luxury resort, and along with Don Farling, the director of food and beverage services, were Maria Pontalba, a fastidious woman who Astin had lured away from Caesars Palace in Las Vegas to serve as his head of housekeeping; Trisha York, the consummate concierge—a woman who could get absolutely anything accomplished that was asked of her and done in record time; Peter Rembrioso, a former Olympic skier from northern Utah who was in charge of all outdoor activities; and Melody Evers, director of live entertainment.

"Any more questions?" Astin asked as he scanned the faces of his trusted employees.

"You mentioned that Ms. Londres wants access to the stage?" Melody prompted.

"Yes, she plans to rehearse some of her dance routines for her upcoming play . . . when it's convenient, of course."

"Just make sure I'm notified in advance," Melody told Astin. "Security, you know?"

"Sure. Any more questions? Issues?" When no one spoke up, he said, "Okay. That's it. Thank you all for coming and let's get back to work."

Once his staff members had left, Astin remained in the empty conference room, tilted back in his chair, thinking. When he had given Niya Londres his business card so long ago, he had never dreamed she would actually visit his resort one day, or that she would be considered one of the most promising new actresses to take to the New York stage. He had read all about her stunning debut in *Rise*, in the *New York Times*, as well as her acclaimed performance on Broadway in *Morning Stars*. He had felt a surge of pride; he had known her long before she became a famous actress and he could truthfully say that he had danced with her on stage.

He had never forgotten that evening in Orlando and, apparently, never had she.

Swiveling in his chair, he faced the floor-to-ceiling windows that provided him a majestic view of the Stillwater Mountains and the expansive complex that made up Diamond Marsh Resort.

Nestled in the foothills of the rugged, snow-topped mountains, his luxury resort was a magical oasis of shimmering glass, gleaming steel, flowering shrubs and trees, and strategically placed natural rock fountains. Three towers of bubbling water gushed forth around the clock and also served as directional markers among the three main areas of the property: the hotel and spa, the outdoor recreational areas, and the authentic western-style dance hall/saloon where a variety of entertainment took place in evenings.

The dance hall, complete with a theatrical stage, a live band, two long bars, and gaming rooms was housed in the only remaining structure that had been part of the original town of Diamond Marsh, founded by Astin's great-great-grandfather, Bill John Spence, in 1864.

Bill John Spence had been part of an adventurous band of free blacks who fled the lower South at the height of the Civil War. When their food gave out and their wagons broke down and their mules refused to go another step toward the treacherous Nevada mountains, they had simply stopped where they were and put down roots, establishing their town on the edge of a swampy salt marsh. They built homes of adobe mud brick and raw pine, a general store for trading, a one-room school house, a mail stop for the Pony Express and, of course, a dance hall and saloon.

The land they settled on was cracked and dry, there was little to no rain, and every crop they planted refused to flourish. The only thing of value in the area, the settlers sadly determined, was salt, which they began mining from the nearby marshy flatlands to sell to the pioneers, trappers and explorers who passed by on their way to California and the Pacific Northwest.

Word spread quickly, and soon the tiny settlement of Diamond Marsh became known as a safe place to spend the night in an otherwise hostile land teeming with Indians and thieves, and was designated as a regular stopping place along the Overland Trail.

In a smart move, Bill John Spence decided to build a hotel—a two-story, pine and mud-brick structure with ten rooms, including a dining room and four private bathrooms with tubs of hot spring water. He charged fifty cents a night to sleep in a bed with a corn husk mattress and a thin quilt, and an additional half dollar for a bath in one of his private bathing tubs. Early visitors were extremely grateful for this respite in the desert and often paid him more than he charged.

By the early 1900s, every family in Diamond Marsh had become wealthier than they had ever imagined, but soon the salt played out, the pioneers found better, faster routes to the West, and the town died, deteriorating into a few ramshackle buildings choked with weeds.

The land languished untouched for two generations until Astin got the bright idea to reclaim his heritage and turn the forgotten land and its crumbling structures into a lucrative hotel/resort and tourist attraction, complete with an authentic Western-themed dance hall featuring a musical review starring gorgeous women of color. It had taken four years to complete the complex, which lay fifteen miles east of Carson City, close to the major highway that connected Reno to Las Vegas.

Reservations to stay at Diamond Marsh Resort flooded in as soon as Astin opened the doors, and ticket sales for his exotic dance hall review were brisk, with reservations often made months in advance. Astin felt a great deal of pride in the fact that he had resurrected his family's legacy and was happy to be making a lucrative living. However, he had been thinking that he needed an unusual attraction to keep loyal customers coming back, and he was determined to add a spark to his musical review.

Now, he thought he had found it. What a coup it would be to have Niya Londres appear at Diamond Marsh Resort in a show written and staged just for her. She was gorgeous, provocative, talented, sexual, stylish, and of African origin—exactly the kind of woman he had been looking for to give his venture a boost. He planned to approach Niya about making a guest appearance in a special production to be staged over Labor Day weekend as a benefit show to raise money for the Black Western Heritage Museum, of which Astin was one of the board members. The publicity would be good for her, the fledgling museum, and for Diamond Marsh Resort, too. If he had to, he was willing to pay Niya a handsome fee for her work.

The phone in his adjoining office rang, forcing Astin back to the moment. He sprang to go answer it, suddenly feeling very confident about his plan. "She'll do it," he murmured, nodding. "For some reason I feel sure of it."

Chapter 38

Niya's suite at Diamond Marsh Resort was a two-story cluster of four rooms with huge picture windows that provided gorgeous views of the landscaped grounds and the nearby Stillwater Mountains. The luxury suite had a sunken living room with a white stone fireplace, a master bedroom decorated in muted Southwest colors and real Indian artifacts, a mini modern kitchen, and an enormous bathroom with marble floors and a seductive Jacuzzi in the center.

"This is spectacular!" Niya exclaimed, turning away from the majestic view. With her back to the living room window, she smiled at Astin, her hands clasped together. "I'm so glad I came. You can't imagine how much I'm looking forward to simply lounging on that gorgeous patio and staring at this beautiful blue sky."

"That's exactly what you're supposed to do," Astin replied, taking a step toward her. "I know you have some rehearsing to do for your next play, but we want you to relax, too. My staff is ready and waiting to pamper you, and they're very good at it, I assure you." He extended one hand, which Niya took. "Please, ask for whatever you want or need, and don't hesitate to call on me for anything, promise?"

"I will," Niya replied.

He squeezed Niya's hand and started to let it go, but she placed her other hand on top his and stopped him.

"I want you to know," she began, firming her fingers around his, "that it's wonderful to see you again . . . and you haven't changed at all . . . after all these years."

"Neither have you," he added. "You're more beautiful than I remembered."

Releasing Astin's hand, Niya walked to a tufted cream ottoman beside the window and sank down, crossing her legs. She stared at the mountains, her profile to Astin for a few moments before speaking. "That's nice of you to say, Astin, but I know I'm too thin, I'm looking a bit frazzled, and I'm completely exhausted." She faced him. "My life has been such a whirlwind of rehearsals and performances and interviews and parties over the past few years. I desperately need this escape . . . and time to regroup before facing the hectic schedule that's waiting for me in London." She paused while Astin moved to sit down in a chair opposite her. "I'm engaged now," she said, tilting her left hand upward to show off the huge yellow diamond.

"Yes, I know," Astin told her. "To Granger Cooper, the producer. Congratulations. It's been mentioned more than once in the entertainment trades."

Niya laughed. "You see? The world knows my every move. Seems I've become quite a public person now."

"Good for you."

"Well, it has its good sides, but it has a troubling side, too, as I'm sure you know."

"Oh, yes, I do," Astin replied in a sympathetic tone. "We get quite a few celebrities who come here to escape the craziness of their successful, fast-paced lives."

"And on top of everything, I have a wedding to plan. We're getting married soon after our return from London, so this may be my last chance to really disconnect and do nothing for a while. Granger thought I was crazy for wanting to come out here . . . into the desert just to relax. He wanted me to go to a spa in London, so he could enjoy it with me, but I just couldn't resist the opportunity to see you again . . . and for some reason, coming here alone was important for me."

"Good choice," Astin replied, focusing on her. "Unpack, rest a while. I'll have Chef Don prepare lemon chicken for lunch . . ."

"My favorite," Niya interrupted; pleased that Astin's staff had obviously done their research.

"I know," Astin said, grinning mischievously. "And when you're feeling up to it, I'd love to show you around. Call me . . . dial 4400 on that red phone over there . . . and I'll be here to pick you up."

Niya touched Astin's arm. "Thanks. I'll do just that."

The sun was sinking below the mountains when Niya telephoned Astin, who promptly arrived to show her around the complex. She was intrigued by the luxurious amenities at the ultra-modern resort in its naturally beautiful setting, and impressed by the historical significance of the restored black town that Astin had sculpted into a fabulous entertainment complex.

Behind the sleek high-rise hotel, quaint wooden frame buildings lined a picture-perfect recreation of Diamond Marsh's old main street, where tourists could shop for western-themed souvenirs, buy ice cream, beer, and even period clothing. The town had been accurately reproduced to reflect the past, with hitching posts, shopkeepers dressed in bonnets and fringed jackets, carriages drawn by statuesque horses, and a sound system that recreated the sounds of a bustling pioneer settlement.

As they walked, Astin nodded to tourists and greeted those who passed, while telling Niya about the upcoming charity fund-raiser over Labor Day weekend that he was producing to help finance the Black Western Heritage Museum.

"The fact that this town was founded by freed and escaped slaves, and that my show features—in my opinion—some of the most beautiful women of color in the world, makes Diamond Marsh Resort the perfect venue for such a production. Tourists who are tired of Reno and Las Vegas often make a special trip out here just to try their luck at our casino and see a different kind of show. Adding a cultural component in the form of a museum fund-raiser would add greatly to my marketing abilities," Astin said. He glanced at Niya, as if making sure he had her full attention. "And . . . I'd love it if you could make a guest appearance."

Impressed, Niya smiled, head tilted to one side as she thought about what Astin had just told her. "I am so impressed with your oasis in the desert and I definitely would be interested in helping you out." She moved to stand under the canopy shade at the entrance to an authentic ice-cream parlor. "However, Labor Day weekend won't work. I have to return to New York at the end of August, repack my suitcases, shut down my apartment, take care of a few things and then take off immediately for London. *Perfectly* opens October 8th and, thank God, it's only a short, two-week run."

"I understand," Astin replied as he escorted Niya down the wood-plank sidewalk that led past the sheriff's office to the restored dance hall and saloon. "I know you came here for a rest, and I certainly don't want to impose, but I had to ask, and if you really want to do it, maybe next year."

"Yes, maybe next year," Niya agreed, "and if I do perform, I hope you'll let me mix some Afro-Cuban dance steps into the performance: the rumba, the mambo, and salsa, of course. It might be a lot of fun to add a few flashy tropical costumes and bright colors to your cowboy boots and fringe."

"Exactly what I hoped you'd say," Astin replied. "A guest appearance by Niya Londres would definitely add a much-needed spark to our already lively Western-style production."

Niya chuckled and studied Astin, both brows raised. "Of course, you'd have to agree to at least one mambo on stage with me," she teased.

"No problem," Astin shot back. "You know I can keep up with you, and . . . I've been practicing for an encore performance ever since the last time we danced together."

Niya playfully swatted at Astin. "Oh, right. You expect me to believe that?"

"Yes, I'm serious," Astin admitted, holding up one hand as if making a pledge of truth. "And I hope you'll let me prove it, too."

Niya simply shook her head, thinking that this time away from the pressures of work and away from the strict schedule that Granger made sure she adhered to was just the kind of relaxing experience she needed. How long had it been since she had been able to take a long nap without setting an alarm clock, or eat what she wanted for lunch without worrying about Granger's watchful eye, or stroll along and chat and laugh with an old friend, which she suddenly considered Astin to be although she had only met him one time?

Once Granger entered her life, it seemed that her world had constricted into a small circle, one that surrounded him and his friends, and kept her going around and around the edges in order to make sure she pleased him. Oh, she wasn't bitter . . . she knew that he had her well-being at heart and wanted only the best for her, but this break from her rigid routine was a rare and welcome treat.

Outside the Diamond Marsh Dance Hall they paused beneath a blazing marquee of round lightbulbs set in the pattern of an old-fashioned playbill announcement. Niya looked up into the rapidly darkening sky and read aloud, "Diamond Dolls Review—Authentic Western Dance Hall Beauties."

"I want you to see the stage, though it is dark tonight," Astin told her. "Always is on Mondays, but I keep the marquee lit round the clock. People have told me that on clear nights they can see the marquee from the sky as their planes approach the airport in Carson City." He stepped up to the dance hall entry. "Come on inside," Astin said, opening the heavy pine door with an old-fashioned skeleton key. "I want you to see my creation." He reached in and flipped a switch near the door, lighting the interior of his entertainment complex.

The main room was a large open space with creaky original wooden floors and old-fashioned poker tables scattered around, bound on one side by a long bar with a mirrored wall behind it. An upright piano sat in one corner, next to tall barrels marked whisky, rye, and beer. Heavy iron chandeliers hung from the low ceiling and the walls were decorated with bear skins, bleached steer skulls—their long horns stretching into the room—and brightly colored Indian blankets. Niya felt as if she had stepped into a Western movie set.

"Now, look over here," Astin urged, moving Niya toward an opening to the right of the entrance.

Branching off from the authentic saloon-type setting, beyond a wide arched door, was a very modern gaming room, complete with slot machines, black jack and roulette tables, and a modern well-stocked bar. "And finally," he began, escorting Niya to another widely arched opening opposite the game room, "this is what I really want you to see." He stepped back to let Niya precede him through the door.

Niya took three steps across the threshold, and found herself outdoors again, now facing a huge revolving stage under the stars. Beyond the stage, the audience's seats had been arranged in a terraced fashion along solid rock ledges cut into the side of the mountain. Row after row, the seats ascended the mountainside, like a swirl of thick rope wound around a spool. It was a stunning scene that took Niya's breath away, and she stood there in silence, her lips parted in surprise as she assessed the unusual creation.

Quietly, she ventured out onto the stage, drinking in the fresh desert air and the woodsy night scents that drifted down from the spiky pines that stood in pockets of darkness all over the craggy mountainside. Though the seats were empty, she could feel a human presence, a kind of expectation that made her shiver. Looking up, she gazed at the brilliant white stars and was suddenly jolted back to Havana, where night skies like this one were common. Living in New York, shuttered up for hours inside dark theaters and rehearsal halls, she had forgotten just how beautiful a starry night could be. To be able to dance in a magical venue like this would be heaven.

She turned and looked back at Astin, who had remained just inside the door, and noticed that music had begun to drift from the sound system inside the theater. It was a slow jazz guitar number that fit perfectly with the mood.

Astin strode toward Niya and simply held out his hand. "I told you I've been practicing. Now, let me show you what I've learned."

His move caught Niya by surprise, but she didn't hesitate to place her fingertips to his upturned palm. She closed her eyes and let Astin pull her toward him, and together they stepped into a series of swirling, fluid movements that took them into the center of the stage. Neither spoke as they moved in tandem, in a seamless motion that was as graceful as two doves in flight, ascending toward the stars.

"This is a fairyland of a setting, Astin. You've created a stage any performer would die to work on," she said, admiringly.

"It's yours, any time you want," he replied, splaying his fingers in the small of her back as he executed a triple spin.

"Very good," Niya murmured, easily keeping up with another intricate fan-out and return. Back in his arms, she murmured, "Your practice sessions are showing."

"Good. I wanted to impress you."

Niya giggled, and settled into the rhythm of the dance, but after a few moments of silence, spoke again. "I've been thinking . . . I *might* be able to delay my departure . . . To do your Labor Day benefit," she mused, looking into his eyes. "I'd have to rearrange a few things but I think it could be done."

Before Astin could respond, a voice came to Niya from the far side of the stage. "But *we* wouldn't want to interfere with your schedule," a woman called out.

Startled, Niya jerked back from Astin and turned to see a

cinnamon-skinned woman in a pale green pantsuit standing at the casino entrance, watching them. Her dark hair was shoulder length and natural, fanning out from her face in a frizzy cloud that dwarfed her small features. She appeared to be in her mid-to-late-thirties and had a soft round figure, but her eyes were fixed and hard, and her body language told Niya that she was not happy at discovering her and Astin on the stage.

"Oh!" Astin remarked in disappointment and surprise. "It's you, Melody." He immediately let go of Niya "What are you doing here, Melody?" he asked, suspiciously.

"The security light was flashing in my office. I thought someone . . . maybe vandals had broken in," she said, haughtily. "You remember when that gang spray-painted graffiti all over the stage last year?"

"Oh. Yeah. Sure. But it's just me. Sorry. My fault," Astin stuttered his apology. "I forgot to disarm the alarm."

"Each false alarm costs us money, Astin. Be more careful in the future."

"Yes, yes, I will," he agreed, contritely.

Now, the woman strode over, stopping two feet from Niya, and said, "Ms. Londres, don't let Astin pressure you into making a commitment that might not be in your best interest. He can be very persuasive at times."

Astin shot the woman an annoyed glance before rushing to introduce her.

"Niya, this is Melody Evers, director of entertainment at Diamond Marsh."

"Hello," Niya said offering her hand.

"Welcome to Diamond Marsh Resort, Ms. Londres," Melody replied, giving Niya's fingers a tepid touch. "Sometimes Astin gets carried away," Melody went on. "I warned him not to bother you with his crazy idea about including you in his fund-raiser for the museum. Astin," she turned to him now, "you ought to apologize to Ms. Londres for imposing on her."

A flash of anger widened Astin's eyes, but he did not respond.

"There's no reason to apologize," Niya quickly reassured Melody, watching Astin, who had pressed a curled fist to his chin, clearly embarrassed by Melody's remarks. "And I think his idea for including me in his fund-raiser is brilliant," she finished, suddenly wanting to disarm this woman's obvious sense of self-satisfaction.

"We already discussed the matter at length," Melody objected. "I don't know why he's bothering you. I thought he understood that our entertainment budget is totally allocated. We really can't afford to bring you in."

Now, Astin focused sternly on Melody. "Let me worry about the money."

"But I wouldn't charge a fee," Niya interjected. "I'd be happy to donate my time . . . for such a good cause. I will have to make a few phone calls and shift a few things around. But I'll work it out." Turning to Astin, she went on. "Somehow, I promise to fit your production into my schedule."

Astin grinned and winked at her.

Melody glared at him for several long seconds, and then curled her upper lip in defeat. "So, how long do you two plan on being out here?" she arrogantly snapped. "You know it's my responsibility to make sure . . ."

"Don't worry," Astin interrupted. "I'll make sure everything is properly shut down before I leave."

"Good," Melody tersely shot back. "And the next time you decide to take a twirl out here when the stage is supposed to be dark, let me know in advance, okay?"

"Okay," Astin agreed, shrugging his shoulders as Melody stalked away.

"Whew!" Niya remarked once Melody had disappeared. "She wasn't very happy, was she?"

"She never is," Astin replied. "She does an excellent job

managing the entertainment aspects of Diamond Marsh, but she takes her job way too seriously."

"I can see that," Niya replied, wondering why a wealthy powerful man like Astin Spence would take such crap from one of his employees.

Chapter 39

Granger was outraged when Niya phoned him in London to tell him of her plans, which meant a delay in her arrival by nearly two weeks. They argued bitterly, and Granger demanded that she come immediately to London and forget about this crazy idea of participating in a fund-raiser for a charity to which she had no personal connection.

"I'm disappointed in you," he told Niya. "I'm over here alone, missing you, and working like crazy to get everything perfect before your arrival, and you don't seem to be in much of a hurry to show up. That's pretty selfish of you."

"How can you call me selfish, when all I want to do is help raise money for a good cause? Anyway, you can go ahead with the understudy during rehearsals without me. It's not like I've never performed on stage, and I plan to rehearse my routines while I'm here!"

"But you won't be on *this* stage. I should have insisted that you fly over with me. I want you here by August 26th as we agreed, and not one day later! Understand?"

"Granger, you need to calm down. I miss you, too, but I have to admit that relaxing here in Nevada has really been good for me already. I needed this break . . . maybe we both need a break from each other. I didn't realize how tired I was, or how much I needed to unwind until I got here."

"Unwind? Relax? Sounds to me as if you're planning to work pretty damn hard while you're there . . . and for free."

"A short benefit performance will not be hard work. It'll be fun . . . and for a worthy cause, too."

"I don't want you to do this," Granger decided, and then added, "Contractually, you can't."

"Ha!" Niya laughed. "You're my manager, and you've always said that loopholes exist in any contract. Find one. Work it out. You know you can."

"And why should I?"

"Because you love me . . . you want me to be happy . . . and doing this would make me very happy."

"You can be so damn headstrong!" he muttered.

"And you've told me more than once that that is one of the reasons you feel lucky to have found me."

"Right now I don't feel so lucky," he grumbled, backing down.

After hanging up the phone, Granger poured a generous slug of vodka into a glass and flung himself down on the sofa in his three-room suite at the Gainsborough Hotel. He glared at the script he had been working on that was lying open on the table, suddenly so lonely and restless he wanted to scream. He had to calm down, he knew. He had to go back to moving through each day and night in anticipation of the next, only because it would bring him closer to the day of Niya's arrival. Sure, he could conduct rehearsals with the understudy, and Niya could probably walk in off the street and onto the stage and perform the role with ease, but that was not what he wanted. He wanted her with him, now. Why wasn't she in as much of a hurry to leave Nevada and come to him as he was to see her?

A knot of panic formed inside Granger, making his limbs begin to tremble. He pulled his knees to his chest and wrapped his arms so tightly around them they soon began to ache.

Why was she doing this? To test him? he wondered, realizing that there was little he could do about this sudden need of hers to express her independence. What or who was keeping her so far away from him at a time when he was so fragile? He had no choice but to wait it out. But could he? he worried, struggling with the familiar, but dreaded, sense of urgency that forced him nearly to tears.

Niya lay awake in her suite at Diamond Marsh, thinking about her conversation with Granger. She had known he would not be happy to hear about her change in plans, but had not expected him to sound quite so desperate. He had always clung to her with a kind of quiet desperation that simmered just beneath the surface of his calm personality, and she had always thought of it as a tender expression of his passion, his way of showing her how much he cared.

At times, she would catch him intently watching her, as if worried that she might suddenly evaporate before his eyes. And once she had awakened in the middle of the night and heard him crying—a bad dream, he had told her before sweeping her into his arms and holding her so closely that she had hardly been able to breathe.

For a man so worldly and mature, he often adopted the demeanor of a frightened little boy who was afraid of life, and who could appear strangely isolated in the middle of a crowd. *He'll be fine,* she told herself, feeling slightly proud to have been able to resist his demand that she leave Nevada at once and come to him. *He has to understand that he can't control me completely,* she mused, plumping her pillow and easing quickly toward sleep.

Agitated and restless, Granger poured another hefty shot of vodka into his glass and then grabbed the phone. Ricky answered on the second ring.

"Ricky," Granger started right in. "I just spoke to Niya.

There'll have to be some changes in the rehearsal schedule. She can't get here until after Labor Day."

"What?" Ricky threw back, clearly not happy. "Why?"

"Seems she prefers the dry Nevada air to London's foggy climate."

"You can't be serious," Ricky replied sarcastically. "Pushing rehearsals with Niya back means paying overtime. Unions over here won't let actors and technicians sit around unless we pay them, you know . . . adding thousands to the budget!"

"I know, but there's not much we can do," Granger told his partner, going on to fill him in on the reason for Niya's decision.

"Well, it's not just *your* money, Granger," Ricky tersely replied. "I'm in this, too. Don't mess it up. The sets are complete, the costumes are nearly fitted, and all of the local talent we need has been cast . . . except for two roles I auditioned today. We're ready to go! Get on the phone and tell Niya to get her ass over here! Now!"

"Watch it, Ricky!" Granger tossed back. "That's my future wife you're talking about. I'm not happy about this situation either, but it's not the end of the world. The budget is tight, I know that . . . but we'll manage. Keep cool and I promise to do what I can to get her over here as soon as possible."

Granger could hear Ricky's dispirited sigh of resignation through the phone.

"All right," Ricky finally said. "Okay, we'll deal with the money when we have to."

"Good," Granger replied. "Now, what about today's auditions?"

"I got some video footage of the auditions this afternoon. Only two actors showed up to try out for the role of the salesman. A good-looking red-haired guy who read alone and a pleasant enough thinning blond who did a quick run-through with me. Two different looks and two very different approaches to the role. Wanna come up and take a look at the video?"

"Sure, why not?" Granger decided, pushing himself up off the couch. He gulped down his vodka and ran a hand through his hair. "I really need to get out of this room."

For the next hour, Granger and Ricky critiqued the footage of the day's auditions and finally settled on the redhead for the role of the salesman, agreeing that he looked more suited for the part and had a voice that exuded authority. Just as Granger was about to leave, Ricky's doorbell rang. When Ricky answered it, a very young, strawberry-blonde wearing precariously high heels and too much makeup walked in.

"Hello," Granger nodded, preparing to walk past her and out the door.

The girl, who didn't respond to his greeting, strutted directly into Ricky's hotel room and disappeared into the back without speaking to either of the men.

"You can stay," Ricky quickly offered.

Granger cocked a brow. "Ricky, Ricky. You can't help yourself, can you?"

After a short pause, Ricky placed a hand on Granger's shoulder and, facing him, said, "And neither can you. Come on, Granger. This one is really special. It's been a long time, and Niya is thousands of miles away. Clearly in no hurry to see you. You got nothing else to do."

Granger froze, his eyes locked with Ricky's. The truth cut into his soul. No one knew about Granger's secret addiction to underage girls except Ricky Monroe, with whom he had engaged in many three-ways over the years. Granger had tried repeatedly to break his nasty addiction that had first gripped him during the time that his mother was rejecting every girl he dated. It was not until he met Niya that he had been able to get this insane craving under control and he hadn't had a slipup since. But now, with Niya so far away, and seeming to ignore his need for her presence, he felt vulnerable, agitated, and abandoned. The temptation was great, but he couldn't give in.

"I can't," Granger managed huskily, his voice cracking with the realization that Ricky was offering him the perfect opportunity to feed the familiar hunger that had begun to eat at his insides and clutter his mind as soon as he left New York. However, he couldn't betray Niya, he just couldn't. "I'd better head back to my room," he muttered, emptying his lungs of air.

Ricky shrugged, removed his hand from Granger's shoulder, and vanished into the back of the suite, leaving the door to his bedroom cracked. Unable to help himself, Granger stepped forward, his mouth dry, his ears flooded with the sound of blood rushing through his head. He entered the hallway, walked to the door of the semi-dark bedroom, and peeked inside, automatically scanning the room for one of Ricky's ever-present cameras.

Ricky, who had just finished undressing the girl, looked up and winked at Granger. "Don't worry. No videotaping tonight."

Granger hurriedly stepped inside, shed his clothing and eased down on top of the young girl. He groaned aloud when her silky youthful skin touched his.

Ricky shifted to one side of the king-size bed to make room for Granger, while keeping one eye on the miniature camcorder hidden in the ceiling fan.

Chapter 40

"Miracle Mile Club in Manhattan," said Dejen Ray, Tremont's longtime friend and former guitarist. "That's the last place she worked, man," Dejen went on. "After that I got nothing."

"Did you talk to the manager?" Tremont asked, feeling sick with excitement to finally have a lead on Niya's whereabouts, yet disgusted with himself for having involved Dejen in his search. *But, thank God for Dejen*, he thought, grateful that his friend had visited him faithfully once a month in prison and been there when he was released.

Now that he was out on parole, he was full of regrets: if only he had not been so harsh with Niya. If only he'd read her letters. If only he had married her before he entered that hell-hole.

While incarcerated, he had deliberately hardened his heart, forced himself to shut down emotionally in order to survive, and had been convinced that he was doing right. It had been his choice to break off with her, though a stupid one, he now knew, and he was desperate to know where she was, if she was happy, if she thought of him at all. He was consumed with finding her and was plagued with memories of holding her, kissing her, making love to her. Would he ever recapture the joy they once shared? Was it possible? Or was he only setting himself up for more pain?

Being back in Miami, living alone in G-Daddy's rambling old house, the only thing of value he still owned, brought back memories of happier times with his grandfather, and with Niya, too, who had filled the place with joy. While adjusting to life on the outside, his need for her had come down like a thundering rush of water, driving him to call Dejen and beg him to help track Niya down and find out what she had done with her life.

"Naw, I didn't get to the manager," Dejen replied. "I spoke to some girl who answered the phone and told me that Niya didn't work there anymore."

"That's all?"

"Yeah, I didn't want to ask a lot of questions."

"Well, thanks, Dejen," Tremont replied. "At least I've got a place to start."

"Good. Now, don't go giving up on her. She was meant for you, man. You know that?"

"Yeah . . ." Tremont said, stretching out the word. "I know that now."

"Okay . . . so, you wanna meet me at Club Cariba for a drink?" Dejen went on in a more upbeat tone. "I hear there's a hot new band over there."

"Naw," Tremont answered. "Think I'll stay in and watch the fight on cable."

"Don't go shutting yourself off like some hermit, man. You're free now. You can come and go as you please."

"I know, I know," Tremont said. "But I don't really mind being alone."

After clicking off, Tremont stared at the phone number he had scribbled on the cover of the magazine, wondering how long he could keep from dialing it. If he found Niya, would she speak to him? Would she want to know that he still loved her, even more than when he told her goodbye? Would she listen to his words of regret and apology for all the pain he knew he'd caused her, and himself?

"What the hell," Tremont mumbled as he quickly dialed the

number for the Miracle Mile Club, doing it before he could talk himself out of taking this frightening step.

When a woman answered, he asked to speak to the manager, and was told that the manager was not in.

"I'm Contessa. Maybe I can help you?" the woman stated in a mature, professional voice.

"I'm looking for a dancer named Niya Londres. Does she work there?" Tremont asked.

"Who's calling?"

"Uh . . . Mr. Grant. An old friend from Miami."

"Oh, well, Niya left here a long time ago," Contessa rushed to inform Tremont.

"Do you know where she went?" Tremont boldly asked, not expecting much of an answer. However, the woman was turning out to be pleasantly responsive.

"Yeah, first she got a part in a Broadway play . . . well, off-Broadway, really. It was called *Rise*, and it was great, then she was a smash hit in *Morning Stars*. Now she's going to Europe to be in another play. Niya is probably on her way to London right now."

"London?"

"Yes, and she's recently engaged to Granger Cooper, the show's producer. It's been all in the papers and everything. Where have you been? You must not be into the theater, huh? Well, I gotta say, Niya did pretty good for herself," the chatty woman rambled on. "Pretty damn good."

Tremont sucked back a sharp breath, feeling as if he'd been punched in the stomach.

"If this is important, I know I can get a message to her," Contessa continued. "You see, I used to be her personal assistant, but now . . ."

"No. No message," Tremont interrupted, easing down the phone. He held his breath while he struggled to digest the disturbing news. He'd lost her. She belonged to another man, now. She had gone on to make a life for herself and find love with someone else.

"And why wouldn't she?" he whispered into the cavernous room. "After all, I was the one who drove her away. Isn't this exactly what I wanted her to do?"

Contessa frowned at the handset, annoyed, and then pressed a button to retrieve the caller's number from the caller ID. She hated it when people hung up on her in mid-sentence without as much as a thank you. She ought to call the man back and cuss him out. She had tried to be polite and helpful, as she always was with whoever called, but some folks just didn't have any manners.

In a huff, she flipped open her phone log and made her first entry for the day: Mr. Grant from Miami called for Niya Londres. Phone # 555-192-6699. No message." The phone rang again and she snatched it up, determined to remain upbeat and professional.

Los Angeles

Larry Lo tossed a twenty dollar bill onto the table and stood, anxious to leave the crowded restaurant and get back to the recording studio, where he was overdue to cut the last track of his latest CD, *Down for You.* As soon as he pulled his aviator sunshades over his eyes, an excited shout erupted at the front door of the restaurant and two girls, both dressed in midriff-baring tops that barely contained their enormous breasts and the shortest mini shirts Larry had ever seen, rushed over to him, squealing their demands for his autograph. The most animated of the two, a young Hispanic girl whose jet-black hair hung over her shoulders, grabbed Larry's arm and hung on tightly as she thrust a piece of paper at him, while the other girl waited her turn.

"Hey, calm down, babe," he cautioned the girl, pulling his arm up and away. "You could do a lotta damage with that grip."

"I'd love to do a lotta damage to you, if you know what I mean," she brazenly purred.

"That so?" Larry cocked a brow.

"Yeah," she breathed, pressing her breast against his arm. "And I promise I wouldn't hurt you *too* much." She giggled and winked at Larry.

"Sarita, you need to quit," the girl's friend called out, squinting in disgust.

"Quit what?" Sarita tossed back, blinking innocently at her friend, who threw up her hands and shook her head.

"So, your name is Sarita?" Larry probed.

"Um-hum. Sarita Hernandez," she murmured watching closely as he wrote her name and then scribbled his signature below it. He handed the paper back to Sarita, and then used his Sharpie pen to autograph the bare shoulder of Sarita's friend.

Sandi Lee hung back while the girls continued to fuss over Larry until the waitress came to seat them. They waved goodbye and headed off, but quickly a new crowd gathered as the patrons in the restaurant became aware of the celebrity in their midst. Several approached with their own requests, and Larry signed his name on whatever piece of paper or body part they offered.

Sandi Lee watched the scene with interest, as well as a sense of pride that she was the woman he had arrived with, the one with whom he had eaten lunch, the one he would take back to his limo when he left, and the one who would, hopefully, be in his bed again tonight. She didn't mind standing in the shadows while strangers fawned over Larry. There was no reason to be jealous just because women threw themselves, and all kinds of intimate clothing, at him. He could have any girl he wanted, but he had chosen her, and Sandi Lee had no complaints.

"Let's go," he finally ordered, jerking his head toward his bodyguard and driver, Tiny Fizz, who immediately stepped in front of Larry and cleared a path to the door. Sandi Lee followed dutifully, chin up, shoulders back, her tight red dress clinging to her body as she flashed a smug grin at the girls, who ogled her with envy.

Once they were outside and crossing the hot asphalt parking lot, Larry looked back at Sandi Lee. "Go ahead to the limo," he told her, hanging back, one hand on Tiny Fizz's arm.

Sandi Lee went to the limo, climbed in, and sank back against the cool leather seats, glad to be out of the hot July sun. Her red snakeskin outfit might be fashionable, but it sure as hell wasn't cool.

From behind the dark windows she watched Larry talking to his bodyguard and gesturing with both hands. Tiny nodded, turned around and went back into the restaurant, while Larry entered the limo and flopped down next to Sandi Lee.

"What's going on?" she asked, checking her watch. "I thought you had to be at the studio by one. It's already two-thirty."

Larry shrugged. "Can't nobody do nothin' till I get there, anyway." He leaned forward and looked out the window, as if anxious for Tiny Fizz to return. "Besides, what's it to you?"

"Nothin'" she shrugged. "Just making conversation."

"When you gonna learn? I hate chitchat for chitchat's sake. If you got nothin' important to say, then keep quiet."

His unexpected rebuke burned hotly in Sandi Lee's mind, and her cheeks flushed deep red. However, she was determined not to let him know that he had hurt her. She'd been yelled at all her life, verbally abused by her father since she was a child, and she knew how to let harsh words roll off her back without even blinking. She could take whatever was thrown at her and survive: Look at how far she had come since Oyster Cove. She owned her own business, had money in her pocket, and the attention of the hottest singer around. Oh, yeah, she could take care of herself, all right.

Tiny Fizz returned to the limo, opened the driver's side door and eased his bulky figure behind the wheel. He turned on the

CD player and then reached over his seat back to hand a folded piece of paper to Larry, then started the engine and pulled off.

Larry opened the note and laughed. "Thanks, Fizz," he grinned.

Sandi Lee silently fumed, wanting to keep quiet, yet desperate to let Larry know that she knew what he was up to. Sending Tiny back for that girl's number! What a juvenile thing to do. She inched forward and cut her eyes to the side, trying to read what was in the note.

Suddenly, Larry's head snapped around and he fixed her with a hard, cold stare. "What you lookin' at? This ain't nonna your business," he quipped.

"It's that girl's phone number, isn't it?" Sandi Lee boldly threw back.

"What if it is?" Larry challenged. "What you gonna do about it?"

"Humph. She's probably jailbait," Sandi Lee grumbled under her breath.

"What'd you say?" Larry threw out, his jaw tight.

"Nothing," Sandi Lee told him, clearly exasperated.

Larry grabbed her by the wrist. "What'd I say about talkin' about nothin'? You just don't get it, do you?"

"Oh, yeah. I get it all right. I just hope you know what you're doing. That girl can't be more than fifteen years old. She's trouble. You're crazy if you get involved."

"Get outta my car, bitch," Larry suddenly ordered.

Sandi Lee looked at him blankly, but did not move. He'd yelled at her before and called her a bitch lots of times. His outbursts never lasted long.

"Tiny!" Larry shouted at his bodyguard. "Stop the damn car. Now!"

Tiny Fizz brought the limo to a stop on the shoulder of the freeway.

"I said get out," Larry ordered again, leaning over Sandi

Lee to open the door. "I damn sure don't need you tellin' me how to live my life. I'm Larry Lo. I fuckin' do as I please."

"Yeah? Well you sure as hell need somebody to tell you, you ain't all that," Sandi Lee shouted as she jumped out of the limo and slammed the door. After giving her wilting blonde curls a hard shake, she lifted her chin, shouldered her purse and started off down the freeway exit ramp, wishing like hell she had not worn her best stiletto heels to lunch.

Chapter 41

Nevada

Melody never missed a chance to remind Niya of how much money her appearance was costing in costumes, extra musicians, overtime pay for staff, and promotional materials—all of which cut into her budget. Niya struggled to ignore Melody's snide remarks, and when she complained to Astin, he told her not to take Melody's comments to heart. It was simply the way she was. Everyone just accepted her the way she was.

Niya was dumbfounded and unable to understand why Astin continued to put up with the angry black sister who had made it perfectly clear the first night they met that Niya's presence at Diamond Marsh Resort was not all that welcome. Melody could be cold, cruel, and downright mean, in a sly, calculating manner that she had perfected and clearly enjoyed. No one stood up to her, not even Astin, and it was a puzzle to Niya why not.

When Niya inquired about making an appearance on a local radio program to promote the benefit show, Melody told Niya to stay out of matters that didn't concern her. Promotion was not Niya's job, it was hers. Niya immediately backed away, deciding to focus her energy on her dance rehearsals, the musicians, and selecting her wardrobe.

As work on the production progressed Niya and Astin spent a lot of time together, and after rehearsals often drove over to Carson City to sit in one of the quaint open air cafés and sip wine long into the night, talking and laughing and finding that they enjoyed each other's company very much. Neither was ever in a hurry to say goodnight. For the first time in years, Niya was free of Granger's exacting vigilance, and with Astin, she felt natural—back to her true Afro-Cuban, energetic self.

While in Nevada she let her hair grow out and was wearing it in a free-flowing, naturally wavy style, and was not worried about the few pounds she had put on in her hips, where she preferred a bit of roundness. She was wearing close-fitting, colorful clothing once more and indulging in her favorite Cuban foods—black beans and rice with plantains, which she had taught Chef Don how to prepare for her. She even taught Astin how to make *café con leche,* a combination of strong espresso coffee with warm milk, and felt no guilt about skipping her daily two-hour workout sessions if Astin asked her to go off and explore the area with him.

He kept a stable of horses and loved to ride, so when he invited Niya to go riding with him one Saturday morning, she eagerly accepted.

"Something told me that you were a good rider," Astin told her as they made their way along the path that wound through the forested mountain foothills. He was seated on a beautiful palomino and she was riding a feisty chestnut mare. Before they took off, he asked his stable man to snap two Polaroid photos of them on their mounts, and he gave one of them to her.

They galloped at a brisk pace until they reached the gravel path that wound up the mountainside. They dismounted to let the horses drink from a sparkling creek, and then walked together for a while.

"On Sunday afternoons, my father used to take me and my brother to the countryside to visit an old friend of his who owned six horses," Niya told Astin as they started out, side by side. "The man's name was Rudolfo Castenya, a tiny, wiry little man, and he loved to take me and Lorenzo out to his barn and tell us to choose which horse we wanted to ride. Then he'd throw an old blanket over the horses' backs—he didn't own real saddles like the ones you have—and off we'd go. I loved to ride through the fields of tall sugar cane, or along the beach, where I felt free, and in control of what was happening." She glanced over at Astin. "This is the first time I've been on a horse since my father died. It makes me sad, but happy, too."

When Astin reached out and touched Niya's arm, she leaned closer and let him put his arm around her shoulder, as if it were the most natural thing in the world to do.

"From what you've told me," Astin said, "I can tell that you loved your father very much. Is your mother still alive?"

"Yes," Niya nodded, proceeding to tell Astin about her mother's current situation, as well as her father's activities in the anti-Castro movement and how it destroyed him.

"Your mother sounds like a very brave person," Astin replied.

"She is," Niya agreed. "I'll never be able to repay her for all she sacrificed for me to escape Cuba."

"I don't think parents expect their children to repay them," Astin commented. "They just want them to move forward, make something of their lives, and not forget who they are, where they came from. I know that's why I decided to restore Diamond Marsh. It's been my lifelong dream to re-create the town my people founded, and now it is a reality. I never once thought of leaving this place. It's where I belong. It's who I am."

His words resounded with Niya, who had been silently struggling with a disquieting sense of isolation, a kind of disconnect that began when she arrived in New York. Living as a stranger in a foreign land, while trying to accept a new way of life and hold onto the culture of her birth, had made it difficult for her to remember who she really was sometimes.

She stopped walking and faced Astin. "I've traveled across the United States and met many wonderful people, yet I've never felt at home in any of the cities. You're lucky to live in the place where your ancestors are buried, and to be able to preserve their legacy."

"What about Miami, with its huge Cuban population and tropical weather?" Astin asked. "Didn't that seem a bit like home?"

"At times," Niya replied, "But it definitely was not Havana, though not nearly as foreign as New York. Even Nevada is easier to embrace, with its open spaces and beautiful countryside. I love it here, Astin. So much so that I hate to think about returning to the noisy, cold city."

"You could stay," he ventured.

"Impossible," she laughed, suddenly spinning out from beneath his arm to remount her horse. "You know I can't do that! And since I can't return to Cuba, I have no choice but to muddle along until this country called America becomes my own."

"I guess you know what's best," Astin commented as he swung up onto his sleek palomino. Turning serious, he added, "But don't forget that you're always welcome here at Diamond Marsh. *Mi casa es tu casa*. It would make me happy if you'd think of my home as yours."

They headed back in silence, Astin's remark settling in her mind. Away from the stressful circumstances of her life in New York, Niya realized how much Astin understood her. He sensed her need to be who she was, to connect with what was familiar, and he appreciated the rugged natural beauty of the countryside. He anticipated her every need, often fulfilling it before she let him know what she wanted. He was sweet with her. Tender. He liked troubling himself just for her, and made the effort to listen. He was attentive, yet never a nuisance, and he seldom hovered, in the way that Granger did, who nearly smothered her with his attention.

She loved Granger, but was beginning to wish that he could give her this easygoing, open-ended kind of connection that made her feel grounded and content. Just like Astin, she was forever connected to a land, to a place, to a cause, and to a people even though she was living outside her homeland. Astin understood this, but Granger did not, and she was grateful to Astin for allowing her to play a small part in keeping his family legacy alive.

Chapter 42

Humiliated and emotionally distraught, Sandi Lee sat in her car, which was parked beneath a tree at the end of the gated driveway leading to Larry Lo's house, and silently cursed the singer, who had just emerged from his limo with the raven-haired Hispanic girl, Sarita, hanging onto his arm.

Since their argument on the freeway two weeks ago, Larry had refused to take Sandi Lee's phone calls, had cancelled her company's contract to serve bar at his upcoming party at Century Plaza, and had instructed Tiny Fizz to turn her away when she showed up at his house, demanding to see him.

His cruel rejection incensed Sandi Lee, who began hanging out in places where Larry regularly showed up to watch him from a distance. She went to his gym, his favorite restaurant, lurked outside his recording studio, shopped in the trendy Rodeo Drive area where he spent a lot of his time.

She refused to believe that he did not still think about her, miss her, and crave the great sex that she had been giving him. Every night she prayed that he would come to his senses, call her, tell her he was sorry, and invite her back into his bedroom. So far, her prayers had not been answered.

"That's okay," Sandi Lee told herself as she watched Larry and Sarita disappear into the house. "I know what Larry needs and he knows that I'm the best. I just have to be patient until he realizes that, that little hoochie-mama slut will never take my place."

Chapter 43

August was the height of the tourist season in Nevada, and Diamond Marsh Resort was booked solid straight through Labor Day.

Niya was enjoying her stay immensely, and stayed busy by taking advantage of the many amenities offered, as well as rehearsing not only for her London role, but for Astin's Labor Day benefit show.

When she wasn't working, she relaxed in the spa, took tennis lessons, or passed the time sipping iced tea on one of the hotel's shady patios, chatting with interesting women from around the world who regularly visited Diamond Marsh to be pampered and de-stressed.

The charity show moved forward. The gorgeous dancers, the talented musicians and the competent staff at Diamond Marsh Resort treated Niya like royalty, making her feel pampered, appreciated, and completely at home. Everyone except Melody Evers, who went out of her way to make life as miserable as possible for Niya, treating her with snobbish, cold indifference.

During preparations for the benefit, Melody made it a point to hang around whenever Niya and Astin were alone, often insinuating herself into their conversations and rudely interrupting Niya in mid-sentence. Melody made no effort to hide her displeasure with Astin's infatuation with Niya, and took every opportunity that came along to remind Astin that Niya was engaged to be married and would be flying off to London to join her fiancé as soon as her benefit performance was over.

When Niya asked Astin why Melody seemed so angry and unhappy, he simply shrugged and made some vague excuse about her being overworked and stressed out over the addition of the benefit to her already hectic entertainment schedule. He apologized for her rude behavior far too often, and acted as if he were personally responsible for smoothing any feathers that Melody ruffled. Seeing that he preferred to put up with his employee's moody attitude rather than to call her on it, Niya dropped the subject. After all, it was not her place to tell Astin how to manage his staff.

As Labor Day weekend approached, ticket sales for the Black Western Heritage Museum benefit were swift. With prices ranging up to fifteen hundred dollars a seat, the show quickly sold out.

On the afternoon before the grand event, following the final dress rehearsal, Astin came to see Niya in the temporary trailer he had set up to serve as her dressing room, eager to thank her for all of the hard work she had put in and assure her that this was going to be a show long remembered and talked about in the area for years. Having Niya Londres as the spectacular guest star was such a coup, and he was grateful to her for making it happen.

"I'm glad to do it," Niya assured Astin, "even though Granger is still a tad upset with me for staying here so long."

"I'm sorry your decision to extend your stay caused trouble between you and your fiancé," Astin stated with sincerity.

"Well, it's not your fault. You have nothing to apologize for. Besides, when I get to London, he'll forget all about this and we'll be fine," Niya said, just as Melody burst into the trailer without knocking.

"And?" Niya said, whipping her head around, eyes wide. She had just about had enough of this woman. How dare she burst in without even a tap on the door? "Do you need something, Melody?"

"Yes," she quickly replied. "I need to pick up the two checks I left on your dressing table for Astin to endorse."

A blank expression came over Niya's face. "What checks? And why would you leave them in here?"

"Because this is where he seems to spend most of his time nowadays. I wanted to make sure he didn't forget to sign them."

Niya glanced around. "I haven't seen any checks." She arched a brow at Astin. "Have you?"

He shook his head, "No."

"You must have," Melody insisted. "I left them right there . . ." she jabbed a sharply pointed fingernail toward the center of Niya's dressing table. "They couldn't have simply disappeared."

"I'm sorry, Melody, but I don't know what you're talking about. You must be mistaken . . ."

"I don't make mistakes . . . not where money is concerned, Ms. Londres," Melody threw out.

"Well you made a mistake just now by accusing me of taking your money, which I'm pretty damn sure you never left here in the first place. This is nothing but a crappy setup," Niya slung back, jumping to her feet. She took one long step forward, making sure her eyes were level with Melody's. She was fed up with Melody messing with her mind and not about to sit by and let this woman attack her. "Listen, bitch," Niya growled, "I know you're lying. There never were any checks left in here!"

Astin raced to step between the two women, keeping his back to Niya, placing his angry lips dangerously close to Melody's face. "How dare you insinuate that Niya would steal from us!" Astin lashed out. "Apologize to her . . . and you'd better act like you mean it!"

Melody blew air through her lips and rolled her eyes, clearly dismissing Astin's demand.

"You know you're lying. Apologize right now," Astin ordered again.

"For what?" Melody finally spit out.

"For making such a serious, unfounded accusation. You're deliberately trying to cause trouble. Think I don't know what you're doing? You've been desperate to make Niya miserable since the day she arrived, and you need to quit. Your insane nastiness has to end. Do you understand? It has to end now!"

Finally, Niya thought, *he's putting this bitch in her place*.

As Astin and Melody continued to argue, Niya stalked out of the trailer in a huff, not about to stick around and get further involved in their strange, dysfunctional relationship, whatever it might be. She could hear them screaming at each other as she crossed the complex and headed back to her hotel suite, worried, yet secretly pleased that Astin was standing up to Melody at last.

Later that evening, Astin found Niya sitting alone at a table on the stone patio adjoining the hotel's restaurant, sipping a margarita.

"May I join you?" he asked.

"Please do," Niya told him.

He sank tiredly into a chair and ordered a round of margaritas for them both. Niya sipped her drink and remained quiet as she watched him carefully, having decided not to bring up the incident in her trailer. That was his situation to explain.

They drank margaritas and made small talk about tomorrow's event until Astin asked her to walk with him across the grounds. They made their way to a quiet spot in a secluded rock garden where they stopped and leaned against a rough wooden split-rail fence to gaze at the shadows of the dark mountains in the distance. At last, he brought up Melody's accusation, telling Niya how sorry he was about what happened.

"You were right," he said. "There never were any checks left in your trailer."

"Thank you for supporting me," Niya said. "But I don't understand Melody. What did I ever do to make her hate me so much? Why is she so angry at me?"

Astin sighed, and then hunched over his glass, twirling it as he thought. "She's insecure. She always feels threatened by any new woman who arrives on the scene."

"But I'm not competing with her for your affections."

"I know, but sometimes I wish you were," Astin brashly replied.

"Astin, please don't say things like that," Niya stopped him, beginning to feel uncomfortable. "I think the world of you, and it hurts me to see how much Melody enjoys berating you. The woman has some serious problems."

"You gave me the courage to stand up to her tonight."

"What's it about, Astin? I don't get it. What is it with you two?"

"Melody Evers is my ex-wife."

"Your what?" Niya stepped back to better see Astin's face in the moonlight. "You were once *married* to her?"

"Yes. It was a brief marriage, only lasted a year, and we've been divorced for ten years."

"All right . . ." she stretched out her reply. "So, that's it . . . but why is she still around, let alone on your payroll?"

"Because she received one-half ownership of the Diamond Marsh property in our divorce settlement, along with the right to be involved in any business that I ever created on the property. So when the resort was finished, I brought her on board to run the entertainment division, and she's done a good job. We agreed to keep our past relationship out of our business affairs when the restoration project began. She took back her maiden name, so few people know we were once married, and I prefer it that way. "

"Thanks for finally filling me in."

"I don't want any secrets between us, Niya. I . . . I respect you too much. I don't want you to think that I'd ever put up with a woman like Melody under any other circumstances."

Though surprised, Niya nodded her understanding. "She's a

burden, I can see. If she was like this when you were married, I understand why you divorced her."

"Believe me, she's been worse, whenever she felt threatened."

"You deserve to be treated better, Astin. Ex-wife or not, Melody has no right to belittle you and act so possessive. I appreciate you leveling with me, but I still don't understand why you let her get away with so much."

"I guess I'm tired of fighting with her. It's been like this for years. For me, the best way to handle the situation is to ignore her. I barely pay any attention to her jabs now, but when she started in on you . . . well, I couldn't let that slide."

"Soon, I'll be gone, so she won't have to worry about me taking up your time anymore."

The corners of Astin's eyes crinkled up in an irritated frown. "I hate to see you go, Niya. I'll miss you very much. Having you here, getting to know you, work with you, and relax with you—well, it's been wonderful . . . the most perfect time in my life, I'm sure."

"It has been fun, and I'll miss you, too," Niya replied, taken aback by the sincerity in Astin's tone, as well as the enraptured expression on his face.

He has fallen in love with me, she realized, aware that her feelings for him were slightly more intense than she dared to acknowledge. His charismatic personality, coupled with his uncanny ability to make her feel completely at ease, had brought her back to who she really was, infused her life with a spontaneous joy that she didn't want to lose.

They had bonded instantly, in an uncanny way that had seemed perfectly natural, making Niya think of Astin Spence as a kind of soul mate—a man who had brought the fractured pieces of this new life together and valued who she really was.

"You may miss me, Niya, but not in the same way that I'll miss you," Astin was saying. "For weeks now, we've spent nearly every day together, so you must know that I'm deeply attracted to you."

Niya didn't trust her voice to utter a word.

"Hell. I'm in love with you," Astin blurted out. "Now, I've said it. You captivated me and captured my heart in Orlando when I first held you in my arms, but I dismissed my feelings as impulsive and crazy. But since we've been here together at Diamond Marsh, my first reaction has been validated. I've loved you since that first wonderful night when we met and danced together under the stars. I don't want to let you slip away again. I want to keep you here with me in the desert. Forever."

Niya slowly eased her hand to his chest and touched him lightly. "Don't. Please don't say more. You're only complicating things. It's hard enough for me to leave this place . . . and leave you, without your confession of love racing through my mind. Really, Astin, there's no future for us. I'm engaged to be married, and I've kept my fiancé waiting too long. I need to get back to him, and back to the real world. This has been a fantasy time, a surreal experience that I feel privileged to have had, but it has to end."

"No, it doesn't. It never has to end, and you know that," he softly countered. "I understand you, Niya. You're African, Cuban, and now a bit American. Somewhere along the way, I think you've forgotten who you are and what you need. You're a passionate woman who needs a passionate man to love you, protect you, and walk through life beside you. Right now, I'd love nothing more than to whisk you off to Las Vegas and get married, return to Diamond Marsh and start my life all over with you."

Niya laughed aloud. "Run off to Las Vegas and get married? What an imagination!"

"People do it all the time," he protested seriously. "They face up to the truth of who they are and what they need in a relationship and they act on it before superficial intrusions get in the way. What's wrong with that? You know it's true!"

Now, Niya adopted a somber expression. "There was a time when I might have agreed with you, but I've learned to be more cautious about matters of the heart. If circumstances were different . . . who knows what I might do? But for now, getting back to my fiancé and back to work are all that's on my mind."

Astin stepped closer. "I don't believe you, Niya" he murmured. "I think my proposition *is* on your mind, but I understand your hesitation to admit it."

When he swayed even nearer, Niya did not move. When his breath warmed her neck, she managed to step back slightly, but not far enough to keep his lips from grazing her jaw. She let him kiss the soft spot beneath her chin, and then sweep his lips across her cheek to settle on her mouth. Unable to stop herself, Niya pressed the tip of her tongue to his and then parted her lips to accept him, silently exploding with the release of tension that had been building inside her for weeks.

Never had she imagined that a simple kiss could be so charged full of light, energy and passion. Her desire for it to continue welled quickly inside her body. Soon every inch of her was tingling, her breasts were pinned against Astin's chest and she could feel his heart beating under his shirt. She slipped her arms around his waist and pulled him flush against her.

This is wrong. Granger deserves better, she silently castigated, hating herself for this betrayal. However, this was nothing more than a goodbye between friends, wasn't it? Astin knew that tomorrow, she would walk out of his life forever.

During the long days and nights that they had spent together she had known this moment would come, but had never dreamed that she would respond so easily to his touch. Astin was difficult to resist, with his gentlemanly charm, lively brown eyes, and handsomely rugged face. He was youthful and tender. Wealthy and charitable. Stable, honest, and trustworthy. He wanted her, and for a brief moment, Niya let herself want him.

The kiss took its time playing out, and he continued to hold her afterward, filling her with guilt for remaining in his arms.

She placed her head on his shoulder, exhausted with desire, drained of the energy required to pull away.

"I wish you well, Niya," Astin whispered, his lips against her hair. "My only regret is that I didn't act on my feelings for you when we first met, and that I didn't pursue you with a vengeance earlier. I want you to be my wife, and I'd marry you in a heartbeat if your situation ever changes. If that should ever happen, I hope to God that you'll let me know."

Niya leaned back to look up at Astin, but had no words for him, only a deep, disturbing awareness that she would do exactly that.

The charity fund-raiser was a runaway success that raised a quarter of a million dollars for the museum and was an exhilarating experience that made Niya feel content with her decision to remain in Nevada. The extra work, the delay in her departure for London, even the risk she had taken of upsetting Granger had been worth it. The crowd had stomped and clapped and hooted their appreciation of her performance, demanding that she return to the stage for five curtain calls, and when it was all over, even Melody was grinning and clapping along with the audience, stunning Niya, who had never seen a smile on the dour woman's face.

Niya spent the next day packing and making the rounds of the hotel staff to thank them for such a wonderful stay, and that evening she had dinner with Astin in the privacy of his penthouse suite atop the hotel.

After the meal, during which they talked only about the fund-raiser and self-consciously avoided personal matters, they went, with brandy snifters in hand, out onto the balcony to sit and gaze at the dark purple mountainscape spread out before them.

Astin spoke first. "Delay your marriage to Granger until after the New Year."

Startled, Niya gripped the stem of her glass so hard she worried it might break. "Why?" she managed. "What good would that do?"

"It would give us time to see where our feelings might lead us."

"Not a good idea," she murmured, shaking her head.

"Can I visit you in New York when you return from London?"

"Of course not," she whispered. "There would be no point."

"I won't give up so easily," he told her. "Could you at least please promise to call me as soon as you arrive in New York? Just so I'll know that you arrived home safely."

"Yes," Niya agreed, willing to do that much for him.

Astin set down his glass, took Niya's from her, and then anchored both of his hands on her shoulders. After a long moment of silence while he studied her face, he dropped his chin and bent to kiss her—gently, yet urgently; passionately, yet tender.

When he pulled back, Niya touched his cheek with the palm of her hand, rose, and then left his apartment without ever looking back.

On the plane to New York, Niya studied Granger's engagement ring, knowing she would marry him, even though her heart raced whenever she thought of Astin, even though she could still feel the press of his lips on hers and the blissful touch of his hands in her hair during their brief encounter in the desert.

Chapter 44

There was so much to do that Niya was unsure of where to start. A month's worth of mail, which her New York apartment building manager had held for her, was now piled on the kitchen table, awaiting her attention. A phone call to the answering service that Granger had hired to screen her calls had resulted in a list of messages that needed to be returned. After sorting through the mess, Niya decided that the only ones that she would deal with for now were those from Contessa, Stephanos, and Astin, who had already called twice.

She had shopping and packing to do before leaving for London, and had not yet made her plane reservation. She could not find her passport, which she was sure she had put in the middle drawer of her desk, and she needed to schedule an appointment to get her hair cut before meeting Granger in London. He'd be horrified to see how long she had let it grow.

Niya muted the television that was sitting on the bar between the kitchen and the breakfast area, and with a steaming cup of *café con leche* nearby, began sifting through the pile of mail, most of which was junk. However, one envelope caught her eye right away. It was from the Cuban Immigrant Assistance League in Miami. Quickly, she slit the seal with her letter opener and glanced at the letterhead. It was from Paige Moore. Her heart pounding, Niya began to read.

July 22, 2006

Dear Ms. Londres:
Good news. I have recently received confirmation from the authorities in Havana that your mother, Olivia Londres, was freed from Manto Negro Prison for Women on June 20, 2006. I am happy that her release was granted and am certain that Senator Thorpe's interest in her case was instrumental in speeding up the process. All that I can tell you is that your mother's prison sentence has been satisfactorily completed and that she returned to Havana. I did learn that her home had been confiscated by the government, so I don't know where she is living now. If I am able to secure additional information, I will inform you.

I hope that all is well with you and I send my congratulations for your success in the theater. We've all read about your stunning performance in Morning Stars *in the Cuban-American News and are very proud to say we know you.*

Regards,
Paige Moore

Niya crushed the letter to her chest and let out a scream of delight. "Mama is free!" she shouted into the empty apartment as she jumped up and spun around. "Finally. She's free." Eagerly, Niya ran and snatched up the phone and direct-dialed the number to Granger's London hotel, praying that he would be in. He was.

"Niya. I'm so glad you called. You're back in New York, then?" he started right in.

"Yes, yes," Niya replied, catching her breath, wiping tears of joy from her eyes. "And guess what was here?"

"What?" he asked.

"A letter from the Cuban Immigrant Assistance League in Miami. Mama is out of prison. Granger! Mama is free." There was a beat while Niya let Granger digest the news. "But her apartment was confiscated while she was in prison, so no one knows where she is. Granger, couldn't Senator Thorpe help me find her? Maybe even help her leave Cuba?"

"Whoa," Granger stopped Niya. "That's great news . . . your mother being out of prison, and all, but don't go getting ahead of yourself. It's not easy to leave Cuba."

"What do you mean? I got away, didn't I?"

"And your brother died in the process, remember?"

"That may be true, but it can be done. Why can't you ask your senator friend to get his people to help Mama find a way to escape?"

"I wouldn't *even* ask him for a favor like that," Granger stated flatly.

"What harm can there be in talking to him about it?"

"It doesn't work that way, Niya. You should be content to know that Senator Thorpe helped your mother get out of prison. Now she can go on with her life."

"But I want her here in New York with me."

"Well, I don't think . . . even if it were possible, that it would be such a good idea," Granger objected.

"What did you say?"

"I . . . I think, at her age, it would be too risky, and too difficult an adjustment if she came here. Now, she's back among people she knows, in a familiar environment that she is accustomed to. Beside, once we're married, we'll be traveling a lot, maybe living in Europe for a long stretch if the play gets picked up by some theaters over here. Your mother would be left alone in New York . . . and that would be cruel. She's better off remaining in Cuba."

"I can't believe you just said that. My brother is, most likely, dead. I'm the only living relative my mother has now. Why shouldn't I do everything in my power for us to be together?"

"Because I don't think it'd be a wise thing to do," Granger calmly answered.

"Let me be the judge of that," Niya threw back.

"Listen. I don't want to argue. I'm just being realistic," Granger began, his tone softer and a bit more contrite. "For now, let's let it drop. When you get here, we'll talk it through and see what's realistic. Okay?"

"Fine," Niya relented, feeling totally deflated.

"So, what time does your flight get in tomorrow?"

"I've been so busy, I haven't booked it yet," she admitted, suddenly in no hurry to face Granger.

"What? That's crazy. I'll take care of it on this end," Granger decided, going on to tell her which flight he planned to book her on and which seat he'd try to get for her.

As Niya listened to Granger plan her trip, a slow boil bubbled up inside. He was so damn efficient, when it came to arranging her life, but not at all concerned about what she really needed: her mother. All of her joy over her mother's freedom evaporated as he rattled on. She knew that Granger could be possessive and overly protective of her, but why did he have to micro-manage her every move, as if she were a child? Was he that insecure about their love?

Surely not, Niya thought, tapping her pen on the letter from Paige.

"You know what, Granger?" she interrupted. "I'm not flying out tomorrow."

"You have to," he decided.

"Well, I'm not," she tossed back. "I have to do some checking on my mother's situation . . . make some phone calls. See if there is any way I can contact her."

"Niya," Granger began in a low, serious tone. "You're not talking sense, nor are you taking this play seriously. It's your first musical, and even though you have the script, and say you have been rehearsing the routines, it's not enough. Not being here has already caused serious production delays, and cost us a lot of money, too. Ricky is nervous about the actors, the musicians, the budget, and he's making noise about pulling out of the partnership, and frankly I wouldn't blame him if he did. If you don't show up tomorrow, we may as well shut down production and send everybody home."

"Oh, don't be so dramatic, Granger. I'll be there! But I can't leave tomorrow. I've got too much on my mind. I just need a few days. I'll call you tomorrow evening."

After a curt goodbye, Granger hung up, leaving Niya worried about his reaction, fully aware that she ought to fly out tomorrow. But she couldn't. Not until she talked to Paige Moore.

And why was Granger being so selfish? He could pick up the phone and make a call to any one of his powerful friends and possibly assist her mother. Who knew what the powerful official might be able to accomplish? Granger was always telling her that he knew best. He wanted her to forget about Lorenzo, to consider her brother dead, and she'd tried to do as he asked. But what if he was wrong?

The realization that Granger did not care about what happened to her family made Niya's stomach tighten, and she knew there was only one thing to do: move forward without his knowledge. She wasn't his wife . . . not yet. He didn't own her. If she wanted to establish communication with her mother, who was he to interfere?

Though her hand was shaking, she managed to press the numbers at the top of the letter into the handset of her phone, and immediately asked for Paige Moore. After a short pause, she was buzzed through. The two women exchanged a few pleasantries, and then Niya got right to the purpose of her call.

"Paige, can you help my mother get out of Cuba?"

"That's a very tall order," Paige replied. "As a convicted political dissident she'd have trouble traveling to the other side of the island, let alone escape. I'm certain her movements are watched and restricted. It would not be wise for her to associate with anyone planning an escape."

"So, it's impossible?" Niya asked, defeat in her voice.

Paige paused. "Nothing is impossible. You know how often a boat full of Cuban refugees enters the waters off the Florida coast. Dangerous, complicated, and risky, yes. But not impossible."

"What about her living arrangements? You said in your letter that her apartment has been confiscated by the government. How can I find her? Write to her? Help her? I want to send money," Niya pressed, thinking that if she could at least manage to get much-coveted American dollars into her mother's hands, she'd have funds to negotiate an escape if the opportunity ever arose.

"Umm. I *could* try to find her," Paige began.

"What do I need to do?" Niya eagerly asked.

"Nothing. I've been granted permission to join an official, government-sanctioned task force traveling to Havana next month—with a U.S. congressman, the Mexican Minister of Culture, and several Florida educators. Their goal is to explore the possibility of establishing academic and cultural exchanges between the three countries. I've been asked to serve as an interpreter. If I am able to move about, I might find your mother, or at least get a current address for her."

"If I wire some money to you, will you take it with you? Give it to my mother?"

"I can't promise anything," Paige replied.

"I understand that, Paige. But I'll send it today."

"Niya, I have to be careful and you need to be patient. Things like this take time."

"I don't care how long it takes. Do whatever you can while you're there," Niya replied, delighted that Paige was at least willing to try.

The thought that one day soon she might be able to communicate freely with her mother gave Niya a renewed sense of hope. Granger wouldn't like the fact that she had initiated this plan behind his back, but why did he need to know? Niya would do anything in the world to make life easier for the woman who had loved her enough to risk prison in order to give her a chance at life in America.

If Granger loved me, he'd understand, Niya brooded.

While her mind was on Paige's trip to Cuba, she thought again of her missing passport, and searched her desk one more time. It simply wasn't there. She had taken it to Granger's apartment when they first began planning their trip to London. Had she left it there?"

"The safe," she decided, recalling his offer to hold onto her newly acquired document until it was time to leave for London.

After a short taxi ride to his apartment, she entered his study and searched his Rolodex where he had shown her he kept the combination. Code in hand, she went into the dining room, swung back the painting of Frida Kahlo and began turning the knob on the lock, glad that Granger trusted her enough to let her have access to his safe. He knew she would never violate that trust by poking around in his private papers, and he was right. All she wanted was to find her passport and prayed it was inside.

Once the safe was open, she quickly spied her passport, which was right at the front, exactly where she knew he would have placed it and, smiling with relief, took it out and tucked it into her purse.

After closing the safe, she left the apartment, hailed a taxi and gave the driver the address for Miracle Mile Club, anxious to see Contessa and tell her friend goodbye before leaving for London.

While the taxi crawled through traffic, Niya thought about Astin. Though she had been back in New York less than twenty-four hours, he had already phoned her twice, and she had been happy to hear his voice. The fact that she had chatted so easily with him, and looked forward to speaking with him again was disturbing.

"I am totally smitten with you and have no shame about admitting it," he had told her the last time they talked. "I love you, Niya. I wish you would let me give you a life filled with romance and excitement, if only you'd let me in."

"Are you trying to make yourself irresistible?" Niya had playfully bantered back, unsure of what else to do.

"I am," Astin confessed. "And I don't plan to let up on the charm until you agree to give me a chance."

"A chance to do what?" Niya had asked, feigning innocence.

"The chance to prove that you'd be much happier married to me than to Granger Cooper."

Her heart had stopped, and she had needed to draw in a long breath before continuing. "Is that so?" Niya had teased, though certain that Astin was deadly serious. A mental image of life as Mrs. Astin Spence flitted through her mind: a carefree, vivacious journey filled with music, dancing, great adventures, easy conversation and wonderful food. However, settling down in Nevada with Astin, was not in her future: Her future belonged to Granger.

Niya timed her arrival at Miracle Mile just right. Contessa was about to take her second coffee break of the morning when Niya walked through the door.

"I thought you had already left for London," Contessa said as the two women walked toward the back of the club and sought privacy in Niya's old dressing room, which was empty and not very different from the way she had left it long ago.

"No, but I'll be leaving in a few days. I stayed in Nevada longer than I planned, and now I've got to put a rush on everything to get out of here. But I had to see you . . . tell you about my trip to the desert," Niya started, filling Contessa in on her stay at Diamond Marsh Resort.

"Please stop," Contessa said after hearing all the details of her friend's luxury getaway, complete with a blow by blow account of her confrontation with Melody. She held out a hand, palm toward Niya. "Stop, girl, I can't take it anymore. First of all, you should have kicked that bitch's ass, and then taken off with Astin, if only for one night. What the hell? Why not have one last fling before walking down the aisle? You say he's fine, he's loaded, he's divorced, and he's black? Girl, if you don't want him, I'll sure take him off your hands."

Niya laughed and shook her head. "If only it had been that easy. I didn't want to raise his expectations and then cause a big messy situation when I left. I performed at his charity benefit and raised a ton of money. That was all I was supposed to do. And, yes, you're right. Astin is a wonderful, sensitive, caring man, and . . . just between you and me . . . and don't you ever repeat this," Niya whispered. "If I had been free . . . not engaged to Granger . . . I might have let Astin romance me. He's so handsome, easygoing . . . so likeable . . ."

"Don't you mean loveable?" Contessa cut in. She crossed her long legs, folded her arms across her chest and sat back on the sofa, eyes narrowed at Niya. "You can't fool me, Niya. I can see it in your face. That guy, Astin, got to you." Then she leaned forward, pointing one finger. "Oh. And while we're on the subject of men, you had a call from a Mr. Grant in Miami. Sounded kinda cute, but he hung up on me. He didn't leave a message."

The smile on Niya's face quickly vanished and she curled both hands into fists. "What? Mr. Grant? You're sure?"

"Yeah, I wrote it down in the log book. Along with the number he called from. Who is he? Another one of your mystery men?"

"The only Mr. Grant I know in Miami is dead . . . Tremont's grandfather."

"Oh. Well. I doubt it was *that* Mr. Grant, then."

"Can I see the phone number?" Niya asked.

Nodding, Contessa grabbed the phone off the dressing table and dialed the front desk. "Johnnie. Look in my log book for July for a notation for Niya about a Mr. Grant." She placed one hand over the mouthpiece of the phone while she pointed to a pen and notepad, which Niya quickly handed to her.

"Yeah, that's it," Contessa murmured, scribbling down the number. She hung up and handed the piece of paper to Niya. "Look familiar?"

Niya nodded. "This is the phone number to G-Daddy's house." She stared at Contessa, but remained silent, as if afraid to put the pieces together by verbalizing them.

However, Contessa did it for her. "If Mr. Grant is dead, who would be using his name and calling from his house?" she asked Niya, who did not respond. "Tremont?" Contessa prompted, scooting to the edge of the sofa, zeroing in on Niya's blank expression. "You think Tremont is out of prison and looking for you?"

Slowly, Niya nodded, yes, and then let the air that she had been holding in her lungs escape in a long whoosh. "So it seems," she finally said.

"You gonna call him? See what he wants?" Contessa pressed, her face lit with interest.

"Of course not!" Niya threw back, trying to keep control while every nerve in her body was alive with fear. "I don't want to talk to him!" She stood and walked to the far side of the dressing room, fingertips to her lips in thought.

Contessa stood, too, and moved very close to Niya, making sure she got her friend's full attention. "Why not? You know you still love the guy!"

"No, I don't!" Niya let loose, nearly shouting, and then lowering her voice, told Contessa, "I don't love Tremont Henderson and I never want to see him or talk to him again."

"Yes you do, and you will, too. Mark my words, you will."

"That's crazy. I'm going to marry Granger. I love him."

In a knowing manner, Contessa clucked her tongue and murmured her understanding. "Yes, you probably do love Granger, but you're not *in* love with him. Not like you were in love with Tremont."

"That's a lot of double talk."

"No it's not, it's the truth, though you won't admit it. Tell me again that you don't love Tremont and let me look in your eyes while you say it!"

"Okay!" Niya shouted back. "I admit it . . . I love Tremont. I'll always love him. But he's part of my past and we don't have any reason to re-connect."

"You could, if you'd let yourself feel what you used to feel for him."

"Contessa, I can't deal with this right now."

"I think you'd better deal with it," Contessa said, sounding serious. "There's Granger, ready to walk down the aisle. And Astin, out there in Nevada itching to romance you. And now Tremont, is looking for you. Either you're a very lucky girl, or you're headed for a train wreck, and you've got some serious decisions to make."

"Stop it, Contessa. Let it go. I've got to run," Niya decided, snatching her purse off the dressing table. She gave Contessa a quick, hard hug. "Not a word of any of this to anyone, you hear?"

Contessa nodded.

"Good. I've got tons of errands to finish. See you when I get back from London."

"Right," Contessa said, smugly. "Be safe, be careful, and tell your *fiancé,* Granger, I said hello."

Before Niya had even flagged down a taxi, Contessa was punching in the number she had scribbled on the notepad. "Tremont Henderson, please," she stated in a very professional manner.

"This is Tremont."

"This is Contessa Torino, the receptionist at Miracle Mile Club in New York." She paused long enough to allow him time to make the connection.

"Oh, right," he drew out the words, sounding a bit confused. "I spoke to you last month . . . but how did you get *my* name?"

Ignoring his question, Contessa plunged ahead. "You told me that you were looking for Niya Londres?"

"Yes. And you said she was in London."

"Well, she's in New York now and if you want to see her, I suggest you get your butt on the first plane out of Miami, because she's leaving the country in a few days."

"But how do you know . . ."

"When you get here," Contessa blurted out, "call me at the club. I'll tell you where to go."

Chapter 45

"She's not coming tomorrow," Granger told Ricky as soon as he slipped into a seat in the darkened theater. They were sitting at the back of the auditorium while the director was rehearsing a scene.

"Not coming tomorrow?" Ricky snapped. "When then?"

"In a few days," Granger said. "Don't worry. Everything is going to be fine."

"Don't worry? That's not good enough," Ricky shot back, furious. "What's the problem, Granger? You're the one who approached me about forming a partnership to produce my play, and I went into this project to make money. Now it sounds like Niya's flaking out."

"We'll make money, I always do. And Niya is not flaking out."

"She'd better get her ass over here. I'm in deep-shit debt over this, and I don't have a trust fund to fall back on, like you do."

Granger looked at Ricky with little emotion. "You'll get paid when the production makes money."

"Or not," Ricky tossed back. He stood and hurriedly gathered up his bound script, notepads, and his bulky attaché case from one of the empty theater seats, preparing to leave. "That's easy for you to say, Granger. You don't have everything on the line. I do! If Niya is not here by the day after tomorrow, I'm going home. Count me out of this project. I'll take back the rights to the script, and if this play does not come off, you *are* going to pay me back."

When Ricky arrived at his hotel room, he was shaking with rage. How the fuck did he get into such a mess? But more importantly how was he going to get out? The money he had invested in the partnership had been money partly obtained from the sale of his AT&T stock, and the balance had come from one of his father's many safety deposit boxes, from which Ricky had taken a bundle of cash and some jewelry he had pawned.

Ricky had been given access to his father's many safety deposit boxes long ago in case something nasty happened to his mob-connected, twice-widowed parent. Using his father's cash and jewelry for his own purposes had been risky, and Ricky was going to be in one hell of a situation if he didn't return everything before his father discovered it was missing. Robert Monroe was not the kind of father who would legally prosecute his only son for theft; he was the kind of father who would have him killed.

Ricky snapped open a can of beer from the minibar and downed it in three gulps before noticing that the red message light was blinking on his phone. He punched in the retrieval code and grimaced as he listened—it was from Laurie, the little girl he'd been screwing since his arrival in London, and she was eager to know if he wanted to get together with her that evening.

Not hardly, Ricky thought, not in the mood for fooling around. He had serious thinking to do.

And then he froze. Laurie. The answer to his problem.

With the approval of his probation officer, Tremont quickly made arrangements to leave Miami and fly to New York. He arrived at dusk, secured Niya's address from Contessa, and went to the deli across the street from Niya's apartment building where he sat for an hour and drank three cups of coffee while gathering his courage to face her.

He felt sick with apprehension. Why had he even come to New York? And why should Niya want to talk to him? Just because her gutsy girlfriend thought she ought to? He knew it was mean of him to show up like this and interfere with Niya's new, sophisticated life. But he *had* to see her. He *had* to hear her say that she didn't love him anymore, and that her future husband was the only man who could make her happy.

Tremont was hopeful, but not optimistic, about the outcome of this visit. After all, he had deliberately hurt Niya in hopes of forcing her to forget him. He had not wanted her to waste a single minute of her life worrying about him, visiting him in prison, and sitting around waiting for him while the world passed her by. He had wanted her to go out into the world and grab all the happiness that she deserved . . . and she had done exactly that. How dare he show up unannounced and intrude on the world she had struggled to create?

"Because I have to tell her how sorry I am, and that I will always love her," he whispered, looking over at the building where she lived. He scanned the tiny windows, wondering which ones belonged to her apartment, trying to imagine what she was doing.

"Anything else I can get for you?" the waitress asked, interrupting Tremont's thoughts. She placed a tray with the check on the table.

He dug into his wallet and removed a five dollar bill, which he placed on the small plastic tray. "No. And keep the change."

Swallowing back his anxiety, he left the deli, crossed the street and entered the front door to Niya's building. After locating her buzzer, he pressed his thumb to it, and closed his eyes. When she answered, he sucked down a sharp breath at hearing her familiar, lilting voice again. She sounded just as he remembered, and the memory initiated a current of desire that shot through him like an electric charge and momentarily rocked him back on his heels.

"Yes? Hello?" she repeated into the intercom. "Who is it?"

Tremont licked his lips and lifted his chin. "Tremont," he boldly stated. "Niya, it's Tremont Henderson. Will you see me?" Only silence came back to him over the intercom. "I know this is a shock, and I should have called . . ."

"I'm not shocked," Niya finally spoke. "I guess I've been expecting this. Please. Come up. Sixth floor, number 633."

Though she had told Tremont she was not surprised that he had rung her doorbell, in fact she was in shock that he had arrived so soon. Only one person in New York knew about her connection to Tremont!

"Contessa?" she prompted after Tremont had entered her apartment and was sitting stiffly on a chair across from her in the living room.

He nodded. "Yes. Don't be angry with her. I'm glad she contacted me."

"The sneaky busybody!" Niya commented, trying to lighten the mood while assessing Tremont, who appeared tense, thin, and more mature than when she'd last seen him, but still as handsome as she remembered. However, there was a hollow sadness in his eyes that made her want to go to him, hold him in her arms, and tell him that she understood the misery he had suffered.

"You have a good friend in Contessa," Tremont commented.

Niya nodded. "No one else could have arranged this." *And no one else understands how much I needed to see you, Tremont,* she thought, still struggling with the tangle of emotions that had been with her since her conversation with Contessa the day before. She did not regret admitting to Contessa that she still loved Tremont; saying the words had finally forced her to face the realization that what they had had was a once in a lifetime kind of love. She still missed him, thought about him much too often, and sometimes even craved his touch late at night when she was alone and memories of the past crept into her mind and took over. However, admitting her feelings to Contessa had been one thing, telling Tremont how she felt about him was out of the question. They had already had their chance at love, and lost, and she never wanted to go through that kind of hell again.

"So, how are you, really?" Niya asked, determined to carry on as normal a conversation as possible.

Leaning forward, hands dangling between his knees, Tremont let a slow one-sided smile touch his lips. "Learning to live on the outside again. Getting by."

"So, you're living at G-Daddy's house?"

"Yep. And it's exactly as it was when he was alive. I think of him every day."

"I think of him often, too. What Ace and Sandi Lee did to him was such a horrible thing. I wonder if the police ever found her."

"Sandi Lee was not the mastermind behind G-Daddy's kidnapping," Tremont told Niya.

"How would you know?" Niya warily responded.

"Sandi Lee wrote me a long letter explaining what had happened. She did not want to go along with Ace. I think . . ."

"So, you accepted *her* mail and not mine?" Niya interrupted sarcastically, unable to help herself.

However, Tremont did not react, but plunged ahead. "Sandi Lee explained how Ace forced her to ride in the van to keep G-Daddy quiet and how she begged with him to let my grandfather go. Unable to get him to listen to her, she bailed out of the van when it stopped in front of the bus station and got on a bus and fled out of town."

"You believe her?"

"Yes, I do. And I don't hold any grudges against her. She was a victim, too."

"Where is she now?"

"I don't know. The letter was postmarked from some small town in California, but there wasn't any return address on the envelope."

"If she had listened to me, she never would have gotten mixed up with Ace's awful plot to extort money from you," Niya stated.

"And if I had listened to you, I might not have gone to prison," Tremont finished.

Tensing, Niya decided not to touch that subject, and asked instead, "Are you performing in Miami?"

"No. I'm just glad to be out of prison, to have a place to live, a little cash, and a few friends." He chuckled under his breath. "Dejen has become a real fixture at the house, and he's driving me crazy with his mother-hen act."

"I'm glad to hear that you and Dejen are still friends. You shouldn't be alone right now," Niya said.

"Maybe . . . but I wish you were at the house with me instead of Dejen," Tremont blurted out, suddenly rising. He crossed the room and sat down beside Niya. "Niya, I'm really sorry about the way I acted . . . I didn't know what else to do. I had to push you away, but I hate myself for destroying what we had. At the time, I was scared, I was really scared, and I didn't think I had a choice."

"But, you did," she whispered shifting to focus on him, all of the pain that had built up inside her over the years welling up and ready to spill out. "We could have gotten married before you went to prison. We could have worked it out, stuck together and held onto our love. Other married couples survive more than what was thrown at us and wind up closer than before. Why didn't you trust me, Tremont? Why didn't you want to try? You didn't even care! You didn't love me enough. You only wanted to protect *your* feelings! Well, what about mine?"

"That's not true," Tremont replied, an edge of desperation sharpening his words. "I didn't want you to wind up hating me. I knew you'd eventually resent me for ruining the best years of your life. If I had married you and then gone off to prison, as my wife, you would have been bound to me in a selfish, pain-filled relationship that revolved around me and my prison term. Month after month, year after year, you'd have trudged faithfully up to the prison to see me, and pretty soon you'd have gotten tired of the whole damn business. It would have slowly broken you down and turned you into a shell of yourself. I couldn't accept being stuck in a cell while you spent your life on the outside waiting for the next visiting day, consumed with my situation. Did I want to marry you before I entered prison? Hell, yes, I did. And I still do. I'd marry you tomorrow if you'd have me, Niya. All you'd have to do is say the word."

"That would be impossible, after what you put me through."

"Well, I can't say I'd have done anything differently," Tremont shot back. "All I can say is . . . I love you now . . . more than I did on the day we said goodbye. I hope you believe me. Do you?"

Niya looked away, pained, and then murmured, "Believe you? I've tried to convince myself that you *never* loved me, but even if you did, I hated the way you showed it. Shutting me out was a hurtful thing to do, and you put me in my own kind of hell, you know?"

"Do you hate me?" Tremont asked.

"Hate you? No."

"Is there any way for me to make up for the pain I caused?"

Tears welled in Niya's eyes as she took one of his hands in hers and touched each finger softly. "Yes, there is," she told him. "Leave here and forget about me." Looking up, she captured his eyes with hers. "In a few months I'm going to marry Granger Cooper, and I plan to have a good, decent life with him. Promise me, Tremont, that you won't interfere. If you love me as much as you say, then let me go. We can't get back what we lost."

Tremont grimaced and looked away, and then he turned back and kissed Niya fiercely on the lips, as if filling himself up with her, branding her presence on his soul. Pulling back, he gently kissed both of her tear-stained cheeks, on the middle of her forehead, and then whispered. "You have my word. I won't interfere."

Niya held his face between her hands, drinking in every angle and plane and curve of his features as if trying to memorize them. Then, she turned him loose, stood, and went to the door. Holding it open, she told Tremont, "I *am* glad you came. Really, I am."

He slipped past her without a word and she closed the door, but remained there, listening to his footsteps as he walked down the corridor. When the elevator bell dinged and the doors clattered shut, she gasped and covered her mouth with a fist.

Hurrying to the window overlooking the street, she stared down at the pavement and waited for him to emerge from the building. When she saw him, she leaned heavily against the sill, not taking her tear-filled eyes off of him until he disappeared into the entrance to the subway station on the corner.

Chapter 46

Niya emerged from Customs at Heathrow International Airport and scanned the waiting area for Granger. When she saw him, she hurried over, genuinely relieved and happy that he had come to meet her.

During the seven hour flight from New York, she had worried that he might still be angry at her, that he might simply send a car to pick her up, and be moody and irritable when they met. But, no. There he was, smiling, and holding a small bouquet of flowers, sending her heart racing as it always did when her eyes locked with his.

They embraced and held onto each other for a long moment. Then Niya kissed Granger long and hard. Much too passionately for a public welcome, but she didn't care if the world was watching. It seemed forever since she had felt Granger's arms around her, his lips on hers, his calming strength flowing into her. All their petty arguments vanished as soon as they met and Niya was filled with a sense of pride that she had done the right thing and honored her commitment to Granger, and to Ricky.

"Your hair is a bit too long," Granger commented as they hurried across the crowded airport and out to their waiting car.

"Didn't have time to get it cut," she told him, swallowing her lie. She liked it long and had decided to leave it that way.

"Well, you can get it cut at the hotel salon," Granger tossed back. They got into the car and settled down. "Ricky is about to implode," he continued. "You only have three weeks of rehearsal until opening night, and believe me, you're going to have to work damn hard. You can't let me . . . us down, Niya. You've got to give it your all."

"I will. I promise," she told Granger, sinking back against the seat next to him, pushing everything out of her mind except the task that lay ahead.

Rehearsals for *Perfectly* continued nonstop for the next fifteen days, with Niya giving one-hundred and ten percent of herself to the role of a bored housewife who gets involved with a perfect stranger, a salesman who appears at her door and turns her life upside down. The local actors were easy to work with and she had her lines completely memorized after the first run-through. The troupe meshed immediately and Niya loved being surrounded by wonderfully talented young people who filled her days with laughter and excitement. She was completely at home in her role, which she embraced with great enthusiasm, thankful that her monthlong rest in Nevada had prepared her for the taxing workload.

In addition to the heavy rehearsal schedule, she did media interviews, attended parties hosted by local theater devotees, and appeared on three television shows. And by the time opening night rolled around, both Granger and Ricky were totally convinced that they had a hit on their hands.

Unfortunately, Mother Nature had other plans.

A violent rainstorm swept into London on opening night and stalled over the city, filling the streets with a wild rushing stream of water that forced faithful theatergoers to stay at home. Shops flooded, roofs collapsed, and the streets remained rivers of water day and night.

Inside, the Royal Tower Theatre was dry, and the curtain went up on schedule. Niya and her fellow actors carried on courageously, performing to a house that was less than half-filled. Though discouraged by the small number of people in the audience, Niya was proud and pleased with the cast's opening night performance.

Granger and Ricky huddled in their office backstage and crunched the box office numbers, praying that the bad weather would vanish in time to make up for their loss.

It didn't. The next evening's take was worse, and by the start of the second week they were in deep trouble. Water continued to pour from the sky as if a dam in the heavens had been breached, and the weeks dragged on in a dreary succession of cloudy days. The nights were simply, totally, mired in mud.

The actors struggled to keep their spirits up and carry on with the show but in time, their efforts proved to be futile. With no box office relief, Granger was forced to close down the performance three days ahead of schedule and let everybody go.

Stunned by his first true theatrical failure, Granger was distraught, moody and impatient to find a way to turn a profit from what was left of his venture. He set aside his glass of wine and focused on Niya, who was sitting across the table from him in the hotel restaurant. They had been discussing ways to salvage something from their disaster.

"I've decided to remain in Europe to try to sell the play to other theater owners here who have expressed an interest," he told Niya. "I'll set up an office in my Paris apartment and work from there. I have plenty of connections to get this play back onto the stage."

"Do you think you can?" Niya asked.

"Sure. It's a good script. Great music. The reviewers loved it. We were simply blindsided by a fluke of bad weather. I may have to stay here for a long time, and put up some of my own money to make a deal, but I will if it's what I have to do."

"Should I stay, too?" Niya wanted to know, ready to do whatever Granger asked of her to make up for the losses they had incurred.

"No. You go on home. Start planning our wedding. Just because the play was not a success does not mean I'm letting you off the hook as far as our wedding goes. I want you to make all the decisions . . . don't worry about consulting with me on the details. Whatever you plan will be fine . . . and don't worry about money, either. There's some cash in the safe . . . you know where the combination is, don't you?"

Niya nodded.

"Well, if you need extra money, use it. And when you get home, will you arrange for my mail to be forwarded to this address?" He opened the small leather-bound notebook he always carried in his breast pocket and wrote down the address and phone number of his Paris apartment.

"Sure, Granger, I'll take care of everything, and as for money . . . I have plenty of money of my own. Besides, the bride is supposed to pay for the wedding, isn't she?"

"Oh, Niya, don't be so damn sensitive, or old-fashioned," Granger mumbled. "I've got more money than I can possibly spend in my lifetime. All I meant was, I'd like to help with expenses."

"Okay, okay. I'm sorry." She leaned across the table and kissed him lightly on the lips. "I'll plan the perfect wedding, one that people will talk about for a long time."

"Good. All I need is the date, the time and the location, and I'll show up in my tuxedo. Sure you're okay with me setting up an office in Paris, and remaining here?"

Niya reached out and accepted his hand. "I'm sure. I'll handle everything, but I hate to leave you with so much to do. What about Ricky, is he going to work with you?"

Granger gave up a snort of a laugh, wrinkling his forehead. "Ricky? No. I'm sure he's already back in New York by now. He had to go home and deal with his father, from whom I now understand he stole a chunk of cash."

"For his share of your partnership?"

Granger slowly nodded, "Sadly, yes."

"Oh, my God. That's awful."

"Right," Granger replied. "Ricky's very angry at me . . . and he got pretty damn snippy about the money situation, too. He had the nerve to demand that I refund fifty percent of his investment. Where the hell does he get off asking me for a deal like that? I was clear when we started talking about a partnership that nothing was guaranteed. An investor must be able to bear a loss, if that's what comes down. I thought he understood. He also told me that he'd sold his AT&T stock to get his share of the money, and I believed him. Now he's calling me a crook and a liar."

"God, I hate what this has done to you two . . ." Niya began.

"Don't worry, we'll make up. We always do. Ricky and I have been friends a long time. This isn't going to change things and he's still going to be my best man at our wedding." Granger took another sip of wine. "However, if he pesters you over this money thing while I'm here, call me at once. I'll deal with him." After a beat, he added, "You know, I think it might be best if you didn't spend too much time with Ricky, anyway. Let him cool off, okay?"

"Fine," Niya promised, realizing that she had never seen Granger quite so uneasy.

Chapter 47

From JFK Airport, Niya went directly to Granger's apartment to take care of the things he had asked her to do, and to put her passport back into his safe. Once she had spoken to Alfred, the doorman, and watered Granger's numerous plants, she opened the safe and tucked her passport safely beneath a stack of what looked like charcoal sketches that had been haphazardly tossed inside. She decided to take a peek at Granger's work, thinking this would not betray his trust. She wasn't digging around in his financial documents.

She pulled one out and murmured in surprise. It was very well done. She looked at another, then two more, surprised that each sketch was of a young woman's face.

"And he told me that he had never sketched another woman's portrait before mine. What a lot of bull," she murmured, trying to shake off her irritation, knowing that he most likely had been trying to impress her. "You didn't have to lie," she grumbled, shoving the sketches back inside, suddenly wondering what else Granger might have lied to her about.

She boldly grabbed another packet of papers and rifled through them in anger, not looking for anything specific. When a yellowed funeral program fluttered to the floor, she bent to pick it up, and then scrutinized the face of the woman on the front. She was elegant, aristocratic looking, but her eyes were fierce and her mouth hard. Mercedes Sutton Cooper, it read. Funeral Service 2 P.M. May 23, 2004, at Weselton's Funeral Home, Long Island, NY. She quickly read through the obituary, her hands shaking as she gripped the program.

"Survived by her only son, Granger Cooper," Niya whispered. "His mother died in 2004? The same year that I met him?" Niya's throat closed in confusion. What did this mean? Why had Granger lied to her? He said his mother died when he was a teenager.

She had never doubted Granger's word about anything before, and now it was clear that he had lied to her. Why had she been so quick to trust him? She bit her lip, worried.

She had believed in Tremont's word too. He had vowed to love her forever, and then he'd shut her out of his life for his own selfish reasons. Even Astin had remained silent about his relationship with Melody until he no longer had been able to hide the truth.

Each man's lack of confidence in her was disturbing. She would have laughed, and even been flattered if Granger had confessed that he loved making sketches of the beautiful women he had known. And why lie about his mother?

She would have married Tremont and stuck by him during his incarceration, if he had not pushed her away. And Astin? She would have admired him more if he had come clean with her right away about his and Melody's past rather than let Niya stand by and watch while that woman manipulated him.

Why are men so damn headstrong and difficult to understand? she questioned, as a quiet sadness crept over her. Could anyone ever *really* know a person? she wondered, beginning to doubt her own judgment in men.

Feeling restless and unsettled, Niya left Granger's apartment and headed home. *All a woman wants is a man she can trust. A man who is willing to open up his heart and let his woman see him for who he truly is,* she fretted as the taxi slipped through traffic. *What else don't I know about Granger? Or*

Astin, or Tremont, for that matter? Each man told me that he loves me, and wants me to be his wife, but what do I truly know about them?

Looking out the window, she watched the throng of strangers hurrying along the sidewalk, bundled up against the chilly winds that were swooping down from the north in a signal of winter's fast approach.

What a strange turn of events—to have three different men vying for my love. And why is this happening to me? she wondered. Was this a sign that she needed to slow down? Take a closer look at Granger, maybe cut Tremont some slack, or even stop resisting Astin's campaign to win her heart?

Oh, God, what do I really want to do? she silently asked herself. *And how can I plan a wedding with all of this on my mind?*

The next day, instead of calling Simply Sweets and Such, to start talking wedding cakes and reception menus, she telephoned Bert Kline, the founding partner of Berger, Berger, and Kline Private Investigators, whom she had met at Miracle Mile while he had been working a divorce case for a wealthy client. He was glad to hear from her and assured Niya that he'd put a rush on her request and, though it would be costly, he would get her all the information she asked for.

Chapter 48

Three weeks later

A soft mist had begun to fall, coating the asphalt pavement of the dark alley behind Club Scandalous with a glistening sheen of water. It was not really rain, nor was it bothersome enough to force the knot of fans who were waiting at the private club's back door to leave. Some of them opened big black umbrellas to hold high above the crowd, while others pulled up the head-coverings of their sweatshirts and hoodies and a few held folded newspapers over their heads to ward off the slow drip of water that was falling from the sky.

Inside her dry, warm car, Sandi Lee flicked on the windshield wipers and watched as the crowd grew larger and more restless with each minute that ticked by. She was listening to "Totally Tricked," Larry's latest release, on her CD player, and his voice was so smooth, sexy, and full of his familiar enticing pull that Sandi Lee found herself squirming around in her seat as her panties grew damp with desire. He was irresistible. She missed the hell out of him, and her entire body ached for his touch. If she concentrated hard enough she could actually feel his thumbs on her nipples, his tongue inside her mouth, and his hardness pumping into her.

She missed him so damn much she wanted to cry, but had no tears left to shed. She'd cried herself out long ago and no longer cared about anything other than grasping every opportunity that arose to catch a glimpse of the man she loved.

Sandi Lee shuddered to recall the last time he had spoken to her, when she had intercepted his dash from the gym on La Cienega to his limo, when she had begged him to get rid of Sarita and take her back. He had laughed at her, told her to get lost, and roughly pushed her aside before ducking into his car, where Sandi Lee had spied Sarita sitting self-righteously with her legs crossed, wearing a skirt three sizes too small.

"The brazen hussy," Sandi Lee cursed under her breath. If it hadn't been for Sarita Hernandez's bold come-on, Sandi Lee would still be with Larry, who needed a girl like herself at his side, and not a stupid little star-struck teenager who was totally out of her league. Larry needed a real woman—one with grit and brass and who knew how to deliver for her man. Sandi Lee knew how things worked in his world, and had always been vigilant about making sure that her man was well taken care of. Sarita couldn't do that for Larry—but he'd find out soon enough.

Now, Sandi Lee opened her purse and examined the small pearl handled .22 revolver that she had bought at a pawnshop on Crenshaw Boulevard. She had a permit to own it, knew how to use it, and had loaded it herself. "You're gonna be sorry you ever dumped me for Sarita," she whispered, just as the CD ended. "You need a woman like me, Larry, and one day you'll thank God that I'm still hanging tough."

Sandi Lee glanced back out the window and noticed that the crowd had begun to press closer to the back door of the club. She also noticed that a knot of tough looking guys, whom she recognized as fans of Larry's rival, Ice Blu, had arrived. They hooted and screamed and made a lot of noise demanding that Larry Lo come out and greet them. As if on cue, Larry burst out the back door, Sarita close behind.

Gathering her courage, Sandi Lee grabbed her purse, stepped out of her car and walked straight toward the smiling couple, a determined set to her jaw. "This is where *I* belong," she muttered, shoving her way to the front of the crowd.

Chapter 49

Niya was startled from a half sleep when her doorbell rang. She sat up quickly, surprised that she had nodded off while watching the news. The last thing she recalled was escorting Ginger Drew to the door and sitting down to listen to some special report on TV about the outlandish cost of real estate in Southern California. After that, she must have drifted off.

She hurried to the door and accepted a large envelope from a courier. The return address was Berger, Berger, and Kline and the sight of those three words set her heart racing. At last, Bert Kline's report was here.

She took the envelope back into the living room and picked up the remote control to turn off the TV, eager to read what Bert had found. However, a Special Newscast Alert popped onto the television screen, making her pause. Curious, she increased the volume and sat down to listen, eyes wide with interest as she studied the file photo of a young black male.

"There was a shooting outside Club Scandalous tonight, shortly after rapper Larry Lo's concert in Los Angeles," the newscaster began. "East Coast rapper Cat Morris, whose real name is Clifford Marin, is dead from a gunshot wound, but bad boy Larry Lo was not hurt."

The photo that remained on the screen stunned Niya. She squinted at it, moved closer, gasped aloud, and then let out a scream. "Lorenzo! My brother, Lorenzo! It's you." She flung the private investigator's report aside and concentrated on the news alert. There was no doubt in her mind. The face smiling into the camera was Lorenzo Londres, the brother she had thought long dead.

"Let me tell you what went down," the young man was explaining to the reporter while a live shot sequence replaced his file photo.

Niya gaped in disbelief at the cocky, gold-chain-laden figure who was lounging casually against the graffiti-covered wall of a dark brick building. A misty rain was falling and a huge bear of a man was holding an umbrella over the musician, who jerked his head to one side and jabbed the air with four fingers to emphasize every other word that came out of his mouth. She could hardly believe her eyes.

"You see, I was comin' out the back door of the club, you know, cause I gotta duck the crazies any way I can. When boom! This gunshot comes outta nowhere. You know? I hit the ground, man. I didn't know *what* the you-know-what was goin' down. So I stayed low." He ducked his head, and then looked up at the reporter and grinned. "Then, when I look up I see her!" He pointed out of camera range, and immediately the camera swept to a woman who was standing to the side, and who was obviously very nervous.

"No way!" Niya shouted at the television when the face of her old friend, Sandi Lee Holt, appeared. Niya dropped to her knees in front of the TV and pressed her nose nearly to the screen and stared at the long-lost ghost from her past. This is unbelievable, she thought, listening while Sandi Lee rattled on.

"Yeah, I was sitting in my car in the alley after the concert," she started. "I saw how crazy the crowd was getting and I got worried. I had this feeling that something bad was gonna happen to Larry, so I came prepared. I been watching Larry's back for a long time, now. Ready to defend him if I had to. You see, I know Larry Lo from way back, we been tight forever. I knew Ice Blu was after him. Anyway, when I saw Ice Blu's homeboy aimin' a gun at Larry Lo—over some crazy beef that started a long time ago—I realized what was about to go down. I slammed into the guy and sent his gun-toting ass to the ground, but because I pushed him, I caused him to accidentally shoot and kill Cat Jack Morris."

"But you saved Larry Lo's life," the reporter gushed.

"Yeah," Sandi Lee agreed, looking over at Larry. "That's awesome. I guess I did."

Stunned, Niya jumped up and grabbed the phone, but then stopped. Who the hell was she going to call? Niya slammed down the phone and collapsed on the couch, her mouth hanging open as she stared in shock at the two people who had once meant everything to her. Sandi Lee and Lorenzo? How in the world had that ever happened?

Chapter 50

Acapulco, Mexico—Four weeks later

Niya, wearing her exquisite Stephanos original wedding dress and white orchids in her hair, looked down from her upstairs window into the lush, flower-filled garden of her rented villa by the sea where her wedding guests were anxiously awaiting her arrival. Niya was satisfied. Everyone she had invited had arrived.

The curious guests, who had begun arriving early in the day, were still slightly overwhelmed by the luxurious accommodations at the villa, the unusual wedding invitations, and the massive number of flowers and candles filling the garden. Niya had made it a point to stay out of sight all day, allowing Contessa to serve as her official hostess until after the wedding ceremony.

Now, the guests chatted excitedly among themselves as they waited for the ceremony to begin.

With the exception of Contessa, all twelve of her invited guests were seated in the garden. Sandi Lee and her Jamaican neighbor from the trailer park, Miss Gladys, were there. So was Paige Moore, who was sitting with Olivia Londres, whom she had personally escorted from Cuba to Mexico on a special tourist visa. For the next ten days Olivia would be able to extend the brief reunion she had already had with her daughter. Seated next to Olivia was Lorenzo, who had flown to Acapulco on his private jet, and who, according to Contessa, was in total shock at being so suddenly reunited with his mother, and very anxious to see Niya. Lorenzo, still paranoid about his safety, had gotten permission from Niya to bring both Tiny Fizz and Stevie along as protection. Dejen had arrived late, and brought along Tremont, as Niya had made him promise to do. Seated next to Tremont was Robert York, the man who had launched Niya's career as a dancer in Miami. Behind them sat Niya's heartthrob from Nevada, Astin Spence, who had been pestering Contessa all afternoon for a private moment alone with Niya. Ginger Drew, the graphic artist who had designed Niya's fabulous wedding invitations, had been ecstatic about receiving one herself. And finally, at the back of the garden, Ricky Monroe waited, dressed in a white tuxedo, prepared to serve as Granger's best man.

Now, Niya buzzed the intercom to the outer room and instructed Contessa to ask Granger to come up and see her. She paced the room while waiting for him to arrive and, when he knocked, she eagerly welcomed him into her room.

Granger gazed at her with anticipatory delight, beaming with pride as he closed the door. "You look absolutely radiant," he told her, and then asked, nervously. "Is something wrong? I really shouldn't see you before the ceremony, should I?"

Niya laughed. "I think we can break tradition without worry. And nothing is wrong. I just wanted a few minutes alone with you before the ceremony."

He carefully embraced her with a quick hug and an air kiss, as if afraid he'd muss up her makeup and her dress. "At last, the big day is here. You're going to be my wife. I'm so happy, Niya. With you, my life is complete," he murmured.

"Yes, at last," Niya responded.

"You are extremely beautiful today. More beautiful than ever. Maybe it's because we've been separated for so long."

"Maybe so," Niya agreed, moving to a long table near the

window, where beautifully wrapped wedding presents were piled high. She picked up a small gift box wrapped in blue silk. "For you . . . from me," she whispered, watching as he accepted it, and then turned the box around in his palm.

"For me?" He appeared genuinely touched.

"Yes, I want you to have this before we go downstairs and tie the knot. Please, go ahead. Open it," she urged.

"I'm embarrassed. Let me go and get the gift I have for you . . ." he started.

"Later," Niya interrupted.

With a lift of his shoulder, Granger relented and eased off the silk fabric, opened the box and lifted out three photographs. He pulled them close to his face, and then reached into the breast pocket of his tuxedo and took out his tiny black frame reading glasses, which he put on. "What are these?" he muttered, turning them over to study them from all directions.

"They are pictures of you . . . stills from the videotape of you and Ricky and the pretty young girl in Ricky's hotel room. Your three-way in London, remember?" Niya spoke calmly in a voice with no emotion. "My private investigator, Bert Kline, had to pay Ricky two hundred and fifty thousand dollars for them, but I willingly authorized the payment when Ricky offered them for sale. Ricky had quite a few stories that he was happy to tell Bert, making it easy for me to tell you that I can't possibly be your wife, Granger. I only wish I had learned about your nasty little fetish earlier."

"You can't mean . . ." Granger stuttered. "After all I've done for you. You can't mean we're finished. This is a mistake, Niya. Ricky is just upset over . . ."

"Shhh," Niya hissed, a finger to her lips. "Don't try to explain. And I have no idea why you lied to me about your mother's death . . . and at this point, I don't really care. You'll only make a fool of yourself if you say anything else and no explanation will make those photographs or my disappointment in you disappear."

She tilted her chin down and peered up at Granger from beneath her thick mascara-covered lashes as she pulled off the yellow diamond ring he had given her from her finger and handed it to him. "Goodbye, Granger . . . and I am truly grateful for what you've done for me. I am. But I don't need you anymore."

Incensed, Granger pocketed the ring, threw the photos to the floor, gave Niya a frigid, furious stare and then rushed from the room, leaving the door open.

"And Ricky can leave with you," Niya rushed to the open door to call out as Granger disappeared down the wide spiral staircase.

Back in her room, Niya went limp. This plan of hers was turning out to be much more taxing than she had imagined, but she had to press on.

After taking a deep breath to clear her mind, Niya buzzed Contessa with a request that Astin come up to see her. When he arrived, Niya approached, a sweet smile on her lips.

"I'm so glad you came, Astin. I've missed you terribly. I know now that I misjudged you, but I couldn't tell you how I felt over the phone. I had to see you personally, and tell you how wrong I was. I asked you to come up here so that I could tell you . . . I have called off my wedding to Granger."

"What? Called it off?"

"Yes. Just now."

"What does that mean? That you do care for me?" he asked, grasping both of her hands.

Niya simply smiled.

"I knew it!" he gushed, squeezing her hands. "I knew something was up when you sent me that wedding invitation without the name of the groom on it, and then when you telephoned me to make sure I'd be here . . . well, I suspected something was up. You never were going to marry Granger, were you?"

Niya blinked and inclined her head slightly. "That's right. After leaving Nevada I couldn't stop thinking about you . . . about what it would be like to be your wife. You were right. I should have allowed us time to fully explore our feelings. But now, at last, we can."

"Then, it's me you want to marry, isn't it?" Astin pressed ahead. "I knew you could never be happy with Granger. He was all wrong for you. Do you want me to go and tell everyone to go home? That there'll be no ceremony?" he asked nervously.

"Don't worry. I'll have Contessa take care of everything," Niya said, and then motioned him closer. "Come here. I have something I want to give you on this special day." She kissed him harder than she had planned to and then handed him a flat box wrapped in shiny white paper.

"You should have waited until later," Astin started. "I have a gift for you, too. I brought it with me . . . in case I had a chance to speak to you alone. Niya, why don't we wait . . ."

"No, no. Please, open it now," she softly urged.

Overcome with happiness, Astin tore away the wrapping paper and lifted out a sheaf of papers. He studied them, perplexed, and then groaned.

"Look familiar?" Niya asked.

Slowly, Astin nodded as his eyes darted over the dense script covering the pages. He leafed through the document very quickly, and then let his hand drop to his side, still gripping the pages.

"They should," Niya prompted, her words as hard as flint. "Those are your divorce papers from Melody Evers, papers which you *never* finalized, which my private investigator uncovered. Melody is *still* your wife, isn't she, Astin?"

He widened his eyes and licked his lips, but didn't speak.

"You never divorced her because your finances are so intertwined that a divorce would bankrupt you. You planned to divorce Melody only after I agreed to marry you, ensuring your continued financial comfort."

"Niya, you don't understand," Astin started, looking confused and angry.

"Oh, I understand completely," she told him, going to the door, which she held open, a calm expression on her face. "As tempted as I was to run off to Las Vegas with you last summer, thank God I was smart enough to resist your charms. I took my time getting to know you, and it paid off. I was devastated to learn just how much of a charmer you really are. So, you can leave now, Astin. I have a car waiting to take you to the airport."

Giving Niya a knowing but sad nod, he touched his index finger to his lips, held it out toward her, and then left.

Once he was gone, Niya collapsed onto the side of the bed, her whole body shaking. First Granger, then Astin, and now all she had to do was deal with Tremont, and she'd have finally cleaned her emotional house. It was not in her nature to intentionally hurt people, and bringing these three men, all of whom had professed to love her, together under false pretenses was a nerve-wracking ordeal that she was eager to be finished with.

Niya checked her makeup, brushed the creases from her dress, and told Contessa to bring Tremont up to her room. This would be the first time she had seen him since sending him away from her apartment last month, and she was apprehensive about how he would react to what she planned to tell him.

"What's this about?" he asked cautiously as he entered her room and shut the door.

"I wanted to see you," Niya said.

"For what? To gloat?" Tremont tossed back. "Look, Niya, I did *not* want to come to Mexico in the first place, but Dejen kept goading me and messing with my mind. Telling me I was afraid of seeing another man take you from me and all that crap. I am not afraid to let you go. I did it once before, remember? So here I am. Bring it on. I'm happy that you are happy, okay? And you know what? Now, I'm glad you sent me an invitation because I want to watch you make the biggest mistake of your life."

"I understand how you feel, Tremont, but I'm glad you're here," Niya calmly admitted, watching Tremont closely. "This day would not have been complete if you hadn't shown up. There have been things . . . difficult things that I've had to do in order to find peace of mind. I had to see you because you are a part of this process, whether you want to be or not."

"Well, as I said, I'm here." He frowned at her, tears glistening in his eyes. "You've seen me. Satisfied? Go ahead and say what you gotta say and let's leave it there, okay? Anyway, why aren't you downstairs getting married?"

Niya picked up a small white orchid from a box on her dresser and twirled it between two fingers. "Because, Tremont," she began, "we're going downstairs together."

"Why would I want to go down there with you?"

"So that preacher in the garden can make me your wife."

Tremont's lips parted as he stared at Niya, puzzled by her remark. "Make you *my* wife?"

Niya stepped close to him, pinned the white orchid to his lapel, and then kissed him tenderly on the lips. "If you'll have me," she murmured. "It has taken me a long time to face up to the fact that you are the only man I will ever truly love. You were my first love and, even though you made mistakes, I made mistakes, too. I was a hardheaded fool to think that I could ever recapture the kind of love we shared with anyone other than you. Granger protected me, and used me to keep his own demons at bay. Astin wooed me, with a plan to use me for his own selfish reasons. But you . . . you simply loved me for who I was and were willing to sacrifice what we shared for my best interest. I never stopped loving you, Tremont. We fit together, we belong together and I've missed the hell out of you . . . and Miami. I want to live there in peace with you, my love."

"Are you for real?" Tremont stuttered, paling at the realization that he was the man Niya had chosen.

"As real as these flowers in my hair," Niya replied, linking her arm through Tremont's. "Will you marry me? Today?"

"But we don't have a license . . . and what about . . ."

"Don't worry so much," she interrupted. "We're in Mexico. Things like that can be taken care of later when we're back in the States."

"Niya, I'm too overcome to say anything but, let's do it. Right now, before you change your mind," Tremont decided, beaming with love, his hand over hers.

"I'll never change my mind about you, Tremont. Never again," Niya promised as she started down the spiral staircase to join her anxious wedding guests.

Epilogue

After the wedding, the guests who had remained for the ceremony stayed on at Villa Tropical for an extra ten days, basking in the hot sun, enjoying the water, and seeing the sights. Niya and Lorenzo and Olivia had a good time catching up and enjoyed a real family reunion before it was time for Olivia to return to Cuba.

Instead of letting Paige escort Olivia home, Lorenzo, using the name Larry London and a fake Mexican passport that he somehow managed to acquire, accompanied his ailing mother back to Cuba.

Once there, he was detained, questioned, and prevented from leaving the island. He went on to become a national singing sensation and a popular tourist attraction at the Imperial Hotel in Havana. He bought a big white house for himself and his mother, who had a full-time job keeping the women away from her son.

Sandi Lee, having mended her relationship with Niya, returned to Los Angeles where she purchased a bar on Venice Beach with the money that Lorenzo gave her for saving his life. It quickly became *the* hangout for rappers, hip-hop artists and the flashy music crowd, with everyone anxious to get close to the woman who saved the life of the famous singer, Larry Lo.

After returning to New York, Niya and Tremont had a civil

ceremony at City Hall, where Dejen and Contessa (who had become inseparable in Acapulco) served as witnesses. Then the newlyweds flew to Miami, threw a wild coming-home party, and invited all of their musician friends to G-Daddy's newly restored mansion.

A READING GROUP GUIDE

BETWEEN GOODBYES

Anita Bunkley

The following questions are intended to enhance your group's discussion of this book.

DISCUSSION QUESTIONS

1. Niya and her brother, Lorenzo, immigrated illegally to the United States. If Lorenzo had been caught at sea, he would have been returned to Cuba. What are your feelings about this policy?

2. Olivia was imprisoned for helping her children escape Cuba. Would you have risked imprisonment for your children's freedom?

3. How would you describe Niya's and Sandi Lee's friendship? What kept them together?

4. What did Sandi Lee want most in life? Why wasn't she able to find it?

5. Tremont had little respect for money and his cavalier attitude caused many problems. Do you know anyone like him?

6. Do you think Tremont was correct to sacrifice his love for Niya when he went to prison?

7. What made Larry Lo tick? Why did he become so successful?

8. Discuss the benefits that both Niya and Granger received from their relationship. Do you think Granger truly loved Niya? Why or why not?

9. What single word would you use to describe Astin? Do you think Astin expected too much, too soon from Niya? Why or why not?

10. If you could rewrite the story who would Niya have married?